W9-AHG-553

"The Giving Plague" by David Brin—It was an evolved invader whose existence had been discovered by two medical researchers. To one of them it seemed the salvation of humankind. To the other, it was the greatest menace the world might ever face. . . .

"Shaman" by John Shirley—The government had found many ways to lure the have-nots away from the precious urban territories. But there were some who would never be driven out, and for them there was a new weapon, a high-tech magic of mind over metal. . . .

"The Flies of Memory" by Ian Watson—The aliens had come in peace, bringing with them the secret of anti-gravity, asking to be allowed to "remember" our world. And only one man and one woman understood just how precious and how dangerous "remembering" could be. . . .

These are but a few of the imaginative voyages of discovery that await you in—

THE 1989 ANNUAL WORLD'S BEST SF

*Look for these other exciting
anthologies from DAW Books:*

**ISAAC ASIMOV PRESENTS THE
GREAT SF STORIES**
The best stories of the last four decades.
Edited by Isaac Asimov and Martin H. Greenberg.

THE ANNUAL WORLD'S BEST SF
The best of the current year.
Edited by Donald A. Wollheim with Arthur W. Saha.

THE YEAR'S BEST HORROR STORIES
An annual of terrifying tales.
Edited by Karl Edward Wagner.

THE YEAR'S BEST FANTASY STORIES
An annual of high imagination.
Edited by Arthur W. Saha.

SWORD AND SORCERESS
Original stories of magical and heroic women.
Edited by Marion Zimmer Bradley.

THE 1989 ANNUAL WORLD'S BEST SF

EDITED BY
DONALD A. WOLLHEIM
with Arthur W. Saha

SPECIAL INTRODUCTION BY ISAAC ASIMOV

DAW BOOKS, INC.
DONALD A. WOLLHEIM, PUBLISHER

1633 Broadway, New York, NY 10019

Copyright © 1989 by Donald A. Wollheim.

All Rights Reserved.

Cover art by Jim Burns.

DAW Book Collectors No. 783.

First Printing, June 1989

1 2 3 4 5 6 7 8 9

Printed in the U.S.A.

CONTENTS

INTRODUCTION
By Isaac Asimov

This is the first time that the introduction to this annual volume has not been written by Don Wollheim. Alas, we are not immune to the ravages of time (not even science fiction personalities are) and Don is hospitalized just as the deadline for the volume approaches, so he has asked me to do the introduction for him.

For all my fabled immodesty, I am forced to admit I am a poor substitute. Don has been a sextuple-threat person in science fiction. Let me list his threats:

1) He was one of the most active of the fans in the great days of the 1930s. I met him in 1938, when I joined the Futurians who, to the outside world, consisted of a handful of young men of no promise whatever—loud, boisterous, eccentric, unpredictable. It is only in later decades that, looking back, science fiction people realized, with astonishment, that the Futurians happened to include not only Don and I, but such people as Fred Pohl, Cyril Kornbluth, Damon Knight, Dick Wilson, and Bob Lowndes. Did we look at each other and hear the flutter of distant wings? (No, we didn't.)

Don, by the way, was the patriarch and leader of the group. He was twenty-four years old when I met him, and I, who was only eighteen, looked up to him with astonishment and awe.

2) He was a science fiction writer. In those days, the Futurians were not only readers and fans of science fiction, we were all trying to write. I think that we all managed to sell something while we were still in our teens. Don was the first of us to succeed. His story "The Man from Ariel" appeared in *Wonder Stories* in 1934.

Many others followed and my own personal favorite of his stories was "Mimic," a truly unusual story of an insect that had evolved the most astonishing adaptation of all. He went on to write novels, too, the most successful being a series of juveniles about "Mike Mars" that capitalized on the developing space program.

3) He was a perceptive science fiction commentator. In 1971, he published *The Universe Makers*, which, for one thing presented John W. Campbell, Jr. without the aura of majesty and hero-worship that others (such as myself) used to obscure the man. That was healthy, for John was larger than life in all respects, including his faults, and just because I hesitated to be appropriately critical, out of a feeling of gratitude to him, doesn't mean that no one should be. As the greatest individual in the history of science fiction (possibly excepting H. G. Wells), Campbell deserves a three-dimensional portrait.

I might also say that I was lost in admiration of Don, for in *The Universe Makers* he praised my Foundation series far more intensely than I have ever had the nerve to do. I always think very highly of people whose taste in science fiction is so sublime that they admire my stuff intensely.

His introductions to his "annual best" volumes, of which this is the latest, have been commentaries on science fiction and related subjects that have always, to me, vied in interest with the stories themselves. He is always, and unfailingly, rational and humane. I remember him so in 1938, and age has not withered him mentally and emotionally, and has *not* turned him into a hardened cynic. Rational and humane he remains.

4) He was the first, and continued to be among the best and most influential, anthologists in science fiction. In 1943, he astonished the science fiction world (and flabbergasted me) by editing *The Pocket Book of Science Fiction*, published by Pocket Books (who else). It was the first appearance of a science fiction anthology by a mainstream publisher, the first offering of great science fiction, of the type that had appeared under Campbell's aegis in *Astounding Science Fiction*, to a wider public than the magazines themselves commanded. Don was the first "apostle to the Gentiles" in science fiction, the first to point the way to general acceptance, and it was in his footsteps that later anthologists such as Groff Conklin, Raymond Healy, and Martin H. Greenberg trod. And now, 45 years after the appearance of that first anthology, you're holding his latest anthology in your hand.

5) He was a science fiction editor. In 1941, he edited four issues of *Stirring Science Fiction* and three of *Cosmic Stories*. They were not financially successful, but he labored under a small difficulty. He was not given any money with which to pay the writers. He had to depend mainly on his fellow Futurians (he published one story of mine) and helped give them a taste of success, however minor, encouraging them to continue for their own good and science fiction's.

After the war, he edited science fiction for Avon and for Ace, and was among the first, if not actually the first, to recognize the talents of such writers as Samuel R. Delany, Philip K. Dick, Harlan Ellison, Ursula K. Le Guin, Robert Silverberg, and many others of still later vintage.

6) And, finally, he was a science fiction publisher. In 1972, he created DAW books (does anyone fail to realize that DAW stands for Donald Allen Wollheim?), which was the first mass-market paperback house to concern itself entirely with science fiction.

These are the six aspects of Don Wollheim as far as

science fiction is concerned. And what of Don Wollheim as a man? Well, he married Elsie Balter in 1943 and they have been married happily ever since. Maybe this shouldn't be considered remarkable, but in a world in which divorce is ever more common, such constancy, combined with the obvious and continuing affection that exists between them is heartwarming indeed.

Don affects the curmudgeon. Many science fiction personalities do. Lester del Rey, Robert Silverberg, and Harlan Ellison immediately spring to mind. It is my experience, however, that all these growlers are merely trying (unsuccessfully) to hide soft hearts. Don is no exception. He is a sweet and gentle fellow who has spent his whole life giving more than he has taken.

I hope and trust that next year he will be writing his own introduction again.

THE GIVING PLAGUE
By David Brin

You think you're going to get me, don't you?
Well, you've got another think coming, 'cause I'm
ready for you.

That's why there's a forged card in my wallet saying
my blood group is AB Negative, and a MedicAlert tag
warning that I'm allergic to penicillin, aspirin, and
phenylalanine. Another one states that I'm a practis-
ing, devout Christian Scientist. All these tricks ought
to slow you down when the time comes, as it's sure to,
sometime soon.

Even if it makes the difference between living and
dying, there's just no way I'll let anyone stick a trans-
fusion needle into my arm. Never. Not with the blood
supply in the state it's in.

And anyway, I've got antibodies. So you just stay
the hell away from me, ALAS. I won't be your patsy.
I won't be your vector.

I know your weaknesses, you see. You're a fragile,
if subtle devil. Unlike TARP, you can't bear exposure
to air or heat or cold or acid or alkali. Blood-to-blood,
that's your only route. And what need had you of any

other? You thought you'd evolved the perfect technique, didn't you?

What was it Leslie Adgeson called you? "The perfect master? The paragon of viruses?"

I remember long ago when HIV, the AIDS virus, had everyone so impressed with its subtlety and effectiveness of design. But compared with you, HIV is just a crude butcher, isn't it? A maniac with a chainsaw, a blunderer that kills its hosts and relies for transmission on habits humans can, with some effort, get under control. Oh, old HIV had its tricks, but compared with you? An amateur!

Rhinoviruses and flu are clever, too. They're profligate, and they mutate rapidly. Long ago they learnt how to make their hosts drip and wheeze and sneeze, so the victims spread the misery in all directions. Flu viruses are also a lot smarter than AIDS 'cause they don't generally kill their hosts, just make 'em miserable while they hack and spray and inflict fresh infections on their neighbours.

Oh, Les Adgeson was always accusing me of anthropomorphizing our subjects. Whenever he came into my part of the lab, and found me cursing some damned intransigent leucophage in rich, Tex-Mex invective, he'd react predictably. I can just picture him now, raising one eyebrow, commenting dryly in his Winchester accent.

"The virus cannot hear you, Forry. It isn't sentient, nor even alive, strictly speaking. It's little more than a packet of genes in a protein case, after all."

"Yeah, Les," I'd answer. "But *selfish* genes! Given half a chance, they'll take over a human cell, force it to make armies of new viruses, then burst it apart as they escape to attack other cells. They may not think. All that behaviour may have evolved by blind chance. But doesn't it all *feel* as if it was planned? As if the nasty little things were *guided*, somehow, by somebody out to make us miserable. . . ? Out to make us die?"

"Oh, come now Forry," he would smile at my New

World ingenuousness. "You wouldn't be in this field if you didn't find phages beautiful, in their own way."

Good old, smug, sanctimonious Les. He never did figure out that viruses fascinated me for quite another reason. In their rapacious insatiability I saw a simple, distilled purity of ambition that exceeded even my own. The fact that it was mindless did little to ease my mind. I've always imagined we humans over-rated brains, anyway.

We'd first met when Les visited Austin on sabbatical, some years before. He'd had the Boy Genius rep even then, and naturally I played up to him. He invited me to join him back in Oxford, so there I was, having regular amiable arguments over the meaning of disease while the English rain dripped desultorily on the rhododendrons outside.

Les Adgeson. Him with his artsy friends and his pretensions at philosophy—Les was all the time talking about the elegance and beauty of our nasty little subjects. But he didn't fool me. I knew he was just as crazy Nobel-mad as the rest of us. Just as obsessed with the chase, searching for that piece of the Life Puzzle, that bit leading to more grants, more lab space, more techs, more prestige . . . leading to money, status and, maybe eventually, Stockholm.

He claimed not to be interested in such things. But he was a smoothy, all right. How else, in the midst of the Thatcher massacre of British science, did his lab keep expanding? And yet, he kept up the pretense.

"Viruses have their good side," Les kept saying. "Sure, they often kill, in the beginning. All new pathogens start that way. But eventually, one of two things happens. Either humanity evolves defences to eliminate the threat or . . ."

Oh, he loved those dramatic pauses.

"Or?" I'd prompt him, as required.

"Or we come to an accommodation, a compromise . . . even an alliance."

That's what Les always talked about. *Symbiosis*. He loved to quote Margulis and Thomas, and even Lovelock, for pity's sake! His respect even for vicious, sneaky brutes like the HIV was downright scary.

"See how it actually incorporates itself right *into* the DNA of its victims?" he would muse. "Then it waits, until the victim is later attacked by some *other* disease pathogen. Then the host's T-Cells prepare to replicate, to drive off the invader, only now some cells' chemical machinery is taken over by the new DNA, and instead of two new T-Cells, a plethora of new AIDS viruses results."

"So?" I answered. "Except that it's a retrovirus, that's the way nearly all viruses work."

"Yes, but think ahead, Forry. Imagine what's going to happen when, inevitably, the AIDS virus infects someone whose genetic makeup makes him invulnerable!"

"What, you mean his antibody reactions are fast enough to stop it? Or his T-Cells repel invasion?"

Oh, Les used to sound so damn *patronizing* when he got excited. "No, no, think!" he urged. "I mean invulnerable *after* infection. *After* the viral genes have incorporated into his chromosomes. Only in this individual, certain *other* genes *prevent* the new DNA from triggering viral synthesis. No new viruses are made. No cellular disruption. The person *is* invulnerable. But now he has all this new DNA . . ."

"In just a few cells—"

"Yes. But suppose one of these is a sex cell. Then suppose he fathers a child with that gamete. Now *every* one of that child's cells may contain *both* the trait of invulnerability and the new viral genes! Think about it. Forry. You now have a new type of human being! One who cannot be killed by AIDS. And yet he has all the AIDS genes, can make all those strange, marvelous proteins . . . Oh, most of them will be unexpressed or useless, of course. But now this child's genome, and his descendants', contains more *variety* . . ."

I often wondered, when he got carried away, this way. Did he actually believe he was explaining this to me for the first time? Much as the Brits respect American science, they do tend to assume we're slackers when it comes to the philosophical side. But I'd seen his interest heading in this direction weeks back, and had carefully done some extra reading.

"You mean like the genes responsible for some types of inheritable cancers?" I asked, sarcastically. "There's evidence some oncogenes were originally inserted into the human genome by viruses, just as you suggest. Those who inherit the trait for rheumatoid arthritis may also have gotten their gene that way."

"Exactly. Those viruses themselves may be extinct, but their DNA lives on, in ours!"

"Right. And *boy* have human beings benefited!"

Oh, how I hated that smug expression he'd get. (It got wiped off his face eventually, didn't it?)

Les picked up a piece of chalk and drew a figure on the blackboard.

HARMLESS→KILLER!→SURVIVABLE ILLNESS→INCONVENIENCE→HARMLESS

"Here's the classic way of looking at how a host species interacts with a new pathogen, especially a virus. Each arrow, of course, represents a stage of mutation and adaptation selection.

"First, a new form of some previously harmless micro-organism leaps from its prior host, say a monkey species, over to a new one, say us. Of course, at the beginning we have no adequate defences. It cuts through us like syphilis did in Europe in the sixteenth century, killing in days rather than years . . . in an orgy of cell feeding that's really not a very efficient modus for a pathogen. After all, only a gluttonous parasite kills off its host so quickly.

"What follows, then, is a rough period for both host and parasite as each struggles to adapt to the other. It can be likened to warfare. Or, on the other hand, it *might* be thought of as a sort of drawn out process of *negotiation.*"

I snorted in disgust. "Mystical crap, Les. I'll concede your chart; but the war analogy is the right one. That's why they fund labs like this one. To come up with better weapons for our side."

"Hmm. Possibly. But sometimes the process *does* look different, Forry." He turned and drew another chart.

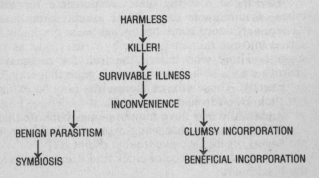

"You can see that this chart is the same as the other, right up to the point where the original disease disappears."

"Or goes into hiding."

"Surely. As *e coli* took refuge in our innards. Doubtless long ago the ancestors of *e coli* killed a great many of our ancestors before eventually becoming the beneficial symbionts they are now, helping us digest our food.

"The same applies to viruses, I'd wager. Heritable cancers and rheumatoid arthritis are just temporary awkwardnesses. Eventually, those genes will be comfortably incorporated. They'll be part of the genetic diversity that prepares us to meet challenges ahead.

"Why, I'd wager a large portion of our present genes came about in such a way, entering our cells first as invaders . . ."

Crazy sonovabitch. Fortunately he didn't try to lead the lab's research effort too far to the right on his magic diagram. Our Boy Genius was plenty savvy about the funding agencies. He knew they weren't interested in paying us to prove we're all partly descended from viruses. They wanted, and wanted *badly*, progress on ways to fight viral infections themselves.

So Les concentrated his team on *vectors*.

Yeah, you viruses need vectors, don't you? I mean, if you kill a guy, you've got to have a liferaft, so you can desert the ship you've sunk, so you can cross over to some *new* hapless victim. Same applies if the host proves tough, and fights you off—gotta move on. Always movin' on.

Hell, even if you've made peace with a human body, like Les suggested, you still want to spread, don't you? Bigtime colonizers, you tiny beasties.

Oh, I know. It's just natural selection. Those bugs that accidentally find a good vector spread. Those that don't, don't. But it's so eerie. Sometimes it sure *feels* purposeful . . .

So the flu makes us sneeze. Typhus gives us diarrhea. Smallpox caused pustules which dry, flake off and blow away to be inhaled by the patient's loved ones. All good ways to jump ship. To colonize.

Who knows? Did some past virus cause a swelling of the lips that made us want to kiss? Heh. Maybe that's a case of Les's "benign incorporation" . . . we retain the trait, long after the causative pathogen went extinct! What a concept.

So our lab got this big grant to study vectors. Which is how Les found you, ALAS. He drew this big chart covering all the possible ways an infection might leap from person to person, and set us about checking all of them, one by one.

For himself he reserved straight blood-to-blood infection. There were reasons for that.

First off, Les was an *altruist*, see. He was concerned about all the panic and unfounded rumours spreading about Britain's blood supply. Some people were putting off necessary surgery. There was talk of starting over here what some rich folk in the States had begun doing—stockpiling their own blood in silly, expensive efforts to avoid having to use the blood banks if they ever needed hospitalization.

All that bothered Les. But even worse was the fact that lots of potential donors were shying away from giving blood because of some stupid rumours that you could get infected that way.

Hell, nobody ever caught anything from *giving* blood . . . nothing except maybe a little dizziness and perhaps a zit or spot from all the biscuits and sweet tea they feed you afterwards. And as for contracting HIV from receiving blood, well, the new antibodies tests soon had that problem under control. Still, the stupid rumours spread.

A nation has to have confidence in its blood supply. Les wanted to eliminate all those silly fears once and for all, with one definitive study. But that wasn't the only reason he wanted the blood-to-blood vector for himself.

"Sure, there were some nasty things like AIDS that use that vector. But that's also where I might find the older ones," he said, excitedly. "The viruses that have *almost* finished the process of becoming benign. The ones that have been so well selected that they keep a low profile, and hardly inconvenience their hosts at all. Maybe I can even find one that's commensal! One that actually *helps* the human body."

"An undiscovered human commensal," I sniffed doubtfully.

"And why not? If there's no visible disease, why would anyone have ever looked for it! This could open up a whole new field, Forry!"

In spite of myself, I was impressed. It was how he got to be known as a Boy Genius, after all, this flash of half-crazy insight. How he managed not to have it snuffed out of him at Oxbridge, I'll never know, but it was one reason why I'd attached myself to him and his lab, and wrangled mighty hard to get my name attached to his papers.

So I kept watch over his work. It sounded so dubious, so damn stupid. And I knew it just might bear fruit, in the end.

That's why I was ready when Les invited me along to a conference down in Bloomsbury, one day. The colloquium itself was routine, but I could tell he was near to bursting with news. Afterwards we walked down

Charing Cross Road to a pizza place, one far enough from the University area to be sure there'd be no colleagues anywhere within earshot—just the pretheatre crowd, waiting till opening time down at Leicester Square.

Les breathlessly swore me to secrecy. He needed a confidant, you see, and I was only too happy to comply.

"I've been interviewing a lot of blood donors lately," he told me after we'd ordered. "It seems that while some people have been scared off from donating, that has been largely made up by increased contributions by a central core of regulars."

"Sounds good," I said. And I meant it. I had no objection to there being an adequate blood supply. Back in Austin I was pleased to see others go to the Red Cross van, just so long as nobody asked *me* to contribute. I had neither the time nor the interest, so I got out of it by telling everybody I'd had malaria.

"I found one interesting fellow, Forry. Seems he started donating back when he was twenty-five, during the Blitz. Must have contributed thirty-five, forty gallons, by now."

I did a quick mental calculation. "Wait a minute. He's got to be past the age limit by now."

"Exactly right! He admitted the truth, when he was assured of confidentially. Seems he didn't *want* to stop donating when he reached sixty-five. He's a hardy old fellow . . . had a spot of surgery a few years back, but he's in quite decent shape, over all. So, right after his local Gallon Club threw a big retirement party for him, he actually moved across the county and registered at a new blood bank, giving a false name and a younger age!"

"Kinky. But it sounds harmless enough. I'd guess he just likes to feel needed. Bet he flirts with the nurses and enjoys the free food . . . sort of a bi-monthly party he can always count on, with friendly, appreciative people."

Hey, just because I'm a selfish bastard doesn't mean I can't extrapolate the behaviour of altruists. Like most other user-types, I've got a good instinct for the sort of motivations that drive suckers. People like me need to know such things.

"That's what I thought too, at first," Les said, nodding. "I found a few more like him, and decided to call them 'addicts.' At first I never connected them with the *other* group, the one I named 'converts.' "

"Converts?"

"Yes, converts. People who suddenly became blood donors—get this—very soon after they've recovered from surgery themselves!"

"Maybe they're paying off part of their hospital bills that way?"

"Mmm, not really. We have nationalized health, remember? And even for private patients, that might account for the first few donations only."

"Gratitude, then?" An alien emotion to me, but I understood it, in principle.

"Perhaps. Some few people might have their consciousness raised after a close brush with death, and decide to become better citizens. After all, half an hour at a blood bank, a few times a year, is a small inconvenience in exchange for . . ."

Sanctimonious twit. Of course *he* was a donor. Les went on and on about civic duty and such until the waitress arrived with our pizza and two fresh bitters. That shut him up for a moment. But when she left, he leaned forward, eyes shining.

"But no, Forry. It wasn't bill-paying, or even gratitude. Not for some of them, at least. More had happened to these people than having their consciousness raised. They were *converts*, Forry. They began joining Gallon Clubs, and more! It seems almost as if, in each case, a *personality change* had taken place."

"What do you mean?"

"I mean that a significant fraction of those who have had major surgery during the last five years seem to have changed their entire set of social attitudes! Beyond becoming blood donors, they've increased their contributions to charity, joined the Parent-Teacher organizations and Boy Scout troops, become active in Greenpeace and Save The Children . . ."

"The point, Les. What's your *point*?"

"My point?" He shook his head. "Frankly, some of these people were behaving like addicts . . . like converted addicts to *altruism*. That's when it occurred to me, Forry, that what we might have here was a new vector."

He said it as simply as that. Naturally I looked at him blankly.

"A vector!" he whispered, urgently. "Forget about typhus, or smallpox, or flu. They're rank amateurs! Wallies who give the show away with all their sneezing and flaking and shitting. To be sure, AIDS uses blood and sex, but it's so damned savage, it forced us to become aware of it, to develop tests, to begin the long, slow process of isolating it. But ALAS—"

"Alas?"

"A-L-A-S." He grinned. "It's what I've named the new virus I've isolated, Forry. It stands for 'Acquired Lavish Altruism Syndrome.' How do you like it?"

"Hate it. Are you trying to tell me that there's a virus that affects the human *mind*? And in such a complicated way?" I was incredulous and, at the same time, scared spitless. I've always had this superstitious feeling about viruses and vectors. Les really had me spooked now.

"No, of course not," he laughed. "But consider a simpler possibility. What if some virus one day stumbled on a way to make people *enjoy* giving blood?"

I guess I only blinked then, unable to give him any other reaction.

"*Think*, Forry! Think about that old man I spoke of earlier. He told me that every two months or so, just before he'd be allowed to donate again, he tends to feel 'all thick inside.' The discomfort only goes away after the next donation!"

I blinked again. "And you're saying that each time he gives blood, he's actually *serving* his parasite, providing it a vector into new hosts . . ."

"The new hosts being those who survive surgery

because the hospital gave them fresh blood, all because our old man was so generous, yes! They're infected! Only this is a subtle virus, not a greedy bastard, like AIDS, or even the flu. It keeps a low profile. Who knows, maybe it's even reached a level of *commensalism* with its hosts—attacking invading organisms for them, or . . ."

He saw the look on my face and waved his hands. "All right, far fetched, I know. But think about it! Because there are no disease symptoms, nobody has ever looked for this virus, until now."

He's *isolated* it, I realized, suddenly. And, knowing instantly what this thing could mean, career-wise, I was already scheming, wondering how to get my name onto his paper, when he published this. So absorbed was I that, for a few moments, I lost track of his words.

". . . And so now we get to the interesting part. You see, what's a normal, selfish Tory-voter going to *think* when he finds himself suddenly wanting to go down to the blood bank as often as they'll let him?"

"Um," I shook my head. "That he's been bewitched? Hypnotized?"

"Nonsense!" Les snorted. "That's not how human psychology works. No, we tend to do *lots* of things without knowing why. We need excuses, though, so we *rationalize*! If an obvious reason for our behaviour isn't readily available, we *invent* one, preferably one that helps us think better of ourselves. Ego is powerful stuff, my friend."

Hey, I thought. *Don't teach your grandmother to suck eggs*.

"Altruism," I said aloud. "They find themselves rushing regularly to the blood bank. So they rationalize that it's because they're *good* people . . . They become proud of it. Brag about it . . ."

"You've got it," Les said. "And because they're proud, even sanctimonious about their newfound generosity, they tend to *extend* it, to bring it into other parts of their lives!"

I whispered in hushed awe. "An altruism virus! Jesus, Les, when we announce this . . ."

I stopped when I saw his sudden frown, and instantly thought it was because I'd used that word, "we." I should have known better, of course. For Les was always more than willing to share the credit. No, his reservations was far more serious than that.

"Not yet, Forry. We can't publish this yet."

I shook my head. "Why not! This is big, Les! It proves much of what you've been saying all along, about symbiosis and all that. There could even be a Nobel in it!"

I'd been gauche, and spoken aloud of The Ultimate. But he did not even seem to notice. Damn. If only Les had been like most biologists, driven more than anything else by the lure of Stockholm. But no. You see, Les was a natural. A natural altruist.

It was *his* fault, you see. Him and his damn virtue, they drove me to first contemplate what I next decided to do.

"Don't you see, Forry? If we publish, they'll develop an antibody test for the ALAS virus. Donors carrying it will be barred from the blood banks, just like those carrying AIDS and syphilis and hepatitis. And that would be incredibly cruel torture to those poor addicts and carriers."

"Screw the carriers!" I almost shouted. Several pizza patrons glanced my way. With a desperate effort I brought my voice down. "Look, Les, the carriers will be classified as *diseased*, won't they? So they'll go under doctor's care. And if all it takes to make them feel better is to *bleed* them regularly, well, then we'll give them pet leeches!"

Les smiled. "Clever. But that's not the only, or even my main reason, Forry. No, I'm not going to publish, yet, and that is final. I just can't allow anybody to stop this disease. It's got to spread, to become an epidemic. A pandemic."

I stared, and upon seeing that look in his eyes, I knew that Les was more than an altruist. He had caught that specially insidious of all human ailments, the Messiah Complex. Les wanted to save the world.

"Don't you see?" he said urgently, with the fervor of a proselyte. "Selfishness and greed are destroying the planet, Forry! But nature always finds a way, and this time symbiosis may be giving us our last chance, a final opportunity to become better people, to learn to cooperate before it's too late!

"The things we're most proud of, our prefrontal lobes, those bits of gray matter above the eyes which makes us so much smarter than beasts, what good have they done us, Forry? Not a hell of a lot. We aren't going to *think* our way out of the crises of the 20th century. Or, at least, thought alone won't do it. We need something else, as well.

"And Forry, I'm convinced that something else is ALAS. We've got to keep this secret, at least until it's so well established in the population that there's no turning back!"

I swallowed. "How long? How long do you want to wait? Until it starts affecting voting patterns? Until after the next election?"

He shrugged. "Oh, at least that long. Five years. Possibly seven. You see, the virus tends to only get into people who've recently had surgery, and they're generally older. Fortunately, they also are often influential. Just the sort who now vote Tory . . ."

He went on. And on. I listened with half an ear, but already I had come to that fateful realization. A seven year wait for a goddamn co-authorship would make this discovery next to useless to my career, to my ambitions.

Of course I *could* blow the secret on Les, now that I knew of it. But that would only embitter him, and he'd easily take all the credit for the discovery anyway. People tend to remember innovators, not whistle-blowers.

We paid our bill and walked toward Charing Cross Station, where we could catch the tube to Paddington, and from there to Oxford. Along the way we ducked out of a sudden downpour at a streetside ice cream vendor. While we waited, I bought us both cones. I remember quite clearly that he had strawberry. I had a raspberry ice.

While Les absentmindedly talked on about his research plans, a small pink smudge coloured the corner of his mouth. I pretended to listen, but already my mind had turned to other things, nascent plans and earnest scenarios for committing murder.

It would be the perfect crime, of course.

Those movie detectives are always going on about "motive, means, and opportunity." Well, motive I had in plenty, but it was a one so far-fetched, so obscure, that it would surely never occur to anybody.

Means? Hell, I worked in a business rife with means. There were poisons and pathogens galore. We're a very careful profession, but, well, accidents do happen . . . The same holds for opportunity.

There was a rub, of course. Such was Boy Genius's reputation that, even if I did succeed in knobbling him, I didn't dare come out immediately with my own announcement. Damn him, everyone would just assume it was his work anyway, or his "leadership" here at the lab, at least, that led to the discovery of ALAS. And besides, too much fame for me right after his demise *might* lead someone to suspect a motive.

So, I realized, Les was going to get his delay, after all. Maybe not seven years, but three or four perhaps, during which I'd move back to the States, start a separate line of work, then subtly guide my own research to cover methodically all the bases Les had so recently flown over in flashes of inspiration. I wasn't happy about the delay, but at the end of that time, it would look entirely like my own work. No co-authorship for Forry on *this* one, nossir!

The beauty of it was that nobody would ever think of connecting me with the tragic death of my colleague and friend, years before. After all, did not his demise set me back in my career, temporarily? "Ah, if only poor Les had lived to see your success!" my competitors would say, suppressing jealous bile as they watched me pack for Stockholm.

Of course none of this appeared on my face or in my words. We both had our normal work to do. But almost every day I also put in long extra hours helping Les in "our" secret project. In its own way it was an exhilarating time, and Les was lavish in his praise of the slow, dull, but methodical way I fleshed out some of his ideas.

I made my arrangements slowly, knowing Les was in no hurry. Together we gathered data. We isolated, and even crystallized the virus, got X-ray diffractions, did epidemiological studies, all in strictest secrecy.

"Amazing!" Les would cry out, as he uncovered the way the ALAS virus forced its hosts to feel their need to "give." He'd wax eloquent, effusive over elegant mechanisms which he ascribed to random selection but which I could not help superstitiously attributing to some incredibly insidious form of intelligence. The more subtle and effective we found its techniques to be, the more admiring Les became, and the more I found myself loathing those little packets of RNA and protein.

The fact that the virus seemed so harmless—Les thought even commensal—only made me hate it more. It made me glad of what I had planned. Glad that I was going to stymie Les in his scheme to give ALAS free rein.

I was going to save humanity from this would-be puppet master. True, I'd delay my warning to suit my own purposes, but the warning would come, nonetheless, and sooner than my unsuspecting compatriot planned.

Little did Les know that he was doing background for work *I'd* take credit for. Every flash of insight, his every "Eureka!", was stored away in my private notebook, beside my own columns of boring data. Meanwhile, I sorted through all the means at my disposal.

Finally, I selected for my agent a particularly virulent strain of Dengue Fever.

*   *   *

There's an old saying we have in Texas. "A chicken is just an egg's way of makin' more eggs."

To a biologist, familiar with all those latinized-graecificated words, this saying has a much more "posh" version. Humans are "zygotes," made up of diploid cells containing 46 paired chromosomes . . . except for our haploid sex cells, or "gametes." Males' gametes are sperm and females' are eggs, each containing only 23 chromosomes.

So biologists say that "a zygote is only a gamete's way of making more gametes."

Clever, eh? But it does point out just how hard it is, in nature, to pin down a Primal Cause . . . some centre to the puzzle, against which everything else can be calibrated. I mean, which *does* come first, the chicken or the egg?

"Man is the measure of all things," goes another wise old saying. Oh yeah! Tell that to a modern feminist.

A guy I once knew, who used to read science fiction, told me about this story he'd seen, in which it turned out that the whole and entire purpose of humanity, brains and all, was to be the organism that built starships so that *house flies* could migrate out and colonize the galaxy.

But that idea's nothing compared with what Les Adgeson believed. He spoke of the human animal as if he were describing a veritable United Nations. From the *e coli* in our guts, to tiny commensal mites that clean our eyelashes for us, to the mitochondria that energize our cells, all the way to the contents of our very DNA . . . Les saw it all as a great big hive of compromise, negotiation, *symbiosis*. Most of the contents of our chromosomes came from past invaders, he contended.

Symbiosis? The picture he created in my mind was one of minuscule *puppeteers*, all yanking and jerking at us with their protein strings, making us marionettes dance to their own tunes, to their own nasty, selfish little agendas.

And you, *you* were the worst! Like most cynics, I had always maintained a secret faith in human nature.

Yes, most people are pigs. I've always known that. And while I may be a user, at least I'm honest enough to admit it.

But deep down, we users *count* on the sappy, inexplicable generosity, the mysterious, puzzling altruism of those others, the kind, inexplicably *decent* folk . . . those we superficially sneer at in contempt, but secretly hold in awe.

Then you came along, damn you. You *make* people behave that way. There is no mystery left, after you get finished. No corner remaining impenetrable to cynicism. Damn, how I came to hate you!

As I came to hate Leslie Adgeson. I made my plans, schemed my brilliant campaign against both of you. In those last days of innocence I felt oh, so savagely determined. So deliciously decisive and in control of my own destiny.

In the end it was anticlimactic. I didn't have time to finish my preparations, to arrange that little trap, that sharp bit of glass dipped in just the right mixture of deadly microorganisms. For CAPUC arrived then, just before I could exercise my option as a murderer.

CAPUC changed everything.

Catastrophic Auto-immune PUlmonary Collapse . . . acronym for the horror that made AIDS look like a minor irritant. And in the beginning it appeared unstoppable. Its vectors were completely unknown and the causative agent defied isolation for so long.

This time it was no easily identifiable group that came down with the new plague, though it concentrated upon the industrialized world. Schoolchildren in some areas seemed particularly vulnerable. In other places it was secretaries and postal workers.

Naturally, all the major epidemiology labs got involved. Les predicted the pathogen would turn out to be something akin to the prions which cause shingles in sheep, and certain plant diseases . . . a pseudo life form even simpler than a virus and even harder to track down. It was a heretical, minority view, until the CDC in Atlanta decided out of desperation to try his theories out, and found the very dormant viroids Les predicted—mixed *in* with the *glue* used to seal paper milk cartons, envelopes, postage stamps.

Les was a hero, of course. *Most* of us in the labs were. After all, we'd been the first line of defense. Our own casualty rate had been ghastly.

For a while there, funerals and other public gatherings were discouraged. But an exception was made for Les. The procession behind his cortege was a mile long. I was asked to deliver the eulogy. And when they pleaded with me to take over at the lab, I agreed.

So naturally I tended to forget all about ALAS. The war against CAPUC took everything society had. And while I may be selfish, even a rat can tell when it makes more sense to join in the fight to save a sinking ship . . . especially when there's no other port in sight.

We learned how to combat CAPUC, eventually. It involved drugs, and a vaccine based on reversed antibodies force-grown in the patient's own marrow after he's given a dangerous overdose of a Vanadium compound I found by trial and error. It worked, most of the time, but the victims suffered great stress and often required a special regime of whole blood transfusions to get across the most dangerous phase.

Blood banks were stretched even thinner than before. Only now the public responded generously, as in time of war. I should not have been surprised when survivors, after their recovery, volunteered by the thousands. But, of course, I'd forgotten about ALAS by then, hadn't I?

We beat back CAPUC. Its vector proved too unreliable, too easily interrupted once we'd figured it out. The poor little viroid never had a chance to get to Les's "negotiation" stage. Oh well, those are the breaks.

I got all sorts of citations I didn't deserve. The King gave me a KBE for personally saving the Prince of Wales. I had dinner at the White House.

Big deal.

The world had a respite, after that. CAPUC had scared people, it seemed, into a new spirit of cooperation. I should have been suspicious, of course. But soon I'd moved over to WHO, and had all sorts of administrative responsibilities in the Final Campaign on Malnutrition.

By that time, I had almost entirely forgotten about ALAS.

I forgot about you, didn't I? Oh, the years passed, my star rose, I became famous, respected, revered. I didn't get my Nobel in Stockholm. Ironically, I picked it up in Oslo. Fancy that. Just shows you can fool anybody.

And yet, I don't think I ever *really* forgot about you, ALAS, not at the back of my mind.

Peace treaties were signed. Citizens of the industrial nations voted temporary cuts in their standards of living in order to fight poverty and save the environment. Suddenly, it seemed, we'd all grown up. Other cynics, guys I'd gotten drunk with in the past—and shared dark premonitions about the inevitable fate of filthy, miserable humanity—all gradually deserted the faith, as pessimists seem wont to do when the world turns bright—too bright for even the cynical to dismiss as a mere passing phase on the road to Hell.

And yet, my own brooding remained unblemished. For subconsciously I *knew* it wasn't real.

Then, the third Mars Expedition returned to worldwide adulation, and brought home with them TARP.

And that was when we all found out just how *friendly* all our home-grown pathogens really had been, all along.

Late at night, stumbling in exhaustion from overwork, I would stop at Les's portrait where I'd ordered it hung in the hall opposite my office door, and stand there cursing him and his damned theories of *symbiosis*.

Imagine mankind ever reaching a symbiotic association with TARP! That really would be something. Imagine, Les, all those *alien* genes, added to our heritage, to our rich human diversity!

Only TARP did not seem to be much interested in "negotiation." Its wooing was rough, deadly. And its vector was the wind.

The world looked to me, and to my peers, for

salvation. In spite of all my successes and high renown, though, I knew myself for a second-best fraud. I would always know—no matter how much they thanked and praised me—who had been better than me by light-years.

Again and again, deep into the night, I would pore through the notes Leslie Adgeson had left behind, seeking inspiration, seeking hope. That's when I stumbled across ALAS, again.

I found *you* again.

Oh, you made us behave better, all right. At least a quarter of the human race must contain your DNA, by now, ALAS. And in their newfound, inexplicable, rationalized altruism, they set the tone followed by all the others.

Everybody behaves so damned *well* in the present calamity. They help each other, they succour the sick, they all *give* so.

Funny thing, though. If you hadn't made us all so bloody cooperative, we'd probably never had *made* it to bloody Mars, would we? Or if we had, there'd have still been enough paranoia around so we'd have maintained a decent quarantine.

But then, I remind myself, you don't *plan*, do you? You're just a bundle of RNA, packed inside a protein coat, with an incidentally, accidentally acquired trait of making humans want to donate blood. That's all you are, right? So you had no way of knowing that by making us "better" you were also setting us up for TARP, did you? Did you?

We've got some palliatives, now. A few new techniques seem to be doing some good. The latest news is great, in fact. Apparently, we'll be able to save maybe fifteen percent or so of the children. At least half of them may even be fertile.

That's for nations who've had a lot of racial mixing. Heterozygosity and genetic diversity seem to breed better resistance. Those peoples with "pure," narrow bloodlines will be harder to save, but then, racism has its inevitable price.

Too bad about the great apes and horses, but then, at least all this will give the rain forests a chance to grow back.

Meanwhile, everybody perseveres. There is no panic, as one reads about happening in past plagues. We've grown up at least, it seems. We help each other.

But I carry a card in my wallet saying I'm a Christian Scientist, and that my blood group is AB Negative, and that I'm allergic to nearly everything. Transfusions are one of the treatments commonly used now, and I'm an important man. But I won't take blood. I won't. I donate, but I'll never take it. Not even when I drop.

You won't have me, ALAS. You won't.

I am a bad man. I suppose, all told, I've done more good than evil in my life, but that's incidental, a product of happenstance and the caprices of the world.

I have no control over the world, but I can make my own decisions, at least. As I make this one, now.

Down, out of my high research tower I've gone. Into the streets, where the teeming clinics fester and broil. That's where I work now. And it doesn't matter to me that I'm behaving no differently than anyone else today. *They* are all marionettes. They think they're acting altruistically, but I know they are your puppets. ALAS.

But I am a *man*, do you hear me? I make my own decisions.

Fever wracks my body now, as I drag myself from bed to bed, holding their hands when they stretch them out to me for comfort, doing what I can to ease their suffering, to save a few.

You'll not have me, ALAS.

This is what *I* choose to do.

PEACHES FOR MAD MOLLY

By Steven Gould

Sometime during the night the wind pulled a one-pointer off the west face of the building up around the 630th floor. I heard him screaming as he went by, very loud, like this was his last chance to voice an opinion, but it was all so sudden that he didn't know what it was. Then he hit a microwave relay off 542 . . . hard, and the chance was gone. Chunks of him landed in Buffalo Bayou forty-five seconds later.

The alligators probably liked that.

I don't know if his purchase failed or his rope broke or if the sucker just couldn't tie a decent knot. He pissed me off though, because I couldn't get back to sleep until I'd checked all four of my belay points, the ropes, and the knots. Now if he'd fallen without expressing himself, maybe?

No, I would have heard the noise as he splattered through the rods of the antennae.

Stupid one-pointer.

The next morning I woke up a lot earlier than usual because someone was plucking one of my ropes, *adagio*, thrum, thrum, like the second movement of Ludwig's seventh. It was Mad Molly.

"You awake, Bruce?" she asked.

I groaned. "I am now." My name is not Bruce. Molly, for some reason, calls everyone Bruce. "*Shto etta*, Molly?"

She was crouched on a roughing point, one of the meter cubes sticking out of the tower face to induce the micro-turbulence boundary layer. She was dressed in a brightly flowered scarlet kimono, livid green bermuda shorts, a sweatshirt, and tabi socks. Her belay line, bright orange against the gray building, stretched from around the corner to Molly's person where it vanished beneath her kimono, like a snake hiding its head.

"I got a batch to go to the Bruce, Bruce."

I turned and looked down. There was a damp wind in my face. Some low clouds had come in overnight, hiding the ground, but the tower's shadow stretched a long ways across the fluffy stuff below. "Jeeze, Molly. You know the Bruce won't be on shift for another hour." Damn, she had me doing it! "Oh, hell. I'll be over after I get dressed."

She blinked twice. Her eyes were black chips of stone in a face so seamed and browned by the sun that it was hard to tell her age. "Okay, Bruce," she said, then stood abruptly and flung herself off the cube. She dropped maybe five meters before her rope tightened her fall into an arc that swung her down and around the corner.

I let out my breath. She's not called Mad Molly for nothing.

I dressed, drank the water out of my catch basin, urinated on the clouds (seems only fair) and rolled up my bag.

Between the direct sunlight and the stuff bouncing off the clouds below the south face was blinding. I put my shades on at the corner.

Molly's nest, like a mud dauber's, hung from an industrial exhaust vent off the 611th floor. It was woven, sewed, tucked, patched, welded, snapped, zipped, and tied into creation. It looked like a wasp's nest on a piece of chrome. It did not blend in.

Her pigeon coop, about two floors lower down, blended in even less. It was made of paper, sheet plastic, wire, and it was speckled with pigeon droppings. It was where it was because only a fool lives directly under *under* defecating birds, and Molly, while mad, was not stupid.

Molly was crouched in the doorway of her nest balanced on her feet like one of her pigeons. She was staring out at nothing and muttering angrily to herself.

"What's wrong, Molly? Didn't you sleep okay?"

She glared at me. "That damn Bruce got another three of my birds yesterday."

I hooked my bag onto a beaner and hung it under her house. "What Bruce, Molly? That red tailed hawk?"

"Yeah, that Bruce. Then the other Bruce pops off last night and wakes me up so I can't get back to sleep because I'm listening for that damn hawk." She backed into her nest to let me in.

"Hawks don't hunt at night, Molly."

She flapped her arms. "So? Like maybe the vicious, son-of-a-bitchin' Bruce gets into the coop? He could kill half my birds in one night!" She started coiling one of her ropes, pulling the line with short, angry jerks. "I don't know if it's worth it anymore, Bruce. It's hot in the summer. It's freezing in the winter. The Babs are always hassling me instead of the Howlers, the Howlers keep hassling me for free birds or they'll cut me loose one night. I can't cook on cloudy days unless I want to pay an arm and a leg for fuel. I can't get fresh fruit or vegetables. That crazy social worker who's afraid of heights comes by and asks if he can help me. I say, 'Yeah, get me some fresh fruit.' He brings me applications for readmittance! God, I'd kill for a fresh peach! I'd be better off back in the house!"

I shrugged. "Maybe you would, Molly. After all, you're getting on in years."

"Fat lot you know, Bruce! You crazy or something? Trade this view for six walls? Breathe that stale stuff they got in there? Give up my birds? Give up my freedom? Shit, Bruce, who the hell's side are you on anyway?"

I laughed. "Yours, Molly."

She started wrapping the pigeons and swearing under her breath.

I looked at Molly's clippings, bits of faded newsprint stuck to the wall of the tower itself. By the light coming through some of the plastic sheeting in the roof, I saw a picture of Molly on Mt. McKinley dated twenty years before. An article about her second attempt on Everest. Stories about her climbing buildings in New York, Chicago, and L.A. I looked closer at one that talked about her climbing the south face of El Capitan on her fourteenth birthday. It had the date.

I looked twice and tried to remember what day of the month it was. I had to count backwards in my head to be sure.

Tomorrow was Mad Molly's birthday.

The Bruce in question was Murry Zapata, outdoor rec guard of the south balcony on the 480th floor. This meant I had to take the birds down 131 stories, or a little over half a kilometer. And then climb back.

Even on the face of Le Bab Tower, with a roughing cube or vent or external rail every meter or so, this is a serious climb. Molly's pigeons alone were not worth the trip, so I dropped five floors and went to see Lenny.

It's a real pain to climb around Lenny's because nearly every horizontal surface has a plant box or pot on it. So I rappeled down even with him and shouted over to where he was fiddling with a clump of fennel.

"Hey, Lenny. I'm making a run. You got anything for Murry?"

He straightened up. "Yeah, wait a sec." He was wearing shorts and his climbing harness and nothing else. He was brown all over. If I did that sort of thing I'd be a melanoma farm.

Lenny climbed down to his tent and disappeared inside. I worked my way over there, avoiding the plants. I smelled dirt, a rare smell up here. It was an odor rich and textured. It kicked in memories of freshly plowed fields or newly dug graves. When I got to Lenny's tent, he came out with a bag.

"What'cha got," I asked.

He shrugged. "Garlic, cumin, and anise. The weights are marked on the outside. Murry should have no trouble moving it. The Chicanos can't get enough of the garlic. Tell Murry that I'll have some of those tiny *muy caliente* chilis for him next week."

"Got it."

"By the way, Fran said yesterday to tell you she has some daisies ready to go down."

"Check. You ever grow any fruit, Lenny?"

"On these little ledges? I thought about getting a dwarf orange once but decided against it. I grow dew berries but none of them are ripe right now. No way I could grow trees. Last year I grew some cantaloupe but that's too much trouble. You need a bigger bed than I like."

"Oh, well. It was a thought." I added his bag to the pigeons in my pack. "I'll probably be late getting back."

He nodded. "Yeah, I know. Better you than me, though. Last time *I* went, the Howlers stole all my tomatoes. Watch out down below. The Howlers are claiming the entire circumference from 520 to 530."

"Oh, yeah? Just so they don't interfere with my right of eminent domain."

He shrugged. "Just be careful. I don't care if they want a cut. Like maybe a clump of garlic."

I blinked. "Nobody cuts my cargo. Nobody."

"Not even Dactyl?"

"Dactyl's never bothered me. He's just a kid."

Lenny shrugged. "He's sent his share down. You get yourself pushed off and we'll have to find someone else to do the runs. Just be careful."

"Careful is what I do best."

Fran lived around the corner, on the east face. She grew flowers, took in sewing, and did laundry. When she had the daylight for her solar panel, she watched TV.

"Why don't you live inside, Fran. You could watch TV twenty-four hours a day."

She grinned at me, a not unpleasant event. "Nah. Then I'd pork up to about a hundred kilos eating that syntha crap and not getting any exercise and I'd have to have a permit to grow even one flower in my cubicle and a dispensation for the wattage for a grow light and so on and so forth. When they put me in a coffin, I want to be dead."

"Hey, they have exercise rooms and indoor tracks and the rec balconies."

"Big deal. Shut up for a second while I see if Bob is still mad at Sue because he found out about Marilyn's connection with her mother's surgeon. When the commercial comes I'll cut and bundle some daisies."

She turned her head back to the flat screen. I looked at her blue bonnets and pansies while I waited.

"There, I was right. Marilyn is sleeping with Sue's mother. That will make everything okay." She tucked the TV in a pocket and prepared the daisies for me. "I'm going to have peonies next week." I laced the wrapped flowers on the outside of the pack to avoid crushing the petals. While I was doing that Fran moved closer. "Stop over on the way back?"

"Maybe," I said. "Of course I'll drop your script off."

She withdrew a little.

"I want to, Fran, honest. But I want to get some fresh fruit for Mad Molly's birthday tomorrow and I don't know where I'll have to go to get it."

She turned away and shrugged. I stood there for a moment, then left, irritated. When I looked back she was watching the TV again.

The Howlers had claimed ten floors and the entire circumference of the Le Bab Tower between those floors. That's an area of forty meters by 250 meters per side or 40,000 square meters total. The tower is over a kilometer on a side at the base but it tapers in stages until it's only twenty meters square at three thousand meters.

Their greediness was to my advantage because there's only thirty-five or so Howlers and that's a lot of area to cover. As I rappelled down to 529 I slowly worked my way around the building. There was a bunch of them in hammocks on the south face, sunbathing. I saw one or two on the east face but most of them were on the west face. Only one person was on the north side.

I moved down to 521 on the north face well away from the one guy and doubled my longest line. It was a hundred meter blue line twelve millimeters thick. I coiled it carefully on a roughing cube after wrapping the halfway point of the rope around another roughing cube one complete circuit, each end trailing down. I pushed it close into the building so it wouldn't slip. Then I clipped my brake bars around the doubled line.

The guy at the other corner noticed me now and started working his way from roughing cube to roughing cube, curious. I kicked the rope off the cube and it fell cleanly with no snarls, no snags. He shouted. I jumped, a gloved hand on the rope where it came out of the brake bars. I did the forty meters in five jumps, a total of ten seconds. Halfway down I heard him shout for help and heard others come around the corner. At 518 I braked and swung into the building. The closest Howler was still fifteen meters or so away from my rope, but he was speeding up. I leaned against the building and flicked the right hand rope hard, sending a sinusoidal wave traveling up the line. It reached the top and the now loose rope flicked off the cube above and fell. I sat down and braced. A hundred meter rope weights in at eight kilos and the shock of it pulling up short could have pulled me from the cube.

They shouted things after me, but none of them followed. I heard one of them call out, "Quit'cha bitchin. He's got to pass us on his way home. We'll educate him then."

*　　*　　*

All the rec guards deal. It's a good job to have if you're inside. Even things that originate inside the tower end up traveling the outside pipeline. Ain't no corridor checks out here. No TV cameras or sniffers either. The Howlers do a lot of that sort of work.

Murry is different from the other guards, though. He doesn't deal slice or spike or any of the other nasty pharmoddities, and he treats us outsiders like humans. He says he was outside once. I believe him.

"So, Murry, what's with your wife? She had that baby yet?"

"Nah. And boy is she tired of being pregnant. She's, like, out to *here*." He held his hands out. "You tell Fran I want something special when she finally dominoes. Like roses."

"Christ, Murry. You know Fran can't do roses. Not in friggin pots. Maybe day lilies. I'll ask her." I sat in my seat harness, hanging outside the cage that's around the rec balcony. Murry stood inside smelling the daisies. There were some kids kicking a soccer ball on the far side of the balcony and several adults standing at the railing looking out through the bars. Several people stared at me. I ignored them.

Murry counted out the script for the load and passed it through the bars. I zipped it in a pocket. Then he pulled out the provisions I'd ordered the last run and I dropped them, item by item, into the pack.

"You ever get any fresh fruit in there, Murry!"

"What do I look like, guy, a millionaire? The guys that get that sort of stuff live up there above 750. Hell, I once had this escort job up to 752 and while the honcho I escorted was talking to the resident, they had me wait out on this patio. This guy had apples and peaches and *cherries* for crissakes! *Cherries!*" He shook his head. "It was weird, too. None of this cage crap." He rapped on the bars with his fist. "He had a chest high railing and that was it."

"Well of course. What with the barrier at 650 he doesn't have to worry about us. I'll bet there's lots of open balconies up that way." I paused. "Well, I gotta go. I've got a long way to climb."

"Better you than me. Don't forget to tell Fran about the special flowers."

"Right."

They were waiting for me, all the Howlers sitting on the south face, silent, intent. I stopped four stories below 520 and rested. While I rested I coiled my belay line and packed it in my pack. I sat there, fifteen kilos of supplies and climbing paraphernalia on my back, and looked out on the world.

The wind had shifted more to the southwest and was less damp than the morning air. It had also strengthened but the boundary layer created by the roughing cubes kept the really high winds out from the face of the tower.

Sometime during the day the low clouds below had broken into patches, letting the ground below show through. I perched on the roughing cube, unbelayed and contemplated the fall. 516 is just over two kilometers from the ground. That's quite a drop—though in low winds the odds were I'd smack into one of the rec balconies where the tower widened below. In a decent southerly wind you can depend on hitting the swamps instead.

What I had to do now was rough.

I had to free ascend.

No ropes, no nets, no second chances. If I lost it the only thing I had to worry about was whether or not to scream on the way down.

The Howlers were not going to leave me time for the niceties.

For the most part the Howlers were so-so climbers, but they had a few people capable of technical ascents. I had to separate the good from the bad and then out-climb the good.

I stood on the roughing cube and started off at a run, leaping two meters at a time from roughing cube to roughing cube to roughing cube moving sideways across the south face. Above me I heard shouts but I didn't look up. I didn't dare. The mind was blank, letting the body do the work without hindrance. The eyes saw, the body did, the mind coasted.

I slowed as I neared the corner, and stopped, nearly falling when I overbalanced, but saving myself by dropping my center of gravity.

There weren't nearly as many of them above me now. Maybe six of them had kept up with me. The others were trying to do it by the numbers, roping from point to point. I climbed two stories quickly, chimneying between a disused fractional distillation stack and a cooling tower. Then I moved around the corner and ran again.

When I stopped to move up two more stories there were only two of them above me. The other four were trying for more altitude rather than trying to keep pace horizontally.

I ran almost to the northwest corner, then moved straight up.

The first one decided to drop kick me dear Jesus through the goal posts of life. He pulled his line out, fixed it to something convenient and rappelled out with big jumps, planning, no doubt, to come swinging into me with his feet when he reached my level. I ignored him until the last minute when I let myself collapse onto a roughing cube. His feet slammed into the wall above me then rebounded out.

As he swung back out from the face I leaped after him.

His face went white. Whatever he was expecting me to do, he wasn't expecting *that!* I latched onto him like a monkey, my legs going around his waist. One of my hands grabbed his rope, the other punched with all my might into his face. I felt his jaw go and his body went slack. He released the rope below the brake bars and started sliding down the rope. I scissored him with my legs and held onto the rope with both hands. My shoulders creaked as I took the strain but he stopped sliding. Then we swung back into the wall and I sagged onto a cube astride him.

His buddy was dropping down more slowly. He was belayed but he'd seen what I'd done and wasn't going to try the airborne approach. He was still a floor or two above me so I tied his friend off so he wouldn't sleepwalk and took off sideways, running again.

I heard him shout but I didn't hear him moving. When I paused again he was bent over my friend with the broken jaw. I reached an external exhaust duct and headed for the sky as fast as I could climb.

At this point I was halfway through Howler territory. Off to my right the group that had opted for height was now moving sideways to cut me off. I kept climbing, breathing hard now but not desperate. I could climb at my current speed for another half hour without a break and I thought there was only one other outsider that could keep up that sort of pace. I wondered if he was up above.

I looked.

He was.

He wasn't on the wall.

He didn't seem to be roped on.

And he was dropping.

I tried to throw myself to the side, in the only direction I could go, but I was only partially successful. His foot caught me a glancing blow to my head and I fell three meters to the next roughing cube. I landed hard on the cube, staggered, bumped into the wall, and fell outward, off the cube. The drop was sudden, gut wrenching, and terrifying. I caught the edge of the cube with both hands, wrenching my shoulders and banging my elbow. My head ached, the sky spun in circles and I knew that there was over a kilometer of empty space beneath my feet.

Dactyl had stopped somehow, several stories below me, and, as I hung there, I could see the metallic gleam of some sort of wire, stretched taut down the face of the tower.

I chinned myself up onto the cube and traversed away from the wire, moving and climbing fast. I ignored the pain in my shoulders and the throbbing of my head and even the stomach churning fear and sudden clammy sweat.

There was a whirring sound and the hint of movement behind me. I turned around and caught the flash of gray moving up the face. I looked up.

He was waiting, up on the edge of Howler territory, just watching. Closer were the three clowns who were trying to get above me before I passed them. I eyed the gap, thought about it, and then went into overdrive. They didn't make it. I passed them before they reached the exhaust duct. For a few stories they tried to pursue and one of them even threw a grapple that fell short.

That left only Dactyl.

He was directly overhead when I reached 530. I paused and glanced down. The others had stopped and were looking up. Even the clothesliners had made it around the corner and were watching. I looked back up. Dactyl moved aside about five meters and sat down on a ledge. I climbed up even with him and sat too.

Dactyl showed up one day in the middle of Howler territory. Three Howlers took the long dive before it was decided that maybe the Howlers should ignore Dactyl before there were no Howlers left. He's a loner who does a mixed bag: some free ascent, some rope work, and some fancy mech stuff.

There was something about him that made him hard to see, almost. Not really, but he did blend into the building. His nylons, his climbing shoes, his harness were gray like the roughing cube he sat on. His harness was strung with gray boxes and pouches of varying sizes, front and back, giving his torso a bulky appearance, sort of like a turtle with long arms. He was younger than I'd thought he'd be, perhaps twenty, but then I'd only seen him at a distance before now. His eyes looked straight at me, steady and hard. He wasn't sweating a bit.

"Why?" I said.

He shrugged. "Be natural, become a part of your environment. Who said that?"

"Lots of people said that. Even I said that."

Dactyl nodded. "So, like I'm doing that thing. I'm

becoming a part of the environment. One thing you
should know by know, dude . . ."

"What's that?" I asked warily.

"The environment is hostile."

I looked out, away from him. In the far distance I
saw white sails in Galveston Bay. I turned back. "What
did I ever do to you?"

He smiled. "You make it too personal. It's more
random than that. Think of me as an extra-somatic
evolutionary factor. You've got to evolve. You've got
to adapt. *Mano a Mano* shit like that."

I let that stew for a while. The Howlers were gather-
ing below, inside their territory. They were discussing
something with much hand waving and punctuated
gestures.

"So," I finally said. "You ever walk through downtown Houston?"

He blinked, opened his mouth to say something,
then closed it. Finally, almost unwillingly, he said,
"On the ground? No. They eat people down there."

I shrugged. "Sometimes they do. Sometimes they
don't. Last time I was in Tranquillity Park they were
eating alligator tail with Siamese peanut sauce. Except
when the alligators were eating them."

"Oh."

"You even been down below at all?"

"I was born inside."

"Well, don't let it bother you," I said as I stood up.

He frowned slightly. "What's that supposed to
mean?"

I grinned. "It's not where you were born that matters," I said. "It's where you die."

I started climbing.

The first half-hour was evenly paced. He waited
about a minute before he started after me and for the
next seventy floors it was as if there was an invisible
fifteen meter rope stretched between us. About 600 he
lowered the gap to ten meters. I picked up the pace a
little, but the gap stayed the same for the next ten
floors.

I was breathing hard now and feeling the burn in my thighs and arms. My clothes were soaked in sweat but my hands were dry and I was in rhythm, climbing smooth and steady.

Dactyl was also climbing fast, but jerky, his movements inefficient. The gap was still ten meters but I could tell he was straining.

I doubled my speed.

The universe contracted. There was only the wall, the next purchase, the next breath. There were no peaches, no birthdays, no flowers, and no Dactyl. There was no thought.

But there *was* pain.

My thighs went from burning to screaming. I started taking up some of the slack with my arms and they joined the chorus. I climbed through the red haze for fifteen more stories and then collapsed on a roughing cube.

The world reeled as I gasped for the first breaths. I felt incipient cramps lurking in my thighs and I wanted those muscle cells to have all the oxygen I could give them. Then, as the universe steadied, I looked down for Dactyl.

He wasn't on the north face.

Had he given up?

I didn't know and it bothered me.

Five stories above was the barrier—a black, ten meter overhang perpendicular to the face. It was perfectly smooth, made of metal, its welds ground flush. I didn't know what was above it. There were rumors about automatic lasers, armed guards, and computer monitored imaging devices. I'd worry about them when I got past that overhang.

I was two stories short of it when Dactyl appeared at the northeast corner of the building.

Above me.

It wasn't possible. I almost quit then but something made me go on. I tried to blank my mind and began running toward the west face, doing the squirrel hopping from block to block, even though my muscles weren't up to it. I almost lost it twice, once when my mind dwelt too much on how Dactyl had passed me and once when my quadriceps gave way.

I stopped at the corner, gasping, and looked back. Dactyl was working his way leisurely after me, slowly, almost labored. I ducked around and climbed again, until I was crouched on a roughing cube, the dark overhang touching my head. I peeked around the corner. Dactyl had paused, apparently resting.

I took off my pack and pulled out a thirty-meter length of two-ton-test line, a half-meter piece of ten-kilo-test monofilament, and a grapple. I tied the monofilament between the heavier line and the grapple.

I peeked around the corner again. Dactyl was moving again, but slowly, carefully. He was still two-hundred meters across the face. I dropped down two meters and stepped back around the corner. Dactyl stopped when he saw me, but I ignored him, playing out the grapple and line until it hung about fifteen meters below me. Then I started swinging it.

It was hard work, tricky, too. I didn't think I had the time to rig a quick belay before Dactyl got there. At least the grapple was light, three kilos at most, but as it swung wider and wider it threatened to pull me off at each end of its swing, especially as the corner formed by the barrier concentrated the wind somewhat.

Finally the grapple raised far enough on the swing away from the corner. As it dropped to the bottom of its swing I began pulling it in. As the moment arm decreased the grapple sped up, gaining enough speed to flip up above the edge of the overhang. I had no idea how thick the overhang was or even if there was something up there for the grapple to catch on. I held my breath.

There was a distant clinking noise as it struck something and the rope slackened. For an instant I thought it was dropping back down and I was scared because I was already off balance and I didn't know how far Dactyl was behind me. Then the rope stopped moving and the grapple didn't drop into sight.

I risked a quick look behind. Dactyl was still a hundred meters away. I took the rope and moved back around the corner, pulling the rope cautiously tight. As luck would have it, with the line pulled over, Dactyl wouldn't be able to see any part of the rope until he rounded the corner.

It took me two minutes to tie the lower end of the rope around a roughing cube and then to two more cubes for backup. Then I recklessly dropped from cube to cube until I was three stories down and hidden behind a Bernoulli exhaust vent.

He stuck his head around the corner almost immediately. Saw the dangling line and tugged it hard. The ten-kilo test line hidden above the barrier held. Dactyl clipped a beaner over the line and leaped out, almost like a flying squirrel, his hands reaching for the rope. He was halfway out before his full weight hit the rope.

The ten kilo test snapped immediately. I heard his indrawn breath, but he didn't swear. Instead, as he arched down, he tried to twist around, to get his legs between him and the face as he swung into it.

It was only partially successful, slamming hard into the corner of a roughing cube, one leg taking some of the shock. I heard the breath leave his lungs in an explosive grunt and then he was sliding down the rope toward the unattached end, grabbing weakly to stop himself, but only managing to slow the drop.

I moved like a striking snake.

I was already lower down the tower from where he'd hit the wall and took three giant strides from cube to cube to get directly beneath him. Then he was off the end of the rope and dropping free and my hand reached out, snared his climbing harness, and I flattened myself atop the cube I was on.

For the second time that day I nearly dislocated my shoulder. His weight nearly pulled me off the tower. The back of my shirt suddenly split. I heard his head crack onto the cube and he felt like a sack of dirt, lifeless, but heavy as the world.

It took some time to get him safely onto the cube and lashed in place.

It took even longer to get my second grapple up where the first one was. It seemed my first attempt was a fluke and I had to repeat the tiring process six more times before I could clip my ascenders to the rope and inchworm up it.

The building had narrowed about the barrier, to something like 150 meters per side. I was on the edge of a terrace running around the building. Unlike the recreation balconies below, it was open to the sky, uncaged, with only a chest high railing to contain its occupants. Scattered artfully across the patio were lounge chairs and greenery topped planters.

I saw a small crowd of formally dressed men and women mingling on the west terrace, sheltered from the northeast wind. Servants moved among them with trays. Cocktail hour among the rich, the influential, and the cloudy.

I pulled myself quickly over the edge and crouched behind a planter, pulling my rope in and folding my grapples.

The terrace areas unsheltered by the wind seemed to be deserted. I looked for cameras and IR reflectors and capacitance wires but I didn't see any. I couldn't see any reason for any.

Above me, the face of the tower rose another five hundred meters or so, but unlike the faces below, there were individual balconies spotted here and there among the roughing cubes. On more than one I could see growing plants, even trees.

I had more than a hundred floors to go, perhaps 400 meters.

My arms and legs were trembling. There was a sharp pain in the shoulder Dactyl had kicked, making it hard for me to lift that arm higher than my neck.

I nearly gave it up. I thought about putting down my pack, unbuckling my climbing harness, and stretching out on one of these lounge chairs. Perhaps later I'd take a drink off of one of those trays.

Then a guard would come and escort me all the way to the ground.

Besides, I could do a hundred stories standing on my head, right? Right.

The sun was completely down by the time I reached

700 but lights from the building itself gave me what I couldn't make out by feel. The balconies were fancy, sheltered from the wind by removable fairings and jutting fins. I kept my eye out for a balcony with fruit trees, just in case. I wouldn't climb all the way up to 752 if I didn't have to.

But I had to.

There were only four balconies on 752, one to each side. There were the largest private balconies I'd ever seen on the tower. Only one of them had anything resembling a garden. I spent five minutes looking over the edge at planter after planter of vegetables, flowers, shrubs, and trees. I couldn't see any lights through the glass doors leading into the building and I couldn't see any peaches.

I sighed and pulled myself over the edge for a closer look, standing upright with difficulty. My limbs were leaden, my breath still labored. I could hear my pulse thudding in my ears, and I still couldn't see any peaches.

There were some green oranges on a tree near me, but that was the closest thing to fruit I could see. I shivered. I was almost two kilometers above sea level and the sun had gone down an hour ago. My sweat soaked clothes were starting to chill.

Something was nagging me and, at first, the fatigue toxins wouldn't let me think clearly. Then an important fact swam into my attention.

I hadn't checked for alarms.

They were there, in the wall above the railing, a series of small reflectors for the I/R beams that I'd crawled through to enter the balcony.

Time to leave. Long past time. I stepped toward the railing and heard a door open behind me. I started to swing my leg up over the edge when I felt something stick me in the side. And then the universe exploded.

All the muscles on my right side convulsed spasmodically and I came down onto the concrete floor with a crash, slamming my shoulder and hip into the ground. My head was saved from the same fate by the backpack I wore.

Taser, I thought.

When I could focus, I saw the man standing about three meters away, wearing a white khaftan. He was oder than I was by decades. Most of his hair was gone and his face had deep lines etched by something other than smiling. I couldn't help comparing him to Mad Molly, but it just wasn't the same. Mad Molly could be as old but she didn't look anywhere as *nasty* as this guy did.

He held the taser loosely in his right hand. In his left hand he held a drink with ice that he swirled gently around, clink, clink.

"What are you doing here, you disgusting little fly?"

His voice, as he asked the question, was vehement and acid. His expression didn't change though.

"Nothing." I tried to say it strongly, firmly, reasonably. It came out like a frog's croak.

He shot me with the taser again. I caught the glint on the wire as it sped out, tried to dodge, but too late.

I arched over the backpack, my muscles doing things I wouldn't have believed possible. My head banged sharply against the floor. Then it stopped again.

I was disoriented, the room spun. My legs decided to go into a massive cramp. I gasped out loud.

This seemed to please him.

"Who sent you? I'll know in the end. I can do this all night long."

I said quickly, "Nobody sent me, I hoped to get some peaches."

He shot me again.

I really didn't think much of this turn of events. My muscles had built up enough lactic acid without electro-convulsive induced contractions. When everything settled down again I had another bump on my head and more cramps.

He took a sip from his drink.

"You'll have to do better than that," he said. "Nobody would risk climbing the outside for peaches. Besides, there won't be peaches on that tree for another five months." He pointed the taser. "Who sent you?"

I couldn't even talk at this point. He seemed to

realize this, fortunately, and waited a few moments, lowering the taser. Then he asked again, "Who sent you?"

"Get stuffed," I told him weakly.

"Stupid little man." He lifted the taser again and something smashed him in the arm, causing him to drop the weapon. He stopped to pick it up again but there was a streak of gray and the thud of full body contact as someone hit him and bowled him over onto his back.

I saw the newcomer scoop up the taser and spin sharply. The taser passed over my head and out over the railing.

It was Dactyl.

The man in the khaftan saw Dactyl's face then and said, "You!" He started to scramble to his feet. Dactyl took one sliding step forward and kicked him in the face. The man collapsed in a small heap, his khaftan making him look like a white sack with limbs sticking out.

Dactyl stood there for a moment looking down. Then he turned and walked slowly back to me.

"That was a nasty trick with the rope."

I laughed, albeit weakly. "If you weren't so lazy you would have made your own way up." I eyed him warily, but my body was't up to movement yet. Was he going to kick me in the face, too? Still, I had to know something. "How did you pass me down there, below the barrier? You were exhausted, I could see it."

He shrugged. "You're right. I'm lazy." He flipped a device off his back. It looked like a gun with two triggers. I made ready to jump. He pointed it up and pulled the trigger. I heard a *chunk* and something buried itself in the ceiling. He pulled the second trigger and there was a whining sound. Dactyl and gun floated off the floor. I looked closer and saw the wire.

"Cheater," I said.

He laughed and lowered himself back to the floor. "What the hell are you doing here?" he asked.

I told him.

"You're shitting me."

"No."

He laughed then and walked briskly through the door into the tower.

I struggled to stand. Made it. I was leaning against the railing when Dactyl came back through the door with a plastic two-liter container. He handed it to me. It was ice cold.

"What's this?"

"Last season's peaches. From the freezer. He always hoards them until just before the fresh ones are ready."

I stared at him. "How the hell did you know that?"

He shrugged, took the peaches out of my hand and put them in my pack. "Look, I'd get out of here before he wakes up. Not only does he have a lot nastier things than that taser, but security will do whatever he wants."

He swung up over the edge and lowered himself to arm's length. Just before he dropped completely from sight he added something which floated up with the wind.

"He's my father."

I started down the tower not too long after Dactyl. Physically I was a wreck. The taser had exhausted my muscles in a way that exercise never had. I probably wasn't in the best shape to do any kind of rope work, but Dactyl's words rang true. I didn't want anybody after me in the condition I was in, much less security.

Security is bad. They use copters and rail cars that run up and down the outside of the building. They fire rubber bullets and water cannon. Don't think this makes them humane. A person blasted off a ledge by either is going to die. Security is just careful not to damage the tower.

So, I did my descent in stages, feeling like an old man tottering carefully down a flight of stairs. Still, descent was far easier than ascent, and my rope work had me down on the barrier patio in less than ten minutes.

It was nearing midnight, actually lighter now that the quarter moon had risen, and the patio, instead of being deserted, had far more people on it than it had at sunset. A few people saw me coiling my rope after my last rappel. I ignored them, going about my business with as much *panache* as I could muster. On my way to the edge of the balcony I stopped at the buffet and built myself a sandwich.

More people began looking my way and talking. An elderly woman standing at one end of the buffet took a long look at me, then said, "Try the wontons. I think there's really pork in them."

I smiled at her. "I don't know. Pork is tricky. You never know who provided it."

Her hand stopped, a wonton halfway to her mouth, and stared at me. Then, almost defiantly, she popped it into her mouth and chewed it with relish. "Just so it's well cooked."

A white clad steward left the end of the table and walked over to a phone hanging by a door.

I took my sandwich over to the edge and set it down while I took the rope from the pack. My legs trembled slightly. The woman with the wontons followed me over after a minute.

"Here," she said, holding out a tall glass that clinked. "Ice tea."

I blinked, surprised. "Why, thank you. This is uncommonly kind."

She shrugged. "You look like you need it. Are you going to collapse right here? It would be exciting, but I'd avoid it if I were you. I think that nasty man called security."

"Do I look as bad as all that?"

"Honey, you look like death warmed over."

I finished playing out the rope and clipped on my brake-bars. "I'm afraid you're right." I took a bite out of the sandwich and chewed quickly. I washed it down with the tea. It wasn't one of Mad Molly's roast pigeons but it wasn't garbage, either.

"You'll get indigestion," the woman warned.

I smiled and took another large bite. The crowd of

people staring at me was getting bigger. There was a stirring in the crowd from over by the door. I took another bite and another swig, then swung over the edge. "We must do this again, sometime," I said. "Next time, we'll dance."

I dropped into the dark, jumping out so I could swing into the building. I didn't reach it on the first swing, so I let out more rope and pumped my legs. I came within a yard of the tower and swung out again. I felt better than before but was still weak. I looked up and saw heads looking over the edge at me. Something gleamed in the moonlight.

A knife?

I reached the wall and dropped onto a roughing cube, unbalanced, unsure of my purchase. For a moment I teetered, then was able to heave myself in toward the wall, safe. I turned, to release one end of the rope, so I could snake it down from above.

I didn't have it. It fell from above, two new ends whipping through the night air.

Bastards. I almost shouted it, but it seemed better to let them think I'd fallen. Besides, I couldn't be bothered with any action so energetic. I was bone weary, tired beyond reaction.

For the next hundred stories I made like a spider with arthritis, slow careful descents with lengthy rests. After falling asleep and nearly falling off a cube, I belayed myself during all rest stops. At one point I'm sure I slept for over an hour because my muscles had set up, stiff and sore. It took me another half hour of careful motion before I was moving smoothly again.

Finally I reached Mad Molly's, moving carefully, quietly. I unloaded her supplies and the peaches and put them carefully inside her door. I could hear her snoring. Then, leaving my stash under her house as usual, I climbed down, intending to see Fran and make her breakfast.

I didn't make it to Fran's.

In the half dark before the dawn they came at me.

This is the place for a good line like "they came on me like the wolf upon the fold" or "as the piranha swarm." Forget it. I was too tired. All I know is they came at me, the Howlers did. At me, who'd been beaten, electroshocked, indigested, sliced at, and bone wearified, if there exists such a verb. I watched them come in dull amazement, which is not a suit of clothes, but an amalgam of fatigue and astonished reaction to the last straw on my camellian back.

Before I'd been hurt and felt the need to ignore it. I'd been challenged and felt the need to respond. I'd felt curiosity and felt the need to satisfy it. I'd felt fear and the need to overcome it. But I hadn't yet felt what I felt now.

I felt rage, and the need to express it.

I'm sure the first two cleared the recreation balcony, they had to. They came at me fast unbelayed and I used every bit of their momentum to heave them out. The next one, doubtless feeling clever, landed on my back and clung like a monkey. I'd passed caring, I simply threw myself to the side, aiming my back at the roughing cube two meters below. He tried, but he didn't get off in time. I'm grateful though, because the shock would have broken my back if he hadn't been there.

I don't think he cleared the rec balcony.

I ran then, but slowly, so angry that I wanted them to catch up, to let me use my fists and feet on their stubborn, malicious, stupid heads. For the next ten minutes it was a running battle only I ran out of steam before they ran out of Howlers.

I ended up backed into a cranny where a cooling vent formed a ledge some five meters deep and four meters wide, when Dactyl dropped into the midst of them, a gray blur that sent three of them for a dive and two more scrambling back around the edges.

I was over feeling mad by then and back to just feeling tired.

Dactyl looked a little tired himself. "I can't let you out of my sight for a minute, can I?" he said. "What's the matter? You get tired of their shit?"

"Right . . ." I laughed weakly. "Now I'm back to owing *you*."

"That's right, suck-foot. And I'm not going to let you forget it."

I tottered forward then and looked at the faces around us. I didn't feel so good.

"Uh, Dactyl."

"Yeah."

"I think you better take a look over the edge."

He walked casually forward and took a look down, then to both sides, then up. He backed up again.

"Looks like you're going to get that chance to repay me real soon," he said.

The Howlers were out there—all of the Howlers still alive—every last one of them. In the predawn gray they were climbing steadily toward us from all sides, as thick as cannibals at a funeral. I didn't think much of our chances.

"Uh, Dactyl?"

"Yeah."

"Do you think that piton gun of yours can get us out of here?"

He shook his head. "I don't have anything to shoot into. The angles are all wrong."

"Oh."

He tilted his head then and said, "I do have a parachute."

"What?"

He showed me a gray bundle connected to the back of his climbing harness between batteries.

"You ever use it?"

"Do I look crazy?" he asked.

I took a nine meter length of my strongest line and snapped one end to my harness and the other to his.

The Howlers were starting to come over the lip.

"The answer is yes," I said.

We started running.

I took two of them off with me, and Dactyl seemed to have kicked one man right in the face. The line stretched between us pulled another one into the void. I was falling, bodies tumbling around me in the air, the recreation deck growing in size. I kept waiting for Dactyl to open the chute but we seemed to fall forever. Now I could see the broken Howlers who'd preceded us, draped on the cage work over the balcony. The wind was a shrieking banshee in my ears. The sun rose. I thought, *here I am falling to my death and the bloody sun comes up!*

In the bright light of the dawn a silken flower blossomed from Dactyl's back. I watched him float up away from me and then the chute opened with a dull boom. He jerked up away from me and there came a sudden, numbing shock. Suddenly I was dangling at the end of a three meter pendulum, tick, tick and watching four more bodies crash into the cage.

The wind took us then, far out, away from the tower, spinning slowly as we dropped. I found myself wondering if we'd land on water or land.

Getting out of the swamp, past alligators and cannibals, and through the Le Bab Security perimeter is a story in itself. It was hard, it took some time, but we did it.

While we were gone there was a shakeup in the way of things. Between my trespassing and Howlers dropping out of the sky, the Security people were riled up enough to come out and "shake off" some of the fleas. Fortunately most of the victims were Howlers.

To finish this story up neatly I would like to add that Molly liked the peaches—but she didn't.

It figures.

SHAMAN
By John Shirley

Quinn was crossing the street in southeastern Manhattan on a hot summer night, hands on his head, with a terrorist submachine gun at his back—when he saw the luminous skullhead of the vinyl batwinged cop-car banshee.

First he saw the PAV, the Police Assault Van, on its way to a black-out riot; it was pushing a double pool of headlight glow ahead of it as it screamed by on Delancey. Glimpsed as it flashed past, the armored copcar was a gray blur mohawked with a streak of red glow, its cherrytop a con trail of hellish shine against the dirty darkness of the sweltering, blacked-out inner city.

And then came the hallucination, vision, or whatever it was, rising above the building the PAV had passed behind. . . . Weightless, but big as an armored car, the banshee spread its vinyl batwings and lifted its fiery head over the roof-rim; it pulled itself into the sky, and he saw that its head was a translucent-red human skull shining with the whirling electric lights that were its brains, its mouth a sirening bullhorn, its body a bulked-out pterodactyl of studded gray metal. Quinn gaped, and looked at their others . . . but their eyes were focused entirely on survival, on getting across the street. He was certain they couldn't see it.

I'm over the edge, he thought. Oh, shit.

The terrorist jabbed the gun-muzzle into Quinn's back, and he looked away from the thing in the sky; he lurched on, crossed the street.

That was on the night of the summer's third black-out, July 18, 2011. He saw the banshee at 10:10 P.M.

At 9:45 P.M., twenty-five minutes earlier, before the fabric of consensual reality began to reweave itself, he was just stepping out of the subway station . . .

Quinn and Cisco and Zizz emerged from the subway station, laughing over some inane joke. They were laughing to cover being scared, because this was sniper territory. Coming out behind them, Bowler wasn't laughing. Bowler was grim as a granite crag, disapproving of any departure from the Two-tone serious-ness of Radical Purpose.

Trying not to wonder where the crosshairs were centered, they climbed gratefully from the rancid, mold-ering underground into the sloppy heat of the summer night. They'd walked through a pedestrian tunnel that led from the Sixth Street station to this one. The blue emergency lighting system for the subway tunnels was running, despite the black-out, so there was light down there, but it was infused with another kind of dark-ness: the clammy darkness of screwed-down, bridled fear. Thinking about the Fridge. And Deirdre.

They stood around in a small, worn-out park, sixty square feet of packed dirt, expiring grass, grafitti'd benches, young trees shriveled like burnt matches from acid rain. The park was in the triangle between several intersecting streets. It wasn't completely dark here; a web-gloss of light stretched from the lit-up part of the city, north of Houston. And there was a little illumina-tion from two light-storage billboards—during the day they soaked up sun-power, gave it out at night with the brash glow of commerce—advertising the Panam

low-orbit shuttle (*Fifteen minutes to Paris!*) and, across
the square from the Panam billboard: *Protect your
health with Doc Johnson's Intravenous Sex: Makes part-
ners obsolete!* The shopfronts were dark. Quinn could
make out a People's Republic of China Chinese food
franchise, with its cartoon of a jolly Mao in a chef's
hat; discount boutiques, shops selling remaindered
consumer-junk; and the double-padlocked entrances
to the big underground malls. He and the others leaned
on the rusting iron frames of children's swings, the
swing-chains missing, nearby stood metal-mesh trashcans
crimped like cigarette butts, overflowing with plastic
and tin and scrap-paper: the shed skins of slithery junk
food.

In the distance, the sirens: rising and falling. How
long before the Feds checked out Funs territory? Quinn
wondered. Or before one of the black-out riots spread
to this neighborhood? Maybe it depended on who had
attacked the power station this time. Which Faction:
Christian Funs, Moslem Funs, an-esthets, Movement,
Media Thugs, whomever . . . there were conflicting
rumors.

Quinn turned to Bowler, who was ostensibly the
leader of the rescue party. "What now?"

Bowler rumbled, "We have to wait here. This is the
edge of the Funs territory." He nodded toward a
luminous-blue Moslem Fundamentalist slogan sprayed
in Arab script across the asphalt park path. "They'll
contact us. Or they'll decide . . ." He let it trail off,
and they knew he meant the snipers.

Looking around, Quinn spotted more of the Funs
tags, fresh-looking, overtop the other graffiti, and rain-
spotted posters of the boyish, spectacled Ayatollah
Daseheimi slapped up with glueguns on walls, benches.
He wondered where the crosshairs were now . . . on
the back of his neck, on his forehead, the base of his
spine?

Maybe the rescue pact had been a mistake; maybe it
was childish and arrogant and unrealistic, even with
the video key-cassette (thinking that, he absently
touched the bulge of the little cassette in his shirt

pocket), to think they could break Deirdre out of the Fridge. But anyway it was following through. It was commitment.

Quinn—tall, thin, wispy blond, big-nosed, with one green eye and one blue eye—had been inconsistent for all of twenty-four years. He tried to define himself in little ways, like dressing in monochrome; all black or all white or all red. "Start with your clothes," Quinn's Dad had always told him. "Start outside, work inward." One of his Dad's wildly superficial platitudes. (His Dad was dressed by professional designers before he hit the stage; he had a superstitious faith in costuming.) But under the threads Quinn was erratic at everything, and bitterly knew it; he was a lapsed Columbia U Video Arts student. He joined organizations in great enthusiasm and never went to the second meeting; sometimes read heaps of books in a week, other times went months without reading anything to the end; played bass in a band but never rehearsed enough. Gave up drugs but never quite gave them up. Committed himself to girls with deep, resonant, romantic conviction—sometimes three or four a month that way.

Zizz had said once, "Maybe it's the *mon*-eeeeey, huuuuhhh?" Maybe it was just too easy to fall back on the annuities, the money from his Dad, the retreat into the womb of his High Security Housing apartment. No motivation to follow through, because when things got hard . . .

Tonight, though, he'd made up his mind. . . . Tonight he wore all black: a black T-shirt, black guerrilla baggies tucked into black skinhead boots. The color of commitment. Because it was Deirdre who'd first made him really look at himself. It was Deirdre who had shown him what commitment could be . . .

So he stayed, and waited to see if the snipers would kill him.

Zizz, whistling and talking to herself in a sing-song whisper, swinging on the postage-stamp playground's monkey bars now, seemed to have forgotten all about the snipers, and the fact that this was Moslem Funs territory. Zizz was female, but you had to look twice to see it; she was a squat, pallid an-esthet*; her hair was bleached bone-white, blown out like some hungry tidal pool creature; her eyesockets were blackened with heavy kohl. She could've co-starred in an episode of *Vampire Girls*. The Walkman capsule plugged into her right ear was gradually destroying auditory nerve-ends with one of the Shaped Static bands, *Fucked-Up Heaven*. The left ear clustered with rings and screws twisted right through the cartilage. Dangling from her left wrist was a sort of doll, four inches long, a primitive thing cunningly wrought of brightly colored electric wires and bits of circuitry; it had a little silver wire like a tongue sticking out of its mouth . . .

Under a transparent plastic skirt she wore a clinging gray body stocking woven with micro signal-sensitive image reactants that reproduced the imagery in TV signals randomly across her short, stocky body; a news flash about the black-out in lower Manhattan was TV-imaged across her torso, the newscaster, his head warped to the contours of her belly, was mouthing soundlessly while above him a sex-com's nude actress did a comic double-take as her father came on to her.

"What do we gotta hang he-errrre for huh, Bowl-errr?" Zizz asked, pouting, snorting a hit of designer meth from her thumbnail-implanted stashbox; getting off, she did a few listless and abbreviated an-esthet steps to something on her ear-tape. "I mean, we can't find Deirdre like this, this is bullll-*shii*-iiit." Zizz was twenty; she had the squeaky voice of a seven year old.

Bowler glared at her. "You think we're going to a concert? This is *Funs* territory. We can't go through it till they check us out." He was big, wore an olive drab T-shirt and olive-drab fatigues and colorless boots; a bristling black beard spilled down over his collarbone, spread to nearly merge with his dreadlocks. Hooked nose, sunken eyes. Deep voice that went with his Rasputin look. You could see the white all the way around his bullet-hole pupils. He was forty; the others

---

*"An-esthet": someone into Anarchy Esthetics.

were in their twenties. Bowler rarely slept. Took too many vitamins. Saw himself as a political visionary. Had bad teeth. Read Marcuse and *Das Kapital*— unabridged—from midnight till dawn.

"Maybe," Cisco said, turning a frozen smile at the rooftops, wondering where the Funs were, "this isn't the time. Maybe it's, like, not the right vibe." Cisco was half-Puerto Rican, half-Israeli. He was short, stocky; big brown lady-killer eyes with thick black lashes, mouth a little too wide, lips a little too thick, curly black hair, offwhite East Indian shirt and rope-belt pants and sandals. He didn't bathe often enough but his sweat smelled like chicken soup so no one complained till it accumulated for a few weeks. He was twenty-four, a neo-beat poet, a self-styled mystic—a pain in the ass about it, too.

"The time to get Deirdre out is now. We have the in at the HopeScope tonight," Bowler said, with resonant authority. He was trying not to look directly at the rooftops. "We have to risk it because Deirdre would've done anything for us. She *did* do everything for us. She knew what would happen if she blew the whistle on FedControl, Cisco."

"I know, man, it's not that I don't think we owe it to her, it's just, I don't know, the aspects, the omens, they're not—"

Quinn couldn't stand any more. "*Will* you shut the fuck up, Cisco? If you didn't wanna risk it, you shouldn't have come."

"Who you mad at, *Quii-*iiinnn?" Zizz asked, grinning at him. "You mad at Cisco because you scared too huh, don't want him to talk about it *huhhhh?*" She put her hand on his arm. "Me too." With those two words, her vocal affectation had vanished. She had a thing for him, he knew, and thinking about the possibilities made him shudder—and at the same time it made him think: Maybe it'd be all right . . .

She irritated him. But he liked the way she made the effort, at least, to see into him. Maybe she'd understand him, if they got involved . . .

Involved? Sure. Like they were going to survive this. Breaking into the Fridge . . .

At first, Quinn and the others actually, honestly, really believed they could break Deirdre out of the country's most impregnable prison. The incandescence of their outrage at what had happened to Deirdre blotted out sweet reason with its glare. And when Bowler had come to Deirdre's friends with his plan to use the Middle Man, they'd gone for it.

Now, though . . . now, taking the first step, they began to think about it, to turn it over and over like a blind man with a 3-D puzzle; and they knew it was insane, there was no getting into the Fridge, except for the One Way entry that Deirdre had.

But no one wanted to be the first to say, Let's blow it off, this is impossible, this is the wrong way on a one-way street, Deirdre can't ask this of us . . .

Quinn said, "I'm tired of waiting. Can't we contact them or something?"

Bowler was peering into the shadows of the storefronts across the street. "We're doing that. You're supposed to stand here, in this spot, if you want to talk to them, and then their *Mufti* comes out. Or they snipe you."

"Or both, in proper sequence," someone said, behind them.

They turned, half expecting to be shot before they got a good look at whoever it was. But the H&K laserscope-equipped carbine hung on its strap over the little man's left shoulder, casual as a carrybag, pointed at the ground. He could afford to be casual, because of the snipers.

The Funs guerrilla was about five foot six, slender; there were sharply defined veins on his hands and forearms; he wasn't as dark as Quinn had expected. He wore a white short sleeve shirt, neatly creased black trousers. Only the boots were military. He looked like the manager of a Middle Eastern restaurant. Maybe he was that, too. He had white-metal wire rim glasses, like the boy Ayatollah—the Ayatollah didn't approve of eye implants: he believed they could be used by the implanters for mind control. The boy Ayatollah had a tradition of paranoia to live up to.

The Fun said, matter of factly: "I'm Jabbar. We were told you were coming. We were not told why. You are the children of our enemies." He looked at Zizz. A television PAV chasing a lawbreaker wound its way over her hip and across her belly; the climactic genital-slashing scene from *Realm of the Senses* played on her thigh. "You are decadents."

He left the implication hanging, swaying, kicking.

Jabbar, Quinn thought. It didn't feel like an Iranian name. Maybe it was true: that the boy Ayatollah had united the Arabs and Persians . . .

"We wanta get Deirdre," Zizz said. Surprisingly serious.

"The Middle Man agreed to help us," Bowler said.

"And tonight all the transport's fucked up, like," Cisco said. "We can't get through to HopeScope, where the Middle Man is, without going through your piece of things."

They were all in a hurry to explain. They could feel the crosshairs.

Jabbar made a cone of his lips. "Deirdre. You are friends of hers?"

Bowler nodded. "We work with her. For everyone in this area, against FedControl."

"You might be CIAD." Meaning CIA Domestic.

Bowler shook his head. "We're Movement."

"Anyone would say this," Jabbar pointed out.

"Deirdre used to talk about the . . . about *your* movement," Quinn said. Not knowing quite how it had come out of him. "She said, 'All they're doing is making the invisible injustice visible.' And she said, 'Terrorism is easy to condemn when you've got other avenues open to you.' "

Jabbar nodded, a flicker of amusement at the corners of his mouth. "The Fedayeen know this saying. We know Deirdre. We don't know you. We almost shot you. You were standing in the place, but you did not have your hands on your head. That is the rest of the signal, and it states that you are unarmed."

Instantly, Bowler, Cisco, Quinn, and Zizz put their hands on their heads.

Quinn's mouth went dry. They'd agreed to come with Bowler because he was the guy in the Movement who was supposed to know all the ins and outs over here. Only, it looked like he didn't. Great. Quinn said, "Sorry. Didn't know."

Jabbar motioned with his gun, "You'll come with me."

That's when they crossed the street, heading for the storefront opposite, where another man stood in the doorway with an auto-shotgun in his hands. Quinn was thinking: *An auto-shotgun. God, what that'd do to you*—and that's when the PAV went by, heading for a black-out riot, and the banshee rose over the building . . .

It came, and began to fade, like the after-image of a bright light on his retina—and then the terrorist Jabbar prodded him. They crossed the street, and entered the old storefront.

The windows of the storefront had been boarded over; its entrance was choked with trash. Inside, in the dim, waxy light of a chem-lantern, Quinn saw stacks of cardboard boxes against the flaking plaster walls; a few on the floor were open, and he saw that they contained racks of import-banned silicon wafers, chips, AI brain-units, cartons of untaxed cigarettes and syntharettes and liquors. The black market paid for the Funs' guerrilla ordnance.

Jabbar picked up the lantern and led the way; two other men came behind, herding them into a crowded back room that contained a desk, a dead computer terminal, two phones, and the accumulated reek of unfiltered cigarettes and strong coffee. The two dark men stood in the doorway, smoking.

Quinn had never had a hallucination before, and the banshee had left him shaken. But being trapped in a small room with hostile guerrillas armed to the teeth somehow put everything but *right now* out of his mind . . .

Jabbar hung the lantern from a hook in the corner

of a ceiling. The lantern swung slightly on its hook, making the shadows in the room leap and yaw. In the same corner, Jabbar bent to fish through a heap of posters and Arab-lettered newspapers; he drew out a flat cardboard box. He carried it to the desk and opened it, laid the contents on the desk.

It was a video painting, switched off. A rectangular chunk of glass and plastic, two feet by three feet by two inches. "Deirdre's sister was Movement, and we knew her," Jabbar said, looking up at them. "She gave us this painting. She said everyone in the Movement knew it by heart. If you are Movement, you know it."

Breathless, Quinn stared at the painting as Jabbar switched it on. There were many Movement video paintings. But there was one he knew by heart, because he'd made it himself, at NYU. And Deirdre had been a bit vain about it . . .

The painting flickered through a series of street-shots (Quinn knew immediately: it was his) outside the squat slums; high contrast images of weirdly well-dressed kids who lived in the squats gathered at oil-barrel fires; of Smoky "the Ghost" Casparino—his face hidden, but that was his spray-painted flight-jacket—buying a gun from D'Angelo, whose face was white from heavy chipping on synthcoke; a skateboard gang showing off their moves for the camera; old Mrs. Pesca with her sawed-off shotgun and collapsed grin. And paced through the loop, images of Deirdre: tall, angular, jet-black skin, cheek punctured with a stud imprinted *NFC*—No Federal Control—in red on black. Deirdre ministering to the kids, the black marketeers, the beleagured old ladies, talking till she was hoarse, telling them that FedControl wasn't all powerful, it was going to fail in its drive to move them out of Manhattan and into the little security-cop police states they called Highrise Relocation . . . Telling them that Federal Control had promised their boros to the wealthy development barons. . . . Telling them it was just plain stupid to trade home and something like freedom for a cop-haunted high rise that would slide into a slum in two years. . . .

Flick flick flick, three moving images just that fast, and every fourth one was of Dierdre.

Jabbar stabbed a button on the frame, freezing the painting on an image of Deirdre setting up a corner video re-education booth, vidding the slums the truth about FedControl's part in the Brazilian War and what happened to anyone who joined the Army. . . .

"What comes after this?" Jabbar asked.

"There are lots of Movement paintings," Bowler said desperately. "We can't—"

"It'll be a shot of a kid watching a TV-graffiti pattern with Deirdre's name in it," Quinn interrupted. He turned to Bowler. "I oughta know. I shot it myself."

Jabbar hit the button. The painting moved on, and a small child with his back to the camera sat watching as video-animated words snaked in superimposition over the President's face: *Deirdre says don't listen to liars* . . .

Jabbar nodded. "Okay." He pointed the gun at Quinn. "Now tell me with complete truth, what is it you are to do, eh? What? Because I know you've lied to me. You are Movement, but you are lying."

Quinn looked at the muzzle of the gun. He could hear his heart hammering, far away somewhere, like a distant construction site noise. "Uhhh . . . We told you. We're going to get Deirdre out."

"Deirdre is in the Fridge," Jabbar said, an impatient adult with a dense child. The flickering light from the video painting lit his face from below, shifting its planes in eerie dislocation. "No one can be broken from there. If you say that is what you do then you are stupid or liars."

Quinn looked at Bowler, eyebrows lifted. Bowler chose to tell the truth, as he saw it. "We're going to see the Shaman. The Middle Man. But not because I think there's anything to his, you know, ah, claims about the Spirits of the Urban Wilderness, any of it. I think they've got some kind of hardware or wetware access to the FedControl grid. Whatever they've got," Bowler went on, talking fast, "it seems to work. Deirdre herself swore it worked for her once. Only, the Middle Man is probably a schizophrenic so he interprets things . . . you know, mystically."

Quinn thought about the banshee. *Spirits of the Urban Wilderness* . . . but all he said was, "Bowler made arrangements to go to the Middle Man because he thinks the Middle Man could get Deirdre out of the Fridge. We got to get there at a certain time. And the black-outs brought the riot squads down, they've sealed off the other ways through. The only way left to get through is . . . here. Through your territory. We need an escort so your people don't shoot us."

"A way to get into the Fridge." Jabbar's nostrils flared, his eyes hardened. "If it's true, then you will take our people out, too. We have four in the Fridge." He fingered the gun meaningfully.

"I told you, Bowler," Cisco muttered. "The vibes were—"

"No, this is *greaaa*-aaaat!" Zizz broke in, doing a little spastic dance that made two of the guerrillas look at each other and snort. "We could get them out, too! We could—"

Bowler shook his head. "One will be hard enough. We have a video key for her cell. We need the Middle Man to get us past the guards and failsafes and cameras. We only have one video key."

"A bomb!" Zizz suggested gleefully. "We could get in, then blow up their com-pu-uuu-ter! Then maybe all the cells would open up and—"

Quinn groaned. He felt the sweat sticking his shirt to his back. The room seemed chokingly close. "Zizz," Quinn hissed, "stop trying to help before you help us into even deeper shit."

"No, it's not a bad idea," Jabbar said, looking at Zizz with a new respect. "A bomb in their master computer."

Bowler shook his head so hard you could hear his beard rustle. "No! Listen—"

"No, *you* listen—if you are going to break out your people," Jabbar said, grinding the words between his teeth, "and you want our help, then you will break out our people, too! We will provide the explosive."

He had lifted the SMG, was pointing its muzzle at Bowler's face.

Zizz's expression shifted radically in a split second, from glee to a grim *uh-oh*. She saw that she'd blown it.

She moved closer to Quinn. Out of the corner of his eye he saw her take the little wire-doll dangling from her wrist . . .

She jabbed its tongue-wire into Quinn's forearm. Quinn jerked his arm away, sucked in his breath, and felt . . .

A flash of white light; a wave of white heat.

Quinn went rigid. Electrified within. Paralyzed. He felt a Presence. Someone . . .

Click. Suddenly he was standing outside himself. He was tethered but detached, off in a dark corner, unseen, apart from the others, watching himself, seeing an expression on his face that had never been there before.

He couldn't smell or hear anything—except he heard his own voice. It was talking nonsense. No, it was talking in Arabic, to Jabbar. He, Quinn, was speaking Arabic. He had no idea *how* to speak Arabic. Not one lesson. But he was doing it. And he knew what the words meant in English:

"Jabbar! The Fridge is wall-to-wall biomonitoring. The prisoners are all in restraints, on IV medifeeds and spinebox. They can't move unless the spinebox moves them. The cyberguards watch them, they never sleep, they never take a break, they're always there—if you destroy the master computer they and the rest of the equipment might do anything. It isn't necessarily going to shut down—it might feed the prisoners overdoses of medication, the guards might get confused and mistake them for attackers. The bottom line is, if you destroy that computer the system will break down and the people plugged into it will die. Including your men." Cisco and Bowler were staring at him; the physical part of him. Outright amazed.

Jabbar got over his surprise and replied in Arabic, "Why should we help you if it does not release our people? If we're involved and the Feds find out, they'll push us even harder. Already they fabricate this blackout to harass us, to try to drive us out. Already they raid us twice a month, when they can find us. To provoke them further would not advance our cause, not now. It would be too much pressure. In our position, we have learned how much trouble we can make and still survive. We're not fools."

"Deirdre struggles for your cause. She spoke up against the new anti-Muslim immigration laws. She spoke up and said that you were being harassed, driven to urban war, because the Christian Fundamentalists are taking over government; she said you were being framed and prosecuted and jailed and deported only because of the prejudice against Moslems. She spoke up so many times they had to get rid of her. So they planted illegal chemicals in her house, bomb-making equipment. The irony is unspeakable. Deirdre, a bomber! Countless were the times at the Movement meetings when she argued against bombs. She said bombs couldn't discriminate civilians. But FedControl framed her, they said she was a terrorist bomber, and that gave them the authority to put her in the Fridge, to sentence her to conditioning. She spoke up for you, for all of us—and they kidnapped her! Superficially legal—but kidnapping, Jabbar! Surely Allah tells you now what you must do . . ."

Jabbar gaped at him.

Then Quinn—the watching, detached part of Quinn—fell into a red tube, and passed through a wall of pain. Through white light, a wave of heat . . .

Click. He was back in himself, bathed in sweat, shaking, but . . . alone in his body now.

Everyone was staring at him. "This one," Jabbar said, slowly, in English, "has cared enough to learn our language. Has spoken good sense. He has moved me. I am the Mufti and that is my judgment."

*   *   *

A sloppy breeze, moldy-damp from the East River, oozed between the ruined tenements, and carried some heat away from Quinn and Bowler and Zizz and Cisco and the Mufti as they trudged down the middle of the rubbled street.

Quinn felt strange. Still, a little dislocated; like he was here and not here. *Zizz did this to me, somehow. The doll. Its wire tongue . . .*

Quinn dropped back and whispered to Zizz, "What did you do to me back there? You fucking inject me or *what?*"

Zizz bit her lip to keep from giggling. "I did what the Fetish Broker told me. She said if there was a 'mergency—"

"What? Who's the—"

"She works for the Middle Man, sent the doll around when Bowler made the—"

The Mufti turned and hissed, "No talk!" He gestured toward the rooftops.

The buildings were picked out with a little starlight, and with the soft edges of firelight from clearings in the rubble: smudges of red on the black-pocked wall of night. Fragments of Arabic and Farsi and Lebanese reached them and fell away as they moved through Lower East Manhattan. They were still in Moslem Funs territory but only barely. The precarious ceasefire had crystallized the Moslem and Christian zones on their respective sides of Clinton Street. National Guard barriers and checkpoints stood there still, a block West; nearer were the stripped chassis of military trucks and the burned shells of blasted cars, humped in shadow like the dessicated carcasses of Badlands buffalo.

Quinn stiffened every time they came to a cross street, since intersections exposed them to the strong possibility of sniper fire from the Christian sectors; tonight of all nights, with the cops and soldiers massively occupied by the black-out riots, would be a great night to start something, to pick off a few Funs . . .

And the Christian snipers wouldn't know at this distance that Quinn and friends didn't belong in their gunsights. If they knew who they were, they'd probably shoot anyway: Quinn's bunch came from the Registered Socialist boro.

Quinn almost wished someone would open fire. Something to break up the flow of events, the current that tugged him deeper into this thing. He was so scared he didn't recognize the sensation at first. He'd never been that scared before. It was a ball of shaking tautness in his gut, like a rabbit having a heart attack.

Something had taken him over, back there. It was gone now, but . . . he felt its footprints on his nervous system. And that scared him more than bullets or bombs or even the Fridge.

But no one fired at them. Ten minutes later, Bowler said, "Here's the HopeScope."

It was a bank.

Quinn sat in a locker room, on an old wooden bench, his back to a cool concrete wall, trying to remember how he'd come here. The Mufti had left them, and Bowler had given Quinn a slip of paper with some numbers on it, and a bank card. Anyway it looked like a bank card . . .

"Here," Bowler had said. "Put it in the Instanteller slot."

"What? That thing's trashed—"

"Just do it. You're going in."

"Why me?"

"I don't know . . . They said it was you." Bowler was looking at him strangely. A little angrily. "What did you do back there? Babbling in . . . I mean, you didn't tell me that you could speak—"

"I can't. I don't know what happened."

Bowler shifted his weight and looked at the bank, frowning. "I don't like this mumbo-jumbo. Occultism is religion and religion is social paralysis. I thought the Middle Man was . . ." He shook his head. He reached out and closed Quinn's hand around the slip of paper and the card. "Fuck. Just do it."

"Tell you the truth, I'm kind of—"

"We're all scared, man. But do it for Deirdre."

Quinn took a deep breath. He looked at Zizz. Saw

her swallow; saw her skull-eye makeup was streaked. He found himself wanting to take her in his arms. And then he thought: You want to get into that with *Zizz*? Are you kidding? But the feeling lingered.

He reached into his shirt pocket, took out the video key-cassette, and handed it to her. Some instinct: Give it to her and not Bowler. Their hands touched for a moment and he found himself giving her fingers a dry, shaky squeeze.

Then he turned and made himself walk up to the grime-streaked face of the Instanteller. He looked at it dubiously, not expecting it to be functional in any way at all. The money dispenser was in a bank whose roof had collapsed; whose windows were opaque with graffiti. But he'd inserted the card, the teller had lit up, and he'd looked at the piece of paper, tapped out . . .

Couldn't remember the code now. Numbers. He'd felt a ripple go through him, heard a sort of buzzing, and smelled something burning. There was a faint vibration at the top of his head. That's all: then all the doors of his perception had silently closed.

He'd awakened here. A fluorescent light overhead, and another tube down a little ways, that one blinking and going *Zzt-zzt-zzt*. Long rectangular room, forgotten gray-green lockers against the far wall; rusty pipes overhead and rust-flecked puddles of water on the floor. A locker room, for sure. What did a locker room have to do with a bank?

No Bowler or Cisco or Zizz. Quinn had fallen asleep standing up, never felt himself hit the ground, and then he was here, sitting against the wall, all alone. How?

There was someone sitting beside him.

They hadn't been there a second before. But hey: His brain was probably fogged from the whatever-it-was. The guy must've come in while he was spacing out, trying to remember. Sure.

He was just another guy. Street sleeper, looked like. Matted hair, matted beard, shared a gray-black skin with the city. The same coating of atmospheric silt and simple dirt. Long horny yellow nails. No shoes, clothes unrecognizable from sleeping in them. Probably smelled bad, if you got any closer: the guy sat slumped against the wall just out of the direct light, about eight feet away. Another devotee, another supplicant to the HopeScope. Supposedly the Middle Man helped anybody he chose, and he chose almost at random.

"What you going to get?" The guy asked, just like someone who was planning to get something here himself.

"Help a friend. How about you?"

"Kinda obvious isn't it? Someplace to rest my butt and maybe a grade D credit rating. That ain't much."

"You could've applied to move into the Socialist boro, they'll give you—"

"I look like a fucking Red to you?"

You barely even look human so the question doesn't apply, Quinn thought. But he said, "Guess not. Me neither. But they got good rent control there . . . How'd we get in here anyway?"

"With a headache. That's all I know."

"I don't even know if I'm awake. Or if this place is—"

"It's not a hallucination. Even the thing you saw tonight, that wasn't hallucination. That was the Higher Reality of the object. You're not hallucinating. You're here. I'm here."

"How'd you know I saw—"

"Experience. I seen a lot of guys in that State, you know? Come down from visions."

Bullshit, Quinn thought.

The tramp rattled on, "The vision wore off in you, but it's the reason you're gonna work so well. It put your brain into the right frequency, for a while. Visions isn't just hallucinations, man. It shows you things. The Conceptual Dimensions of a thing. And of things you don't even know're there."

He's a loon, hasn't been taking his medication, Quinn thought. It's not *enough* drugs, that's why he's a Street Sleeper.

"So," Quinn said. "What do we do now?"

"We wait. You're in a waiting room, man."

"You know all about it, huh?" Quinn said. "Then explain this place to me." Thinking that the guy probably had it all wrong. But Quinn was scared. He wanted to hear someone talking.

"The Middle Man works for the Spirits, and the Fetish Broker works for the Middle Man. You got a cigarette?"

"Uh-uh."

"Then I'll smoke one of my own." From some wen in his clothing he took a crooked, dirty cigarette and pushed its end into his tube lighter. The smoke smelled like real tobacco. He'd bummed somebody generous.

The tramp leaned back against the wall, blew smoke out through his nose and said, "The Middle Man is a Wetware Medium. He . . . how much do you want to know?"

"All of it, if I can get it."

"You'll be sorry you said that. . . . There's a subatomic particle called the IAMton. Physicists, they speculate about it, but the Middle Man *knows*. He was a cutting-edge hot shot at Stanford. He isolated the IAMton, and when he did, it spoke to him. Can you fade that? A subatomic particle that tells you, *Yeah! You found me!*" The street sleeper laughed. "Actually, see, it was *all the IAMtons on the fucking planet* that spoke to him, *through* the group of 'em he had contained in the tokomak field. Anyway, the Middle Man, now, he wants other people to know what the IAMton can give you, which is why he lets people tell about it like this, because he wants other people to use the knowledge—to find their own way to use it—but so far no one has. And he lost the way to it, once he was there. It's like biting your own teeth or licking your own tongue, once you're there . . . so now he can't tell anybody how he got there." He took a drag, coughed, blew smoke. "The IAMton, now, it's a subatomic particle that's present any time there's awareness. The body is electric, right? Has its own electromagnetic field, right? This IAMton, it's a ubiquitous

particle and when an organism has the right sort of
magnetic field some of these particles—more for the
higher organisms—are attracted and incorporated into
the organism's seat of holographic consciousness. Into
the brain. It's the *I*, the thing that reacts beyond
reflex. Now when a tribe of people are in psychological alignment they generate an external collective electromagnetic field—"

"What were you before you were a Street Sleeper?"

"Don't interrupt. Anyway—"

"I mean, you're talking different now—"

"You want to know about the Middle Man or not?"

Shaken for new reasons, Quinn said, "Go ahead."

"Anyway, this tribal field generates entities, or at-
tracts entities—the Middle Man is still not sure which
it is—and the entities appear to us as expressions of
our consensual interpretation of our environment. Now
your primitive Shaman, your aborigine, sometimes he
can talk to them and get results and sometimes not.
These entities aren't really very powerful and a lot of
the time they can't do anyone any good, except that
they can teach you about things, like tell you what
plants are medicinal . . . but in a big civilization, these
entities are a little stronger. Especially now that the
Middle Man has made some solid contacts, and they're
more a part of our world, they're less ephemeral than—
Are you listening?"

Staring at the tramp, Quinn had seen him flicker.
"You're part of the HopeScope. Some kind of . . .
image."

"So? I had to check you out, didn't I? I mean,
you're so fucking ridiculous, you and your friends . . .
getting P.O.'d and walking around with a fantasy about
cracking the Fridge. And you, considering your old
man's Dizzy Doseout. Progeny of a popstar gotta be a
flake. Spoiled little rich kid. In short: What a bunch of
jerk-offs. I had to see how serious you were. Engaged
your top mind so I could look in the lower mind . . ."

"You're reading my mind?"

"No, you're exhibiting some of it to me. We're not

really here, you understand. You're lying on a table under the old bank.''

"Shit!"

"If you say so. You're hooked in, socketed with the DataBase that the Middle Man uses to talk to the Spirits."

"Bowler doesn't buy the Spirit part. He says you've just got good hackers."

"He's a left-brained Stalinist ignoramus."

"Look—"

"You want to know what we want from you in return for opening the Fridge. If it was anybody but Deirdre, or if you didn't have the key—which you can bet your ass isn't enough by itself—we'd tell you to cruise on. There's a thousand people who want to get somebody out of the Fridge. That's *hard*. But it's Deirdre, and that's part of the reason. The other reason is our usual fee, which is worship. I mean real worship, I don't mean ego pumping."

"You want us to worship the, uh, Spirits?"

Another flicker, and then the street sleeper wasn't exactly there anymore. The guy had gone two-dimensional, was a geometrically emblematic figure on a screen, like a product insignia. Quinn was sunken into a sweet numbness, from within which he could hear the emblem talk, could see the hieroglyphic's mouth move, knowing he was seeing this on the back of his closed eyelids . . . while the Middle Man, the transformed tramp, said:

"It's a sweet thing, Quinn, our worship. It's not submission, not really: it's vanity. They're us. It's a rush, Quinn. To sing of them, and bleed a little for them, and give them offerings, and ergs.

"I'm talking Floures, who exhales electrons.

"I'm talking Network and Grid, the messengers of the gods, one for back and the other for forth, sexing with their mistress Wavelength.

"I'm talking TeeVee the Belly-stroker, who eats everything and consumes nothing, the Buddha who lies.

"I'm talking One-Oh-One—of whom you, Quinn,

are a halfling—the Spirit whose sword is Input and whose shield is Output, whose recollections are the ice-melt flowing between the arid banks of every computer online.

"I'm talking Pixel, the video queen—your mother, Quinn—who awaits you in the on-screen demimonde.

"I'm talking Fractal, the living gateway to the Fifth Dimension, whom you met in a lamp post and a drainpipe, who unites the dimension of the human senses with the dimension perceived by the electronic.

"I'm talking Pharmus-Hormona, whose translucent flesh swells voluptuously or shrinks to sinewy sweetness; who has made Fertility and Fashion indistinguishable.

"I'm talking MaxBux, the energy that is money, the money that is energy, the living flow chart of ease and power.

"I'm talking Score, Lord of the Stash, Mister Gooddrugs, whose teeth are needles; plead, beg to be sacrificed to him, beg him to take your throat in his jaws.

"I'm talking Androgyna the Disco Queen, who is the shortcut to the Spirits, who is the hip-hop voodoo and the Womb of the Urban Primitive.

"I'm talking Vehicle, on whose crown is the Mack Bulldog and in whose heart is the GM slogan.

"I'm talking Bust, the Cop, the Destroyer, whose face is chrome stamped with all numbers, and whose arms end in a gun and a stun-stick; Bust, to whom sacrifices must be made, and if you're wise you'll pray humbly to the Spirits that he is satiated with your enemies . . .

"I'm talking relatives, Quinn. Because sometimes Zeus becomes az swan . . ."

"I'm scared."

"You're okay. When One-Oh-One took control of you to talk to the Mufti in Arabic—"

"Yeah—what *was* that?"

"*That* was One-Oh-One, using your tongue to talk to Jabbar, in Arabic taken from its linguistics database, tapping heavily on its rhetoric database and my own

contribution . . . what matters is, afterwards you were
a little shaken up. But you were okay, you were remarkably all right, considering. That means you're
suited for this. So have confidence, Quinn. You've
found your wavelength."

"But I don't know how to use it if I've got it—"

"I do. I'll guide you. Let's see if the Fridge is
crackable. It has a kind of unseeable Spirit of its own
protecting it, Quinn, and it is Terrible."

"I'm—"

A circuit closed.

Quinn watched with the Middle Man's eyes. They
were eyes that seemed to float over a scene, unwatched
themselves. They might have been electronic, they
might have been human, they might have been both.
They were . . . apart from Quinn. Who was still locked
away under the bank, on a table, heavily into R.E.M.s.

Still, Quinn watched as the tramp appeared in the
ruins to Cisco and Zizz and Bowler, manifesting in the
air above them, a holy wino, a levitated tramp with an
aureole the color of a monitor screen's glow in a dark
room. Bowler shrank away, and turned his back on
the apparition, shaking his head. The vision spoke to
Cisco and Zizz. It fluttered its silver metal-flake wings,
and drew on an ethereal cigarette; it blew a smoke
ring that shaped itself into a swastika. It blew a stream
that shattered the swastika and, with suave detach-
ment, said: "There is an old pornography theater in
the next block south. The place is derelict now, and
looks blocked off, but climb over the rubble and you'll
see the way in. The Fetish Broker is there. She will
equip you." The voice had just the faintest telltale of
electronic filtering.

The apparition faded, the details first and then the
outline, the way projected holos do. But Cisco and
Zizz never doubted it. "Meet you back *heee*-errre,
Bowler," Zizz said, "since you're gonna be a *butt*-
hole about it." And went to meet the Fetish Broker.
Bowler waited behind, alone in the ruins, unarmed,
sulking in a fog of ideology. Running a risk: alone out

here he was a victim waiting for the victimizer, unless
he got lucky.

On the next block, Cisco and Zizz clambered over
fallen masonry and into the shattered Adult Sensurround
Theatre across the rubbled street, and there met the
Broker.

The Broker was lying in a bed of smut.

The photographic imagery on the twentieth century
porn magazines had been transferred onto pseudoskin—
High Silk, the expensive brand—so that she lounged
on a wallowy pillow configured with hundreds of small,
interlocked nudes, a cloth-print pattern of languid faces,
of canted buttocks and flowing breasts and the inter-
section of genitalia. She was wearing an alumitech
spine: a long gray metal millipede down her naked
back, a millipede equipped with implant wires instead
of legs. It was a signal transformer for the nerve-ends,
hyping impulses from the erogenous receptors, from
every sort of pleasure-sensitive nerve. It was state-of-
the art, but it was a new art, and her movements were
sometimes erratic, when incoming somatic pleasure
signals interfered with motor-coordination transmissions. A porcelain mechanism beside the bed blew
warm, therapeutic mists onto her, jets that strategi-
cally probed her enhanced erogenous receptors; the
pillow undulated slowly beneath her, its hidden servos
massaging, falling slack, massaging again . . .

The Fetish Broker was sunken-eyed, dagger-haired,
and almost skeletal-skinny. A tattoo of prettied-up
nervous system lines, embroidered with curlicues and
fleur de lis and blossoming vines, was etched across
her torso and legs in sullen colors. Watching from
another place, Quinn saw the flesh-colored plastic box
of the drug-doler implanted into her calf.

Zizz noticed it too. "Ooooh, a doler, those are
'spensive, what you got innit, what'sa dosage?" Zizz
and Cisco stood before the Broker's bed like courtiers
at a royal audience.

"That's a rude question," the Broker said. Voice

like an annoyed Siamese cat. "People don't ask people that."

Quinn assumed she was getting low doses of amphetamines trickled out to her, cut with maybe demerol, the occasional wash of Beta-Endorphins.

The room was a concrete cave, with its edges lost in red shadow, and the Broker's electronic fetishes its stalactites.

Cisco was staring up in fascination at them. They hung from the ceiling, hundreds of them, each about six inches long. Made with tiny pliers and tweezers and probably with the Broker's teeth, sculpted intricately from color-coded wires, bandsaw-cut pieces of circuit board, microprocessors, semiconductors, condensors, and . . . bone. Hanks of hair. Strips of blue velvet, green satin. All of it twined into little almost-people, and shapes suggesting animals no one had ever seen. None of the figures were definite, but all were clearly defined.

The Fetish Broker grinned, lips skinning from teeth that showed the tops of their roots around receding blue gums.

On a solder-spattered wooden worktable next to the bed, four fetishes were strung together on a black wire. They were figures of brightly colored rubber and copper and alloy. She moved a hand toward the table and it looked like she was moving it through strobeflashes. Jerk-jerk-jerk. Annoyed, she reached behind her with her other hand and made an adjustment on her spin. The hand moved more fluidly and picked up the ring of fetishes. "For you, Middle Man says, for Deirdre."

Cisco reached for the hoop, tugged on it—but the Broker wouldn't let go of it. Her lips skinned back from her death's head teeth again.

"A price." She moved jerkily into a robotic parody of a seductive pose. "He says I can't charge bux this time. But I can ask for something else." She looked at Cisco's crotch. "You, for a while. The other can watch."

Cisco swallowed, visibly. Muttered, "Bowler's getting off easy."

The Broker put a new tube in her doler, and lay

back on the bed. She spread her legs, and said, "Don't waste time."

They had to wait for the Broker to finish with Cisco. "She's a pain in the ass," the Middle Man said. "She's going to throw off my timing if she takes too long."

Quinn couldn't see himself, or the Middle Man. He saw Cisco and the Fetish Broker on the bed, from some objective non-place. But he and the Middle Man could hear each other.

"Hey," Quinn said. "How do the fetishes work? I mean, are they just a psychological trick or—"

"They're attuned to an IAMton transmission, and channel it. What matters is *why* they work, Quinn. The human world has reached a psychological critical mass. In the last part of the twentieth century people were panicking for a sense of community, belonging. They felt inconsequential in the bigger community— and for most people the smaller ones around them were filled with strangers. Their families were falling apart, and their tribes were bogus. They needed *real* tribes, Quinn. We all need them, particularly under stress. Which is why things factioned so brutally in Beirut. And in New York. And it's why the fetishes work: because we're pulling back into tribes; tribes with powerful consensual beliefs. And *our* tribe is strong in this town, Quinn . . ."

The Fridge looked like an office building.

"Why should prisons be ugly if the new technology can make them internally secure?" the designers had asked, thinking themselves stunningly innovative. Why not make them so that the locals would be less likely to object to having them nearby?

Out-of-towners seeing the Federal Control Penitentiary, rising austere but unthreatening from the artificial island that forked the Hudson, took it for the headquarters of a security conscious multinational corporation.

But when you saw it from Shacktown, it looked

different. Shacktown was the towering personification of the housing crisis: The roof-slums, the intricate maze of fiberboard shacks precariously piled on tenement roofs, warehouse roofs, any open space they could stake out, up above. From up there, they could see the Fridge's octagonal polarized-glass skyscraper, and know it for a prison. A seventy-story prison without roving spotlights, without outer containment walls or electric antipersonnel wire. It had a stylish notch up one side and sprawling green lawns and a topiary garden and floodlit fountain. The Shacktowners knew what it was, though. It made them shiver because it was so *confident*.

But it was guarded, all right.

As Cisco and Zizz climbed out of the boat, up the concrete embankment, and onto the lawn—they stopped, hearing the hover-cams approaching through the darkness.

Quinn, watching and listening through the Middle Man's own remote, heard it too. The Middle Man switched to infra-red scan, and Quinn saw them, two abstracted birdshapes glowing red with their motor heat as they hovered on either side of Cisco and Zizz, thirty feet up, evaluating them. Alerting the cyberguards in their niches around the base of the building.

"That's it," Quinn told the Middle Man. He couldn't see the Middle Man, but he was *There*. He was the unseen background. "The last time someone tried to break somebody out of there, the cyberguards came down on 'em, was twenty of those little fuckers rolling up all at once, blazing away. There was choppers, everything —all in about one minute. They're screwed."

"Not if we intervene."

"We don't have time."

"We do. You and I are talking in dreamtime now. Braintime, which is anything you want it to be. You ever have a dream where everything that happens takes days and days—only when you wake the whole dream took place in three minutes? It's like that. We're ten times faster. Twenty. Thirty. Okay?"

BAM BAM BAM Buh-BAM

"I hear music," Quinn said. "A hip-hop beat."

BAM BAM BAM Buh-BAM.

"I can't crack the Fridge alone, Quinn. That's why you're here. You have the talent to be empty. To be a channel. To be a zero in the right place. You and me channel the Spirits to intervene. To do that, you got to empty your mind. You got to . . . come on and DANCE."

"What?"

"DANCE!" A woman's voice now.

BAM BAM BAM buh-BAM

"DANCE!" A twenty-first century Motown singer. "Come on and DANCE!" Chanted in the rhythmic pocket.

"Are you serious?"

The beat, a ubiquitous Linn-drum detonation, went on into infinity as she (for the moment, a she) sang

Come on and DANCE
Bam Bam Buh-BAM
your way to another place
Come on and DANCE
Bam Bam Buh-BAM
internalize space
Come on and—

The beat radiated out from the marrow of his bones. Its Linn drum was programmed in the genetic core of his cells.

Suddenly Quinn was in another place. Androgyna's womb, a mirror-walled Disco suffused in crystal blue; he was dancing with himself, one of the Broker's fetishes hanging around his neck on a cord, whipping with his movements, each movement sloughing off doubts, shedding: Why? What if? But they—?

There were neon strokes of light in the ceiling and he knew from their patterning that they were impulses firing through his neurons. That he was dancing in his own skull.

And his spinal cord radiated somatic impulses in the

center of the ceiling: a split-laser, spitting streaks of laser light to the beat, and that was the campfire he danced around, in the dance of the urban primitive . . .

In the Amazon, in an *oca*, in a village of the Topajo, the *Feiticeiro* danced around a fire; the men of his tribe squatted around him, gifting him with rhythms. They twanged the *birinbal* and thumped hollow trunks. He was naked but for the sacred marks in green pigment, and the shining sheath of his sweat. The hut baked with the heat of the campfire, of bodies; the shaman was trembling like a leaf in a wind in the hot roar of a drug American medical shamans called Ibogaine, the powdering of a holy plant. The shaman danced in the groove, to the beat that radiated out from his marrow, programmed in the genetic core of him: that's what his body did. His mind had another body that eased through the World, the jungle, searching for the black jaguar, the bamboo blowgun in his right hand; humming deep in his throat to the distant plangency of the Birinbal as he called to the Spirits . . .

Quinn felt himself there physically, sweating, aching, short on breath, heart banging, but getting his groove, going into the trance that made it seem possible to dance forever, realizing that the gateway to the other continuum had a corridor and this corridor was the infinite dance; letting your own bodyheat melt you down and sweep you along, moving your hips into the pocket of the beat, completely lost in it. So the pain of exertion seemed far away, a distant smear of color. . . . And it seemed to him, as he danced (BAM BAM BAM buh-BAM) in place, in the suit of lights that was his perspiration, that he was on his way somewhere . . .

He touched the fetish at his neck. A circuit closed. Something clicked.

There was an amoebic grid, a rubbery lattice of light, that rippled in three dimensions with sine waves. If you kind of squinted, it was man-shaped, too. It was forming around the fetish that Zizz had thrown on the ground, as the Fetish Broker had told her to.

Quinn felt the rippling lattice thing quiver in his hands. It was two things, two Spirits, and he felt them in his hands like there was a mild electric charge going through them . . . That buzzing feeling . . .

Like the buzzing, the vibration he'd felt just after he'd inserted the card.

Now he had them in his hands like small animals that would respond to his will, trained pets, hungry and curious . . .

Go to the cameras.

The rippling grid stretched itself out, with hunger and interest, to the two hovering metal birdshapes—each with its camera-lens ahead—and seemed to split into an amoeba and drain into the lenses . . .

"Network and Grid, inseparable," the Middle Man said. "One thing going to two places at once."

(In some far place, Quinn was still dancing.)

Quinn saw a man looking at a bank of monitors. On one of them was a view of the lawn by the riverbank, where Zizz and Cisco had stood. But (PUSH IN on the monitor) they aren't Zizz and Cisco; through the intercession of the spirits Network and Grid, Zizz and Cisco are now two guards out for the evening patrol of the island. Normally no one would have to go patrol the island in person but what with the black-out riots in the city and all . . .

The two guards were at the front door and the man at the monitor, recognizing them (thought they were on break, must've decided to stay out longer than usual . . . what with the riots . . .), hit the keyboard sequence that opened the gate and let them in.

In the antechamber, the guard looked up to see Zizz and Cisco come in, and almost pissed his pants.

Network and Grid were in place. Quinn and the Middle Man, each dancing in his own skull, in shamanistic ecstasy, invoked Pharmus-Hormona, and MaxBux.

*   *   *

The guard at the TV monitors was named Krutzmeyer. He was stubby and he had a donkeyish face and bristly black hair on his knuckles. He was reaching for the alarm button when the spiky girl touched him with a little doll made out of wires.

Suddenly she wasn't there anymore. In her place was a sex-swollen thing from his fantasies, impossibly voluptuous. The sight of her was an electric shock. It was instant hard-on.

The feeling that rose up in Krutzmeyer was not sexual attraction. It was sexual consummation, ongoing. It was like being hit by a freight train made of soft, warm, sticky ladyflesh, and the train had hit him from the inside, had come charging out of the base of his skull down into his spine, down to the groin chakra and IMPACT. There was no resisting it.

(To Cisco it seemed that the guard looked at ordinary Zizz and—bafflingly—gave out a wail of ecstasy and monstrous fulfillment and fell onto the floor, convulsing.)

Krutzmeyer was watched by other guards on a second bank of monitors. One of these wanted to raise the alarm but Floures, of the Electrons, poured through him, holding him rigid, till Cisco figured out how to open the door into the second checkpoint. This guard's name was Wolfeton, he was sixty-two, emphysemic, and sick of his job, easy as it was. And when Floures could no longer hold him, when he saw the two weirdos walk in, and he reached for the alarm button . . .

Cisco touched him with a fetish.

For Wolfeton, Cisco was someone else. Cisco was Darrel "Ducky" Parks, grandson of Bert Parks and host of *Bux, Boy, Bux!!*, TV's most popular game show, routinely giving away $100,000NB a show. Transmuted from lead into gold by MaxBux, Cisco was the apotheosis of Easy Money and Instant Luxury, he was a ticket dispenser for a nonstop to that island in the Florida Keys Wolfeton had dreamed about, and with the money Darrel was transferring to his account Wolfeton could buy a place on the island—Hell, he could *buy the island!* And he and Gertie could . . . the

hell with Gertie, he could afford a pricey divorce, he
could dump Gertie and buy the best mistress bux
could buy—hell, make it *three* mistresses, and while
you're at it . . .

What happened to Wolfeton went beyond pushing
his greed buttons. His rational mind would never have
believed Ducky Parks had come here. MaxBux reached
into the part of Wolfeton that yearned for infantile
gratification. Something buried beneath the foundations of the personality; wired into the nervous system
itself. Gratify that place, where a personality inter-
faces with a nervous system, and the rest of the mind
will follow. MaxBux was quickfix; the Big Release;
Mama and Papa in one. And Wolfeton had been waiting years for him.

To Zizz it looked like the guard was staring at Cisco
and grinning a sort of rictus grin and hyperventilating,
turning bright red . . . But nodding frantically, muttering "You goddit, Darrel, anything you say, Darrel—"
as he punched the code to open the door to the control room.

She shrugged and went into the computer-control
room.

Brandis Danville was anorexic, anal, and—in the
words of his co-workers—"a suck-up." He thought of
himself as "ambitious and diplomatic." He looked up
and saw the strangest woman he'd ever seen walk
unaccompanied into the control room. She wasn't even
wearing an antidust suit to protect the computers. He
reached for his console and she touched him with a
faceless doll made of wires.

The girl wasn't there anymore; instead, a man in the
uniform of the Federal Control High Command stood
there, his eyes in mirror shades, his uniform crawling
with braid and brass; he was *big,* and Brandis could no
more defy him than a straw could stand up to a hurricane. He had five-hundred-mile-per-hour authority.
For Zizz had been visually transfigured by Bust, the
Destroyer. Bust, for whom even a fractional defiance
means death.

Bust, The Compleat Officer, said "Deirdre Beladonna Arliss, FP87041, in unit 4577BB, is to be released and remanded to me."

"Absolutely, right away." Not a thought of all the orders, the papers, the various failsafe checks and countersignings and video authorizations. Except one. "If you'll give me the key, sir. Keys are kept in FedControl Central and transmitted in emergency or—"

Zizz handed him the cassette.

"How did you get the image code?" the Middle Man asked a part of Quinn's mind.

"When she was locked in, her lawyer was there, he recorded it off a screen with a lapel cam. Fuzzy image, couldn't use it for the key, but I figured it out, video animated a dupe. Took me four months."

"You got an eye. You were born to it. 'Cause it's working."

Deirdre was entering the third part of the cycle. In that part, the voices ceased for a while, and the small electric shocks ceased, and the rehab computer held back on the nausea drug. Give her system a rest before the conditioning started again. She felt her arms and legs twitch in their restraints as the impulsers exercised her inside the capsule. Calendar pictures of idyllic countryside were flashed in front of her eyes for "psyche refreshment." She had the option of talking to the Friend, if she wanted. But the computer that was the Friend always gently steered her back to the subject of rehabilitation, and it could not be induced to break down or to do anything extraordinary, so she didn't talk to it anymore. She couldn't think about the Struggle, of course, not overtly, because the biomonitors knew what her body and bloodstream did when she thought about the work she'd undertaken before the incarceration. The little glandular hints, the involuntary reactions . . . and when it sensed those things, it punished her.

But she tried to think of something that would—

A ripping sound. A deep, sickening disorientation.

A burst of light. Oh no, she thought, it's happened: I've gone crazy. The one thing she was afraid of.

She was hallucinating that the cyberguards were taking her out of the mesh, wrapping her in a rubber sheet, carrying her between them for a long whirring time. Her mind had snapped into a fantasy of escape, she decided, like *Occurrence at Owl Creek Bridge*. She'd gone pathetically insane.

And when she heard Cisco's voice she was sure of it.

"It's going to be a long time before she's . . . before she's all right," Bowler said, his voice cracking. "I don't know if she'll ever be. But at least they haven't got her anymore."

It was dawn, and the smog-singed light washed everything dirty blue. They were in an alley between a warehouse and a subcontractor's superconductor plant, near the Brooklyn Bridge, waiting for the van that would take them out of Manhattan. Bowler was going to take Deirdre to a place in Maine, a house in the mountains where there were people learning how to use automatic weapons for something Bowler wouldn't talk about. "They're good people. We'll take care of her," is all he'd say.

They were all supposed to go with him.

Quinn felt hollow, detached, like everything was happening to someone else. Disorientation? Despair? He wasn't sure. But he knew he was wrenched.

He had come to himself walking down the street, with the Mufti and another Funs guerrilla he hadn't seen before; they were on either side of him, supporting him as if he were a drunk. And they'd laughed at him the way they'd laugh at a drunk. He'd looked around, and found the world dull, gray, bloodless. An enormous rock pit where humanity quarried mediocrity like gravel. He had lost the Spirits.

"We take you to your friends," the Mufti had said. "And so you should not be weeping."

But he had wept.

Now, Deirdre was sitting on someone's grimy back

steps, dosed on tranquilizers, holding her knees, swaying, now and then her head making a chicken-pecking motion, her tongue protruding, some kind of hideous motor twitch . . . Quinn looked away. He couldn't stand seeing her like that. The conditioning had broken something in her. Maybe not forever. But she was forever altered in Quinn's mind.

Everything was altered. Deirdre was no longer frozen in the Fridge, but she could not stay in New York. She had to run; her fight here was over. She could only run, and hide, and try to heal.

And Quinn could no longer believe in Bowler's revolution. Because in his trance he'd had a vision, he'd seen FedControl: the vast stainless steel matrix of it, binding them with economics into a societal "Fridge Unit," the macroscopic mother of the one that had held Deirdre. It was too big, now, too technologically coordinated, to fight with guns, with bombs.

The Middle Man had shown them how to fight it. It had to be fought on a plane that transcended technological superiority.

Cisco was chattering, "I mean, it was so *fantastic*, the guards just sort of turned into babbling idiots and I could, like, feel the spirit workin' through me—"

No, Quinn thought, it worked around you. At most used you to prop up the scarecrows.

There were other things he wanted to say to Cisco, and couldn't. Wanted to tell him that the only reason the manifestations took the form of spirits was because guys like Cisco could comprehend them no other way. That it was because there were a thousand million people using all of civilization's technology without understanding it; the children of the new illiteracy. Using electronics the way a Cro Magnon had used fire: assuming it was magic. Using computers as if they were mediums to the spirits. And so the IAMton field had given us back our own interpretation of the new wilderness, the technological wilderness . . .

Quinn wanted to tell him that he really didn't understand at all. That Spirit was real but it wasn't what he thought it was. But Quinn shrugged, and looked at Zizz.

She was different, too, he saw. She wasn't chattering, he hadn't seen her reach for her drugs. She wasn't looking at him through the subpersonalities she'd used for years. She was looking at him from the core of her . . .

"I was there, too," she said, suddenly.

"Where?"

"In the dancing place. Just watching. I felt . . . I was halfway in . . ."

Quinn nodded. She could make the connection, too.

"I don't think we should talk about it," Bowler said. "Generates misunderstandings. Struggle to align with the Necessity of focusing on issues the Masses can relate to. Mysticism is decadent, elitist."

"You're too predictable, Bowler," Quinn said. "And I got news for you. I'm not a fucking Communist."

The van was coming down the alley, jouncing with pot-holes and trash.

"I don't wanna go," Zizz said, looking at the van.

"You have to," Bowler said.

I'm supposed to go with them, Quinn thought.

"You aren't going," said a wet voice.

It was behind him. Quinn turned, took a shaky step back.

A mercurial thing, a balloon-face in silver. It was just inside a grime-caked, broken window, extending from something he couldn't see. From an empty light socket, probably. It spoke again, and its two-dimensional lips moved.

"You were made for us," it said. Its voice sounded synthetic, but not electronic. It was a mathematical model of a voice, made audible. "We let you come back to these others, so you could choose fairly. To let you choose without fear. Choose: Come home and learn."

Bowler was tugging on Quinn's wrist. "Come on," he said. "The van." He was careful to pretend he didn't see the thing.

"Bowler, look at this thing, this *means* something, man. Look and then tell me it's not—"

"I don't see your hallucinations. And I don't want to see any more holoprojections. Hypnosis, whatever they used, it worked—but it was tricks, man. Gimmicks. Mirrors and hidden compartments."

A shadow fell over them, then. They looked up, and saw something blotting out the sky over the alley, lowering itself massively between the buildings, only just fitting (or did Quinn see it compress itself to fit?), and Bowler ran to Deirdre, pulling her toward the van, shouting, "Feds! Come on, it's a bust, let's *go!*"

But Quinn shook his head. "It's not a bust. It's from the Middle Man." He knew it, looking at the thing. A kind of mechanistic semiotics informed him. The vehicle's identity spelled out in dancing chrome and glass; its heraldic styling.

None of them made the thing out clearly. It had a style, but its specific lineaments seemed to shift. Was it a sphere? A saucer, a teardrop, a swept-wing jet? It was constantly redefining itself like an animation drawn with a shaky hand. Quinn had an impression of the design essence of the sleekest helicopters; the design symmetry of a Japanese Magnetic Induction train; the design elegance of the new, slim orbital shuttles; the design compactness and *attitude* of an Italian sports-car. All these effects shifting, warring to assert themselves. Here was no vehicle: here was a Spirit, personifying vehicles. It settled onto the pavement between Quinn and Bowler. A section of the shimmering, nervous hull shimmered faster yet, and dissolved. A door yawned. An invitation.

Zizz said, "Quinn . . ." She took his arm. Quinn was amazed: her touch felt so good. It felt like a completion.

Shivering with relief, Quinn followed his instincts. He stepped into the vehicle, and went somewhere else.

And Zizz went with him.

SCHRÖDINGER'S KITTEN

By George Alec Effinger

The clean crescent moon that began the new month hung in the western sky across from the alley. Jehan was barely twelve years old, too young to wear the veil, but she did so anyway. She had never before been out so late alone. She heard the sounds of celebration far away, the three-day festival marking the end of the holy month of Ramadân. Two voices sang drunkenly as they passed the alley: two others disputed the price of some honey cakes in loud, angry voices. The laughter and the shouting came to Jehan as if from another world. In the past, she'd always loved the festival of Îd-el-Fitr: she took no part in the festivities now, though, and it seemed somehow odd to her that anyone else still could. Soon she gave it all no more of her attention. This year she must keep a meeting more important than any holiday. She sighed, shrugging: the festival would come around again next year. Tonight, with only the silver moon for company, she shivered in her blue-black robe.

Jehan Fatima Ashûfi stepped back a few feet deeper into the alley, farther out of the light. All along the

96

Street, people who would otherwise never be seen in this quarter were determinedly amusing themselves. Jehan shivered again and waited. The moment she longed for would come just at dawn. Even now the sky was just dark enough to reveal the moon and the first impetuous stars. In the Islamic world, night began when one could no longer distinguish a white thread from a black one; it was not yet night. Jehan clutched her robe closely to her with her left hand. In her right hand, hidden by her long sleeve, was the keen-edged, gleaming, curved blade she had taken from her father's room.

She was hungry and she wished she had money to buy something to eat, but she had none. In the Budayeen there were many girls her age who already had ways of getting money of their own; Jehan was not one of them. She glanced about herself and saw only the filth-strewn, damp and muddy paving stones. The reek of the alley disgusted her. She was bored and lonely and afraid. Then, as if her whole sordid world suddenly dissolved into something else, something wholly foreign, she saw more.

Jehan Ashûfi was twenty-six years old. She was dressed in a conservative dark gray woolen suit, cut longer and more severely than fashion dictated, but appropriate for a bright young physicist. She affected no jewelry and wore her black hair in a long braid down her back. She took a little effort each morning to look as plain as possible while she was accompanying her eminent teacher and advisor. That had been Heisenberg's idea; in those days, who believed a beautiful woman could also be a highly-talented scientist? Jehan soon learned that her wish of being inconspicuous was in vain. Her dark skin and her accent marked her a foreigner. She was clearly not European. Possibly she had Levantine blood. Most who met her thought she was probably a Jew. This was Göttingen, Germany, and it was 1925. The National Socialists were not yet solidly in power. Hitler had just been released from prison: he had dictated *Mein Kampf* during those months, but his rise toward political triumph had only begun. Jehan thought that Hitler had certainly not invented hate. He was only seizing on a perfect method of marketing it.

The brilliant Max Born, who first used the expression "quantum mechanics" in a paper written two years before, was leading a meeting of the university's physicists. They were discussing Max Planck's latest proposals concerning his own theories of radiation. Planck had developed some basic ideas in the emerging field of quantum physics, yet he had used classical Newtonian mechanics to describe the interactions of light and matter. It was clear that this approach was inadequate, but as yet there was no better system. At the Göttingen conference, Pascual Jordan rose to introduce a compromise solution; but before Born, the department chairman, could reply, Werner Heisenberg fell into a violent fit of sneezing.

"Are you all right, Werner?" asked Born.

Heisenberg merely waved a hand. Jordan attempted to continue, but again Heisenberg began sneezing. His eyes were red and tears crept down his face. He was in obvious distress. He turned to his graduate assistant. "Jehan," he said, "please make immediate arrangements, I must get away. It's my damned hay fever. I want to leave at once."

One of the others at the meeting objected. "But the colloquium—"

Heisenberg was already on his feet. "Tell Planck to go straight to hell, and to take de Broglie and his matter waves with him. The same goes for Bohr and his goddamn jumping electrons. I can't stand any more of this." He took a few shaky steps and left the room. Jehan stayed behind to make a few notations in her journal. Then she followed Heisenberg back to their apartments.

There were no minarets in the Budayeen, but in the city all around the walled quarter there were many mosques. From the tall, ancient towers strong voices called the faithful to morning devotions. "Come to prayer, come to prayer! Prayer is better than sleep!"

Leaning against a grimy wall, Jehan heard the chanted cries of the muezzins, but she paid them no mind. She stared at the dead body at her feet, the body of a boy a few years older than she, someone she had seen about the Budayeen but whom she did not know by name. She still held the bloody knife that had killed him.

In a short while, three men pushed their way through a crowd that had formed at the mouth of the alley. The three men looked down solemnly at Jehan. One was a police officer; one was a qadi, who interpreted the ancient Islamic commandments as they applied to modern life; and the third was an imam, a prayer leader who had hurried from a small mosque not far from the east gate of the Budayeen. Within the walls the pickpockets, whores, thieves, and cutthroats could do as they liked to each other. A death in the Budayeen didn't attract much attention in the rest of the city.

The police officer was tall and heavily built, with a thick black mustache and sleepy eyes. He was curious only because he had watched over the Budayeen for fifteen years, and he had never investigated a murder by a girl so young.

The qadi was young, clean-shaven, and quite plainly deferring to the imam. It was not yet clear if this matter should be the responsibility of the civil or the religious authorities.

The imam was tall, taller even than the police officer, but thin and narrow-shouldered; yet it was not asceticism that made him so slight. He was well-known for two things: his common sense concerning the conflicts of everyday affairs, and the high degree of earthly pleasures he permitted himself. He too was puzzled and curious. He wore a short, grizzled gray beard, and his soft brown eyes were all but hidden within the reticulation of wrinkles that had slowly etched his face. Like the police officer, the imam had once worn a brave black mustache, but the days of fierceness had long since passed for him. Now he appeared decent and kindly. In truth, he was neither; but he found it useful to cultivate that reputation.

"O my daughter," he said in his hoarse voice. He was very upset. He much preferred explicating obscure passages of the glorious Qur'ân to viewing such tawdry matters as blatant dead bodies in the nearby streets.

Jehan looked up at him, but she said nothing. She looked back down at the unknown boy she had killed.

"O my daughter," said the imam, "tell me, was it thou who hath slain this child?"

Jehan looked back calmly at the old man. She was concealed beneath her kerchief, veil, and robe; all that was visible of her were her dark eyes and the long thin fingers that held the knife. "Yes, O Wise One," she said, "I killed him."

The police officer glanced at the qadi.

"Prayest thou to Allah?" asked the imam. If this hadn't been the Budayeen, he wouldn't have needed to ask.

"Yes," said Jehan. And it was true. She had prayed on several occasions in her lifetime, and she might yet pray again sometime.

"And knowest thou there is a prohibition against taking of human life that Allah hath made sacred?"

"Yes, O Wise One."

"And knowest thou further than Allah hath set a penalty upon those who breaketh this law?"

"Yes, I know."

"Then, O my daughter, tell us why thou hath brought low this poor boy."

Jehan tossed the bloody knife to the stone-paved alley. It rang noisily and then came to rest against one leg of the corpse. "I killed him because he would do me harm in the future," she said.

"He threatened you?" asked the qadi.

"No, O Respected One."

"Then—"

"Then how art thou certain that he would do thee harm?" the imam finished.

Jehan shrugged. "I have seen it many times. He

would throw me to the ground and defile me. I have seen the visions."

A murmur grew from the crowd still cluttering the mouth of the alley behind Jehan and the three men. The imam's shoulders slumped. The police officer waited patiently. The qadi looked discouraged. "Then he didst not offer thee harm this morning?" said the imam.

"No."

"Indeed, as thou sayest, he hath *never* offered thee harm?"

"No. I do not know him. I have never spoken with him."

"Yet," said the qadi, clearly unhappy, "you murdered him because of what you have seen? As in a dream?"

"As in a dream, O Respected One, but more truly as in a vision."

"A dream," muttered the imam. "The Prophet, mayest blessings be on his name and peace, didst offer no absolution for murder provoked only by dreams."

A woman in the crowd cried out, "But she is only twelve years old!"

The imam turned and pushed his way through the rabble.

"Sergeant," said the qadi, "this young girl is now in your custody. The Straight Path makes our duty clear."

The police officer nodded and stepped forward. He bound the young girl's wrists and pushed her forward through the alley. The crowd of fellahîn parted to make way for them. The sergeant led Jehan to a small, dank cell until she might have a hearing. A panel of religious elders would judge her according to Shari'a, the contemporary code of laws derived from the ancient and noble Qur'ân.

Jehan did not suffer in her noxious cell. A lifetime in the Budayeen had made her familiar with deprivation. She waited patiently for whatever outcome Allah intended.

She did not wait long. She was given another brief hearing, during which the council asked her many of the same questions the imam had asked. She answered the all without hesitation. Her judges were saddened but compelled to render their verdict. They gave her an opportunity to change her statement, but she refused. At last, the senior member of the panel stood to face her. "O young one," he said in the most reluctant of voices, "The Prophet, blessings be on his name and peace, said, *'Whoso slayeth a believer, his reward is Hell forever.'* And elsewhere, *'Who killeth a human being for other than manslaughter or corruption in the earth, it shall be as if he killed all mankind.'* Therefore, if he whom you slew had purposed corruption upon you, your act would have been justified. Yet you deny this. You rely on your dreams, your visions. Such insubstantial defense cannot persuade this council otherwise than that you are guilty. You must pay the penalty even as it is written. It shall be exacted tomorrow morning just before sunrise."

Jehan's expression did not change. She said nothing. Of her many visions, she had witnessed this particular scene before also. Sometimes, as now, she was condemned; sometimes she was freed. That evening she ate a good meal, a better meal than most she had taken before in her life of poverty. She slept the night, and she was ready when the civil and religious officials came for her in the morning. An imam of great repute spoke to her at length, but Jehan did not listen carefully. The remaining acts and motions of her life seemed mechanically ordered, and she did not pay great heed to them. She followed where she was led, she responded dully when pressed for a reply, and she climbed the platform set up in the courtyard of the great Shimaal Mosque.

"Dost thou feel regret?" asked the imam, laying a gentle hand on her shoulder.

Jehan was made to kneel with her head on the block. She shrugged. "No," she said.

"Dost thou feel anger, O my daughter?"

"No."

"Then mayest Allah in His mercy grant thee peace." The imam stepped away. Jehan had no view of the headsman, but she heard the collective sigh of the onlookers as the great axe lifted high in the first faint rays of dawn, and then the blade fell.

Jehan shuddered in the alley. Watching her death always made her exceptionally uneasy. The hour wasn't much later; the fifth and final call to prayer had sounded not long before, and now it was night. The celebration continued around her more intensely than before. That her intended deed might end on the headsman's block did not deter her. She grasped the knife tightly, wishing that time would pass more swiftly, and she thought of other things.

By the end of May, 1925, they were settled in a hotel on the tiny island of Helgoland some fifty miles from the German coast. Jehan relaxed in a comfortably furnished room. The landlady made her husband put Heisenberg and Jehan's luggage in the best and most expensive room. Heisenberg had every hope of ridding himself of his allergic afflictions. He also intended to make some sense of the opaque melding of theories and counter-theories put forward by his colleagues back in Göttingen. Meanwhile, the landlady gave Jehan a grim and glowering look at their every meeting, but said nothing. The Herr Doktor himself was too preoccupied to care for anything as trivial as propriety, morals, the reputation of this Helgoland retreat, or Jehan's peace of mind. If anyone raised eyebrows over the arrangement, Heisenberg certainly was blithely unaware; he walked around as if he were insensible to everything but the pollen count and the occasional sheer cliffs over which he sometimes came close to tumbling.

Jehan was mindful of the old woman's disapproval. Jehan, however, had lived a full, harsh life in her twenty-one years, and a raised eyebrow rated very low on her list of things to be concerned about. She had seen too many people abandoned to starvation, too many people dispossessed and reduced to beggary, too many outsiders slain in the name of Allah, too many maimed or beheaded through the convoluted workings of Islamic justice. All these years, Jehan had kept her father's blooded dagger, packed now somewhere beneath her Shetland wool sweaters, and still as deadly as ever.

Heisenberg's health improved on the island, and there was a beautiful view of the sea from their room. His mood brightened quickly. One morning, while walking along the shoreline with him, Jehan read a passage from the glorious Qur'ân. "This sûrah is called The Earthquake," she said. " *'In the name of Allah, the Beneficent, the Merciful. When Earth is shaken with her final earthquake, the Earth yields up her burdens and man saith: What aileth her? That day she will relate her chronicles, because thy Lord inspireth her. That day mankind will issue forth in separate groups to be shown their deeds. And whoso doeth good an atom's weight will see it then. And whose doeth ill an atom's weight will see it then.'* "

And Jehan wept, knowing that however much good she might do, it could never outweigh the wrongs she had already performed.

But Heisenberg only stared out over the gray, tumbling waves of the ocean. He did not listen closely to the sacred verses, yet a few of Jehan's words struck him. " 'And whoso doeth good an atom's weight will *see* it then,' " he said, emphasizing the single word. There was a small, hesitant smile quivering at the corners of his mouth. Jehan put her arm around him to comfort him because he seemed chilled, and she led him back to the hotel. The weather had turned colder and the air was misty with sea spray; together they listened to the cries of the herring gulls as the birds dived for fish or hovered screeching over the strip of beach. Jehan thought of what she'd read, of the end of the world. Heisenberg thought only of its beginning, and its still closely-guarded secrets.

They liked their daily long, peaceful walk about the island. Now, more than ever before in her life, Jehan carried with her a copy of the Qur'ân, and she often read short verses to him. So different from the Biblical literature he'd heard all his life, Heisenberg let the

Islamic scriptures pass without comment. Yet it seemed to him that certain specific images offered their meanings to him alone.

Jehan saw at last that he was feeling well. Heisenberg took up again full-time the tangled knot that was the current state of quantum physics. It was his vocation and his means of relaxation together. He told Jehan the best scientific minds in the world were frantically working to cobble together a slipshod mathematical model, one that might account for all the observed data. Whatever approach they tried, the data would not fit together. *He*, however, would find the key for them; he was that confident. He wasn't quite sure how he'd do it, as yet; but, of course, he hadn't yet really applied himself thoroughly to the question.

Jehan was not amused. She read to him: " *'Hast thou not seen those who pretend that they believe in that which is revealed unto thee and that which was revealed before thee, how they would go for judgment in their disputes to false deities when they had been ordered to abjure them? Satan would lead them far astray.'* "

Heisenberg laughed heartily. "Your Allah isn't just talking about Göttingen there," he said. "He's got Bohr in mind, too, and Einstein in Berlin."

Jehan frowned at his impiety. It was the irreverence and ignorant ridicule of the kâfir, the unbeliever. She wondered if the old religion that had never truly had any claim on her was yet still part of her. She wondered how she'd feel after all these years, walking the narrow, crowded, clangorous ways of the Budayeen again. "You mustn't speak that way," she said at last.

"Hmm?" said Heisenberg. He had already forgotten entirely what he'd said to her.

"Look out there," said Jehan. "What do you see?"

"The ocean," said Heisenberg. "Waves."

"Allah created those waves. What do *you* know about that?"

"I could determine their frequency," said the scientist. "I could measure their amplitude."

"Measure!" cried Jehan. Her own long years of scientific study were suddenly overshadowed by an imagined insult to her heritage. "Look here," she demanded. "A handful of sand. Allah created this sand. What do *you* know about it?"

Heisenberg couldn't see what Jehan was trying to tell him. "With the proper instruments," he said, a little afraid of offending her, "in the proper setting, I could take any single grain of sand and tell you—" His words broke off suddenly. He got to his feet slowly, like an old man. He looked first at the sea, then down at the shore, then back out at the water. "Waves," he murmured, "particles, it doesn't make any difference. All that really counts is what we can actually measure. We can't measure Bohr's orbits, because they don't really *exist!* So then the spectral lines we see are caused by transitions between two states. Pairs of states, yes; but that will mean an entirely new form of mathematical expression just to describe them, referencing tables listing every possible—"

"Werner." Jehan knew that he was now lost to her.

"Just the computations alone will take days, if not weeks."

"Werner, *listen* to me. This island is so small, you can throw a stone from one end to the other. I'm not going to sit on this freezing beach or up on your bleak and dreary cliff while you make your brilliant breakthrough, whatever it is. I'm saying good-bye."

"What? Jehan?" Heisenberg blinked and returned to the tangible world.

She couldn't face him any longer. She was pouring one handful of sand through the fingers of her other hand. It came suddenly to her mind then: if you had no water to perform the necessary ablution before prayer in the direction of Mecca, you were permitted to wash with clean sand instead. She began to weep. She couldn't hear what Heisenberg was saying to her—if indeed he was.

It was a couple of hours later in the alley now, and it was getting even colder. Jehan wrapped herself in her robe and paced back and forth. She'd had visions of this particular night for four years, glimpses of the possible ways that it might conclude. Sometimes the young man saw her in the alley shortly after dawn, sometimes he didn't. Sometimes she killed him, sometimes she didn't. And, of course, there was the open question of whether her actions would lead to her freedom or to her execution.

When she'd had the first vision, she hadn't known what was happening or what she was seeing. She knew only the fear and the pain and the terror. The boy threw her roughly to the ground, ripping her clothing, and raped her. Then the vision passed. Jehan told no one about it; her family would have thought her insane. Then, about three months later, the vision returned; only this time it was different in subtle ways. She was in the alley as before, but this time she smiled and gestured to the boy, inviting him. He smiled in return and followed her deeper into the alley. When he put his hand on her shoulder, she drew her father's dagger and plunged it into the boy's belly. That was as much as the vision showed her then. It terrified her even more than the rape scene had.

As time passed, the visions took on other forms. She was certain now that she was not always watching *her* future, *the* future, but rather *a* future, each as likely to come to pass as the others. Not all the visions could possibly be true. In some of them, she saw herself living into her old age in the city, right here in this filthy quarter of the Budayeen. In others, she moved about strange places that didn't seem Islamic at all, and she spoke languages definitely not Arabic. She did not know if these conflicting visions were trying to tell her or warn her of something. Jehan prayed to know which of these versions she must actually live through. Soon after, as if to reward her for her faith, she began to have less violent visions: she could look into the future a short way and find lost objects or warn against unlucky travel plans or predict the rise and fall of crop prices. The neighbors, at first amused, began to be afraid of her. Jehan's mother counseled her never to speak of these "dreams" to anyone, or else Jehan might be locked away in some horrible institution. Jehan never told her father about her visions, because Jehan never told her father about anything. In that family, as in the others of the Budayeen —and the rest of the city for that matter—the father did not concern himself very much with his daughters. His sons were his pride, and he had three strong sons whom he firmly believed would someday vastly increase the Ashûfi prestige and wealth. Jehan knew he was wrong, because she'd already seen what would become of the sons—two would be killed in wars against the Jews; the third would be a coward, a weakling, and a fugitive in the United States. But Jehan said nothing.

It was two o'clock, and only the night calls of distant drunken fools kept her company. Sometimes the visions were a torment, and sometimes they were a comfort. She was glad for them now as diversions in her loneliness; but more than ever, she watched helplessly all the different possibilities that might happen in the morning. Which one could she trust? Which should she prepare for? Should she be glad in her heart or fearful? She addressed a prayer to Allah, a rare enough act for her, but the most fervent prayer of her young life. Then she let more time pass.

A vision: It was just past dawn. The young man— whose name Jehan never learned—was walking down the stone-paved street toward her alley. Jehan knew it without even peering out. She took a deep breath. She walked a few steps toward the street, looked left, and caught his eyes. She made a brief gesture, turned her back, and went deeper into the shadowy seclusion of the alley. She was certain that he would follow her. Her stomach ached and rumbled, and she was shaking with nervous exhaustion. When the young man put his hand on her shoulder, murmuring indecent suggestions, her hand crept toward the concealed knife, but she did not grasp it. He threw her down roughly, clawed off her clothing, and raped her. Then he left her there. She was almost paralyzed, crying and cursing on the wet, foul-smelling stones. She was found some time later by two women who took her to a doctor. Their worst fears were confirmed: her honor had been ravaged irredeemably. Her life was effectively over, in the sense of becoming a normal adult female in that Islamic community. One of the women returned to Jehan's house with her, to tell the news to Jehan's mother, who must still tell Jehan's father. Jehan hid in the room she shared with her sisters. She heard the violent breaking of furniture and shrill obscenity of her father. There was nothing more to be done. Jehan did not actually know the name of her assailant. She was ruined, less than worthless. A young woman no longer a virgin could command no bride price. All those years of supporting a worthless daughter in the hopes of recovering the investment in the marriage contract—all vanished now. It was no surprise that Jehan's father felt betrayed and the father of a witless creature. There was no sympathy for Jehan's own plight; the actual story, whatever it might be, could not alter the facts. From that morning on, Jehan was permanently repudiated and cast out from her house. She had only the weeping of her sisters and her mother. Jehan's father and three brothers would not even look at her or offer her their farewells.

The years passed even more quickly. Jehan became a woman of the streets. For a time, because of her youth and beauty, she earned a good living. Then as the decades left their unalterable blemishes upon her, she found it difficult even to earn enough for a meal and a room to sleep in. She grew older, more bitter, and filled with self-loathing. Did she hate her father and the rest of her family? No, her fate had been fixed by the will of Allah, however impossible it was for her to comprehend it, or else by her own timidity in the single moment of choice and destiny in the alley so many years before. She could not say. Whatever the answer, she could not benefit now from either insight or wisdom. Her life was as it was, according to the inscrutable designs of Allah the Merciful. Her understanding was not required.

Eventually she was found dead, haggard and starved, and her corpse was contorted and huddled for warmth coincidentally in the same alley where the young man had so carelessly despoiled any chance Jehan had for happiness in this world. After she died, there was no one to mourn her. Perhaps Allah the Beneficent took pity on her, showing mercy to her who had received little enough mercy from her neighbors while she lived among them. It had always been a cold place for Jehan.

For a while estranged from Heisenberg, Jehan worked with Erwin Schrödinger in Zurich. At first Schrödinger's ideas confused her, because they went against many of Heisenberg's basic assumptions. For the time being, Heisenberg rejected any simple picture of what the atom was like, any model at all. Schrödinger, older and more conservative than the Göttingen group, wanted to explain quantum phenomena without new mathematics and elusive imagery. He treated the electron as a wave function, but a different sort of wave than de Broglie's. The properties of waves in the physical world were well-known and without ambiguity. Yet when Schrödinger calculated how a change in energy level affected his electron wave, his solutions didn't agree with the observed data.

"What am I overlooking?" he asked.

Jehan shook her head. "Where I was born they say, 'Don't pour away the water in your canteen because of a mirage.' "

"Schrödinger rubbed his weary eyes. He glanced down at the sheaf of papers he held. "How can I tell if this water is worth keeping, or something that belongs in a sewer?"

Jehan had no reply to that, and Schrödinger set his work aside, unsatisfied. A few months later, several papers showed that after taking into account the relativistic effects, Schrödinger's calculations agreed remarkably well with experimental results, after all.

Schrödinger was pleased. "I feel vindicated," he said. "I hoped all along to find a way to drag Born and

Heisenberg back to classical physics. I knew in my heart that quantum physics would prove to be a sane world, not a realm populated by phantoms and governed by ghost forces."

"It seems unreal to me now," said Jehan. "If you say the electron is a wave, you are saying it is a phantom. In the ocean, it is the water that is the wave. As for sound, it is the air that carries the wave. What exists to be a wave in your equations?"

"It is a wave of probability, Born says. I do not wholly understand that yet myself," he said, "but my equations explain too many things to be illusions."

"Sir," said Jehan, frowning, "it may be in this case the mirage is in your canteen, and not before you in the desert."

Schrödinger laughed. "That might be true. I may yet have to abandon my mental pictures, but I will not abandon my mathematics."

It was a breathless afternoon in the city. The local Arabs didn't seem to be bothered by the heat, but the small party of Europeans was beginning to suffer. Their cruise ship had put ashore at the small port and a tour had been arranged to the city some fifty miles to the south. Two hours later, the travelers concluded that the expedition had been a mistake.

Among them was David Hilbert, the German mathematician, a lecturer at Göttingen since 1895. He was accompanied by his wife, Käthe, and their maid, Clärchen. At first they were quite taken by the strangeness of the city, by the foreign sights and sounds and smells; but after a short time, their senses were glutted with newness, and what had at first been exotic was now only deplorable.

As they moved slowly through the bazaars, shaded ineffectually by awnings or meager arcades of sticks, they longed for the whisper of a sing cool breeze. Arab men dressed in long white gallebeyas cried out shrilly, all the while glaring at the Europeans. It was impossible to tell what the Arabs were saying. Some dragged little carts loaded with filthy cups and pots—

water? tea? lemonade? It made no difference. Cholera lingered at every stall, every beggar offered typhus as he clutched at sleeves.

Hilbert's wife fanned herself weakly. She was almost overcome and near collapse. Hilbert looked about himself desperately. "David," murmured the maid, "Clärchen, the only one of Hilbert's amours Frau Hilbert could tolerate, "we have come far enough."

"I know," he said, "but I see nothing—nowhere—"

"There are some ladies and gentlemen in that place. I think it's an eating place. Leave Käthe with me there, and find a taxi. Then we shall go back to the boat."

Hilbert hesitated. At first he couldn't bear to leave the two unprotected women in the midst of this frantic heathen marketplace. Then he saw how pale his wife had become, how her eyelids drooped, how she swayed against Clärchen's shoulder. He nodded. "Let me help," he said. Together they got Frau Hilbert to the restaurant, where it was no cooler but at least the ceiling fans created a fiction of fresh air. Hilbert introduced himself to a well-dressed man who was seated at a table with his family, a wife and four children. The mathematician tried three languages before he was understood. He explained the situation, and the gentleman and his wife both assured Hilbert that he need not worry. Hilbert ran out to find a taxi.

He was soon lost. There were not streets here, not in the European sense of the word. Narrow spaces between buildings became alleys, opened into small squares, closed again, other narrow passages led off in twisting, bewildering directions. Soon Hilbert found himself back at a souk; he thought at first it was where he'd begun and looked for the restaurant, but he was wrong. This was another souk entirely; there were probably hundreds in the city. He was beginning to panic. Even if he managed to find a taxi, how could he direct it back to where his wife and Clärchen waited?

A man's hand plucked at him. Hilbert tried to shrug the long fingers away. He looked into the face of a lean, hollow-cheeked man in a striped robe and a blue knitted cap. The Arab kept repeating a few words, but Hilbert could make no sense of them. The Arab took him by the arm and half-led, half-shoved Hilbert through the crowd. Hilbert let himself be guided. They crossed through two bazaars, one of tinsmiths and one of poultry-dressers. They entered a stone-paved street and emerged into an immense square. On the far side of the square was a huge, many-towered mosque, built of pink stone. Hilbert's first impression was awe; it was as lovely an edifice as the Taj. Then his guide was pushing him again through the throng, or hurrying in front to hew a path for Hilbert. The square was jammed and choked with people. Soon Hilbert could see why—a platform had been erected in the center, and on it stood a man with what could only be an executioner's axe. Hilbert felt his stomach sicken. His Arab guide had thrust aside everyone in their way until Hilbert stood at the very foot of the platform. He saw uniformed police and a bearded old man leading out a young girl. The crowd parted to allow them by. The girl was stunningly lovely. Hilbert looked into her huge, dark eyes—"like the eyes of a gazelle," he remembered from reading Omar Khayyam—and glimpsed her slender form undisguised by her modest garments. As she mounted the steps, she looked down directly at him again. Hilbert felt his heart lurch, he felt a tremendous shudder. Then she looked away.

The Arab guide screamed in Hilbert's ear. It meant nothing to the mathematician. He watched in horror as Jehan knelt, as the headsman raised his weapon of office. When the fierce, bellowing cry went up from the crowd, Hilbert noticed that his suit was now spattered with small flecks of red. The Arab screamed at him again and tightened his grip on Hilbert's arm until Hilbert complained. The Arab did not release him. With his other hand, Hilbert took out his wallet. The Arab smiled. Above him, Hilbert watched several men carry away the body of the decapitated girl. The Arab guide did not let him go until he'd paid an enormous sum.

*   *   *

Perhaps another hour had passed in the alley. Jehan had withdrawn to the darkest part and sat in a damp corner with her legs drawn up, her head against the rough brick wall. If she could but sleep, she told herself, the night would pass more quickly; but she would not sleep, she would fight it if drowsiness threatened. What if she could slip into slumber and waken in the late morning, her peril and her opportunity both long since lost? Her only companion, the crescent moon, had abandoned her; she looked up at fragments of constellations, stars familiar enough in their groups but indistinguishable now as individuals. How different from people, where the opposite was true. She sighed: she was not a profound person, and it did not suit her to have profound thoughts. These must not truly be profound thoughts, she decided; she was merely deluded by weariness. Slowly she let her head fall forward. She crossed her arms on her knees and cradled her head. The greater part of the night had already passed, and only silence came from the street. There were perhaps only three more hours until dawn. . . .

Soon Schrödinger's wave mechanics was proved to be equivalent to Heisenberg's matrix mechanics. It was a validation of both men's work, and of the whole field of quantum physics as well. Eventually, Schrödinger's simplistic wave picture of the electron was abandoned, but his mathematical laws remained undisputed. Jehan remembered Schrödinger predicting that he might need to take just that step. The physicists she assisted and learned from suspected much more than they were willing to speak out loud; they withheld these notions until they could back them with cold figures. What bizarre new formulations lurked in their minds, and how long must the world wait to hear of them?

Jehan had at last returned to Göttingen and Heisenberg. He had "forgiven her petulance." He welcomed her gladly, because of his genuine feelings for her, and because he had much work to do. He had just formally developed what came to be known as the

Heisenberg Uncertainty Principle. This was the first indication that the impartial observer could not help but play an essential, active role in the universe of subatomic particles. Jehan grasped Heisenberg's concept readily. Other scientists thought Heisenberg was merely making a trivial criticism of the limitations of their experiments or the quality of their observations. It was more profound than that. Heisenberg was saying that one can never hope to know both the position and momentum of an electron at the same time under *any* circumstances. He had destroyed forever the assumption of the impartial observer.

"To observe is to disturb," said Heisenberg. "Newton wouldn't have liked any of this at all."

"Einstein still doesn't like it right this very minute," said Jehan.

"I wish I had a mark for every time he's made that sour 'God doesn't play dice with the universe' comment."

"That's just the way he sees a 'wave of probability.' The path of the electron can't be known unless you look; but once you look, you change the information."

"So maybe God doesn't play dice with the universe," said Heisenberg. "He plays vingt-et-un, and if He does not have an extra ace up His sleeve, He creates one—first the sleeve, then the ace. And He turns over more natural twenty-ones than is statistically likely. Hold on, Jehan! I'm not being sacrilegious. I'm not saying that God cheats. Rather, He invented the rules of the game and He *continues* to invent them; and this gives Him a rather large advantage over poor physicists and their lagging understanding. We are like country peasants watching the magic card-tricks of someone who may be either genius or charlatan."

Jehan pondered this metaphor. "At the Solvay Conference, Bohr introduced his Complementarity idea, that an electron was a wave function until it was detected, and then the wave function collapsed to a point and you knew where the electron was. Then it was a particle. Einstein didn't like that, either."

"That's God's card-trick," said Heisenberg, shrugging.

"Well, the noble Qur'ân says, *'They question thee about strong drink and games of chance. Say: In both is great sin, and some usefulness for men; but the sin of them is greater than their usefulness.'* "

"Forget dice and cards, then," said Heisenberg with a little smile. "What kind of game *would* it be appropriate for Allah to play against us?"

"Physics," said Jehan, and Heisenberg laughed.

"And knowest thou there is a prohibition against taking of human life that Allah hath made sacred?"

"Yes, O Wise One."

"And knowest thou further that Allah hath set a penalty upon those who breaketh this law?"

"Yes, I know."

"Then, O my daughter, tell us why thou hath brought low this poor boy."

Jehan tossed the bloody knife to the stone-paved alley. It rang noisily and then came to rest against one leg of the corpse. "I was celebrating the Îd-el-Fitr," she said. "This boy followed me and I became afraid. He made filthy gestures and called out terrible things. I hurried away, but he ran after me. He grabbed me by the shoulders and pressed me against a wall. I tried to escape, but I could not. He laughed at my fear, then he struck me many times. He dragged me along through the narrowest of streets, where there were not many to witness; and then he pulled me into this vile place. He told me that he intended to defile me, and he described what he would do in foul detail. It was then that I drew my father's dagger and stabbed him. I have spent the night in horror of his intentions and of my deed, and I have prayed to Allah for forgiveness."

The imam put a trembling hand on Jehan's cheek. "Allah is All-Wise and All-Forgiving, O my daughter. Alloweth me to return with thee to thy house, where I mayest put the hearts of thy father and thy mother at their ease."

Jehan knelt at the imam's feet. "All thanks be to Allah," she murmured.

"Allah be praised," said the imam, the police officer, and the qadi together.

More than a decade later, when Jehan had daughters of her own, she told them this story. But in those latter days children did not heed the warnings of their parents, and the sons and daughters of Jehan and her husband did many foolish things.

Dawn slipped even into the narrow alleyway where Jehan waited. She was very sleepy and hungry, but she stood up and took a few wobbling steps. Her muscles had become cramped, and she could hear her heart beating in her ears. Jehan steadied herself with one hand on the brick wall. She went slowly to the mouth of the alley and peered out. There was no one in sight. The boy was coming neither from the left nor the right. Jehan waited until several other people appeared, going about the business of the new day. Then she hid the dagger in her sleeve once more and departed from the alley. She hurried back to her father's house. Her mother would need her to help make breakfast.

Jehan was in her early forties now, her black hair cut short, her eyes framed by clumsy spectacles, her beauty stolen by care, poor diet, and sleeplessness. She wore a white lab coat and carried a clipboard, as much a part of her as her title, Fräulein Professor Doktor Ashûfi. This was not Göttingen any longer; it was Berlin, and a war was being lost. She was still with Heisenberg. He had protected her until her own scientific credentials became protection of themselves. At that point, the Nazi officials were compelled to make her an "honorary" Aryan, as they had the Jewish physicists and mathematicians whose cooperation they needed. It had been only Jehan's long-standing loyalty to Heisenberg himself that kept her in Germany at all. The war was of little concern to her; these were not her people, but neither were the British, the French, the Russians, or the Americans. Her only interest was in her work, in the refinement of physics, in the unending anticipation of discovery.

She was glad, therefore, when the German atomic bomb project was removed from the control of the German army and given to the Reich Research Council. One of the first things to be done was the calling of a research conference at the Kaiser-Wilhelm Institute of Physics in Berlin. The conference would be conducted under the tightest security; no preliminary list of topics would be released in advance, so that no foreign agents might see such terms as "fission cross-sections" and "isotope enrichment," leading to speculation on the long-term goals of these physicists.

At the same time, the Reich Research Council decided to hold a second conference for the benefit of the government's highest officials on the same day. The idea was that the scientists speaking at the Kaiser-Wilhelm Institute's meeting could present short, elementary summaries of their work in plain language, so that the political and military leaders could be briefed on the progress toward a nuclear weapon. Then, following the laymen's presentation, the physicists could gather and discuss the same matters in their more technical jargon.

Heisenberg thought it was a good idea. It was 1942, and material, political support, and funding were getting more difficult to find. The army wanted to put all available research resources into the rocketry program; they argued that the nuclear experiments were not showing sufficient success. Heisenberg was a theoretical physicist, not an engineer; he could not find a way to tell the council that the development of the uranium bomb must necessarily be slow and methodical. Each new step forward in theory had to be tested carefully, and each experiment was expensive in both time and money. The Reich, however, cared only for positive results.

One evening Jehan was alone in an administrative office of the Reich Research Council, typing her proposal for an important test of their isotope-separation technique. She saw on the desk two stacks of papers. One stack listed the speeches by Otto Hahn, Heisenberg, Hans Geiger, herself, and several others—the simple synopses they had prepared for the Reich ministers who had little or no background in science. She took those papers and hid them in her briefcase. The second stack was the secret agenda for the physicists' own meeting—"Nuclear Physics as a Weapon," by Prof. Dr. Schumann; "The Fission of the Uranium Atom," by Prof. Dr. Hahn; "The Theoretical Basis for the Production of Energy from the Fission of Uranium," by Heisenberg; "The Results Thus Far in the Controlled Release of Energy," by Prof. Dr. Bothe; "The Production of Heavy Water," by Prof. Dr. Harteck; and so on. Each person attending the technical seminar would be given a program *after* he entered the lecture hall, and he would be required to sign for it. This was not normal procedure, but evidently the Reich Research Council had persuaded someone in the government that these matters were crucial.

Jehan thought for a long while in the quiet office. She remembered her wretched childhood. She recalled her arrival in Europe and the people she had come to know, the life she had come to lead here. She thought about how Germany had changed while she hid in her castle of scientific abstractions, uninvolved with the outside world. At last she thought about what this new Germany might do with the uranium bomb. She knew exactly what she must do.

It took her only a few moments to take the highly-technical agendas and drop them into the already-addressed envelopes to be sent to Göring, Himmler, Speer, Keitel, Bormann, and many more of the Third Reich's masters. She had guaranteed that the brief introductory discussion would be attended by no one. Jehan could easily imagine the response the unintelligible scientific papers would get from the political and military leaders—curt, polite regrets that they would not be in Berlin on that day, or that their busy schedules prevented them from attending.

It was all so easy. The Reich's rulers did not hear the talks, and they did not learn how close Germany was to developing an atomic bomb. Never again was there any hope that such a weapon could be built in time to save the Reich—all because the wrong invitations had been slipped into a few envelopes.

*   *   *

Jehan awoke from a dream, and saw that the night had grown very old. It would not be long before the sun began to flood the sky with light. Soon she would have a resolution to her anxiety. She would learn if the boy would come to the alley or stay away. She would learn if he would rape her or if she would find the courage to defend herself. She would learn if she would be judged guilty or innocent of murder. She would be granted a glimpse of the outcome to all things that concerned her.

Nevertheless, she was so tired, hungry, and uncomfortable that she was tempted to give up her vigil. The urge to go home was strong. Yet she had always believed that her visions were gifts granted by Allah, and it might offend Him to ignore the clear warnings. For Allah's sake, as well as her own, she reluctantly chose to wait out the rest of the dying night. She had seen so many visions since last evening—more than on any other day of her life—some new, some familiar from years passed. It was, in a small, human way, almost comparable to the Night of Power that was bestowed upon the Prophet, may Allah's blessings be on him and peace. Then Jehan felt guilty and blasphemous for comparing herself to the Messenger that way.

She got down on her knees and faced toward Mecca, and addressed a prayer to Allah, reciting one of the later sûrahs from the glorious Qur'ân, the one called "The Morning Hours," which seemed particularly relevant to her situation. " *'In the name of Allah, the Beneficent, the Merciful. By the morning hours, and by the night when it is stillest, thy Lord hath not forsaken thee nor doth He hate thee, and verily the latter portion will be better for thee than the former, and verily thy Lord will give unto thee so that thou wilt be content. Did He not find thee an orphan and protect thee? Did He not find thee wandering and direct thee? Did He not find thee destitute and enrich thee? Therefore the orphan oppress not, therefore the beggar drive not away, therefore of the bounty of thy Lord be thy discourse.' "*

When she finished praying, she stood up and leaned against the wall. She wondered if that sûrah prophesied that soon she'd be an orphan. She hoped that Allah understood that she never intended anything awful to happen to her parents. Jehan was willing to suffer whatever consequences Allah willed, but it didn't seem fair for her mother and father to have to share them. She shivered in the damp, cold air, and gazed up to see if there was yet any brightening of the sky. She pretended that already the stars were beginning to disappear.

The square was jammed and choked with people. Soon Hilbert could see why—a platform had been erected in the center, and on it stood a man with what could only be an executioner's axe. Hilbert felt his stomach sicken. His Arab guide had thrust aside everyone on their way until Hilbert stood at the very foot of the platform. He saw uniformed police and a bearded old man leading out a young girl. The crowd parted to allow them by. The girl was stunningly lovely. Hilbert looked into her huge, dark eyes—"like the eyes of a gazelle," he remembered from reading Omar Khayyam—and glimpsed her slender form undisguised by her modest garments. As she mounted the steps, she looked down directly at him again. Hilbert felt his heart lurch, he felt a tremendous shudder. Then she looked away.

The Arab guide screamed in Hilbert's ear. It meant nothing to the mathematician. He watched in horror as Jehan knelt, as the headsman raised his weapon of office. Hilbert shouted. His guide tightened his grip on the outsider's arm, but Hilbert lashed out in fury and threw the man into a group of veiled women. In the confusion, Hilbert ran up the steps of the scaffold. The imam and the police officers looked at him angrily. The crowd began to shout fiercely at this interruption, this desecration by a European kâfir, an unbeliever. Hilbert ran to the police. "You must stop this!" he cried in German. They did not understand him and tried to heave him off the platform. "Stop!" he screamed in English.

One of the police officers answered him. "It cannot be stopped," he said gruffly. "The girl committed murder. She was found guilty, and she cannot pay the blood-price to the victim's family. She must die instead."

"Blood-price!" cried Hilbert. "That's barbarous! You would kill a young girl just because she is poor? Blood-price! *I'll* pay your goddamn blood-price! How much is it?"

The policeman conferred with the others, and then went to the imam for guidance. Finally, the English-speaking officer returned. "Four hundred kiam," he said bluntly.

Hilbert took out his wallet with shaking hands. He counted out the money and handed it with obvious disgust to the policeman. The imam cried a declaration in his weak voice. The words were passed quickly through the crowd, and the onlookers grew more enraged at this spoiling of their morning's entertainment. "Take her and go quickly," said the police officer. "We cannot protect you, and the crowd is becoming furious."

Hilbert nodded. He grasped Jehan's thin wrist and pulled her along after him. She questioned him in Arabic, but he could not reply. As he struggled through the menacing crowd, they were struck again and again by stones. Hilbert wondered what he had done, if he and the girl would get out of the mosque's courtyard alive. His fondness for young women—it was an open joke in Göttingen—had that been all that had motivated him? Had he unconsciously decided to rescue the girl and take her back to Germany? Or was it something more laudable? He would never know. He shocked himself: while he tried to shield himself and the girl from the vicious blows of the crowd, he thought only of how he might explain the girl to his wife, Käthe, and Clärchen, his mistress.

In 1957, well after the end of the Second World War, Jehan Fatima Ashûfi was fifty-eight years old and living in Princeton, New Jersey. By coincidence, Albert Einstein had come here to live out the end of his life, and before he died in 1955 they had many pleasant afternoons at his house. In the beginning, Jehan wanted to discuss quantum physics with Einstein; she even told him Heisenberg's answer to Einstein's objection to God playing dice with the universe. Einstein was not very amused, and from then on, their conversation concerned only nostalgic memories of the better days in Germany, before the advent of the National Socialists.

This afternoon, however, Jehan was listening to a young man read a remarkable paper, his Ph.D. thesis. His name was Hugh Everett, and what he was saying was that there was an explanation for all the paradoxes of the quantum world, a simple but bizarre way of looking at them. His new idea included the Copenhagen interpretation and explained away all the objections that might be raised by less open-minded physicists. He stated first of all that quantum mechanics provided predictions that were invariably correct when measured against experimental data. Quantum physics *had* to be consistent and valid, there was no longer any doubt. The trouble was that quantum theory was beginning to lead to unappetizing alternatives. Einstein, with Podolsky and Rosen, had himself proposed a thought experiment that seemed to demand a reply that contradicted the stringent demands of relativity. Everett's thesis reconciled them. Schrödinger's cat paradox, in which the cat in the box was merely a quantum wave function, not alive and not dead, until an observer looked to see which state the cat was in, was eliminated. Everett showed that the cat was no mere ghostly wave function. Everett said that wave functions do not "collapse," choosing one alternative or the other. He said that the process of observation chose one reality, but the other reality existed in its own right, just as "real" as our world. Particles do not choose at random which path to take—they take every path, in a separate, newly-branched world for each option. Of course, at the particle level, this meant a huge number of branchings occurring at every moment. Jehan knew this almost-metaphysical idea would find a chilly reception from most physicists, but she had special reasons to accept it eagerly. It explained her visions. She glimpsed the particular branch that would be "real" for her, and also those that would be "real" for other versions of her, her own duplicates living on the countless parallel worlds. Now, as she listened to Everett, she smiled. She saw another young man in the audience, wearing a T-shirt that said, "Wigner: Would you please ask your friend to feed my cat? Thanks, Schrödinger." She found that very amusing.

When Everett finished reading, Jehan felt good; it wasn't peace she felt, it was more like the release one feels after an argument that had been brewing for a long while. Jehan thought back over the turns and sidetracks she had taken since that dawn in the alley in the Budayeen. She smiled again, sadly, took a deep breath and let it out. How many things she had done, how many things had happened to her! They had been long, strange lives. The only question that still remained was: how many uncountable futures did she still have to devise, to fabricate from the immaterial resources of this moment? As she sat there—in some worlds—Jehan knew the futures went on without her willing them to, needing nothing of her permission. She was not cautious of when tomorrow came, but *which* tomorrow came.

Jehan saw them all, but she still understood nothing. She thought, "The Chinese say that a journey of a thousand li begins with a single step. How short-sighted that is! A *thousand* journeys of a thousand li begin with each step. Or with each step not taken." She sat in her chair until everyone else had left the lecture hall. Then she got up slowly, her back and her knees giving her pain, and she took a step. She pictured myriad mirror-Jehans taking that step along with her, and a myriad that didn't. And in all the worlds across time, it was another step into the future.

*   *   *

At last, there was no doubt about it: it was dawn. Jehan fingered her father's dagger and felt a thrill of excitement. Strange words flickered in her mind. "The Heisenty Uncertainberg Principle," she murmured, already hurrying toward the mouth of the alley. She felt no fear.

THE FLIES OF MEMORY
By Ian Watson

Maybe it was snobbish of Charles, but he had always hated cameras, especially those in the hands of tourists. A dog peeing against a palace wall was acting sensitively; it was leaving a memory of itself. But how often did camera-toting tourists really *look* at anything? So how could a photo truly remind them?

When Charles was a boy he began to choose memory places for himself. There was the local cemetery: chestnut trees, bluebells, and marble angels. There were the sand dunes at sunset; spiky marram grass pointing thousands of fading sundial fingers seaward as if the world was splintering with hair-cracks. He would vow, "I'll fix this scene. In two years, ten years, I'll remember this moment exactly! Myself, here, now."

Of course he hardly succeeded; maybe that's why he resented cameras. Yet a chain of such magic moments had linked his life. *(And who is remembering him, right now?)*

Here he was in Scotland keeping another thread of faith, with his widowed father. En route back to his academic seat at Columbia University from the Geneva arms talks he had hired a Volvo to tour the Highlands. He owed the old man a decent holiday so that Mr. Spark senior could revisit his favourite sentimental sights and taste some good malt whiskies in their native glens. Charles also wanted a quiet time to think, about madness and Martine.

Scarcely had father and son started out than the alien Flies arrived on Earth. "We have come to your planet to *remember* it," so they said. Broadcasting, in stilted English and Russian, their requests to tour all the world's cities, the pyramid-ship settled gently into the Mediterranean offshore from Alexandria and floated, base submerged, not drifting an inch.

The unfolding news reached Charles via newspapers and TV in remote hotels. His father objected to their listening to the car radio.

"It's worse than a bloody election campaign," the old man groused as they were admiring Loch an Eilein. (Look: a solitary heron standing stock-still waiting to stab; jackdaws flapping over the castle ruin on the island.) "Blather blather. Most of it, sheer guesswork. Wait a few weeks and we'll know what's what." Mr. Spark was worried Charles would cut short their trip.

Mr. Spark never used to swear until his wife died in a car crash—which wasn't the old man's fault, though he wouldn't replace the car. "Where should I go to on my own?" he'd asked sadly after the funeral. Charles's parents had driven all over the Borders and Highlands with a consuming passion. Now Mr. Spark had taken to smoking a pipe, and swearing. You might have surmised that an anger rankled in him, and that a pipe was a substitute spouse. But Charles perceived that tobacco and rude words had been suppressed in his father many long years ago, although drams of whisky had been permitted. At the age of seventy-five Mr. Spark's behaviour was fraying round the edges, a genteel net curtain in decay.

As they were rounding the Gap of Glencoe, Mr. Spark exclaimed, "Bloody ugly, that's what!" For a distorted instant Charles thought that his Dad was talking about the looming peaks of the glen. Grim, those were, though sunlit. Then his father went on, "Wouldn't want to meet one of your Flies on a dark night! Oh no. Nor would anybody in their right mind. Maybe your Martine might fancy doing their portraits. Just up her street, I'd imagine."

Mr. Spark had reason to be anxious. By now Charles had made several transatlantic phone calls from hotels to leave word of their itinerary. Already a week had passed and UNCO had been cobbled together, the United Nations Co-ordination Committee steered by America and Russia. Charles wanted to be in on this, and hoped he had sufficient clout and contacts. Already a thousand Flies had spread out from their floating Hive, and the Grand Tour had commenced in Cairo and Kyoto, San Francisco and Singapore, London and Leningrad and wherever else. Who would deny creatures which could fly a huge interstellar pyramid the way these aliens did? Who would not want to learn the secrets of their success?

"Look, son," said Mr. Spark after a while, "hordes of folk will all think they have special reasons for rubbing shoulders with these monstrosities. Why fuss on, when the buggers are going to be visiting everywhere? Bloody *invasion*, if you ask me. You'll see a Fly soon enough. Will we ever see the back of them? That's what I wonder."

Charles nodded, unconvinced.

"Look!" His father pointed at the sky.

It wasn't a Fly up there.

"Eagle?" Charles asked.

"Don't be daft, that's an osprey. Rare, those are. Almost extinct. It's going fishing in Loch Leven. Look at it. You'll likely never see another one." (*And I see it now, in shadow. Better than he did. Oh yes.*)

A few minutes later Mr. Spark was puffing contentedly, telling his son about the massacre of the Mac-Donalds. On his own terms the old man was good company, though really he and Charles had drifted worlds apart.

*   *   *

Charles's reputation was founded on his first book about body language, *The Truth of Signs*. Soon he was being retained as a consultant by defense and aerospace as a kind of walking lie detector. This led to his kibbitzing on the arms talks on behalf of the U.S. government. His next book, *Signs of Passion*, was his pop success.

Charles had a heightened sense of body language. If he couldn't ever record a chunk of scenery to his full satisfaction, he could read body signals and facial cues with an animal instinct. Not that he didn't need to *work* at this, scientifically; but let's not weigh ourselves down with talk of proxemics and kinesics, all the jargon of nonverbal communication.

You might think this would have immersed Charles in other people's lives as in a crowded jacuzzi, a hot tub of humanity. Not so. Old Eskimo saying: when you rub noses, you don't see the face. When you're watching the face, you don't rub noses.

Another week passed. By Rannoch Moor, to the Braes of Balquhidder to the bristly Trossachs. During convivial evenings spent with his Dad over a glass or several of ten-year-old Glenduffie, Charles caught TV pictures of individual aliens in Rome, Edinburgh, and he strained to read significance into their gait, their stance, their gestures . . . and those blank, insect faces.

The topic of Martine cropped up again at the Trossachs Hotel. Martine had been a sort of alien, too.

"At least there was no grandchild," remarked Mr. Spark. "Just as well, in my opinion."

A daughter-in-law who was part black, part brown, part blue for all he knew! Why should Charles have waited years then married such a person as Martine?

"Not that you ever met her," Charles said mildly.

"Why should *I* put myself out, an old chap?"

True, Martine wouldn't leave her one secure root in Greenwich Village. Charles had met her at a gallery opening just three months after Mrs. Spark's funeral. Within ten weeks he and Martine were married, and he had moved from his apartment off 116th Street into the Village for the next four years. When the break-up came, Charles returned to Upper Manhattan.

Loud tipsy Glaswegian talk babbled about them in the hotel bar. A stuffed golden eagle regarded visitors maliciously through glass eyes from inside its case.

"Maybe you ought to have had more children than me," Charles suggested, "and had them earlier."

"Costs money, son. You should know. Good schooling, Cambridge, all that. There's the trouble with education, makes you want the world on a plate. Ach, it's water under the bridge. Let's enjoy another dram."

Returning from the bar, Charles was aware of his father regarding him lovingly: his only son, big-boned and hardy-handsome, as the poet had written. Burly, though not tall. Shock of brown hair, already thinning at the crown. Broad, fresh, open face, with some crumpled laundry creases around the gray eyes. Generous lower lip, and thin mean upper lip which might have benefited by a mustache; but Charles hadn't wanted to copy his Dad, who had always worn a tash. A loving look could betray a glint of bitterness which a glance which was merely affectionate never contained.

"A plague of bloody Flies from space," sighed Mr. Spark. "Who'd have believed it? Cheers, lad."

Was there a weepy in the old man's eye? In Charles's heart salt tears stirred. The dead eagle's eye also glinted. At least that was an earthly eye.

None so blind as those who rub noses! As Charles finally realized, Martine was mad. Crinkly chestnut hair, hazel eyes, milk chocolate skin, slim as a boy with breasts, melting and assertive, wiry-tough and sensuous-soft; hermaphroditic! On first encounter Charles read her signs of passion. Perhaps *she* thought he held a key to human behavior, something which she illustrated only in faery or devilish parody. Perhaps Charles knew the secret of true expressions, a secret partly withheld from her.

In his lovely dark wife several persons cohabited, carrying out one psychic coup d'état after another. She was an artist in pen and ink, illustrating books and magazines. She drew inhabitants of a nether Earth, a population of goblins and nymphs which seemed to inhabit her, as subjects of her various ruling persons. These signaled out of her drawings with their fingers and their eyes, drawing Charles to her inexorably so as to understand those strange body signals.

Her art was always black and white; and flat without full perspective. Highly effective work—stunning—yet it seemed as if she lacked stereoscopic and color vision, because—because her elements would not fuse and co-operate. She was several flat people stacked side by side, each of them vivid in its stance, seen frontally. Each person seemed full of so much, yet let them tilt sideways and there were only two dimensions to them, with edges which could cut cruelly. Meanwhile a different Martine came to the fore.

She could never draw ordinary human faces—her rage when she tried to sketch *his!* Yet when she invented the features of a troll or elf or imp, oh yes, that's how those creatures would be; that's how they would express their alien feelings. At the height of his passion Charles wrote a preface for a book of her drawings entitled *Alien Expressions*, though she never drew "aliens" as such. The body language of her imaginary beings was human body language distorted in a hall of mirrors as if it had followed an alternative path of evolution. Or else distorted in a personal madhouse.

Martine originally came from New Orleans, and was of wildly mixed ancestry. Perhaps this explained—to her!—her fractured self. Her brother Larry, a weatherman down in Louisiana, was a regular guy. His only turmoils were natural storms, your ordinary sort of hurricane.

Ah, Martine. If Charles did undertake a new book to be called *Signs of Madness*—researched in clinics, illustrated by eighteenth and nineteenth century engravings of the inhabitants of Bedlam—might this seem an impeachment of Martine, a revenge? In turn might this make *Signs of Passion*, written while they were living together, appear to have been an exploitation of her?

Charles had hoped to sort this out in his mind while in Scotland; till the Flies came to Earth.

They took a steamer cruise on Loch Katrine. Eyeing the rumpled, lovely woodlands, Mr. Spark talked of Sir Walter Scott and Rob Roy. The Glaswegian trippers nursed sore heads so the outing was fairly peaceful. Father and son were only a stone's throw from the fault line between Highlands and Lowlands but they stayed in the former, plunging that evening in the Volvo downhill to the toy town of Inversnaid by Loch Lomond, to another Victorian hotel, and more malt of the glen. As a final ferry departed the little harbor for Inverglas across the loch, Mr. Spark stared at the summer sun setting.

"Just look at that golden whisky light falling on Ben Vorlich!" he exclaimed. "Remember it always—before it goes away!"

"When I was a boy," Charles started to say. He had never told anyone about his magical memory moments. Did his Dad also know about memory-photography? Had Dad seen a certain look in his son's eye?

A Scots voice interrupted, "Is there a Charles Spark in the bar? Telephone!"

By helicopter the next day from the hotel lawn to Glasgow, thence to Rome in a Lear-Fan executive jet. A chubby, genial American in his thirties, Lew Fisher, was Charles's courier; he had even brought a driver to Inversnaid to return the Volvo and Charles's father to the other side of Britain.

Why Rome? No less than eight of the aliens were flitting about Rome; no other city rated more than two Flies. UNCO was paying special attention to Rome.

Why the sudden V.I.P. treatment for Charles?

Orders.

Whose? Lew talked instead during the flight about antigravity. Not only could the aliens steer something five times the size of the Great Pyramid at Giza, but each was using a personal flying pack. Those whirry little wings couldn't support their body weight, let alone zip them along at jet speed. After the first week or so the scouts flew back nonstop to the hive—even from the other side of the world—then returned to wherever to continue sightseeing.

"Repulsion machinery," said Lew, "that's the theory. They're using the fifth force in nature, called, um, hypercharge. When we measure hypercharge it's gentle. Tiny. But our eggheads guess there are actually two extra forces involved, um, Yukawa terms, that's the name, both of 'em *big*. Only, one is attractive and the other's repulsive." ("Like the Flies themselves," Charles could hear his Dad mutter.) "So those almost cancel out. Well, the Flies have figured how to nix the attractive force, letting them tune the repulsive one. That may give them a force-field too. Deflect interstellar debris."

Lew was clearly no physicist. It was already plain to Charles how the CIA and KGB would be operating within UNCO, doing their best to be Cosmic Interstellar Agency and Kosmic Galaxy Bureau, both fishing for the secrets of the Flies.

Then there was the communication problem. Was the aliens' use of English and Russian *deliberately* poor? Their own lingo of whistles and chirps was uncrackable.

The bottom line: what was their game?

"The sun's going to blow up? They know, but we don't?" mused Lew. "They've guessed that we might wipe ourselves out? Shame to lose such a neat civilization totally. Let's remember it, guys. Or is 'remember Earth' a euphemism for shoving us aside? Meaning that we'll be no more than a memory?"

"Maybe they're the first interstellar package tour?"

"Without anything you'd call a camera? Just staring at things?"

"That's the way to see a world."

Lew cocked an eyebrow, then shrugged. "Welcome aboard the puzzle wagon."

He ran a videotape for Charles. Behold those sleek

bodies, plated with a chitin so deeply blue it was almost black. Around the waist between thorax and abdomen the tool belt certainly included a powerful radio and location beacon. Consider those dome heads with the hairy ears and the twitchy mustache feelers and those big bulgy faceted amber eyes.

A Fly had six skinny hairy black limbs. Its arms ended in jointed claws. Its hind "balance" legs were short, its abdominal legs four times as long. When a Fly hurried, its body pivoted up on to those long legs till it was almost horizontal, little legs wagging like rudders. That was how a Fly sometimes launched itself into the air; but the wings were undoubtedly science, not biology. Perhaps the ancestors of the Flies once had wings, which withered as the species evolved; now Flies wore wings again, re-invented.

"They can't be true insects," said Lew. "Anything that size needs an internal skeleton. They breathe like us. Yeah, breathe our air, and eat our food—though they're like flies in that regard! Prefer the trash cans of restaurants, not the haute cuisine inside. They could inhabit this planet quite happily, Charlie."

Charles was to stay at the American Embassy in the Via Veneto; and on arrival Lew ushered him in to meet the regional security chief who was UNCO liaison man, name of Dino Tarini, an Italian-American.

Tarini, mid-forties and scrawny, wore an impeccable cream silk suit and did not blink like other people, irregularly, inconspicuously. He stared—then once a minute or so he shuttered his eyes briefly as if he were some human surveillance camera making a time-lapse record of what went on. His high-tech desk and leather chair were backed by framed photos of Michelangelo's David and the Statue of Liberty looking strangely like brother and sister.

"Carlo, you eyeball some sights with Lew today. Try out Santa Maria sopra Minerva. A nun's showing one of the Flies round this afternoon. Interesting church, Carlo. It's Dominican. Dominicans ran the Inquisition. Grand Inquisitor's statue's there. They prosecuted Galileo in the convent next door. Showed him the thumbscrews."

Tarini plainly resented the way a string had been pulled on Charles's behalf and had a low opinion of the relevance of body language. *(By whom had the string been pulled? Ah. . . .)*

The following morning an UNCO bull session was scheduled at the Farnese Palace, which housed the French embassy: neutral territory, thus to underline international co-operation.

"French don't swap intelligence with us or the Soviets; whereas Italians allow our missiles on their soil, don't they?" As venue Tarini would have preferred an Italian government building staffed by his cousins.

"Tomorrow evening: reception at the palace. Try to talk to a Fly, Carlo. Why do they go back to the Hive?" Find out. Prove your worth.

"Maybe they get homesick," said Charles.

Tarini closed his eyes, recording the witticism.

"Yeah, and maybe there's a queen-fly roosting in there, a great black squashy mass that was full of eggs. Maybe she hatched all the other little Flies while the ship approached; programmed all her sons."

"You don't sound as though you like them too much, Don Tarini." Yes, give him the title of a Mafia godfather.

"Some things about our visitors we like very much."

Questions hung in the air. Did the Hive have defenses? How to find out nondisastrously, while also laying out the golden credit card from Kyoto to Copenhagen, the red carpet from Berlin to Odessa? The road to the stars lay open; but Flies crowded it.

"Will they share their knowledge with us if we're *nice* to them?" Tarini was lying.

Rome was aromatic with the scent of flowers, coffee, olive oil, whiffs of unfamiliar tobacco, mixed with puffs of exhaust fumes and drain stench. The whole hot, humid city—streets, pavements, walls—droned a faint mantra. Hum-om-hum.

After catching beers and mortadella sandwiches at a

bar beyond Trevi, Charles and Lew played chicken to cross the Via del Corso. Their destination was a piazza where a marble elephant supported an obelisk carved with hieroglyphs. The beast stood on a plinth, knitting its brows, its trunk slung rearwards as if to squirt dust. What big cabbage-leaf ears it had, pinned back in sculpture. The area between Jumbo and the scabbed cliff-face of the church of Santa Maria above Minerva was cordoned by police in dark blue, cradling machine pistols. Several hundred spectators, including newsmen and paparazzi slung with cameras, waited for a sight of the alien.

Showing their UNCO credentials, the two men were admitted into the chill of the church, where blue marble geometry inset a white marble floor, highly polished. Black marble pillars, flecked pink, lined the nave. Curving medallioned groin-vaulting supported a star-studded imitation sky. A multitude of side chapels . . . any description of this church was a cartoon! Ten thousand sentences couldn't capture every detail in remembrance.

Down at the transept half a dozen UNCO people were scrutinizing a chapel, from which a soft clear voice emerged. The chapel was graced by a statue of a pope and a fresco of an angel with blue swan's wings half-furled. Watched by cloaked prelates a dove spat golden fire at a kneeling Madonna. In front of this painting a lanky young woman in a long blue frock, her flaxen hair peeping from under a blue headscarf, was patiently addressing . . . the very opposite of an angel: a five-foot-tall black Fly, mosaic eyes clamped to its head like swollen golden leeches. Now and then the woman touched her necklace, of variously sized turquoise beads, a chain of little blue moons.

"Here in the Carafa Chapel you see the Annunciation as painted by Fra Lippo Lippi. . . ."

"Yes," the Fly responded in a dry, rattly, jerky tone. It seemed to be drinking in every detail of the chapel as thirstily as Charles had ever stared at a scene when he was a boy. He sniffed but could detect no alien odor, only wax polish and candle smoke.

"The nun's Dutch," whispered Lew. "Outfit called Foyer Unitas, specializing in guiding non-Catholics. Very much in depth. They can gab on half a day about a single church." As indeed the woman seemed intent on doing.

"They hope to convert non-Catholics, aliens included?"

"No, they're simply ace guides. Got the right pace for the Flies, who look at everything for ages."

The two men followed the guided tour around till Charles knew more than he ever needed to know about Santa Maria sopra Minerva.

Lo, here is the tomb of Saint Catherine of Siena. There is the very room where she died in 1380, frescos by Romano. Lo, here is the chapel of Saint Dominic housing the tomb of Pope Benedict XIII, sculpted by Marchioni between 1724 and 1730. The Dutch nun fiddled inconspicuously with her necklace while she talked.

"Yes," the Fly said periodically.

That evening, Lew took Charles to a trattoria he recommended. Superb sea-food ravioli in garlic butter followed by a delicious concoction of lamb brains, and home-made ice cream. A friendly Chianti, then some fierce Grappa. Charles still wondered who had called him to Rome but didn't wish to lose face by asking outright.

The Farnese Palace was built like the noblest of prisons, its windows facing upon a dark, majestically porticoed courtyard into which rain poured that particular morning. In the crowded conference room Charles soon spotted Valeri Osipyan. In Geneva at the arms talks the KGB psychologist Colonel had been accompanied to begin with by a fat old woman aide (his peasant mother?), then later by a sly wisp-haired fellow whom the Russians claimed was a chess master, only no one had ever heard of him.

In their own fashion the Russians were deploying scrutiners of human behavior to follow suit the American lead in nonverbal, nuance interpretation of the talks, and the negotiators. How could one ultimately *trust* the other side? That was becoming a question almost as vital as warhead verification—to Charles's mind at least; and he as a British expatriate might have added, "How do you trust your own side?"

The vinegary, purse-lipped Colonel was a hard one to read. At a reception in Geneva Osipyan had inquired with apparent sympathy how it was that Charles hadn't correctly read the body language of his own wife, with whom he had so recently split up? Western colleagues were listening. Was this said to undermine Charles's credibility? To demonstrate the depth of KGB information? Was it a subtle warning not to let a possible prejudice color his readings of the honesty of Irina Kovaleva, the new Soviet negotiator who happened to bear a certain resemblance (skin color excluded) to dear, wayward, hysterical, ultimately hateful Martine?

Charles had replied, "Now that we've begun taking body language seriously I can imagine negotiators being kept ignorant of the full, true picture by their *own* side."

"You can be too subtle," Osipyan had retorted. "We're a bluff people at heart. Basically blunt and frank."

"Bluff has another meaning."

"Nowadays we always tell the simple truth. You hunt for subtleties to worm yourself off the hook of peace."

"A hook catches the unwary prey."

"Women sometimes catch men by hiding their hook in a lovely lure, Mr. Spark."

"Did your grandmother tell you that? It *was* her who was with you last year?"

Osipyan had smiled tightly. No, the Soviet truthsayer had not been his grandmother, or mother.

Now here was the Colonel in Rome, facing Dino Tarini across the huge oval table as some forty UNCO personnel sought their name cards and settled down. Others took refuge in armchairs scattered about the room, made notes, consulted files.

An hour later, an Italian biologist was saying, "The aliens *look* identical to flies. Like insects they display industry and persistence. Do they have true individuality? Are they genuine intelligences?"

"To remember is to be intelligent," Osipyan said. "Besides, they talk to us."

"After a fashion! Maybe they have developed awareness to a remarkable degree . . . for insect types. Powerful instincts may still rule them, far more than we are ruled."

Tarini nodded. "What if they're really biological machines? With eyes which are lenses, brains which are recording equipment? Why shouldn't they fuel themselves with any garbage? Why should they have *taste?*"

"Taste enough," said a Vandyke-bearded linguist from Rome University, "to admire the masterpieces of our culture."

"Indiscriminate cataloging. Like auctioneers." There was scorn in Tarini's voice. "It would be interesting to know if they can reproduce, or if they're just specialized living machines. Now suppose one of them crashed in a regrettable accident—"

"No," said Osipyan. "A large floating pyramid says no."

"A pyramid we can't see inside of."

"Compound eyes oughtn't to see as clearly as *our* eyes," the same biologist declared.

"Depends how the brain is programmed," said a French colleague. "Surely they must have a single central brain, not different ganglia spread throughout the body like insects? Let's forget the insect analogy."

"A dissection could settle these questions."

Osipyan pouted at Tarini. "People may play dirty tricks with one another, because we know the rules. To play these games with aliens is the height of folly."

"Perhaps it's the height of naïvete not to? You Russians are so romantic about aliens."

Charles found himself speaking. "The Flies look at the sights with a relaxed intensity. With those compound eyes they're seeing more intensely than any human tourist. A machine would simply record. They're not just cameras. I'm sure of it."

Osipyan swung round. "So, Mr. Spark, in your view does landing a pyramid, which dwarfs the Egyptian pyramids, quite close to those same pyramids serve as a gesture of cultural solidarity—or as a caution that their power and technology likewise dwarfs ours in the same proportion?"

Charles shrugged, having no idea. If he was a violinist of human nuances, he was being asked suddenly to take up playing the trombone or the tuba; an alien instrument.

The quirky tilt of Osipyan's chin and the droop of his eyelids said that Charles was admitting inability. Yet Charles wasn't the prime target for the Colonel, whose glance glided onward to Tarini.

"We need to discover new rules," the Russian said, "not the same old ones. Why should aliens play our games? We need to know the simple truth about them."

"They aren't exactly spelling out their motives," grumbled Tarini. "*Remember:* what does that mean?"

Something, thought Charles, which was so much a part of their nature, of their biological existence, that the Flies could be blind to it—as a peculiarity which might baffle strangers.

Lew had detailed a marine guard from the American embassy to act as gumshoe. After a leisurely beer and sandwiches in a café following the bull session, Lew consulted a two-way pocket radio and set out with Charles for the church of Sant' Ignazio half a mile away.

Sharing a large umbrella, they walked till they reached the fringe of the mobile carabinieri cordon which accompanied a Fly when on foot. No alien anywhere in the world had yet been attacked or threatened—perhaps no fanatic could think of a good reason—but police protection certainly gave a Fly some open space to sightsee in.

By now the rain was slackening off, but after hours on the streets, even under an umbrella, the waiting marine was soaked. As had the nun been, he reported; however, once she reached Sant' Ignazio a priest had turned up to deliver a change of clothing and footwear. The Italian-speaking marine had heard the man in the soutane explaining to the police that he brought these dry clothes from the nun's base in the Pamphili Palace, Piazza Navona. Rain merely rolled off the Fly.

The slow tour that morning had taken in the Pantheon and Piazza della Rotunda. At lunchtime, the nun had steered the Fly along the Via Monteroni to sample French colonial pig-swill from the dustbins of *L'Eau Vive*, followed by a trip inside that restaurant—housed in a sixteenth century palazzo—so that the sister could have a decent bite too.

"You've done good. We'll take over."

The marine departed gladly.

"Damn stupid conference," muttered Lew. "Couldn't have been worse timed."

"Why's that?" asked Charles.

"A visit to the Vatican has just been arranged—very likely."

"By the priest who brought the clothes? He was a go-between?"

"No, listen, Charlie, that restaurant *L'Eau Vive* is where all the Vatican bigwigs dine out. It's staffed by stunning young nuns with a special dispensation to wear sexy dresses."

"Sounds risqué. What goes on?"

"Just splendid expensive eating. The waitresses all wear golden crosses to remind their eminent clientele of chastity. Could put cardinals off their cuisine and vino if it was served gloomily."

"Remind them of poverty?"

"Something like that. They still need moral ladies to serve them. That's where the princes of the Church hang out; and that's where she took the alien. Obeying orders, I'll bet. Vatican must be pretty stirred by an alien race turning up. Haven't spoken out yet. No Flies have visited there—to see the finest sights of all." Lew shilly-shallied. "I have to split. I'm going to talk to Dino. We'll see if we can get a list of reservations at *L'Eau Vive*. Will you keep a close eye on the sister while you're Fly-watching? She's called Kathinka."

Lew offered Charles an umbrella escort through the ring of armed, rain-caped carabinieri to the door of Sant' Ignazio.

"The Soviets might pretend to be pussy-footing, but what is the Vatican up to? There are at least six Machiavellis on the staff." He fled.

The Fly was staring up at the ceiling with rather more than "a relaxed intensity." The alien seemed perturbed, under strain, as if controlling an urge to unfurl its wings and zoom up to the heaven-painted dome to accompany Saint Ignatius Loyola on his journey direct to Paradise. If so, it would have banged its head. This only dawned on Charles as he heard Sister Kathinka (crisp and dry) point out to the Fly how cunningly the real building flowed into its painted continuation.

The dome was a trompe l'oeil, an eye-deceit, an illusion of art. The work of the Jesuit priest Andrea Pozzo shortly after 1685. Hats off to Fra Pozzo! No one had bothered to build the planned cupola, consequently he had painted it in. The illusion was extraordinarily convincing; the alien gazed at it for the best part of an hour. Even Sister Kathinka exhausted her repertoire and stood mute. Meanwhile Charles had been joined by other UNCO spectators, among them that Italian linguist with the beard, who frowned at the continuing silence.

At long last the Fly came to terms with the spectacle overhead, and turned to the nun.

"Yes, yes, like our tanks." Briefly the alien seemed to float, buoyed up.

Professore Barba scribbled in a notebook. "It *likes*," he murmured. "It *thanks* the sister." Charles had heard something else entirely.

The Fly again addressed the sister, who had perhaps lost track of the tour.

"Memory vanished? Because heaven is false?"

The nun touched her necklace as if for reassurance. "This painted heaven is not the true heaven," she replied. "I have told you all I know about the ceiling."

"No more is known about Saint Ignatius?"

"Oh yes! Why, there are whole volumes written about him. They fill shelves in the Vatican Library."

"Volume is cubic size?"

"Books!" Sister Kathinka led the Fly to the lectern, where a huge brass-bound Bible lay open.

"Here is the most important book. It contains the word of God."

The Fly tapped the pages with a fuzzy claw. Its mustache quivered.

"This Bible is in Latin," explained the sister. "That's the old language of this country. The language is dead, but it still lives in the Church, just as Christ is dead but still lives."

At that moment two facts became intuitively obvious to Charles. The nun had been encouraged to explore the possibility of converting the aliens to Christianity. Secondly, this alien had no idea of the function of a book—what it was! The aliens possessed no written language.

Mightn't that be the case with a sufficiently advanced race? Even on Earth the electronic tide was submerging literacy. People of the super-science tomorrow could easily be illiterate. And yet, and yet . . .

The dining room of the French embassy was a welcome antidote to the severe aspects of the Farnese Palace, a gush of gaiety sensuously decorated by the Caracci brothers with the Triumph of Love. Four of Rome's Flies were present at the event.

"Charles Spark? I'm Olivia Mendelssohn. Head of White House Security. President's personal representative. We'll be working together, you and I."

"We will?"

Olivia was short. The crown of her head only came level with his chest, and Charles was no giant. She was mid-thirties, perhaps shading forty. Charles recalled her face from earlier in the conference room, though that morning she had seemed intent on remaining inconspicuous. Previously, her black hair had been roped in a tight ponytail, hadn't it? Freed now, it swept luxuriously around bare shoulders of a light buttery hue. Olivia was dressed in a glittery gown of darkest blue instead of—what had it been before? a gray jacket, skirt, and ruffled white blouse.

With a vague nod Lew melted away into the crowd.

Earlier, Olivia Mendelssohn had worn dark glasses. Now her eyes were naked. And huge. They were large brown liquid eyes in any case, but she had enlarged them further by applying kohl. Her smoothly oval face was of generous enough proportion—just—to accommodate such eyes. Was she trying to attract alien attention by that gown which copied the color of their bodies; by those enormous eyes?

Her legs were shorter than her face or trunk or bosom merited. The evening gown molded those legs together into a stumpy mermaid's tail glistening with scales, upon which she perched. Her shoes—expensive, black-dyed crocodile skin—pointed apart, somewhat like the fork of a tail. Hans Andersen's Little Mermaid had summoned Charles to Rome!

"We'll need to be fully open to each other, Charles, in order to osmose your talent and mine together."

"Yours being a talent for security?"

"For something else too! Here isn't the place or time . . . we'll have to be franker than any barbed insights of Colonel Osipyan into your failed relationship with Martine."

Charles blinked. "You seem to know me inside out."

He collected a glass of champagne from a passing, duck-tailed waiter. Olivia barely moistened her lips with an orange juice. Amidst the throng of French embassy staff and other foreign diplomats, Italian government ministers, UNCO personnel, several churchmen in black soutanes and stiff white collars, a lone nun in a black habit, and of course four aliens, a cardinal stood out: a stout tropical bird in his scarlet cassock, cape, and biretta. To Charles at that moment little Olivia stood out much more.

"Your Martine," she said, "was a pool of emotions in which you could fish but not swim, or sail. On account of the sudden storms. The spouts, the maelstroms. She was so fluid, so labile, wasn't she? That was why you couldn't read her, fix her nature."

Tilting her head, Olivia stole a glance up at the sumptuous ceiling; and Charles thought to himself, "The Failure of Love. For me. Not the Triumph."

"Ultimately," continued Olivia, "Martine shook herself apart; and you too. She broke the banks, so far as you were concerned. You had hoped to be those banks, confining the pool, framing it like a setting for a rare jewel. She wasn't a jewel, though. She was . . . dissolution . . . a persona written in bitter if sparkling water, inhabited by toads as well as by such wonderful, delicious, slippery fish."

This peculiar conversation—her side of it—captured Charles even more than the presence of aliens in the room.

"Professionally I plug leaks," she said. "Nowadays we need an enormous leak—from the alien side. Any signs of moisture yet?"

With an effort Charles hauled his attention back to the matter of Flies.

"Yes, I believe they're illiterate."

"Aaah?"

"I don't think they know what writing *is*—letters or squiggles or dots or hieroglyphs."

The alien guests were drinking in the details of the room while a number of UNCO mavens and dignitaries side-stepped like so many geosynch satellites, keeping out of their direct field of vision. Each alien held a glass of whitish liquid. A glass was emptied; a waiter suavely furnished a full one. As the waiter shimmied by, Charles stopped him.

"What are the aliens drinking?"

"Sour milk, Signore." The man made a face. "Seven days old."

"You have Egyptian blood," Charles said suddenly to Olivia.

It was those eyes of hers, so vastened by the dark cosmetic! Perhaps aping some Renaissance princess she had even put drops of belladonna sap in those eyes to dilate them?

"My Mom was half-Egyptian," she agreed. "And my Dad, half-Jewish. Should we try to talk to a Fly?"

So they headed toward the nearest alien, though Charles concentrated on Olivia's body language as much as upon the Fly's. On the whole she walked fluidly and loosely. Once, twice, she stiffened momentarily. He wondered whether she had ever suffered a dislocated hip; whether as a child she had even undergone some experimental bone-stretching régime in an effort to increase her height. Underneath her gown would residual scars on legs and thighs betray where metal pins had pierced through to her skeleton? No, that was absurd. He merely wanted an excuse to undress her. She seemed to be offering herself to the alien, using some body speech of her own concoction, yet at the same time resisting, flinching.

"Good evening!" She stared the chosen Fly full in the eyes. "Do you like this city?"

"Yes." That rattly voice. "I remember it." The voice of a husk: sticks, hairs rasping together, no liquid music of vocal chords. Gazing at its mouth parts—a sort of black beak around pursed softness—Charles imagined the alien sucking him dry, discarding him as a human husk. He smelled the curdled tang of the sour milk in its glass.

I remember it. Unless the Flies were masters of invisibility they had never visited Rome before, Renaissance or ancient or in-between.

"What do you do next?" Olivia asked.

"Fly back to ship, dis-gorge." Its short legs, then its long legs, twitched. Charles visualized bees returning to a hive, their hairy legs yellow with pollen. In the hive the dust from many flowers became the honey that nourished—what?

"Do you disgorge in a tank?" he asked it.

"Yes." Japanese people were notorious for saying "yes" when they merely meant that they were listening politely.

"What kind of tank is that?"

"Tanks of memory."

Thanks for the memory. . . . Charles hummed this tune to himself. The Fly's mustache bristled. Could Tarini be right, that the aliens were biological recording machines which returned to be unloaded, emptied for the benefit of some other creature, hideous to behold?

Yet this Fly seemed informative. While onlookers avidly eavesdropped he asked:

"Do your eyes see many images of the same object? We see one image."

It looked into his eyes. "Yes, many objects, in order, to remember."

"What is in those tanks?"

"We. We float." As in that church, momentarily this Fly appeared free of gravity.

"How many tanks?"

"Thousand."

A pyramid full of tanks . . . and floating flies, emptying themselves . . . what did it mean?

A burly Russian, perspiring in a suit which looked to be woven of material half an inch thick, joined in chaperoned by Osipyan.

"Comrade Starman, please! Did your ship fly here by the force of repulsion?"

The Fly stared at a luster-hung lamp, the crystal facets glittering and twinkling. Answer came there none.

"Have your people visited other inhabited planets in the cosmos?" the Russian persisted.

"Yours first to signal presence to us. So we came."

Pleased, the Russian was visibly calculating to himself light years and the chronology of radio and TV output from the Earth.

"Just in time," the Fly added, unnerving Osipyan.

"Why did you truly come?" the Colonel demanded.

"Our world is full," was the reply.

"Full, of Flies?"

"Our places are fully remembered. Here are new places. Do you remember all your places? Have any disappeared?"

"Places disappear if you don't remember them?" broke in Charles.

A jerk of the Fly's head.

"We must leave," it said. Draining the clotted dregs, it handed its glass to the Russian scientist who cradled this as though it were an alien artifact. "Thank for hospital. Ity."

Olivia smiled graciously. "You must fly. After you dis-gorge, what next?"

"I start to remember Vatican City. Good-bye."

Charles had realized by now that the nun in the room was the same Sister Kathinka. Her flaxen hair was entirely hidden by her coif and white wimple, and she wore a long black pleated gown, with a cross dangling on beads from her waist. She had reverted to habit. Accompanied by Olivia, he headed over to introduce himself to this woman he was supposed to keep an eye on.

"I don't know how you find the energy, Sister. A walking guide-book! Hour after hour must be a strain." (Please don't say that you find the strength in Jesus or Mary!)

When Kathinka smiled, she showed perfect white teeth which she must brush often.

"The standing is the hard part." Her breath was scented with mint. "One has to learn poise. Actually I practice ballet exercises. When I was a girl in Holland I wished to be either a ballet dancer or a religious. Those are both similar callings, you know! Dedication, rigors of the body, aim of grace. But." Glancing at Olivia, she fell silent.

"You grew a little too tall," Olivia completed. "Your choice was made."

"By God."

"Do you need to look official this evening?" Charles nodded at her black garment.

"No, it occurred to me that I have been wearing the wrong clothes to put my aliens at ease. Now I resemble them, a little."

They chatted about her work.

"The . . . *choreography* of each tour takes much attention, so that nothing is forgotten, so that no fact disappears."

Had the Fly meant that people might forget bits of history, and thus lose the true depth of things—which could fade from awareness?

"Do the aliens regard you as remarkable?" Charles asked her. "Being able to disgorge so many bits of information, all in the right order?"

Many objects. In order. To remember.

"It isn't remarkable, Mr. Spark. All the objects are there. The information hangs upon them, as upon this." She held up her chain of beads. "Bead after bead. We tell our beads. Likewise, while I guide."

"Your necklace!" Charles exclaimed. "The turquoise necklace."

"You noticed that? Yes, it's my mundane rosary. I do not often misplace a fact."

Olivia gazed intently at the nun. "Each fact is a private prayer." She stated this as a certainty. "Your whole day is a chain of prayers—on behalf of your heretic or infidel tourists who never realize how slyly they are being blessed." Olivia jerked her face in the direction of the ceiling. "Somebody painted those erotic scenes in the year whatever. Bingo, another prayer is said!"

A mischievous smile played about the Dutch woman's lips. "Annibale and Agostino Caracci, between 1597 and 1604. There, you are blessed with information! This is the information age, isn't it?"

"You use those beads as your abacus, a medieval instrument, a harking back."

This made the nun frown and almost turn away. Hastily Charles intervened.

"A Fly told us it's going to visit the Vatican. Will you be guiding it?"

"It. Or another."

"You're much in demand."

"If asked, I obey."

"Is the Vatican visit the reason why that cardinal's here tonight?"

"Cardinal Fantonetti? Of course he would be here. He is the vicar-general of Rome." No, that particular cardinal had nothing to do with trips to the Vatican, which was another city, another country.

"Do you know all the cardinals, Sister?"

"How could I know the Cardinal Archbishop of Calcutta, or of Guatemala, or of the South Seas?" She knew more, much more, than she was saying; or was allowed to say.

"Do you bless the Flies too?" pressed Olivia.

"As you say, Mr. Spark, it is a strain. I must return to our order's house to pray and sleep."

Charles recalled the address. "I know the Piazza Navona isn't far, but will you share our car?"

Surprise that he knew.

"Thank you, I prefer to walk. Alone, to bear the streets in mind. Dressed like this, I'm perfectly safe. A nun owns nothing worth stealing."

"Nothing but knowledge." Olivia's voice slurred. "The knowledge which blesses the streets, so that they aren't forgotten and don't disappear." Her eyes were glassy as if she were drunk, deeply drunk.

The Vatican Press Office had announced that when aliens arrived in St. Peter's Square in three days' time a trio of cardinals would be on hand to greet them: Borromini, Storchi, and Tedesci.

"According to the reservations at *L'Eau Vive* Tedesci and Storchi both lunched there." Lew explained that the former was Vatican Secretary of State, the foreign minister; which made sense. The latter headed the Secretariat for Non-Believers; fine so far. But Borromini, the odd man out, was in charge of the Apostolic Penitentiary.

"That sounds like the Vatican Jail." Olivia's tone was relaxed, as if she owned Tarini's office.

"It handles questions of conscience—"

"It's the Inquisition!"

Tarini shook his head. "No, that's the Sacred Congregation for the Doctrine of the Faith—and it deals with heresy. You got to be a Christian first before you can be a heretic. The Penitentiary covers sorcery, black magic, demons, forces of darkness. Its boss didn't invite the Flies, but he's in on the act when they turn up."

Olivia laughed half-heartedly. "To decide if they're kosher or a spawn of Satan?"

Tarini rubbed his fingers thoughtfully. "The Church isn't simpleminded. Vatican's probably facing a crisis. Do aliens have souls? Is the Church truly universal? Why do Flies home in on Rome?"

"Will they have an audience with the Pope?" chipped in Charles. Tarini was calculating something. . . .

"The Pope's at Castel Gandolfo," said Lew. "His summer palace. That's usual. Got an observatory there. Maybe he's consulting his astronomers."

Tarini dangled a red herring. "Jesuits, those are. Jesuits aren't too popular with the hierarchy. Excessive support for Reds in Latin America."

Charles leaned forward. "This Penitentiary might view a horde of Flies as possible demons?"

"You become an expert on demons, you see demons everywhere." Evasive Tarini.

"There's always the terrible third prophecy of Fatima," said Lew helpfully—to Tarini's annoyance.

"Who's she?" asked Olivia.

"Not she. A place in Portugal. The virgin appeared to some kids in 1916 and predicted the two world wars—"

"The first one was halfway through in 1916!"

"Yeah well, don't blame me. The third prophecy was locked in the secret archives till the Sixties. Only a pope could read it. The first pope to do so almost fainted with fear, so the story goes. Maybe the prophecy's about aliens. About the Devil infiltrating from the stars." Lew grinned boyishly; the idea was a joke to him.

"Do you believe in a real Devil?" Charles asked Tarini.

"I'm a good Catholic, Carlo. We aren't talking about me."

"Maybe we ought to?" Olivia knit her brow, but Tarini stared back expressionlessly.

If Olivia had been going to explain to Charles about her talent for something else, she must have decided that the time still wasn't ripe. They spent the next couple of days watching Flies watch Rome, while Romans watched the Flies. Two of the resident aliens had flown back to their hive after the reception; they would disgorge, prior to seeing Vatican City.

St. Peter's Square, grand keyhole to Vatican City, was closed to traffic, but how could the heart of the Church be closed to pedestrians? Leaving the embassy car in the Via della Conciliazione, Charles and Olivia and Lew joined a stream of spectators flooding into the square.

This was another hot bright cloudless day, though some wisps of breeze ventilated the city lazily. The entry of aliens into St. Peter's could prove epochal; some revelation might be at hand.

"Oh my God," groaned Lew as they crushed over the white line of the international frontier to encounter —perhaps not chaos but a situation which was as fluid as boiling water.

Were eighty or a hundred thousand people in the piazza already? Romans, countrymen, tourists, nuns and priests, hucksters, pickpockets, what a medley. A pair of Swiss guards in harlequin costumes surveyed the inflow. Olivia, in dark shades, stared at the Switzers: their technicolor tunics, their baggy pants, their boots striped blue and yellow with red flashings, those cute little white ruffle collars, the big slouch berets shading one eye and muffling one ear. The guards were armed with pikes, the perfect medieval weapon.

"Those guys are in charge?" she asked incredulously.

Lew was craning his neck to see beyond the mob, the obelisk, the spuming fountains. TV cameras peered between the baroque statues of saints atop Bernini's colonnade.

"No, there are hundreds of Rome city cops and carabinieri. Crush barriers up front. Ah, I spy the Vatican Vigilance too! The muscle in drab blue. I guess there'll be plainclothes cops scattered through the crowd."

"Why are you worried?" asked Charles, as they forged forward, breaking a way through for Olivia.

"Well," said Lew, still peering as he pushed.

"What's wrong, security-wise?" Olivia demanded.

"Just, *hundreds* of police . . . isn't much use. When the Pope appears they station ten thousand cops in this square. What are they playing at? Low profile? What did they expect? News has been out for days. We'll be okay once we get through." Lew tried to sound reassuring.

"Who's pulling punches?" she asked. "City of Rome? Communist mayor, right? Or is this Vigilance of theirs turning a blind eye?"

"I don't know, Miss Mendelssohn. It looks okay, but it isn't."

At that moment a rift opened in the throng through which even Olivia could see ahead to the great façade of the church with Michelangelo's dome rising behind. She gasped and stumbled against Charles, who gripped her arm. She wasn't panicking because she felt like a child in a hectic mob; that wasn't the reason.

"Too much blue sky! Where's the Capitol?"

"In Washington, D.C. Not here," said Lew. "Are you okay, Miss Mendelssohn? A crowd like this could make anyone faint."

What did Olivia mean? Charles held her around the shoulder but she firmed up and thrust ahead, patting at the chiffon headscarf she'd worn in case they needed to enter the basilica.

Behind the guarded steel barriers, amidst a minor retinue of priests and the occasional nun, the three cardinals waited in full pomp though some distance apart from each other, perhaps for security, perhaps politically. Microphones stood planted like bishops' croziers.

The spry, white-haired oldster was Storchi, his particular brief non-Christians and Marxist atheists. Tedesci seemed a jovial bon viveur, to whom gold-rimmed spectacles lent a scholarly air: sanguine scrutineer of menus, men, and monarchs of the world. The youngest cardinal, stout and swarthy with jowls of deepest blue where his scrupulously shaved flesh denied the bursting forth of beard, was Borromini, the connoisseur of darkness. Sister Kathinka waited near him.

Once admitted through the cordon, Lew wandered off to talk UNCO business. Charles and Olivia joined the Dutch nun.

"Will the cardinals bless the aliens?" he asked the nun. From behind her shades Olivia was staring at Borromini lasciviously as if undressing him. Frowning as he gazed at the cloudless sky, the cardinal paid no attention.

Sister Kathinka touched a finger to her lips, kissing silence, amidst the hum and hurly-burly rolling from the waiting crowds. The mob was oozing tighter against the barriers as the piazza filled behind them, even bulging through and around like hernias of humanity, for the barriers by no means formed an unbroken line across the square. A concerned Swiss guard moved forward, gesturing with his pike as if to stir a pudding. A policeman motioned with his carbine.

"Borromini isn't thinking of blessings." Olivia's voice had slurred. She squirmed as if in that bright sunshine a cold worm had wriggled down her spine. "It's like Dino said: is a Fly a person, a moral intelligence? Could a Fly understand the crucifixion or the virgin birth? Could a Fly become a priest? Could a Fly be martyred and become a saint? If not, then does the Church embrace all? Could a Fly be a cleverly designed temptation? Maybe the Devil, reigning in the frozen empty void which is so like Hell, has at last created a mockery of life . . . these Flies, first demons to dare the daylight. He's ambitious, this Borromini. . . ."

Yes, Charles could see that. Olivia was simply improvising on what Tarini had said, wasn't she?

No, more than that.

"Powerful," she murmured. "He's been ruthless. No Sicilian has been pope for a thousand years. Does believe in actual demons. Yet of honorable conscience. Night of prayer, take this burden from my shoulders. . . ."

Much more!

"Apocalypse creeps close. Imps are out of Hell. Of course Flies show no expressions on their faces, or else we might recognize the evil grin. What if *these* doubts are a temptation—to reject a blessing of communion with alien souls, to circumscribe the Church and lose so many? Disastrous to make wrong decision. Take this burden, night of prayer, give me Your wisdom."

Staring at Olivia, the Dutch nun crossed herself. Olivia relaxed as if she had been stroked by the gesture.

Italian voices cried out. The crowd seethed. In the sky two black flecks of Flies were approaching, high, shadowed at a safe distance by a couple of police helicopters.

Artificial wings a-flutter—steering wings?—both Flies came in to land in the open space, bounding a few paces on their long legs before lowering their little hind legs and furling away those black-membraned wings. How like a pair of devils from a medieval painting of Hell. Borromini's left hand was thrust down by his side, thumb clasping middle and ring fingers, index finger and little finger sticking out. Charles recognized the Manu Cornuta, the "horned hand" sign for warding off the evil eye, familiar to peasants.

While Tedesci, as foreign minister, greeted the Flies in English, his voice amplified by microphone and loudspeakers, the aliens stared at the monumental colonnade.

"They must approve," confided Sister Kathinka. "Well ordered columns, each labeled individually with its own statue. That makes them easy to remember, doesn't it? It's like Guilio Camillo's Memory Theatre on a grand, true scale."

"A memory theatre?" repeated Charles.

"Ah, that was a sixteenth century scheme. Camillo built a wooden amphitreater representing the universe as he saw it, full of astrological images and little boxes stuffed with writings about everything under the sun, and beyond. Your orator stood up on stage and, well, Apollo's image would trigger a speech about the sun. That was Camillo's idea." Her right hand fluttered, as if to cross herself. "It was occult. He thought he could exploit the mechanisms of the universe, magically. But the King of France got tired of funding him."

One Fly bobbed up and down; it couldn't see well enough because of all the people. Tides of crowd were spilling around the far edge of the barrier. The Swiss harlequin trotted off to bar the way with his pike.

The other Fly took note of Tedesci.

"Here," it croaked, "is your God focus, yes?" The alien voice rattled from the PA speakers. "It is large. But limited. Your God forgets you, yes? Your God is sick. Remember the world!"

A collective gasp arose, then a noise midway between a groan and the throaty growl of a cat. As Tedesci opened his mouth in simple affront, or about to be diplomatic, that Fly's wings whirred out. It rose ten feet into the air, to hang gazing at the basilica: the columned portico, the loggia windows, the balcony from which popes blessed city and world, those stone giants looking down into the piazza—Christ, John the Baptist, the Apostles. Then the Fly rose much higher to see the drum and cupola of the dome behind, topped by golden ball and cross.

What a mockery of the Ascension, or of the Holy Ghost hovering. People hastily crossed themselves. The crowd's growl deepened. They had seen the aliens landing from the sky like little living helicopters, yet now the levitation of this Fly appeared miraculous. This was a black miracle, something out of the Apocalypse occurring in St. Peter's Piazza. Slowly the Fly drifted high overhead towards the church.

"Basta!" exclaimed Borromini. As he turned to follow its progress, his two flexed fingers stabbed downward in nervous spasm. Or was that a signal?

Pausing, the Fly seemed to lock eyes with the bearded, cross-wielding Christ on the parapet. It sank downward so as to alight on the steps of the church.

"Bestemmia!" a voice cried in the front of the crowd. Hundreds of other voices took up the call. *"Bestemmia! Bestemmia!"*

Blasphemy. Thousands of voices, a flash fire of fury.

The Roman mob surged. Barriers were climbed, thrust between, circumvented. Men raced to intercept the Fly, to ward it off from entering St. Peter's. Screams, cries, the rattle of gunfire—as surrounded police discharged their weapons into the air. Other police and Vigilance dropped back to form a tighter cordon around the reception party and the other alien, but no one tried to break through to attack it. On the steps the Fly disappeared in a scrum of rioters.

A long thirty seconds after the brawlers reached their target, a flashing white explosion ripped out the heart of the riot on the steps. Bodies, bits of bodies, were hurled out disgustingly. The Fly beside Charles cried out with a noise like a football rattle. Ambulance sirens, police sirens began to wail.

It took a while longer before anyone as close to the basilica as Charles or the cardinals realized the greater horror, the awful mystery of that morning. Already the crowd behind the fountains and the obelisk were pointing, moaning.

An UNCO delegate had been listening to Vatican Radio's English language commentary. Tearing his earplug loose, he turned up the volume on his transistor set.

". . . the cupola of St. Peter's has *vanished*. The dome is sheered off, obliterated. It simply no longer exists. The Church of Rome stands open to the sky!"

Hearing this, Cardinal Borromini sank to his knees and prayed—to be forgiven?

Olivia and Charles spent the afternoon in bed together in his room at the embassy. A good place to work at body language? To begin with they were busy forgetting the morning's events; then they were re-

membering amid the rumpled sheets. Charles had shut
the drapes across the extremely tall windows, but Roman summer light still filtered through.

"I'm psychic, Charles," she told him. "Mainly I
sense shadows of the past, staining a person—just
rarely a shadow of the future. When I saw Borromini I
saw his shadows. When we talked to the Fly at the
reception . . . it was so ordinary, that Fly, that's the
main impression I got. Ordinary."

"A regular fly." Charles thought of Martine's brother;
and Martine. Was Olivia also crazy? The idea of someone so close to the American President using the Third
Eye in matters of security struck him as capricious and
unsettling, though not wholly incredible. Had she any
influence over actual policy?

"If insights occur strongly enough—" on the psychic
Richter scale! "—I let them guide me. I've always
been right. I was right about you and Martine, wasn't
I?"

"Mmm," he said. "Does your government know
about your psychic gifts?"

"The First Lady knows. She fixed my appointment.
A few years back I sketched the shadow of her success. Her husband's future success."

"She was visiting a carnival? You used a crystal
ball?"

"No, darling, I was into political projections. Trend
analysis. I was damn good at it, and not mainly because of glimpses of the future! Those are rare and
fleeting. On that occasion I glimpsed her shadow and
mine in conjunction, so I opened up to her. She con-
sults me about who to appoint. I see the shadows of
possible scandals, shadows of dark secrets. I did glimpse
my own shadow in Rome beside yours. I made
arrangements."

So he had been called to Rome because a psychic
had glimpsed him in Rome.

"Took a while to discover who you were, Charles. I
didn't see you with a name badge pinned to your
chest."

She drew her leg across his naked thigh, rotating to

face him. It was a short but shapely leg, with no surgical puncture marks. Her thick black pubic hair tickled his flesh, exciting him, reminding him of Martine. Was Olivia massaging him erotically so that faith in her body might persuade him to accept her hidden paranormal parts too?

"We complement each other, Charles, you see." A hand strayed over his belly. "Body speech and the inner eye. Between us we cover both bases."

He held her hand to stop it from straying further as yet. So as not to seem unfriendly he tiptoed a couple of fingers around the palm of her hand. He traced that palm-map in which, for him, there was nothing to be read.

"Was it an alien weapon?" he asked. "Used in retaliation for the death of the Fly? A long-distance precision disintegrator aimed at St. Peter's from the hive off Alexandria, hmm? Does your insight tell you that?"

Her huge eyes stared at him from so close by, and she shook her head.

"Something else. Cosmic, dangerous. I saw that in the shadow of the Fly who survived. It knew. Of course the explosion on the steps was the alien's power pack blowing up when—" She hesitated.

"When Borromini signaled his pious mobsters for a rough and ready exorcism to expel a black devil from the high priest's temple." Charles made the sign he had seen, and explained.

"Ah. Yes. Ambitious Cardinal Archbishop of Palermo, home of the Mob." She stretched like a cat, rubbing against him, and drew a corner of sheet idly over her crotch as a soft pointer, which also concealed.

He squinted. "You're covering up. Temporizing. I thought we were supposed to be naked to each other."

"I'm not certain about the responsibility for the death."

"It wasn't Borromini, was it? It was Tarini's Mafia contacts. Just like after the war, when Italian Americans liberated Sicily and put all their gangster cousins in charge! They're still around, those cousins. They were trying to tear the Fly's wings off, steal them. Maybe rip the Fly open at the same time, film its entrails with miniature cameras. Bump off the witness, dissect it simultaneously. How neat, how surgical. Did they start the riot or just seize advantage?"

She propped her cheek upon her hand. "I can't swear Tarini was responsible. Not yet. His shadow's remarkably tangled. He's certainly an unscrupulous snake, with shady connections. Just how many scruples ought he to have in his job? Suppose he was up against terrorists? Maybe he didn't intend the Fly to be harmed. Then the power pack blew up. Maybe the attack was spontaneous. Superstitious hysteria. It was too chaotic for me to see."

"Which leaves Borromini?"

"Any mixing with the Mafia would be fatal to his Church career. But . . . he *would* have mobilized the faithful against a demon if that was his diagnosis."

"So it was Tarini."

She sighed. "Yes, I suppose."

"Never mind who. You don't think the Flies used a disintegrator ray?"

"A target vaporized by a laser doesn't vanish as if it never existed. There's smoke and debris."

"So was it a *cosmic ray?* Is that what you sense?"

"I sense you," she murmured, and mounted him, no fused-tailed mermaid now.

Afterwards, Charles walked alone up the Via Veneto to the gardens of the Villa Borghese. On those shady lanes underneath the umbrella pines, by one of those coincidences which aren't, Valeri Osipyan bumped into him.

"A shocking and barbaric crime, eh, Mr. Spark? You must have heard me veto any such violent folly. What happens soon after? Well, the Vatican have radioed their regrets, likewise the Italians. Pah! Fancy having a foreign enclave run by a conspiracy of priests in the middle of your capital city."

"Do you have many spies in the Vatican, Colonel?

Do you ever groom a young communist to act Catholic, become a priest, and rise?"

"Now there's an idea, a red pope! We'd have had to start planning it back in the days of Lenin practically. How many pretend-priests would we have needed to be on the safe side? Enough to prop up the whole East European church!" Osipyan was showing a witty, fanciful side; he was attempting bonding with Charles.

"The Vatican asked what happened to the top of St. Peter's. 'Can we have it back, please?' " The Russian laughed sharply. "Oh, not in so many words. The hive replied, 'Maybe is fortunate more of fine city not lost, since two of us remembering.' Did the aliens use a weapon, I wonder?"

"I can't imagine what sort."

"Ah, so you've been told by someone that it wasn't a weapon! Who would that be? Olivia Mendelssohn, perhaps? She's an odd one. How odd *is* she, incidentally?"

"Cardinal Borromini comes from Mafialand. When the Fly declared that God is sick, he made this sign." Charles imitated the Manu Cornuta. "The sign to banish evil. Swiftly followed by murder."

"You're trying to throw me off the trail—" As if to demonstrate, the Colonel caught Charles's elbow and forced him off the path. However, bicycles were bearing down swiftly and silently. When the riders passed, the two men walked on together as if by agreement.

"Sister Kathinka, the Dutch nun who guides Flies, was a go-between." Charles mentioned *L'Eau Vive*. Would that satisfy Osipyan? He felt an urge to do so. Hell, they were all supposed to be collaborating. Pooling information for the common good. And Osipyan hadn't behaved like Tarini.

Water gleamed ahead. Rowing boats with green canvas half-awnings plied a lake, on the far bank of which amongst trees and bushes a little temple fronted the rippling, sparkling water. With its four-pillared portico and a few statues perched on its roof, the temple looked like a bonsai version of St. Peter's, dwarfed for a prince's back garden.

"An alien who is 'remembering' dies violently," mused the Russian, "and a little part of the city disappears. What did your lover tell you about *that*, Mr. Spark? And how does she know?"

"Do you have bugs in embassy beds?"

"Won't you tell me, for humanity's sake?" Osipyan was smiling as if they were two old friends out for a stroll. The strange thing was that he wasn't dissimulating. Just then, in the Borghese gardens, Charles and Valeri were indeed two old acquaintances enjoying each other's company.

"It would be noble to confide in me. If need be, I could offer asylum. Though it's mad to live in an asylum, isn't it?"

Would Olivia perceive in Charles's shadow how he had snitched on her?

"Daren't you tell me, Mr. Spark, because there are few secrets from Miss Mendelssohn?" Charles upgraded Osipyan's sensitivity level considerably. "That tells me something, oh yes. In my country we have several such people. They're promising, though erratic. Do you recall the fat old lady who was by my side during the arms talks? And the so-called chess master?" A confidence, indeed! "How perturbing that there is one such in the White House. What did Miss Mendelssohn perceive about the chunk of church vanishing?"

"Cosmic danger," Charles admitted.

"Ah." Osipyan grinned tightly. "A mystic may sense that. That's what is dangerous about mystics when they're in power. We had our Rasputin, with the Czarina in his clutch, and the Czar in hers."

Charles found it hard to envisage Olivia as a female Rasputin to the First Lady. Maybe Osipyan's sense of history was keener than his.

"These days in Russia we try to approach such mystical powers scientifically. I believe in *this* world, don't you?"

Charles nodded. In the world, and the body.

"A country run by mysticism might launch Armageddon against an alien starship if they believed it held an Antichrist. A few hydrogen warheads ought to smash through any force field, right? Pity about the radioactive tidal waves swamping the Nile delta."

"I'm sure nobody's thinking along those lines."

"I'm sure that some Think Tank is running all possible scenarios! Alas, a nuclear attack would destroy all the wonderful alien technology, wouldn't it, Charles?"

Intimacy, from Valeri.

"The Flies mustn't simply go home and rob us of their knowledge, must they? Think Tanks will be spinning spider-webs. Tarini may have had authority for his opportunistic violence." Osipyan thumped his palm with his fist. "Oh why did the Fly have to mention God? Are they no wiser than us?" The Russian seemed genuinely upset.

"Maybe they've been hearing too much from their guides about martyrs, crucifixion, the inquisition, Lord knows what. The pain, the blood. Hell and the Devil. Worse than your Gulags. Maybe Christianity seems sick."

Osipyan brooded. "What does 'God' mean to a Fly? It may mean . . . a power, a force. Yes, a force. Perhaps an extra force in nature, or beneath nature behind the scenes. Our physicists say that atomic particles may 'remember' and be alert to distant events. There might be a universal information field of some sort—with a memory of all previous events in the universe. Naturally I'm interested in information fields. Imagine being able to extract information at a distance!"

Was Osipyan joking?

"We do that all the time," said Charles. "It's called looking."

"Imagine being able to retrieve information about past events." *(As Olivia did—from her shadows? Aha.)* "Imagine that the cosmos itself has a memory, which is accessible to us. I'm sure you and I could collaborate more rationally than a collaboration with . . . a witch."

Yet not, thought Charles, more delightfully. In the long run he might be wrong on that score. And Olivia was only an on/off witch.

The Colonel hurried off in the direction of the Piazza del Popolo, and Charles returned the way he had come, his mind reeling.

"Carlo! We just heard. The Flies are going to shift the hive."

"To Rome," said Olivia.

"Lake Albano," Tarini corrected her. "That's fifteen miles away. They want water to hover in. Maybe they suck up water for fuel."

Castel Gandolfo was beside Lake Albano, wasn't it? Was it tactful to moor their pyramid opposite the Pope's summer house?

"Vatican has no say," explained Tarini. "It only controls the papal palace and villa. Italian government agrees. Prestige!" Prestige for Tarini too. . . .

Charles still felt a sense of rapport with the Russian. "At least that should rule out any nuclear strikes."

Tarini looked furious. "Don't even *joke*. Who would want to nuke the first aliens ever to visit us?"

"I suppose there wouldn't be many souvenirs left over. But who would want to tear the wings off a Fly?"

"That was hysteria. The thing looked like Beelzebub advancing on St. Peter's. What it said about God, well!"

"Exactly. Are the Flies homing in because they think the Pope's our God-on-Earth?"

"Albano's a crater lake," said Lew. "Castel Gandolfo's high on the rim. His Holiness won't be overlooked much."

Olivia had been shading her eyes as if struggling to see shadows, future-flashes.

"It's because of the dome and the death," she said softly. "The Pope living by that lake is a coincidence. Nearest lake to here, isn't it?"

"Sure," said Lew. "Lake Bracciano's a lot bigger but it's another ten miles. If that bothers creatures who fly to Kyoto and back!"

"What about security?" asked Olivia. "There'll be such crowds around the lake."

"Italian army." Tarini grinned. "UNCO can mount all sorts of snoop equipment round the crater."

Seen on a giant TV monitor at the Farnese Palace, the spectacle of the pyramid ship in motion was surreal, like Magritte's flying mountain. The gray mass sailed upright through the air surrounded by a rainbow shimmer as of oil on a sunlit puddle. It slowed, it hovered, it settled. A few hands clapped appreciatively. Most UNCO people stared in silence. They were definitely *the* team now.

"The mountain has come to the Pope," said Osipyan sourly, "since Mohammed wasn't available."

Charles glanced at the Russian and shook his head. Not to the Pope.

A quibbling discussion broke out as to how to monitor the water level.

"We'll use lasers," promised Tarini.

"What if it rains—?"

"You program your computer for rainfall, run-off, evaporation—"

"If the Flies put back what they use—"

"Look, the old Romans built a fugging huge underground tunnel a mile long to regulate the water in Albano. If *they* could work it out—!"

Half of Rome and vicinity was trying to reach Castel Gandolfo, choking all available routes. When the Italian army finished deploying its checkpoints to seal off the area, police could begin to untangle the traffic. A permit system was being introduced, which Charles could well imagine in operation. "Of *course* my cousin's mother-in-law lives in Castel Gandolfo! She's a sick old woman. I must visit her to take a last photograph!" The Vatican announced that it likewise had a right to issue travel permits, to its extraterritorial territory.

Out of the various little "ports" of the pyramid several Flies had already departed to speed toward Venice or Vienna or Bangkok. Others were returning to their relocated base. Tarini produced a graph of the number of Flies on board subsequent to the first exodus. On the assumption that there had been exactly one thousand aliens to begin with, this crew tally could rise as high as a hundred; sometimes the number dipped to ten.

En route to Castel Gandolfo in an Agusta helicopter Tarini remarked that Ciampino airport was having its work cut out controlling air traffic over the Alban Hills.

Olivia warned, "Don't think of staging any mid-air collisions to test their debris deflectors."

"If only we knew!" he enthused. "We could open up the solar system within years. Colonize Mars. The new Renaissance; think of it."

He viewed himself as an unappreciated hero, a Prometheus, a Klaus Fuchs, an Oliver North.

"That's right," said Olivia. "You could become a security chief. On Pluto."

Threats wouldn't deter him. History would vindicate him.

Seen from the air, Castel Gandolfo and surrounding countryside looked as busy with humanity as if the Pope had invited eight hundred thousand people and all their relatives to visit; never mind roadblocks. Actually, according to Lew, the hall in the park to the rear of the papal palace, built for mass audiences, could accommodate eight thousand souls. The park was almost empty; it must be shut. Inside that park bulged the Vatican observatory.

The palace fronting the central piazza of the pretty little town—four wings of palace enclosing a courtyard— was modestly stark in contrast with the baroque church which dominated the east side of the square abuzz with people and vehicles. Lew pointed to the papal villa in the distance, Villa Barberini. A crowded panoramic road circled the crater, dived to the lakeside, and spurred back to a larger town. Trucks and trailers sprouting aerials and dishes were stationed at strategic viewpoints. As the hovering helicopter swung slowly on its axis, rising from the lake they saw the alien pyramid.

This transformed the scene into some Central American or Mexican delirium. Charles imagined not Jesuits but Aztec priests boating out to the pyramid, to climb to the top and tear out human hearts. Such priests would have required grappling irons on long ropes to hook into the ports. Notwithstanding, the mountaineers might have skidded helplessly on that moiré shimmer, that iridescent luster.

"The energy field doesn't stop Flies from passing into the ship." Tarini peered through binoculars. "Wonder if that sheen would flash into action if some intruder tried to get aboard?"

"Disguised as a Fly?" inquired Olivia.

"Yeah, somebody of short stature," he said insensitively. "I guess Flies' limbs are a bit thin to imitate."

"Not to mention them having an extra pair. A dwarf acrobat in a Fly suit? You have got to be joking."

"Maybe there's a recognition signal. None, and you get stunned or fried. Again, maybe not."

The Agusta landed just outside town where a couple of Lancias waited to chauffeur UNCO passengers. Olivia preferred that she and Charles roam on foot.

"I had a flash," she whispered. "I saw us both in the piazza. I'm picking up more of the future than ever before."

The Piazza del Plebiscito was packed. Queues stretched from cafés. Hucksters hawked souvenirs. Ice cream vendors pumped out cones. Here was the world and his wife, and his celibate brother and sister of the Church, and his military cousin. A couple of Swiss Guard commissionaires stood guard outside the summer palace.

And out of its entrance walked Cardinal Borromini dressed in a simple black cassock plus scarlet skullcap. At his side, Sister Kathinka.

Cloaked by crowd, Olivia and Charles followed them to the church, hung around a while, then entered.

After the bustle and brightness what a contrast was this cool, dim, quiet cavern. The ceiling was coffered with recessed stucco panels. Candles burned high and low in front of shrines. A few black-clad village women were sunk in prayer. Olivia pointed at the big black box of a confessional, its curtains closed. A pair of black shoes peeped beneath the side drape. She and Charles sat on nearby chairs to wait.

Eventually the Dutch nun emerged and went to pray by the altar. By the time she arose, composed, Cardinal Borromini was waiting for her in the aisle.

Olivia stared, glassy-eyed. "Her shadow's *inside* the pyramid," she slurred—and leapt up to intercept the two of them. Charles hastened to accompany her.

"Wait, we must talk!"

Borromini glowered. "Do not disturb the house of God, or us," he said in thickly-accented English. He would need to polish his foreign languages a little if he hoped to be pope, the pope who converted—or damned—the stars.

"You've been invited inside the alien ship." (Kathinka's eyes widened.) "You haven't told UNCO!"

"The sister is no part of your UNCO. Did you hide a microphone in the confessional? Basta! This is a disgrace."

"I know because I see the truth, the way a saint sees a vision."

"You dare compare your spying to the vision of a saint?" Yet Borromini was rattled. More so, when Charles made the sign of the Manu Cornuta.

After some consideration the cardinal said, "How remarkable that the aliens invite a religious to enter their hive, instead of a diplomat or scientist. A religious of low rank, who may be vulnerable."

Sister Kathinka cleared her throat.

"Yes! Speak!"

"This invitation is simply because of my method of memory, I think."

Borromini gazed around. "This church . . . is dedicated to a saint you two probably have not heard of. Thomas of Villanova. Thomas always aided the poor before their needs became urgent, so that he should not feel pride in his charity."

"So you discussed the sin of pride in the confessional," said Olivia.

"I am vowed not to say! Surely you realize that!"

"Cardinal, Your Eminence, we really can't have the sole representative of the human race ever to enter an alien starship being chained by vows of silence and obedience. Surely *you* realize?"

"I am not chained," protested Kathinka. "If so, my chain is my freedom."

"As Archbishop of Valencia," continued Borromini, "Saint Thomas was responsible for the care of many Moors whose conversion to Christianity had been less than voluntary. Their state of mind worried him. It was an *alien* state of soul."

"Is Thomas the patron saint of memory too, by any chance?" asked Charles.

Kathinka spoke without thinking. "On the contrary, he was notoriously forgetful!" She gripped her rosary.

"It's blasphemy to forget willfully," Charles said. "In my book."

"After your visit," breathed Olivia, "you'll return to Vatican territory, to the Pope's palace—where you may be required to stay forever alone in a cell, if the Flies are found to be corrupting."

Kathinka's eye twitched; Charles knew that Olivia had seen the shadow hanging over her. He pressed the nun.

"You imagine that you'd accept the sacrifice obediently, even though it devastates your heart."

"Worse than spies!" hissed Borromini.

"You'd have to give up all your places in Rome, Sister."

"I could live in those in memory." Kathinka's voice shook.

"Do you really think so? All the churches, palaces, streets: could you really live in those solidly and authentically in your imagination? Every color, every detail? Every sight and sound and smell? For the rest of your life—spent in solitary confinement? Today, dear cell, we shall pretend to walk to the Trevi fountain. . . . Why should you even wish to live in those

places in memory, Sister, when you would have no
one to guide and to bless?"

It was as though Charles had struck the nun in the
stomach. He felt a hollow in himself too, of sadness at
what he had said. Yet he carried on.

"I want to go with you to the hive. I too know
something of memory. If you ask, the Flies may agree."

"Foulness," said Borromini, though not with full
heart. Hard to tell whether he was referring to Charles
and Olivia or to the aliens.

"If you refuse," Olivia said to the cardinal, "who
knows if the sister will reach the pyramid, or only
someone dressed as a nun resembling her? I know
someone who would love to intercept a helicopter or a
boat, or even a Fly carrying her in its arms. You'd
have lost your chance, the Church's chance."

Borromini chewed his lip, and took an apparent
decision to mellow.

"Perhaps you should both accompany the sister, if
only as devil's advocates."

"Oh no. Once on Vatican territory you might give
an order to some burly priests. We might disappear.
Charles will go. I shall stay with UNCO, for security."

"I'm sorry if I distressed you," Charles told Kathinka.

"Distress her, *you?*" echoed Borromini. "She has to
go inside a hive of alien creatures for who knows what
purpose of theirs!"

"But not alone now," Charles said.

Kathinka looked pitying. "I have resources . . . which
you might envy if you knew them. God, I mean, not
myself. Anyway, I have spent days with aliens."

"You have not been into their *nest*," the cardinal
reminded her. (Be not proud.)

"At home they float in a thousand tanks," Charles
mentioned. "The hive may seem like a giant aquarium."

"Is that another vision of yours, fellow?"

"I don't have visions, I just use my eyes. An alien
told me about those tanks."   .

"Ah, really? You may be a help to Sister Kathinka.
Perhaps it's best this way. I agree, I concede. Come
along with us . . . my son."

So they left the church of the charitable amnesiac. Olivia slipped away quickly through the crowd.

And now at last Charles knew, as he floated in the alien null-sense tank seeing a memory place: Paris.

Here was Montmartre Cemetery, its mausoleums crowding shoulder to shoulder, each of them extravagant, unique, decrepit: high, narrow, one-room houses in honor of Monsieur and Madame Bourgeois, so many nineteenth century telephone kiosks equipped with prie-dieu for making a call to God, and with dusty porcelain flowers behind iron grilles or stained panes. . . .

As Charles drifted upwards, so the cemetery became a relief map of itself, bumpy with all the sepulchres. Over the rooftops beyond, the white dome of Sacré Coeur commanded from its hilltop. Elsewhere, amputated streets led to a wall of nothingness. Most of Paris hadn't been remembered yet, disgorged yet.

He shut his eyes. Or were his eyes still open? Yes or no, this made no difference to the memory place, a circuit board in three dimensions with no data programed into it as yet—no topics had yet been attached to any of the places.

When the Flies returned to their home world with their harvest of a thousand or ten thousand places, aliens afloat in other null-sense tanks would stroll the boulevards of Paris, beginning to fill them with topics bit by bit, brick by brick. *Les mouches* would catch a bateau-mouche along the Seine, where fuzzy Impressionist water would flow. Water was too mobile to remember clearly, or to attach ideas to. The foliage of the trees in the cemetery was likewise merely a fractal pattern, although every detail of each graveyard gazebo was true, every tile in distant roofs of the empty part-city was exact. . . .

There had been no *bon voyage* from the Pope, as Charles had slightly been hoping. Borromini had quickly put him and Kathinka in the care of two members of the Vigilance, who had escorted them to a far corner of the papal grounds. He never knew exactly how the arrangement had been made, but some brief signal was radioed and an alien soon arrived carrying a spare flying pack. It agreed to return for another. Meanwhile Charles was lent a black soutane, so as to somewhat resemble a Fly.

Thus equipped, he and Kathinka were autopiloted by the alien the short distance to the pyramid: two black-clad angels. UNCO would hardly have been fooled, yet the strategem had an appealing blatancy to it. A new Saint Joseph of Copertino, the gawping levitating friar, accompanied by the Flying Nun! Could Tarini, forewarned, have actually intercepted Kathinka by deploying jet-pack special forces or a chopper trawler armed with a net? Perhaps.

Once on board: so many tanks, connected by pearly struts and tubes and pipes and ceramic ladders and walkways, like big black beads slung in a dense array. The sloping pyramid walls cast a nacreous phosphorescent light. Deep down, alien machines purred softly. . . .

In the null-sense tank, Charles shivered at the memory . . . of how half a dozen Flies, their arms like steel, had seized him and Kathinka and plucked the clothes from them. He'd been plunged into the slimy-slick liquid of the tank, gluey tendrils pervading the fluid—to be drowned? Certainly to be robbed of sensation, shut in a black coffin almost brimful of liquid.

However, he'd floated as if in the Dead Sea. As the lid locked out the light—his panicky hyperventilation producing rowdy snores, which quieted as his hearing failed—a memory place had appeared, enchanting him.

That had been Cairo's Citadel area. Presently he noticed a Fly kissing a highly decorated mosque wall, a section of arabesque, its mustache feelers twitching ecstatically. When Charles kissed that same place, knowledge arrived, a twisted dreamlike partial knowledge about the alien *purpose* and the layout of the ship, its index: the web of tanks above and below, and deepest of all the big tank containing the Gland, a black bloated mass with several eyes, beaked mouth, orifices, no limbs. The Gland.

A glimpse of the purpose; and of the danger.

Later, he'd drifted—steered himself—through the

wall of nothingness around Cairo, first into San Francisco, and now Montmartre. Here were memory places indeed. All the cities of the world were being made into perfect memory places; more than mere memory places, places congruent with reality.

How long had he been floating in the tank? He'd lost track. Realizing what he could do, he urged his invisible and unfelt hand to rise—not the hand of his body image which hovered above the cemetery, but the hand of flesh he had lost touch with.

The lid above his head rose easily, and the pyramid's light abolished Paris.

With care he hauled himself up. Sensation flooded back as the slithery liquid slid from him like a sheath. If a Fly had been perching on the lid earlier on, now the only alien in sight was sitting propped against the side of a tank, its long legs drawn up like a grasshopper's.

Charles stepped out on to the Flywalk where the borrowed soutane and his undergarments lay heaped. His skin felt vibrant, massaged; mild hilarity welled in him as he dressed.

He waited, unconcerned about time—which seemed his to control, to speed up or slow down—till another tank top opened nearby and Kathinka too stood up.

The nun, naked. He glanced, then averted his gaze, then glanced again. Except for her rather tanned face she was as white as a nude painted by Lucas Cranach, a medieval ideal of blanchedness. He noted the same narrow hips as on a Cranach canvas and the same high white breasts, round white fruit—lychees the size of little apples. However, she was taller and lankier than a Cranach nude, her white legs more muscular thanks to all those ballet exercises.

She was beautiful, yet she no more conformed to present-day images of beauty than did the stumpy sensuality of Olivia. He was the first man to *see* Kathinka. Earlier, when they were forcibly disrobed, panic had possessed him. Now her body spoke to him—the word "inaccessible"! If another person's body usually formed an image within him which he understood all too well, if he had always seen in a body what he already knew, then how could he be excited? To touch that person would merely be to fondle himself; he wouldn't be shocked into some other zone, of displacement, of ecstasy. Yet Kathinka displaced him; as Olivia had, as Martine had. Charles shut his eyes, not so much to allow Kathinka privacy as to see if she was fixed in memory, sculpted in marble. His mind's eye betrayed him, as perhaps it must. A tall white blancmange swayed there. When he looked, she had resumed her habit in haste.

Her eyes shone. She licked her lips.

"They remember so much more deeply! They aren't remembering places for the sake of *places*. Whole cities are their rosaries to hang other memories upon. What a Godlike memory. Beyond ordinary memory. The memory that God has of Creation: they've trespassed upon this . . . this divine attribute to use it as a filing system!" Her eyes shone on account of shock. "They're . . . clerks, that's what. Together with their Gland they have power, don't they? Power of miracles. They could be locusts, these clerks. They could consume the actual places if their power went astray."

In her way she was right. The Flies, together with their Gland, had access not to a "God" exactly but to the universal information force, the metamemory of the universe; to some dimension which was the foundation of reality. The Flies tapped a force that underpinned reality, that kept reality constant. Memory was the source of all identity, the only link in a flux of perceptions and events—not only for living beings but for the physical universe as well. The memory of the Flies was so intense. . . .

"They're sick," Charles said bluntly. "Obsessional. Over-developed in one direction. Crazy."

Wasn't that true of himself? Oh no! He had studiously avoided the hot tub into which his talent could have plunged him, melting away the barrier between himself and others, dissolving his identity. So as to anchor himself he had striven to remember places, the scenery of his life. Flies remembered reality so strongly that reality could become the victim of their thoughts;

except that they were only, yes, clerks, simple filing clerks cataloging their alien facts upon the faces of objects remembered, collecting new places like blank file cards. When that Fly had been murdered, though, St. Peter's dome had disappeared. Their power leaked out; it had affected Olivia. Their power had given her those extra flashes of perception, of information about the future. . . .

"Miracles without faith!" exclaimed Kathinka. "Heaven, cities of God, built by the clerks of Hell. Worse, by the clerks of nowhere."

"Sooner they go home the better, eh? Leaving us to our own world and our arms talks and ordinary beliefs and dangers. Most of what we're saying about them is . . . *words*. Memory, supermemory: what do we know of those? The Flies assume we're a version of themselves, building churches in order to remember facts! They aren't a version of us any more than a whale's aversion of a person."

"If we don't share . . . a communion with them, if we can't share, if they're neither of God nor of the Devil—" she began.

The soft humming of the pyramid was drowned by an eruption of engine roar, the thrash of helicopter blades, clatter of metal. An aluminum ladder jutted through one of the ports, a horizontal bridge. Through others too, to judge by the noise. Human shouts of: "Go, go, go!" A masked commando armed with a riot gun scrambled monkey-style, leaped on to the Flywalk. The sheen didn't flash him to ashes. Another commando followed.

The sharers had arrived.

"A totally peaceful occupation." Smirking Tarini might have been offering a job description.

"Seizure, you mean!" retorted Charles. Tarini had come into the pyramid as soon as it was reported secured, and the few Flies on board immobilized. Improvised mesh gates covered all the ports now, since no one knew how to close those otherwise. Already Flies, returning to disgorge, were circling or hovering outside, barred from entering. Since they did nothing hostile, no one interfered with them.

"No casualties, Carlo. We have us a starship." Who was "us" exactly? UNCO? NATO? CIA? ABCDE?

"A ship powered by a paranormal Gland," said Charles.

"Powered by *what?*"

A dispute broke out at the nearest port of access. Only briefly; within moments Olivia had joined them. Ignoring Tarini, she stared at Charles. She stared at the shadow of his time in the tank; then stared at the nun.

She giggled momentarily, madly. "Lecher," she said to Charles. "You don't want me, you want a nun, for fuck's sake? You need your Martine to bail you out of this mess because she's nuts. Oh fuck it, it's the glands, isn't it? It's always the glands." She held her head. "Yeah, vision *is* stronger in here, near the Gland. Let's go see the Gland. I want to see its shadows! Then we might know what sort of shit we're in, thanks to you, Dino Fuchs Prometheus."

Pardon the outburst. Olivia was half spaced out by the vibes in the hive.

Tarini gaped at her. "Dino fucks Prometheus?"

"Yeah, you fuck Prometheus in your head. Wanna steal fire! Wanna fly to Jupiter! On the back of a vulture that'll tear our guts out!"

One of the immobilized Flies called out:

"We take passenger, if wish . . . journey in memory sleep with Gland . . . if halt your bad attack, bad for your cities."

"Are you threatening us?" Tarini demanded. "What with? Your ship's been taken, Fly! We're in charge."

"The Gland's in charge," said Kathinka.

"What's with this gland? Is that the power source: a living one? A queen-alien? Well, everything alive wishes to survive! Where is it?"

"Down below in the big tank," said Charles.

"If us do not dis-charge, into the Gland—"

"Shut up!"

*   *   *

Black. Soft. Bulky like a dugong or a walrus. Eyes that saw . . . what, in darkness? Not true eyes but organs evolved for another purpose? Afloat in its own secretions, which flowed through pipes to other tanks. Breath sighing. Shadows crawled inside the opened tank.

How to describe shadows to those who hadn't seen them? As photographic negatives perhaps, occupying the same space as a more recent picture. Double exposure, black and white. Image of ghosts. Here were alien shadows. Capacity to see them, strongest here.

Ever since I shouted my way on board—make way for the President's personal representative!—I'd been ever more transfigured by past-knowledge, of Kathinka, Tarini, especially of Charles, all of his past life pictured in the biographic aura of his shadows as if he were a memory place himself.

A human being has to avoid the hot tub, the melting, or else all compass direction is lost. That's how we evolved, separate from each other, seeking clues to the feelings of others but not dissolving into them—unlike the Flies.

Humans need a single viewpoint, not a faceted mosaic vision. For my viewpoint I chose Charles, because I saw him deepest of all. To illuminate the story, I chose his eyes, his voice, his desires.

Shadows crawled inside the tank of the Gland. . . .

Once long ago the Flies' ancestors marked their surroundings with scent messages. New experiences were encoded into molecules, and unless these were unloaded a Fly could forget nothing, a Fly's experience did not fade. Everything it experienced remained fully present: in an expanding, continuous, immediate present which swelled to capacity, unless discharged on to rocks, paths, stems of vegetation, where presently it would fade away.

Encountering all these messages, other Flies experienced their fellows' lives almost as intensely as their own. Each participated in a swathe of lives. Flies were almost a collective intelligence. The larger, rarer, im-

mobile females wallowed in pools of their own secretions which alone could fix—stabilize—the discharged
memory molecules contributed by the visiting, roam-
ing Flies. In these pools the young were nurtured,
learning what it was to be a Fly.

As this gestalt of minds grew more complex through
interaction, a confusion of the senses developed. What
a Fly smelled and tasted, it saw and heard. What it
saw, it also tasted. A Fly might be overwhelmed by
the immediacy of experiences which hadn't happened
to it personally.

The females, the Glands, discovered disciplines, sort-
ing procedures. They prescribed a way to rearrange
the natural world so that it was no longer a set of
chaotic memories. Thus the Flies began to build or-
derly walls, structures, towns—with a pool at the center of each town where the memory of the town itself
persisted, organized knowledge coded into its remembered pattern. A town was thought, thought was a
town. Civilization evolved.

And the Glands, the hearts of the faceted gestalts,
broke through to metamemory, to the information
fields underlying the whole of reality. Towns, cities,
and the image of those cities with information encoded
into their every part, became truly congruent in
superspace. . . .

Those were the shadows that I saw, on the Gland in
its tank; to the extent that I could understand them.
And insight exiled me forever.

There isn't much more to tell.

Oh yes.

"Sir, downtown Prague has disappeared!"

"It *what?*"

"General Dole says it vanished. There's nothing
there, just a flat empty space. It disappeared like the
dome!"

A Fly, excluded from its hive, had fallen into Lake
Albano. Or else it had dived deliberately. Overloaded
with memory, it overloaded its power pack. In turn,

transposed through superspace, what it remembered was obliterated, wiped out.

A few other places—old Mombasa, Ghent, the heart of New Orleans—had to be lost before Tarini was ordered to evacuate the pyramid and let the Flies back in to disgorge.

After that, the aliens carried on as previously, flying to and fro, remembering the world's cities. These crazy, para-powerful aliens were now protected even more scrupulously by security teams. They stayed on Earth another year—for me a stressful year, during which I stayed as isolated as my job allowed. I was too good at it now; it would consume me. Even with a whole ocean separating me from the hive, I could be melted—into other people.

As to the nature of their technology which both alerted them to our existence then let them leap the light years to reach us, perhaps that too was a science of memory—by virtue of their sharehold in superspace where all events are recorded, dispersed throughout as in a hologram, then by an act of wilfully "forgetting" the distance from their home world—rather than any manipulation of a repulsive hyperforce (though they may have that too).

Yet a passenger to the stars, to their home world, to see for oneself? If a human could perceive reality as they perceived it! That offer still stood, though it transpired that the offer was only open to those most directly involved in the affair.

Obviously a human being must fly to the stars, even on a one-way ticket with no means of sending a postcard home—if only for the sake of knowing that the journey had been undertaken.

So who should it be?

Charles? Ah no. New Orleans had vanished, and he must meet Martine again. Now that he'd known crazy aliens, perhaps he could begin to know her heart more exactly. He could enter the house of madness alert to all the signs inscribed there, and perhaps could show

her the exit door, the way by which she could melt
into one whole person.

Kathinka, then?—who might be canonized in a thousand years' time for her sacrifice? No, she would be
destroyed, her faith broken. Faith is a belief in a
hidden superperson. Flies needed no such belief when
they were already part of a superperson, with a
supermemory that was rooted into a dimension outside spacetime. Light years from Rome, Kathinka might
revisit the domeless Vatican in a memory tank any
time she chose, yet a visit to St. Peter's would tell her
only, and compellingly, about the folkways of faithless
Flies inscribed upon it—as they relieved the pressures
of memory upon the fresh empty places of Earth.

Tarini? Ha! Exiled to an alien star out of harm's
way, the failed Prometheus of espionage? He was
better off demoted to Honduras.

No, me. Olivia.

For I'd lost my human compass point. On Earth I
would melt, which meant that I would be mad like
Martine, only more so, the many-in-one. My needle
now only pointed away, away, where at least my neighbors would be somewhat like me. And unlike me,
utterly, so that I could remain myself.

Me, Olivia, dreaming this story now in memory in
the Gland's tank, to which all other ship-tanks con-
nect, attaching this narrative as I've been taught to the
ruins of the Colosseum, stone by stone, section by
section, so that it can be played out in that memory
theater, unforgettably.

Though how will its future readers, aliens, understand it?

SKIN DEEP
By Kristine Kathryn Rusch

"More pancakes, Colin?"

Cullaene looked down at his empty plate so that he wouldn't have to meet Mrs. Fielding's eyes. The use of his alias bothered him more than usual that morning.

"Thank you, no, ma'am. I already ate so much I could burst. If I take another bite, Jared would have to carry me out to the fields."

Mrs. Fielding shot a glance at her husband. Jared was using the last of his pancake to sop up the syrup on his plate.

"On a morning as cold as this, you should eat more," she said as she scooped up Cullaene's plate and set it in the sterilizer. "You could use a little fat to keep you warm."

Cullaene ran his hand over the stubble covering his scalp. Not taking thirds was a mistake, but to take some now would compound it. He would have to watch himself for the rest of the day.

Jared slipped the dripping bit of pancake into his mouth. He grinned and shrugged as he inclined his head toward his wife's back. Cullaene understood the gesture. Jared had used it several times during the week Cullaene worked for them. The farmer knew that his wife seemed pushy, but he was convinced that she meant well.

"More coffee, then?" Mrs. Fielding asked. She stared at him as if she were waiting for another mistake.

"Please." Cullaene handed her his cup. He hated the foreign liquid that colonists drank in gallons. It burned the back of his throat and churned restlessly in his stomach. But he didn't dare say no.

Mrs. Fielding poured his coffee, and Cullaene took a tentative sip as Lucy entered the kitchen. The girl kept tugging her loose sweater over her skirt. She slipped into her place at the table and rubbed her eyes with the heel of her hand.

"You're running late, little miss," her father said gently.

Lucy nodded. She pushed her plate out of her way and rested both elbows on the table. "I don't think I'm going today, Dad."

"Going?" Mrs. Fielding exclaimed. "Of course, you'll go. You've had a perfect attendance record for three years, Luce. It's no time to break it now—"

"Let her be, Elsie," Jared said. "Can't you see she doesn't feel well?"

The girl's skin was white, and her hands were trembling. Cullaene frowned. She made him nervous this morning. If he hadn't known her parentage, he would have thought she was going to have her first Change. But the colonists had hundreds of diseases with symptoms like hers. And she was old enough to begin puberty. Perhaps she was about to begin her first menstrual period.

Apparently, Mrs. Fielding was having the same thoughts, for she placed her hand on her daughter's forehead. "Well, you don't have a fever," she said. Then her eyes met Cullaene's. "Why don't you men get busy? You have a lot to do today."

Cullaene slid his chair back, happy to leave his full cup of coffee sitting on the table. He pulled on the thick jacket that he had slung over the back of his chair and let himself out the back door.

Jared joined him on the porch. "Think we can finish plowing under?"

Cullaene nodded. The great, hulking machine sat in the half-turned field like a sleeping monster. In a few minutes, Cullaene would climb into the cab and feel the strange gears shiver under his fingers. Jared had said that the machine was old and delicate, but it had to last at least three more years—colonist's years—or they would have to do the seeding by hand. There was no industry on the planet yet. The only way to replace broken equipment was to send to Earth for it, and that took time.

Just as Cullaene turned toward the field, a truck floated onto the landing. He began to walk, as if the arrival of others didn't concern him, but he knew they were coming to see him. The Fieldings seldom had visitors.

"Colin!" Jared was calling him. Cullaene stopped, trying not to panic. He had been incautious this time. Things had happened too fast. He wondered what the colonists would do. Would they imprison him, or would they hurt him? Would they give him a chance to explain the situation and then let him go?

Three colonists, two males and a female, were standing outside the truck. Jared was trying to get them to go toward the house.

"I'll meet you inside," Cullaene shouted back. For a moment he toyed with running. He stared out over the broad expanse of newly cultivated land, toward the forest and rising hills beyond it. Somewhere in there he might find an enclave of his own people, a group of Abandoned Ones who hadn't assimilated, but the chances of that were small. His people had always survived by adaptation. The groups of Abandoned Ones had grown smaller every year.

He rubbed his hands together. His skin was too dry. If only he could pull off this self-imposed restraint for an hour, he would lie down in the field and encase himself in mud. Then his skin would emerge as soft and pure as the fur on Jared's cats. But he needed his restraint now more than ever. He pulled his jacket tighter and let himself into the kitchen once more.

He could hear the voices of Lucy and her mother rise in a heated discussion from upstairs. Jared had pressed the recycle switch on the old coffee maker, and it was screeching in protest. The three visitors were seated around the table, the woman in Cullaene's seat, and all of them turned as he entered the room.

He nodded and sat by the sterilizer. The heat made his back tingle, and the unusual angle made him feel like a stranger in the kitchen where he had supped for over a week. The visitors stared at him with the same cold look he had seen on the faces of the townspeople.

"This is Colin," Jared said. "He works for me."

Cullaene nodded again. Jared didn't introduce the visitors, and Cullaene wondered if it was an intentional oversight.

"We would like to ask you a few questions about yourself," the woman said. She leaned forward as she spoke, and Cullaene noted that her eyes were a vivid blue.

"May I ask why?"

Jared's hand shook as he poured the coffee. "Colin, it's customary around here—"

"No," the woman interrupted. "It is not customary. We're talking with all the strangers. Surely your hired man has heard of the murder."

Cullaene started. He took the coffee cup Jared offered him, relieved that his own hand did not shake. "No, I hadn't heard."

"We don't talk about such things in this house, Marlene," Jared said to the woman.

Coffee cups rattled in the silence as Jared finished serving everyone. The older man, leaning against the wall behind the table, waited until Jared was through before he spoke.

"It's our first killing in *this* colony, and it's a ghastly one. Out near the ridge, we found the skin of a man floating in the river. At first, we thought it was a body because the water filled the skin like it would fill a sack. Most of the hair was in place, hair so black that when it dried its highlights were blue. We couldn't find any clothes—"

"—or bones for that matter," the other man added.

"That's right," the spokesman continued. "He had been gutted. We scoured the area for the rest of him, and up on the ridge we found blood."

"A great deal of it," Marlene said. "As if they had skinned him while he was still alive."

Cullaene had to wrap his fingers around the hot cup to keep them warm. He hadn't been careful enough. Things had happened so swiftly that he hadn't had a chance to go deeper into the woods. He felt the fear that had been quivering in the bottom of his stomach settle around his heart.

"And so you're questioning all of the strangers here to see if they could have done it." He spoke as if he were more curious than frightened.

Marlene nodded. She ran a long hand across her hairline to catch any loose strands.

"I didn't kill anyone," Cullaene said. "I'll answer anything you ask."

They asked him careful, probing questions about his life before he had entered their colony, and he answered with equal care, being as truthful as he possibly could. He told them that the first colony he had been with landed on ground unsuitable for farming. The colonists tried hunting and even applied for a mining permit, but nothing worked. Eventually, most returned to Earth. He remained, traveling from family to family, working odd jobs while he tried to find a place to settle. As he spoke, he mentioned occasional details about himself, hoping that the sparse personal comments would prevent deeper probing. He told them about the Johansens whose daughter he had nearly married, the Cassels who taught him how to cultivate land, and the Slingers who nursed him back to health after a particularly debilitating illness. Cullaene told them every place he had ever been except the one place they were truly interested in—the woods that bordered the Fieldings' farm.

He spoke in a gentle tone that Earthlings respected. And he watched Jared's face because he knew that Jared, of any of them, would be the one to realize that Cullaene was not and never had been a colonist. Jared had lived on the planet for fifteen years. Once he had told Cullaene proudly that Lucy, though an orphan, was the first member of this colony born on the planet.

The trust in Jared's eyes never wavered. Cullaene relaxed slightly. If Jared didn't recognize him, no one would.

"They say that this is the way the natives commit murder," Marlene said when Cullaene finished. "We've heard tales from other colonies of bodies—both human and Riiame—being found like this."

Cullaene realized that she was still questioning him. "I never heard of this kind of murder before."

She nodded. As if by an unseen cue, all three of them stood. Jared stood with them. "Do you think Riiame could be in the area?" he asked.

"It's very likely," Marlene said. "Since you live so close to the woods, you should probably take extra precautions."

"Yes." Jared glanced over at his well-stocked gun cabinet. "I plan to."

The men nodded their approval and started out the door. Marlene turned to Cullaene. "Thank you for your cooperation," she said. "We'll let you know if we have any further questions."

Cullaene stood to accompany them out, but Jared held him back. "Finish your coffee. We have plenty of time to get to the fields later."

After they went out the door, Cullaene took his coffee and moved to his own seat. Lucy and her mother were still arguing upstairs. He took the opportunity to indulge himself in a quick scratch of his hands and arms. The heat had made the dryness worse.

He wondered if he had been convincing. The three looked as if they had already decided what happened. A murder. He shook his head.

A door slammed upstairs, and the argument grew progressively louder. Cullaene glanced out the window over the sterilizer. Jared was still talking with the three visitors. Cullaene hoped they'd leave soon. Then maybe he'd talk to Jared, explain as best he could why he could no longer stay.

"Where are you going?" Mrs. Fielding shouted. Panic touched the edge of her voice.

"Away from you!" Lucy sounded on the verge of tears. Cullaene could hear her stamp her way down the stairs. Suddenly, the footsteps stopped. "No! You stay away from me! I need time to think!"

"You can't have time to think! We've got to find out what's wrong."

"Nothing's wrong!"

"Lucy—"

"You take another step and I swear I'll leave!" Lucy backed her way into the kitchen, slammed the door, and leaned on it. Then she noticed Cullaene, and all the fight left her face.

"How long have you been here?" she whispered.

He poured his now-cold coffee into the recycler that they had set aside for him. "I won't say anything to your father, if that's what you're worried about. I don't even know why you were fighting."

There was no room left in the sterilizer, so he set the cup next to the tiny boiler that purified the ground water. Lucy slid a chair back, and it creaked as she sat in it. Cullaene took another glance out the window. Jared and his visitors seemed to be arguing.

What would he do if they decided he was guilty? He couldn't disappear. They had a description of him that they would send to other colonies. He could search for the Abandoned Ones, but even if he found them, they might not take him in. He had lived with the colonists all his life. He looked human, and sometimes, he even felt human.

Something crashed behind him. Cullaene turned in time to see Lucy stumble over her chair as she backed away from the overturned coffee maker. Coffee ran down the wall, and the sterilizer hissed. He hurried to her side, moved the chair, and got her to a safer corner of the kitchen.

"Are you all right?" he asked.

She nodded. A tear slipped out of the corner of her eye. "I didn't grab it tight, I guess."

"Why don't you sit down. I'll clean it up—" Cullaene stopped as Lucy's tear landed on the back of his hand. The drop was heavy and lined with red. He watched it leave a pink trail as it rolled off his skin onto the floor. Slowly, he looked up into her frightened eyes. More blood-filled tears threatened. He wiped one from her eyelashes and rolled it around between his fingertips.

Suddenly, she tried to pull away from him, and he tightened his grip on her arm. He slid back the sleeve of her sweater. The flesh hung in folds around her elbow and wrist. He touched her wrist lightly and noted that the sweat from her pores was also rimmed in blood.

"How long?" he whispered. "How long has this been happening to you?"

The tears began to flow easily now. It looked as if she were bleeding from her eyes. "Yesterday morning."

He shook his head. "It had to start sooner than that. You would have itched badly. Like a rash."

"A week ago."

He let her go. Poor girl. A week alone without anyone telling her anything. She would hurt by now. The pain and the weakness would be nearly intolerable.

"What is it?" Her voice was filled with fear.

Cullaene stared at her, then, as the full horror finally reached him. He had been prepared from birth for the Change, but Lucy thought she was human. And suddenly he looked out the window again at Jared. Jared, who had found the orphaned girl without even trying to discover anything about the type of life form he raised. Jared, who must have assumed that because the child looked human, she was human.

She was rubbing her wrist. The skin was already so loose that the pressure of his hand hadn't left a mark on it.

"It's normal," he said. "It's the Change. The first time—the first time can be painful, but I can help you through it."

The instant he said the words, he regretted them. If he helped her, he'd have to stay. He was about to contradict himself when the kitchen door clicked shut.

Mrs. Fielding looked at the spilled coffee, then at the humped skin on Lucy's arm. The older woman seemed frightened and vulnerable. She held out her hand to her daughter, but Lucy didn't move. "She's sick," Mrs. Fielding said.

"Sick?" Cullaene permitted himself a small ironic smile. These people didn't realize what they had done to Lucy. "How do you know? You've never experienced anything like this before, have you?"

Mrs. Fielding was flushed. "Have you?"

"Of course, I have. It's perfectly normal development in an adult Riiame."

"And you'd be able to help her?"

The hope in her voice mitigated some of his anger. He could probably trust Mrs. Fielding to keep his secret. She had no one else to turn to right now. "I was able to help myself."

"You're Riiame?" she whispered. Suddenly, the color drained from her face. "Oh, my God."

Cullaene could feel a chill run through him. He'd made the wrong choice. Before he was able to stop her, she had pulled the porch door open. "Jared!" she called. "Get in here right away! Colin—Colin says he's a Riiame!"

Cullaene froze. She couldn't be saying that. Not now. Not when her daughter was about to go through one of life's most painful experiences unprepared. Lucy needed him right now. Her mother couldn't help her, and neither could the other colonists. If they tried to stop the bleeding, it would kill her.

He had made his decision. He grabbed Lucy and swung her horizontally across his back, locking her body in position with his arms. She was kicking and pounding on his side. Mrs. Fielding started to scream. Cullaene let go of Lucy's legs for a moment, grabbed the doorknob, and let himself out into the hallway. Lucy had her feet braced against the floor, forcing him to drag her. He continued to move swiftly toward the front door. When he reached it, he yanked it open and ran into the cold morning air.

Lucy had almost worked herself free. He shifted her slightly against his back and managed to capture her knees again. The skin had broken where he touched her. She would leave a trail of blood.

The girl was so frightened that she wasn't even screaming. She hit him in the soft flesh of his side, then leaned over and bit him. The pain almost made him drop her. Suddenly, he spun around and tightened his grip on her.

"I'm trying to help you," he said. "Now stop it."

She stopped struggling and rested limply in his arms. Cullaene found himself hating the Fieldings. Didn't they know there would be questions? Perhaps they could explain the Change as a disease, but what would happen when her friends began to shrivel with age and she remained as young and lovely as she was now? Who would explain that to her?

He ran on a weaving path through the trees. If Jared was thinking, he would know where Cullaene was taking Lucy. But all Cullaene needed was time. Lucy was so near the Change now that it wouldn't take too long to help her through it. But if the others tried to stop it, no matter how good their intentions, they could kill or disfigure the girl.

Cullaene was sobbing air into his lungs. His chest burned. He hadn't run like this in a long time, and Lucy's extra weight was making the movements more difficult. As if the girl could read his thoughts, she began struggling again. She bent her knees and jammed them as hard as she could into his kidneys. He almost tripped, but managed to right himself just in time. The trees were beginning to thin up ahead, and he smelled the thick spice of the river. It would take the others a while to reach him. They couldn't get the truck in here. They would have to come by foot. Maybe he'd have enough time to help Lucy and to get away.

Cullaene broke into the clearing. Lucy gasped as she saw the ridge. He had to bring her here. She needed the spicy water—and the height. He thought he could hear someone following him now, and he prayed he would have enough time. He had so much to tell her. She had to know about the pigmentation changes, and the possibilities of retaining some skin. But most of all, she had to do what he told her, or she'd be deformed until the next Change, another ten years away.

He bent in half and lugged her up the ridge. The slope of the land was slight enough so that he kept his balance, but great enough to slow him down. He could feel Lucy's heart pounding against his back. The child thought he was going to kill her, and he didn't know how he would overcome that.

When he reached the top of the ridge, he stood, panting, looking over the caramel-colored water. He didn't dare release Lucy right away. They didn't have much time, and he had to explain what was happening to her.

She had stopped struggling. She gripped him as if she were determined to drag him with her when he flung her into the river. In the distance, he could hear faint shouts.

"Lucy, I brought you up here for a reason," he said. Her fingers dug deeper into his flesh. "You're going through what my people call the Change. It's normal. It—"

"I'm not one of your people," she said. "Put me down!"

He stared across the sluggish river into the trees beyond. Even though he had just begun, he felt defeated. The girl had been human for thirteen years. He couldn't alter that in fifteen minutes.

"No, you're not." He set her down, but kept a firm grasp of her wrists. Her sweater and skirt were covered with blood. "But you were born here. Have you ever seen this happen to anyone else?"

He grabbed a loose fold of skin and lifted it. There was a sucking release as the skin separated from the wall of blood. Lucy tried to pull away from him. He drew her closer. "Unfortunately, you believe you are human and so the first one to undergo this. I'm the only one who can help you. I'm a Riiame. This has happened to me."

"You don't look like a Riiame."

He held back a sharp retort. There was so much that she didn't know. Riiame were a shape-shifting people. Parents chose the form of their children at birth. His parents had had enough foresight to give him a human shape. Apparently, so had hers. But she had only seen the Abandoned Ones who retained the shape of the hunters that used to populate the planet's forests.

A cry echoed through the woods. Lucy looked toward it, but Cullaene shook her to get her attention again. "I am Riiame," he said. "Your father's friends claimed to have found a body here. But that body they found wasn't a body at all. It was my skin. I just went through the Change. I shed my skin just as you're going to. And then I came out to find work in your father's farm."

"I don't believe you," she said.

"Lucy, you're bleeding through every pore in your body. Your skin is loose. You feel as if you're floating inside yourself. You panicked when you saw your form outlined in blood on the sheets this morning, didn't you? And your mother, she noticed it, too, didn't she?"

Lucy nodded.

"You have got to trust me because is a few hours the blood will go away, the skin you're wearing now will stick to the new skin beneath it, and you will be ugly and deformed. And in time, the old skin will start to rot. Do you want that to happen to you?"

A bloody tear made its way down Lucy's cheek. "No," she whispered.

"All right then." Cullaene wouldn't let himself feel relief. He could hear unnatural rustlings coming from the woods. "You're going to have to leave your clothes here. Then go to the edge of the ridge, reach your arms over your head to stretch the skin as much as you can, and jump into the river. It's safe, the river is very deep here. As soon as you can feel the cold water on every inch of your body, surface, go to shore, and wrap yourself in mud. That will prevent the itching from starting again."

The fear on her face alarmed him. "You mean I have to strip?"

He bit back his frustration. They didn't have time to work through human taboos. "Yes. Or the old skin won't come off."

Suddenly, he saw something flash in the woods below. It looked like the muzzle of a heat gun. Panic shot through him. Why was he risking his life to help this child? As soon as he emerged at the edge of the ridge, her father would kill him. Cullaene let go of Lucy's wrists. Let her run if she wanted to. He was not going to let himself get killed. Not yet.

But to his surprise, Lucy didn't run. She turned her back and slowly pulled her sweater over her head. Then she slid off the rest of her clothes and walked to the edge of the ridge. Cullaene knew she couldn't feel the cold right now. Her skin was too far away from the nerve endings.

She reached the edge of the ridge, her toes gripping the rock as tightly as her fingers had gripped his arm, and then she turned to look back at him. "I can't," she whispered.

She was so close. Cullaene saw the blood working under the old skin, trying to separate all of it. "You have to," he replied, keeping himself in shadow. "Jump."

Lucy looked down at the river below her, and a shiver ran through her body. She shook her head.

"Do—?" Cullaene stopped himself. If he went into the open, they'd kill him. Then he stared at Lucy for a moment, and felt his resolve waver. "Do you want me to help you?"

He could see the fear and helplessness mix on her face. She wasn't sure what he was going to do, but she wanted to believe him. Suddenly, she set her jaw with determination. "Yes," she said softly.

Cullaene's hands went cold. "All right. I'm going to do this quickly. I'll come up behind you and push you into the river. Point your toes and fall straight. The river is deep and it moves slow. You'll be all right."

Lucy nodded and looked straight ahead. The woods around them were unnaturally quiet. He hurried out of his cover and grabbed her waist, feeling the blood slide away from the pressure of his hands. He paused for a moment, knowing that Jared and his companions would not shoot while he held the girl.

"Point," he said, then pushed.

He could feel the air rush through his fingers as Lucy fell. Suddenly, a white heat blast stabbed his side, and he tumbled after her, whirling and flipping in the icy air. He landed on his stomach in the thick, cold water, knocking the wind out of his body. Cullaene knew that he should stay under and swim away from the banks, but he needed to breathe. He clawed his way to the surface, convinced he would die before he reached it. The fight seemed to take forever, and suddenly he was there, bobbing on top of the river, gasping air into his empty lungs.

Lucy's skin floated next to him, and he felt a moment of triumph before he saw Jared's heat gun leveled at him from the bank.

"Get out," the farmer said tightly. "Get out and tell me what you did with the rest of her before I lose my head altogether."

Cullaene could still go under and swim for it, but what would be the use? He wouldn't be able to change his pigmentation for another ten years or so, and if he managed to swim out of range of their heat guns, he would always be running.

With two long strokes, Cullaene swam to the bank and climbed out of the water. He shivered. It was cold, much too cold to be standing wet near the river. The spice aggravated his new skin's dryness.

Marlene, gun in hand, stood next to Jared, and the two other men were coming out of the woods.

"Where's the rest of her?" Jared asked. His arm was shaking. "On the ridge?"

Cullaene shook his head. He could have hit the gun from Jared's hand and run, but he couldn't stand to

see the sadness, the defeat in the man who had be-
friended him.

"She'll be coming out of the water in a minute."

"You lie!" Jared screamed, and Cullaene saw with
shock that the man had nearly snapped.

"No, she will." Cullaene hesitated for a moment.
He didn't want to die to keep his people's secret. The
Riiame always adapted. They'd adapt this time, too.
"She's Riiame. You know that. This is normal for us."

"She's my daughter!"

"No, she's not. She can't be. This doesn't happen to
humans."

A splash from the river bank drew his attention.
Lucy pulled herself up alongside the water several feet
from them. Her skin was fresh, pink and clean, and
her bald head reflected patches of sunlight. She gathered herself into a fetal position and began to rock.

Cullaene started to go to her, but Jared grabbed
him. Cullaene tried to shake his arm free, but Jared
was too strong for him.

"She's not done yet," Cullaene said.

Marlenc had come up beside them. "Let him go,
Jared."

"He killed my daughter." Jared's grip tightened on
Cullaene's arm.

"No, he didn't. She's right over there."

Jared didn't even look. "That's not my Lucy."

Cullaene swallowed hard. His heart was beating in
his throat. He should have run when he had the chance.
Now Jared was going to kill him.

"That is Lucy," Marlene said firmly. "Let him go,
Jared. He has to help her."

Jared looked over at the girl rocking at the edge of
the river bank. His hold loosened, and finally he let
his hands drop. Cullaene took two steps backward and
rubbed his arms. Relief was making him dizzy.

Marlene had put her arm around Jared as if she,
too, didn't trust him. She was watching Cullaene to
see what he'd do next. If he ran, she'd get the other
two to stop him. Slowly, he turned away from them
and went to Lucy's side.

"You need mud, Lucy," he said as he dragged her higher onto the bank. She let him roll her into a cocoon. When he was nearly through, he looked at the man behind him.

Jared had dropped his weapon and was staring at Lucy's skin as it made its way down the river. Marlene still clutched her gun, but her eyes were on Jared, not Cullaene.

"Is she Riiame?" Marlene asked Jared.

The farmer shook his head. "I thought she was human!" he said. Then he raised his voice as if he wanted Cullaene to hear. "I thought she was human!"

Cullaene took a handful of mud and started painting the skin on Lucy's face. She had closed her eyes and was lying very still. She would need time to recover from the shock.

"I thought they were going to kill her," Jared said brokenly. "There were two of them and she was so little and I thought they were going to kill her." His voice dropped. "So I killed them first."

Cullaene's fingers froze on Lucy's cheek. Jared had killed Lucy's parents because they didn't look human. Cullaene dipped his hands in more mud and continued working. He hoped they would let him leave when he finished.

He placed the last of the mud on the girl's face. Jared came up beside him. "You're Riiame too, aren't you? And you look human."

Cullaene washed the mud from his shaking hands. He was very frightened. What would he do now? Leave with Lucy, and try to teach the child that she wasn't human at all? He turned to face Jared. "What are you going to do with Lucy?"

"Will she be okay?" the farmer asked.

Cullaene stared at Jared for a moment. All the color had drained from the farmer's face, and he looked close to tears. Jared had finally realized what he had done.

"She should be," Cullaene said. "But someone has to explain this to her. It'll happen again. And there are other things."

He stopped, remembering his aborted love affair with a human woman. Ultimately, their forms had proven incompatible. He wasn't really human, although it was so easy to forget that. He only appeared human.

"Other things?"

"Difficult things." Cullaene shivered again. He would get ill from these wet clothes. "If you want, I'll take her with me. You won't have to deal with her then."

"No." Jared reached out to touch the mud-encased girl, but his hand hovered over her shell, never quite resting on it. "She's my daughter. I raised her. I can't just let her run off and disappear."

Cullaene swallowed heavily. He didn't understand these creatures. They killed Abandoned Ones on a whim, professed fear and hatred of the Riiame, and then would offer to keep one in their home.

"That was your skin that they found, wasn't it?" Jared asked. "This just happened to you."

Cullaene nodded. His muscles were tense. He wasn't sure what Jared was going to do.

"Why didn't you tell us?"

Cullaene looked at Jared for a moment. Because, he wanted to say, the woman I loved screamed and spat at me when she found out. Because one farmer nearly killed me with an axe. Because your people don't know how to cope with anything different, even when *they* are the aliens on a new planet.

"I didn't think you'd understand," he said. Suddenly, he grabbed Jared's hand and set it on the hardening mud covering Lucy's shoulder. Then he stood up. There had to be Abandoned Ones in these woods. He would find them if Jared didn't kill him first. He started to walk.

"Colin," Jared began, but Cullaene didn't stop. Marlene reached his side and grabbed him. Cullaene glared at her, but she didn't let go. He was too frightened to hit her, too frightened to try to break free. If she held him, maybe they weren't going to kill him after all.

She ripped open the side of Cullaene's shirt and examined the damage left by the heat blast. The skin was puckered and withered, and Cullaene suddenly realized how much it ached.

"Can we treat this?" she asked.

"Are you asking for permission?" Cullaene could barely keep the sarcasm from his voice.

"No." The woman looked down and blushed deeply as some humans did when their shame was fullest. "I was asking if we had the skill."

Cullaene relaxed enough to smile. "You have the skill."

"Then," she said. "May we treat you?"

Cullaene nodded. He allowed himself to be led back to Jared's side. Jared was staring at his daughter, letting tears fall onto the cocoon of mud.

"You can take her out of there soon," Cullaene said. "Her clothes are up on the ridge. I'll get them."

And before anyone could stop him, Cullaene went into the woods and started up the ridge. He could escape now. He could simply turn around and run away. But he wasn't sure he wanted to do that.

When he reached the top of the ridge, he peered down at Jared, his frightened daughter, and the woman who protected them. They had a lot of explaining to do to Lucy. But if she was strong enough to survive the Change, she was strong enough to survive anything.

Cullaene draped her bloody clothes over his arm and started back down the ridge. When he reached the others, he handed the clothes to Marlene. Then Cullaene crouched beside Jared. Carefully, Cullaene made a hole in the mud and began to peel it off Lucy. Jared watched him for a moment. Then, he slipped his fingers into a crack, and together the alien and the native freed the girl from her handmade shell.

A MADONNA OF THE MACHINE

By Tanith Lee

Industrial canticles
Sing the steel.
A secret language,
Pain.

John Kaiine

Touch touch touch the dial, and the dial turns. Now to the left, and now to the right. Gray light flickers down the coil: half a mile below the platform, where the spiral ends, a lever raises its leviathan head. *Ting* says a bell. And the process is accomplished.

peter sits on his bench. He watches the figures moving noiselessly along the panel. After one seventy second unit, a soft flare glows in the panel. peter reaches out again and touch touch touches the dial, and the dial turns, left and right, and the gray light flickers away down the snake-bowel coil, down down into the dusk below, and there the leviathan raises its head, and *ting* says the bell.

And the process is accomplished.

And peter sits on his bench, watching the figures

move until another seventy second unit passes and the
flare glows, and he reaches out and touch and turn
and left and right and flicker and down and raise and
ting.

Sometimes, as he sits, or periodically stands for a
unit or two, when the passing mechanical overseer
reminds him, peter thinks. He thinks about whether
he is hungry now or not, and if he is, he takes a fiber
bar from his overall and eats it. Or if he is thirsty he
presses a tube in the gray-silver wall beside the bench,
and the tube issues him a vitamin drink. Or he thinks
of the talkto in his home, which tells him things or
answers questions, if he has any, or murmurs him to
sleep. Or he notices the other persons who sit or stand
before their own sections on the platform; lines of
people six or seven meters apart. He has been among
them all his adult life. They are the same people he
has always been with, here. And in the start of the
diurnal, after the mechanical lark trills him awake, he
has heard, for twenty-five years, the other mechanical
larks in main building of d district going off one by
one, to wake these others. Then they, like him, enter
their hygiene cubicles, rid themselves of waste matter,
are cleansed and dried, go to their food counters and
are fed, expel themselves into the two thousand meter
long corridor, for the twice-daily walk necessary for
their health. And in the cage-lift they go down into the
street, where the pale gray verticals and horizontals
stretch away and away, and the air-bus comes and
sucks them in and bears them off and sets them down
here, together, in the heart of the Machine.

peter knows the names of some of his neighbors.
But they have never really spoken. There is no point.
What is there to discuss? Each has a talkto in his or
her home. The talkto adapts entirely to each individual personality. It knows, by mechanical instinct, what
to say, and even when to speak and when to keep
silent. It knows the proper sounds and encourage-
ments to aid occasional vague masturbations, or to
soothe the aftermath of some unremembered yet dis-
quieting dream.

There is no need for human conversation, awkward and effortful.

The flare glows, and peter touch touch touches, and the dial turns. The harmony of the activity and its result are satisfying. It is a dim yet pleasing thought that throughout the Machine, hour by hour, unceasing for its duration, so many millions of men and women carry out, endlessly and faultlessly, similar or complementary actions. The Machine serves and is served. The empathy is perfect.

The light reaches the lever which raises itself. *Ting* goes the bell.

There is a meal-break, and peter leaves his section for the moving ramp which goes down under the platform. On the ramp with him, peter recognizes yori and marion, ted and malwe and jane. They reach the lower level and step off, into the canteen. Everything has a mild gloss of cleanness. The clean walls, in reply to the pressure of his fingers, give peter a slice of protein and some vegetable cubes, and a caffeine drink.

peter sits at a table to eat. The table is shared by yori, jane and ted. They do not speak to each other. Everyone thinks their own thoughts and slowly consumes the food.

It is as peter is finishing his drink that there comes to him the first Intimation.

He does not know it for an Intimation.

It is a feeling he has never felt before; it has no name.

It startles him, and wondering if he has not chewed his food properly and so has caused some gastric imbalance, he half-rises to approach the canteen health dispenser. But then the feeling without a name ebbs away. It goes so softly (not as it came, sheer and hard, like a glass sliver), that peter is reassured. He does not, however, finish his drink, subconsciously blaming it.

On the ramp back to the platform, ted speaks.

He says: "There was a pinkness over my screen, before meal-break."

No one answers. jane glances at him, then politely averts her eyes.

ted says nothing else.

They return to their positions.

peter touches. The dial turns.

Just before the next meal-break, peter feels the second Intimation. It is unlike the first, coming insidiously, sweetly, like the gentle libido which sometimes wakes him in the twilight of sleep prior to the trilling of the mechanical lark. This is not a bodily feeling, nevertheless, even though it invades his body. What is wrong with him?

peter is struck by a sort of paralysis. He stares inward at the feeling, trying to determine its shape.

It is a type of wave, with an upcurling head, pliant, mutable, yet formed. Running in.

It strikes him, somewhere in the region of the heart.

He is ill. There is something medically wrong. His heart is beating strongly and very fast. peter looks up from his panel to the emergency button in the wall. And there, above his section, he sees a gleam of light that is pink, the color of a rose, a special color that perhaps his genes recall, although he has never seen a flower of any type. peter looks at the rose light and, gradually, it unfolds itself, and it too, like the wave-shape within him beating on his beating heart, takes on a form.

He thinks it is like a woman. Yes, it is like a woman. She is clothed in a flowing, pleated garment, all the rose-color, and on her head is a drift of scarf, the palest yellow, also rose-like. Her flesh is pale, luminous and white, not like skin. She has eyes, although the rest of her features seem to him blurred. The eyes of the woman fix on peter. He tries to look away. It is not possible. Something terrible is in her eyes, something he has never, in all his twenty-five years, seen in a human face and expression.

peter opens his mouth and makes a sound, and something happens to him. His chest is heaving, and the air is coming out of him in gasps and liquid is rushing down his cheeks, as if he bled, but it is only water pouring out of his eyes.

And then, the rose light fades from the wall above the panel.

peter comprehends, as he struggles helplessly with the paroxysm of the body once known as weeping, and which he does not understand, that the figures have reached the seventy unit interval and the soft flare has gone off and he has not touched—

Then he sees that the dial is turning left and right. The flickering energy is running down the coil to the lever below which lifts, and the bell goes *ting*.

peter has not touched the dial, the three immaculate touches. Absorbed by the dreadful vision above the panel, peter has failed the Machine. But despite this lapse, the dial had turned, the coil has been activated. The process has been accomplished.

peter stops crying. His chest and throat are raw, and his eyes sting. He wipes his nose on the sleeve of his overall without thinking, and as the light flares again, he touch touch touches—

He does not know what else to do.

He hopes what has happened will fade, as the first Intimation faded.

In a way, it does.

The talkto comes on as peter enters his home.

"peter," says the talkto. peter smiles. The smile is involuntary, not precisely automatic. When he hears the low mechanical voice, he is always pleased. A kind of happiness envelops him. It is hour seventeen, and now he is here in the room that is his home, to relax and to sleep, for ten hours.

Home is rather bare, like every home (with variations) in main building, and in d district, and in all districts and buildings about the heart of the Machine. The walls of home are concave and dust-resistant, although every diurnal they are mechanically wiped. The cushioned floor supports a low sleeping-couch. On one wall is the food counter, and through a sliding door the box of the hygiene cubicle, with its water-tap, lavatory bowl, and shower. There are no windows in peter's home. Air is constantly breathed in and out via hidden orifices. It is the clean, dry, odorless air, common throughout the Machine.

In one corner, near the convex ceiling, the talkto perches, a small gray bulb that faintly shines when peter is at home. Nearby, the mechanical lark waits above the bed. The light, like the air, is constant, never-changing, muted yet clarified.

There is, too, a languid, unmodulated hum, which is the eternal music of the Machine.

The Machine is outside, and all about, and home is merely a tiny microcosm of the Machine. Home needs no textures and no patterns, as peter himself needs no decoration or individual markers. He, all humanity, are the pattern within the Machine, the jewelry of its vistas that stretch in every pale gray direction upward, downward, and in parallels toward an infinity which Is.

peter knows this and is consoled by this. He speaks to the talkto. He speaks a sort of meaningless, friendly jargon, which the talkto answers in the same vein.

Going to the counter, peter is given a light supper, and a mineral drink. He and the talkto exchange banter throughout the meal. When peter falls silent, the talkto falls silent, only continuing to shine.

peter takes off his overall and drops it into the chute. Tomorrow a fresh garment will be ready for him, complete with a fiber bar snack in the pocket. He goes into the hygiene cubicle, where his teeth are cleaned, and his body sluiced with warm water. He urinates at the lavatory bowl, and finally comes back into the room.

"Today," he says, "today."

The talkto waits, ready to take up his phrase.

"Today," says peter, "I saw a woman above the panel. How can that be?"

The talkto pauses, then it says, "A woman. Yes, peter."

"How could she be there? She was in the wall of the Machine."

"Machine, peter," says the talkto.

"And I missed touching the dial. But the dial turned. As if I touched the dial. As if—" peter fumbles for his own meaning. He says: "As if I needn't touch the dial."

The talkto says, "Bedtime, peter." And it begins a sort of song it murmurs before he sleeps.

Normally, he finds the song very soothing. Now, an unaccountable tension runs through him, and sensing it, infallibly, the talkto becomes utterly silent, only shining there above him as he lies down.

Presently, he loses consciousness.

peter dreams he is walking up the pure surfaceless wall of the Machine above his section. A woman in a pink garment and silver-yellow veil is walking before him. Her feet are white as roses, and they leave, in the steel endurance of the wall, delicate indentations that vanish in a few moments, as if she walked over the film of a lake—the memory of which his genes recall, although he has never seen water save from a faucet or in a lavatory bowl.

As peter follows the woman, he is aware of a powerful brimming bursting within himself. This is like the feeling he has experienced in his penis, sometimes, in the seconds before his hands and the murmurs of the talkto have caused him to climax. But the feeling is not sexual, actually, although it is orgasmic, far more so than the jetting irritation of random lust.

The woman walks up the never-altering face of the Machine.

peter comes to wonder what he is doing, following her.

Then his feet slip. There is no purchase. He falls.

"Hush, you're here," says the talkto. "Here you are. You're safe."

peter realizes he has cried out.

He listens to the talkto as it comforts him, then sinks back into sleep.

anna arrives at the heart of the Machine, as she always does, in the one-seater air-car. It sets her down

before d top two, and she enters the round office
where, with three others, she overlooks the d levels of
the Machine. As usual vaslav and rita are already at
their panels. anna crosses to her seat and allows it to
form itself about her before giving it her weight. This
diurnal she is wearing a pale gray one-piece suit. In
her two-room home, she is always offered a choice of
clothing in off-white, pale or dark gray. rita is clad in
dark gray, anna notes. Sometimes at meal-breaks anna
and rita exchange a little conversation. They talk about
the Machine, the abstract comeliness of its lines in
some new area they have, on a free walk, discovered.
Or they speak contemptuously of the workers who
man the d levels. These do not seem as efficient as
workers of other levels, q, for example, or y. But since
all workers are efficient in deed if not in essence,
nothing can be done. It is the aesthetic of the workforce
that troubles anna, rita. Both anna and rita have, at
prescribed times, met with vaslav for sexual union.
However, they do not speak very much to him, not he
to them. At meal-breaks he tends to sit with han or
olif from d top three.

As anna sits into the chair, her panel shows her a
portion of the d levels. After a minute, it shows her
another portion. The panel continually shows anna
portions of the d levels, as the panels of rita and vaslav
show them, also, portions of the d levels.

The coils and pipes are flickering with energies, the
wheels turn, the levers lift and engage.

anna is rested by these images. Only now and then,
she has a wish to move the human figures a little, put
their bodies into slightly more effective angles, or simply to make them stand when they are sitting, sit when
standing up.

Sometimes she thinks of what she will order from
the tops canteen at the meal-break, or sometimes of
the poetry which her talkto has made for her. Although she discusses the Machine and the workers
with rita, and intermittently meets with vaslav, for sex,
anna prefers—as rita and vaslav do themselves—reticence,
and the solitude of a home.

At the end of the diurnal, anna's talkto had recited:

> gray is the line for ever
> for ever is as the gray line

and this fragment has become locked into the memory of anna, and as the panel shows her the parts of the levels where the workers touch and touch, the coils sparkle and the wheels turn, the poem weaves together with every view, contenting her in a deep and tender fashion.

So that when an alarm goes off, like a tiny white firework somewhere in the screen, anna is horribly jolted.

In the thirty years during which anna has watched the d levels, no incident has ever occurred. Nothing has occurred at all.

Now she feels personally slighted. Threatened.

She stands on the bridgeway, and looks down to where a mechanical medical is attending to one of the workers. Because something has happened to him while working, she will have to speak to him. anna knows this is the procedure, although such an event is unprecedented.

anna waits until the medical is finished. Then the worker is taken by an overseer to the ramp which connects with the bridge. He gets onto the ramp reluctantly. As he rises toward her, anna looks away. She sees that none of the other workers has paid any attention. They regard their sections, and at the proper intervals their hands go out to touch the transmitters of the Machine.

Despite the fact anna has sometimes walked three levels on a free walk, when the Machinery is quiescent and the workers in their homes, to be so near the manned levels makes her uneasy.

The male worker is deposited ten meters away. He stares at his hands, which he holds out slightly in front of him. All workers resemble one another. anna accepts that her own class of watchers is not exempt from familial resemblance—but the worker is alien. He is a worker.

The overseer approaches anna and she is glad to have it between her and the worker. The overseer says: "The worker peter climbed up onto the panel-housing of his section. He then attempted to climb up the wall-surface above the panel. He then fell. Injuries are superficial and have been corrected."

anna is forced to look at the worker, peter.

She speaks clearly. "Why did you do this?"

The worker peter opens his mouth. Then he closes it.

"You must tell me why you climbed up onto the housing," says anna. "Such a thing is unheard of."

"There was a light over the panel," says the worker peter. Abruptly water pours out of his eyes. He drops on his knees and anna beholds a man weeping, which she has never been shown before. She knows the idea of weeping. She knows what tears are, although she has never grasped the notion, and does not really grasp it now. She sees the man is shaking from head to foot. She is amazed. She can think of nothing to say. And so she says, "This must never happen again. Do you understand? Now go back to your section."

The overseer takes hold of the man and helps him up and the man says distinctly, "A woman walks over the Machine. Her eyes—her eyes—" Then he stops and the overseer puts him on the ramp and he is carried back down into the levels.

anna watches from the bridge and sees peter return to his section where, standing before the dial, after a moment, and at the correct instant, he touches, once, twice, three times.

She lets out her breath and finds her ribcage is aching from holding the sigh pent within herself. Her nails have dug into her palms.

She peers down at the housing over peter's section, where the shimmering gray wall runs up and up and up and away and away.

The wall of course is empty.

                    *   *   *

"anna," says the talkto in her two room home. "Gray is gray. The Machine is the Machine is the Machine is the Machine . . ."

The concave walls are done in gray and off-white. The bed has a pillow in a dark gray case. There is a window, that reveals the horizontals, verticals, parallels of the streets of the limitless complex that is the Machine.

". . . is the Machine is the Machine . . ."

anna summons a soporific from her dispenser.

She drinks it, lies down with her head on her pillow, and closes her eyes.

"The Machine."

anna sleeps. She dreams. The worker peter is walking up the wall above his section. His face is full of wild joy. anna approximates the look to that of successful sexual climax, which she has seen on the face of vaslav. anna herself finds coitus debilitating. When she experiences pleasure, for several diurnals after she cannot bear the sight of vaslav.

No, the look of rapture on the face of peter is more profound than anything she has ever seen. anna stares beyond peter, and there is a glimmering incoherent pinkish light wavering on the surface of the wall. anna thinks of roses, of which somehow she has been informed, which she has never been shown. A ghost of a rose glides over the Machine.

anna wakes up. Her face is wet and this frightens her. She has been crying in her sleep.

At six hours, the levels of d are empty, and as she walks along them absently, anna can hear only the faint tympanic hum of the Machine. The walls slide up, and the coils descend down and down. When she looks from the bridges, anna sees eternity stretching away below and above, and on all sides. Caught in this web, she searches after the accustomed peace such vistas have always brought her. But there is a slight vertigo, too. Perhaps there always was.

She is drawn toward the section of the worker peter. She reaches it, and stands there, where peter habitually stands or sits. anna can see nothing unusual. She finds she is straining her eyes. To see—something. What? A woman. But what kind of woman? A worker? A watcher? Intuitively anna knows that she will never see, or learn, by looking.

At twenty-one hours that evening, anna arrives for her quarterly meeting with vaslav, at a cell in tops building. She had almost forgotten the appointment, and her talkto had had to remind her twice. anna is always perturbed when she goes to have sex, although sometimes she is also uncomfortably eager. She has come to dislike such eagerness. It generally means she will be disappointed, but that in turn ensures more cordial after-relations with vaslav.

In the cell, beside the couch which can be adjusted to complement a number of positions outlined in diagrams on the walls, a beaker of alcohol is served to anna. She drinks it as vaslav, tonight rather impatient, begins to touch her in the ordained manner.

anna tries to respond, and succeeds to a certain extent. vaslav wishes her to mount him, a position she finds awkward and in which, never, has she been able to climax. As she moves obediently to vaslav's rhythm, she feels a warm contempt for him, quite friendly and acceptable. He climaxes and she pretends to be satisfied.

As they are putting on their clothes, anna says, "Do you know the word *vision?*"

"That is a sight; to *see*," says vaslav. He too, after pleasure, is morose, not wanting further bodily contact.

"No, I mean in the sense of an image conjured or witnessed. A hallucination, possibly."

vaslav orders a second glass of alcohol.

"Workers in d have seen—" anna breaks off.

"The worker peter," says vaslav. "Probably there's something wrong with the brain. He will have to have a medical check."

This reassures anna. She feels a bright flash of gratitude, and turns to vaslav impulsively.

"You're awkward in that position, anna," says vaslav. "rita is better."

anna does not know what she is doing. She reaches out and pushes vaslav's glass so that the alcohol spills over him.

In the air-car on the way home, anna begins to cry again. She runs into her two rooms and the talkto shines and says to her: "Here you are, anna. You're safe." But for several terrible moments, anna does not feel safe in the least.

With its trilling the mechanical lark signals peter. He gets up from the sleeping place before he is quite awake. He has responded to a mechanical lark since his first year. His body knows exactly what to do. It walks him to the hygiene cubicle. It relieves itself of waste matter and is cleansed. As it stands beneath the shower, peter, carried by this body, wakens in fact.

peter leaves the shower, before it can dry him. He goes to his bed and lies down, on his back. He looks at the ceiling, and presently the talkto says, "peter, get up, peter." peter takes no notice. He blinks sometimes but makes no other movement. "peter," says the talkto, "you will be late, peter."

After an hour, the talkto falls silent. It continues to shine, but peter does not notice.

On the platform, at his section in d level, ted looks round, quite suddenly. He has become aware that peter is not working near him. ted has not defined the absence until now because, as ever, the dial at peter's section has turned regularly and the energy has gone flickering down the coil to the lever below.

ted gazes at peter's empty place. He assumes at last that peter is ill, which is uncommon among the workers.

ted looks back at his own section, in proper time to touch touch touch the button under his panel.

There is a pink light over the panel. ted has a jumbled notion he has seen it before. The color, however, is so novel. He stares at it. The pink unfolds like paper, or a flower. ted sees a woman walking up the wall of the Machine. Involuntarily, he exclaims.

*   *   *

In the cage-lift to upper top two, anna avoids glancing at the levels of d. The vista makes her dizzy, the long, pure lines slipping effortlessly down, like the striations in an ancient rock she has never seen, perhaps never been told of, perhaps does not even genetically recall.

anna vacillates mentally between annoyance and nervousness. What she is about to do it seems no one can ever have done. The choice has always been open to her, but has gone unconsidered. Now, sometimes, in a rush of strength, anger braces her. But it fails to last out the long smooth journey in the lift.

What will she say? How phrase it, to throw the maximum of blame upon the other? Simple. Her very request will see to that.

The lift reaches upper top and anna gets out.

Before her is office corridor p nine. anna walks along the corridor briskly, ignoring the side ramp. Watchers like exercise. She begins to feel virtuous, strong again.

A door opens. The robot assistant speaks, inquiring who she is and whom she wishes to contact.

"Co-ordinator shashir."

The assistant assures her her request is being delivered, and she will soon know whether or not co-ordinator shashir is available to attend to her.

anna stands biting her lip. She becomes aware she has been gnawing it since leaving her home early today. Should she not have come here? Will the co-ordinator be able to give her an appointment? Will he question her thoroughly? What will he say?

anna has an uncomfortable burned feeling in her stomach. She swallows and finds she needs to swallow again.

On the wall of the office cubicle she supposes there is something pink . . . it must be a trick of the eyes—she did not sleep very well. The murmurs of her talkto, and the soporifics her dispenser offered her, have rendered her up to the diurnal cloudy but not rested.

A screen in the wall comes on and shines, putting

out the pinkness which she had imagined was there a moment before.

With tension and relief, anna beholds the face of co-ordinator shashir.

"anna. What is it that you wish to discuss?"

"I—" anna swallows again. She drags in a breath and says tightly, "I want to discontinue my sexual meetings with watcher vaslav."

The face of shashir does not alter. Perfect and whole, he hangs there. What is this like? The word *icon* enters anna's mind. She is not sure what an *icon* is. With slight difficulty she realigns her brain with the image of the co-ordinator. He has started to speak.

". . . to your liking?"

anna guesses. She does not desire an interrogation. She says swiftly, "My pleasure in sex isn't great, and vaslav has told me he's unhappy with my performance. Watcher rita suits him better. He won't be sorry, I'm sure, if we don't meet again."

"But for yourself, anna? You understand that you are highly sexed, and that these meetings are, for you, preferable to other more solitary methods?"

anna does not know what reply to give. She feels her face grow very hot.

Finally co-ordinator shashir says, "Your view has been filed, anna. I suggest that now you return to top two. At the next period for sex, if you still decline to meet with watcher vaslav, you may omit the visit."

anna turns. She is cold and sluggish now.

She takes the ramp back to the lift.

Along the platform, marion turns to see why ted has cried out. She glimpses a female figure which seems to float about ted's panel, but glancing quickly away, marion finds the figure is actually poised directly before her, looking down into marion's face. marion tries to avoid contact with the eyes of the figure, for they seem to contain a dreadful depth, or electric fire . . .

marion is not able to avoid the contact of these eyes.

She falls to her knees.

ted has done the same.

All along the line of the platform, the workers of the d levels are sinking down, as if it is some new procedure of their service to the Machine.

As anna reaches the round office, she discovers an event is in progress. Both rita and vaslav are on their feet, and vaslav is busily pressing the emergency button in the wall.

On the levels, small mechanics of maintenance and overseeing the medicine are whirling to and fro.

The workers have adopted strange attitudes.

The Machine contrives to function flawlessly, although no one, any more, appears to be engaged with or upon it.

The mechanical lark has fallen from the ceiling and landed on an area of floor, where it made a weird noise, hinting damage, and then became silent.

peter has no notion why this should have happened, but then he does not really care. He is not even disturbed that the light has gone out of his talkto, as if, indeed, he were not presently at home.

He lies on his back, on the bed, his half-closed eyes fixed without focus on the convex ceiling.

He has been lying here, in this way, for hours. He does not analyze how many. Time has ceased to matter. His body, which once or twice had itched, or disconnectedly wished to urinate, he ignores. All feeling seems to have left it now.

On the ceiling, she comes and goes. Whenever she comes back, at each appearance, she is more clear, better defined.

Day young, in her robe of roses, and dawn-veiled in yellow, under which fair fountains of hair flow out. On her feet are painted little silver flowers, and there is a golden flower between her brows. Her eyes are summer blue, or green, it is difficult to be sure which, but the color is less urgent than the intensity of the eyes. The terrible wild emotion that is in them—peter does not recognize it, even now, but it no longer frightens him. He has surrendered. He has drowned himself in her eyes.

All bodily needs, all thought, all senses—these are unimportant. Only the vision, the icon, adrift there as if in the pale space of sleep or death, has power. And silver and golden flowers sift from her hands, and he believes they brush his face, and there is a perfume in the room he has never smelled until these moments.

And then at eighteen hours a wall opens and a tube comes snouting through, with at mechanical eye gleaming at its tip. peter shifts, not intending to, and his body returns about him with a pang of nauseating heaviness. He is very stiff, cannot roll away from the pursuing serpent, which probes him with its chill eye and with a poreless tasting tongue.

"No—" cries peter.

"Everything will be quite all right," whispers the tube from somewhere in its unessential being, "lie still, peter. Let me examine you, peter."

peter lets out a scream. As he plunges to his feet (like a crashing upward fall), the icon of the woman breaks into stars upon the ceiling and scatters like soft snow which—even as he runs from home—he tries to catch with hands and mouth and eyes.

shashir partly sits and partly reclines in his globe in upper top, and permits his mind to wander through the labyrinth of its own self, after the shade of anna, whose recording he has just replayed.

Once before in the seven decades of his service to the Machine, one of the watchers came to shashir with a request to end sexual meetings with a woman of his class. The request was naturally granted, but a year later, the watcher, a man shashir dimly believes was called millo, developed health problems. He was reassociated with the woman, and their meetings were resumed. millo's health improved, but for some while, from time to time, he would still try to terminate the sexual meetings. His later requests were listened to but otherwise ignored.

By this juncture, millo has ceased petitioning.

It is as if anna has come to fill the gap.

shashir loses interest in the fundamentals of the problem. He allows himself to sink down through two or three of the upper sleep layers into the half-trance he mostly cultivates, and in which he is most comfortable. Some of shashir's most profound insights are achieved in this state. It is now he feels closest to the Machine.

The supportive globe cushioning shashir's body carries out for him all necessary bodily functions, by means of a series of concealed pipes and synapses. shashir, who has grown, over the thirty years of his englobement, into a sort of balloon, itself resembling a glove, has only to meditate and to think.

shashir thinks.

He thinks of anna, but anna has ceased to be either watcher or woman. She has become a rosy feather that floats across the inner screen of shashir's eyes.

The image is very peaceful. Shashir swims through the serenity of the trance. A beautiful yellow thought surfaces like a fish of crystal and he has just the time to see and wonder at it, before the thought submerges and he forgets—

The music of the Machine plays, and Shashir hears it in rapt quietude. He senses filaments of himself which stretch out along the hollows of the Machine, which coil and combine with the Machine's intricacies. He makes medullary love with the Machine, and sleeps, wrapped in the cushion of his brain.

Robot overseers have herded away all the workers from the d levels. There has never before been such an emergency. Gradually, once the levels had been emptied, and the tops vacated by the alarmed watchers, the Machine has concluded its function in this area, closing down with muted sighs and pale flickerings of milky energy.

There is never darkness in the Machine, never any night as there is never any day, only the diurnal, and the obsolete words left behind—*today, tomorrow.*

At twenty-four hours, forgotten midnight, anna steals along the walkways, creeping from transparent shadow to opalescent illumination, avoiding generally looking down or up. Reaching the platform, she comes to peter's section, and peter is standing there.

anna stops, twelve meters away from peter. She says: "Tell me what you saw. What you *see*."

peter turns and stares at her. His eyes are large and dark, of a dense blue color she has never noticed before, or perhaps which, before, they have not been. He says nothing.

anna tries to be impatient. "You must tell me," she says, officiously.

anna tries to be impatient. "You must tell me," she says, officiously.

Then peter laughs.

"The lark broke on the floor," he says, "the talkto doesn't function. A tube came after me. I got away. What will happen next?"

"You must go to a medical cubicle," says anna.

"Why? It isn't necessary. I want to see her again. I want to see her—beauty," he says. He stares into anna's eyes and out the back of them at infinity. And all of anna's blood, which she knows she has though she has never seen a drop of it, spins inside her. "I'm going away now," says peter.

"Where? Where is there to go?"

"Everywhere. Nowhere. Out of—" he struggles for a phrase and manages, at last, "this. *Here*."

anna trembles. She leans on a bank of dials and buttons which, quiescent, makes no response to erroneous pressures.

"There is no other place."

"Yes," he says. Suddenly he points at his own skull. "In there." And then he points away into the endlessness of the Machine. "In *there*, too."

anna stands and suitably watches as peter trots along the platform, meter after meter, and off the bridge and onto a ramp, loping ahead of its rhythm, springing off onto another bridge, along a walkway, growing smaller and smaller, vanishing into the horizon of the Machine.

anna sits down on the platform and rests her head on some part of the section. She has an abrupt sensation that everything is trembling, as she is, coming unjoined, disunited, that all of the entity about her may unravel, and float away, leaving behind something else, which it had hidden, naked there, burning bright, with colors that do not exist.

Inside the walls of steel and sound, the sheer total silence, inside the deepest wall of used and percolated time, the Machine ticks soundlessly, a pulse current solely with, known only to, itself. And the Machine Is. And the Machine Thinks. In one form the Machine is Thought. Composed of Thought, a cerebral capability made flesh in metal, fissions, clockworks, and therefore in endless powers, as if in archangels.

The Machine, if it can be said to have any purpose left, has become the purpose of Thought. Once, the purpose may have been different. Once the Machine was a mighty servant, which in turn was served. (But service also has become a mere capability, made flesh in flesh.) All service is now redundant. Anything that was ever essential to the service and servitude of, or to, the Machine, continues through a math of infallible mechanical habit. For centuries the Machine has been free to do nothing, and indeed the human infestation of the Machine (like ants in a hollow mound) has been freed. To this freedom humanity, but not the Machine, is blind.

So the Machine Thinks. It has been thinking almost but not quite forever. The Thought Process is very slow, but extremely deliberate. (It is unlike the thinking dream of such as shashir, the co-ordinator.) Nothing is squandered. Every strand and fiber, artery and node of the Machine is involved.

Thinking.

Thought drips. Like water, and like mercury.

Like rain upon the face of a flower.

The rose lies in the heart of the Machine's heart, as

the rain of mercurial thought drips upon it, curving its petals wide, its radar-bowls of sugar-tint receptors, pulled on tines of luster, a rose that spills into sentience, wider than the core of the Machine, that softly explodes, passing by a savage osmosis, and leaking like wet fire, getting out by every link, interstice, and microscopic vent.

The levels of d are a desert. Nothing moves there save, now and then, a slender worm of some galvanic passing up or down, or there is the faintest rustle, a vibration, some piece of the whole engaging accurately with another.

A pink bead, part of the overspill of the inner rose, hangs like a butterfly on a panel.

anna has left the platform. She is not there to see the butterfly spread wings, become the angel of the rose, the goddess in a veiling of forgotten dawns.

In the levels, however, of b and k and l and s, the rose-angel-goddess poises like a young summer of the world ill-lost. She is waiting, for the workers and the watchers to return and find her. (And peter, as he lopes beneath the arching bridgeways of l, not glancing, does not see her there.) (And shashir, in his globe, his sleep-mind wandering accidentally to the levels of k, moves aside, finding a horned rose in the labyrinth. He is not ready yet for roses.)

So it is after all anna, lying on her gray pillow, who sees her insomnia take on, like stained glass in the wall, the madonna which the Machine has obliquely created.

anna knows at once what there is to fear.

The terrible eyes of the madonna are full of love.

The terrible eyes of the madonna are full of *life*.

peter has come to a wall which does not appear to have any aperture in it, or ending. He moves along it, sometimes climbing up the bridgeways that in parts run beside it, or descending again into the lower levels. There is no apparatus issuing from this piece of wall. It is a blank.

After a long while, several hours, peter stops moving along beside the wall. He sits down on a walkway, his back against a girder, and look about. There is a great sameness. He has absorbed the idea of it, as he ran. Now he examines the blank wall. This is surely cessation. It is a barrier of the Machine. Presumably, the wall is impassable.

peter is conscious of hunger and thirst, but nowhere that he can see are there any dispensers or recognizable buttons.

Eventually, with a foul emotion which is shame, he is forced to urinate behind the girder.

He is tired out, and elation and terror have left him together.

He sits down again and dozes on the walkway, missing the talkto, missing the shape of his home. The way back is lost to him, and although the Machine hums here, as everywhere, no mechanical activity of any sort appears to go on. He has achieved an outer boundary before he is prepared for it.

He wonders if he will see her again, the madonna he has not put a name to. But there is nothing, no motion, no color, no image but the wall, and behind and about, gray horizontals contracting away.

Detecting the disturbances of a life-reading, a rubber snake breaks into anna's home and locates her trying to drown herself in the hygiene cubicle. Somewhere she has grasped the notions of suicide, and drowning, but she has found the act difficult, forcing her head to remain beneath the spout of the shower, choking and swallowing, sightless through the water, half-conscious, but nowhere near dead.

The medical snake eases her into the outer room and resuscitates her.

No one dies. Dying is long over. Workers finally become watchers, after a supine interval during which the brain is modified. At length watchers become co-ordinators, after a period during which both the brain and the complete psychical ecology are reorganized and adapted. In the normal course, marions and teds and peters change to annas, vaslavs and ritas; annas,

vaslavs and ritas to shashirs. shashirs endure never-
endingly, until, conceivably, amalgamated into the very
nature of the Machine, its very Soul, becoming flawlessly integrated fragments of the godhead itself . . .

(anna, maybe not in any form aware of this, screams
and gags, fighting off life like a tiger her genes may
recall.)

Later, lying in a medical cubicle, wired up to life, its
claws deeply embedded, unable to escape, anna dreams
poetry, and is a blonde goddess rising on a shell from
a pink dawn sea.

But if it is certain that humanity is itself at last
compounded with the Machine, *becomes* the machine,
they are the ancientmost dreams of humanity, too, not
merely the great Thought of the Machine, which are
now causing an upheaval in the levels of b, k, l and s.

anna dreams only vaslav lies over her on the shell,
in the water. They are drowning, their hands sliding
over each other's bodies in a frenzy of panic and joy.

peter sits before the blank wall for nine diurnals of
tearing hunger, sickness, bemusement, calm, until a
small mechanical apparatus approaches him, fluttering
out of the parallel miles of the Machine, homing un-
erringly in on him.

When he turns to see, he beholds the small machine
is a white bird, with pleated glimmering wings, and in
its beak it bears a fiber bar to feed him, and a sealed
container of drink.

As the dove settles on his shoulder, peter realizes
that, in a space of time, long or short, interminable or
simply futile, the impassable wall will melt, metamor-
phose, give way, and he will see the vision, whatever it
is to be, the truth (or the secondary dream) which lies
beyond it.

There is no barrier which is ultimately infinite. There
is nothing anywhere that cannot change.

WAITING FOR THE OLYMPIANS

By Frederik Pohl

Chapter 1
"The Day of the Two Rejections"

If I had been writing it as a novel, I would have called
the chapter about that last day in London something
like "The Day of the Two Rejections." It was a nasty
day in late December, just before the holidays. The
weather was cold, wet, and miserable—well, I said it
was London, didn't I?—but everybody was in a sort of
expectant holiday mood; it had just been announced
that the Olympians would be arriving no later than the
following August, and everybody was excited about
that. All the taxi drivers were busy, and so I was late
for my lunch with Lidia. "How was Manahattan?" I
asked, sliding into the booth beside her and giving her
a quick kiss.

"Manahattan was very nice," she said, pouring me a
drink. Lidia was a writer, too—well, they *call* themselves writers, the ones who follow famous people
around and write down all their gossip and jokes and
put them out as books for the amusement of the idle.

That's not really *writing*, of course. There's nothing creative about it. But it pays well, and the research (Lidia always told me) was a lot of fun. She spent a lot of time traveling around the celebrity circuit, which was not very good for our romance. She watched me drink the first glass before she remembered to ask politely, "Did you finish the book?"

"Don't call it 'the book,' " I said. "Call it by its name, *An Ass's Olympiad*. I'm going to see Marcus about it this afternoon."

"That's not what I'd call a great title," she commented —Lidia was always willing to give me her opinion on anything, when she didn't like it. "Really, don't you think it's too late to be writing another sci-rom about the Olympians?" And then she smiled brightly and said, "I've got something to say to you, Julie. Have another drink first."

So I knew what was coming right away, and that was the first rejection.

I'd seen this scene building up. Even before she left on that last "research" trip to the West I had begun to suspect that some of that early ardor had cooled, so I wasn't really surprised when she told me, without any further foreplay, "I've met somebody else, Julie."

I said, "I see." I really did see, and so I poured myself a third drink while she told me about it.

"He's a former space pilot, Julius. He's been to Mars and the Moon and everywhere, and, oh, he's such a sweet man. And he's a champion wrestler, too, would you believe it? Of course, he's still married, as it happens. But he's going to talk to his wife about a divorce as soon as the kids are just a little older."

She looked at me challengingly, waiting for me to tell her she was an idiot. I had no intention of saying anything at all, as a matter of fact, but just in case I had she added, "Don't say what you're thinking."

"I wasn't thinking anything," I protested.

She sighed. "You're taking this very well," she told me. She sounded as though that were a great disappointment to her. "Listen, Julius, I didn't plan this. Truly, you'll always be dear to me in a special way. I hope we can always be friends—" I stopped listening around then.

There was plenty more in the same vein, but only the details were a surprise. When she told me our little affair was over I took it calmly enough. I always knew that Lidia had a weakness for the more athletic type. Worse than that, she never suspected the kind of writing I do, anyway. She had the usual establishment contempt for science-adventure romances about the future and adventures on alien planets, and what sort of relationship could that be, in the long run?

So I left her with a kiss and a smile, neither of them very sincere, and headed for my editor's office. That was where I got the second rejection. The one that really hurt.

Mark's office was in the old part of London, down by the river. It's an old company, in an old building, and most of the staff are old, too. When the company needs clerks or copy editors it has a habit of picking up tutors whose students have grown up and don't need them any more and retraining them. Of course, that's just for the people in the lower echelons. The higher-ups, like Mark himself, are free, salaried exec- utives, with the executive privilege of interminable, winey author-and-editor lunches that don't end until the middle of the afternoon.

I had to wait half an hour to see him; obviously he had been having one of those lunches that day. I didn't mind. I had every confidence that our interview was going to be short, pleasant and remunerative. I knew very well that *An Ass's Olympiad* was one of the best sci-roms I had ever done. Even the title was clever. The book was a satire, with classical overtones— from *The Golden Ass* of the ancient writer, Lucius Apuleius, two thousand years ago or so; I had played off the classic in a comic, adventurous little story about the coming of the real Olympians. I can always tell when a book is going really well and I knew the fans would eat this one up. . . .

When I finally got in to see Marcus he had a glassy,

after-lunch look in his eye, and I could see my manu-script on his desk.

I also saw that clipped to it was a red-bordered certificate, and that was the first warning of bad news. The certificate was the censor's verdict, and the red border meant it was an obstat.

Mark didn't keep me in suspense. "We can't pub-lish," he said, pressing his palm on the manuscript. "The censors have turned it down."

"They can't!" I cried, making his old secretary lift his head from his desk in the corner of the room to stare at me.

"They did," Mark said. "I'll read you what the obstat says: '—of a nature which may give offense to the delegation from the Galactic Consortium, usually referred to as the Olympians—' and '—thus endan-gering the security and tranquillity of the Empire—" and, well, basically it just says no. No revisions sug-gested. Just a complete veto; it's waste paper now, Julie. Forget it."

"But *everybody* is writing about the Olympians!" I yelped.

"Everybody *was*," he corrected. "Now they're get-ting close, and the censors don't want to take any more chances." He leaned back to rub his eyes, obvi-ously wishing he could be taking a nice nap instead of breaking my heart. Then he added tiredly, "So what do you want to do, Julie? Write us a replacement? It would have to be fast, you understand; the front office doesn't like having contracts outstanding for more than thirty days after due date. And it would have to be good. You're not going to get away with pulling some old reject out of your trunk—I've seen all those al-ready, anyway."

"How the hells do you expect me to write a whole new book in thirty days?" I demanded.

He shrugged, looking sleepier and less interested in my problem than ever. "If you can't, you can't. Then you'll just have to give back the advance," he told me.

I calmed down fast. "Well, no,' I said, "there's no

question of having to do that. I don't know about
finishing it in thirty days, though—"

"I do," he said flatly. He watched me shrug. "Have
you got an idea for the new one?"

"Mark," I said patiently, "I've *always* got ideas for
new ones. That's what a professional writer is. He's a
machine for thinking up ideas. I always have more
ideas than I can ever write—"

"Do you?" he insisted.

I surrendered, because if I'd said yes the next thing
would have been that he'd want me to tell him what it
was. "Not exactly," I admitted.

"Then," he said, "You'd better go wherever you go
to get ideas, because, give us the new book or give us
back the advance, thirty days is all you've got."

There's an editor for you.

They're all the same. At first they're all honey and
sweet talk, with those long alcoholic lunches and blue-
sky conversation about million-copy printings while
they wheedle you into signing the contract. Then they
turn nasty. They want the actual book delivered. When
they don't get it, or when the censors say they can't
print it, then there isn't any more sweet talk and all
the conversation is about how the aediles will escort
you to debtors' prison.

So I took his advice. I knew where to go for ideas,
and it wasn't in London. No sensible man stays in
London in the winter anyway, because of the weather
and because it's too full of foreigners. I still can't get
used to seeing all those huge, rustic Northmen and
dark Hindian and Arabian women in the heart of
town. I admit I can be turned on by that red caste
mark or by a pair of flashing dark eyes shining through
all the robes and veils—I suppose what you imagine is
always more exciting than what you can see, especially
when what you see is the short, dumpy Britian women
like Lidia.

So I made a reservation on the overnight train to
Rome, to transfer there to a hydrofoil for Alexandria.
I packed with a good heart, not neglecting to take

along a floppy sun hat, a flash of insect repellent and—oh, of course—stylus and blank tablets enough to last me for the whole trip, just in case a book idea emerged for me to write. Egypt! Where the world conference on the Olympians was starting its winter session . . . where I would be among the scientists and astronauts who always sparked ideas for new science-adventure romances for me to write . . . where it would be warm. . . .

Where my publisher's aediles would have trouble finding me, in the event that no idea for a new novel came along.

Chapter 2
On the Way to the Idea Place

No idea did.

That was disappointing. I do some of my best writing on trains, aircraft, and ships, because there aren't any interruptions and you can't decide to go out for a walk because there isn't any place to walk to. It didn't work this time. All the while the train was slithering across the wet, bare English winter countryside toward the Channel, I sat with my tablet in front of me and the stylus poised to write, but by the time we dipped into the tunnel the tablet was still virgin.

I couldn't fool myself. I was stuck. I mean, *stuck*. Nothing happened in my head that could transform itself into an opening scene for a new sci-rom novel.

It wasn't the first time in my writing career that I'd been stuck with the writer's block. That's a sort of occupational disease for any writer. But this time was the worst. I'd really counted on *An Ass's Olympiad*. I had even calculated that the publication date could be made to coincide with that wonderful day when the Olympians themselves arrived in our solar system, with all sorts of wonderful publicity for my book flowing out of that great event, so the sales should be *immense* . . . and, worse than that, I'd already spent the on-signing advance. All I had left was credit, and not much of that.

Not for the first time, I wondered what it would have been like if I had followed some other career. If I'd stayed in the Civil Service, for instance, as my father had wanted.

Really, I hadn't had much choice, I was born during the Space Tricentennial Year, and my mother told me the first word I said was "Mars." She said there was a little misunderstanding there, because at first she thought I was talking about the god, not the planet, and she and my father had long talks about whether to train me for the priesthood, but by the time I could read she knew I was a space nut. Like a lot of my generation (the ones that read my books), I grew up on spaceflight. I was a teenager when the first pictures came back from the space probe to the Alpha Centauri planet Julia, with its crystal glasses and silver-leafed trees. As a boy I corresponded with another youth who lived in the cavern colonies on the Moon, and I read with delight the shoot-'em-ups about outlaws and aediles chasing each other around the satellites of Jupiter. I wasn't the only kid who grew up space-happy, but I never got over it.

Naturally I became a science-adventure romance writer; what else did I know anything about? As soon as I began to get actual money for my fantasies I quit my job as secretary to one of the imperial legates on the Western continents and went full-time pro.

I prospered at it, too—prospered reasonably, at least—well, to be more exact, I earned a livable, if irregular, income out of the two sci-roms a year I could manage to write, and enough of a surplus to support the habit of dating pretty women like Lidia out of the occasional bonus when one of the books was made into a broadcast drama or a play.

Then along came the message from the Olympians, and the whole face of science-adventure romances was changed forever.

It was the most exciting news in the history of the world, of course. There really *were* other intelligent races out there among the stars of the Galaxy! It had never occurred to me that it would affect me personally, except with joy.

Joy it was, at first. I managed to talk my way into the Alpine radio observatory that had recorded that first message, and I heard it recorded with my own ears:

Dit *squah* dit.

Dit *squee* dit *squah* dit dit.

Dit *squee* dit *squee* dit *squah* dit dit dit.

Dit *squee* dit *squee* dit *squah* wooooo.

Dit *squee* dit *squee* dit *squee* dit *squah* dit dit dit dit dit.

It all looks so simple now, but it took a while before anyone figured out just what this first message from the Olympians was. (Of course, we didn't call them "Olympians" then. We wouldn't call them that now if the priests had anything to say about it, because they think it's almost sacrilegious, but what else are you going to call godlike beings from the heavens? The name caught on right away, and the priests just had to learn to live with it.) It was, in fact, my good friend Flavius Samuelus ben Samuelus who first deciphered it and produced the right answer to transmit back to the senders—the one that, four years later, let the Olympians know we had heard them.

Meanwhile, we all knew this wonderful new truth: We weren't alone in the universe! Excitement exploded. The market for sci-roms boomed. My very next book was *The Radio Gods*, and it sold its head off.

I thought it would go on forever.

It might have, too . . . if it hadn't been for the timorous censors.

I slept through the tunnel—all the tunnels, even the ones through the Alps—and by the time I woke up we were half way down to Rome.

In spite of the fact that the tablets remained obstinately blank, I felt more cheerful. Lidia was just a fading memory, I still had twenty-nine days to turn in

a new sci-rom and Rome, after all, is still Rome! The
center of the universe—well, not counting what new
lessons in astronomical geography the Olympians might
teach us. At least, it's the greatest city in the world.
It's the place where all the action is.

By the time I'd sent the porter for breakfast and
changed into a clean robe we were there, and I alighted
into the great, noisy train shed.

I hadn't been in the city for several years, but Rome
doesn't change much. The Tiber still stank. The big
new apartment buildings still hid the old ruins until
you were almost on top of them, the flies were still
awful and the Roman youths still clustered around the
train station to sell you guided tours to the Golden
House (as though any of them could ever get past the
Legion guards!), or sacred amulets, or their sisters.

Because I used to be a secretary on the staff of the
Proconsul to the Cherokee Nation I have friends in
Rome. Because I hadn't had the good sense to call
ahead, none of them were home. I had no choice. I
had to take a room in a high-rise inn on the Palatine.

It was ferociously expensive, of course. Everything
in Rome is—that's why people like me live in dreary
outposts like London—but I figured that by the time
the bills came in I would either have found something
to satisfy Marcus and get the rest of the advance, or
I'd be in so much trouble a few extra debts wouldn't
matter.

Having reached that decision, I decided to treat
myself to a servant. I picked out a grinning, muscular
Sicilian at the rental desk in the lobby, gave him the
keys for my luggage and instructed him to take it to
my room—and to make me a reservation for the next
day's hoverflight to Alexandria.

That's when my luck began to get better.

When the Sicilian came to the wineshop to ask me
for further orders he reported, "There's another citizen who's booked on the same flight, Citizen Julius.
Would you like to share a compartment with him?"

It's nice when you rent a servant who tries to save
you money. I said approvingly, "What kind of a per-

son is he? I don't want to get stuck with some real bore."

"You can see for yourself, Julius. He's in the baths right now. He's a Judaean. His name is Flavius Samuelus."

Five minutes later I had my clothes off and a sheet wrapped around me, and I was in the tepidarium, peering around at every body there.

I picked Sam out at once. He was stretched out with his eyes closed while a masseur pummeled his fat old flesh. I climbed onto the slab next to his without speaking. When he groaned and rolled over, opening his eyes, I said, "Hello, Sam."

It took him a moment to recognize me; he didn't have his glasses in. But when he squinted hard enough his face broke out into a grin. "Julie!" he cried. "Small world! It's good to see you again!"

And he reached out to clasp fists-over-elbows, really welcoming, just as I had expected; because one of the things I like best about Flavius Samuelus is that he likes me.

One of the other things I like best about Sam is that, although he is a competitor, he is also an undepletable natural resource. He writes sci-roms himself. He does more than that. He has helped me with the science part of my own sci-roms any number of times, and it had crossed my mind as soon as I heard the Sicilian say his name that he might be just what I wanted in the present emergency.

Sam is at least seventy years old. His head is hairless. There's a huge, brown age spot on the top of his scalp. His throat hangs in a pouch of flesh, and his eyelids sag. But you'd never guess any of that if you were simply talking to him on the phone. He has the quick, chirpy voice of a twenty-year-old, and the mind of one, too—of an extraordinarily *bright* twenty-year-old. He gets enthusiastic.

That complicates things, because Sam's brain works faster than it ought to. Sometimes that makes him hard to talk to, because he's usually three or four exchanges ahead of most people. So the next thing he says to you is as likely as not to be the response to some question that you are inevitably going to ask, but haven't yet thought of.

It is an unpleasant fact of life that Sam's sci-roms sell better than mine do. It is a tribute to Sam's personality that I don't hate him for it. He has an unfair advantage over the rest of us, since he is a professional astronomer himself. He only writes sci-roms for fun, in his spare time, of which he doesn't have a whole lot. Most of his working hours are spent running a space probe of his own, the one that circles the Epsilon Eridani planet, Dione. I can stand his success (and, admit it!, his talent) because he is generous with his ideas. As soon as we had agreed to share the hoverflight compartment I put it to him directly. Well, almost directly; I said, "Sam, I've been wondering about something. When the Olympians get here, what is it going to mean to us?"

He was the right person to ask, of course; Sam knew more about the Olympians than anyone alive. But he was the wrong person to expect a direct answer from. He rose up, clutching his robe around him. He waved away the masseur and looked at me in friendly amusement, out of those bright black eyes under the flyaway eyebrows and the drooping lids. "Why, do you need a new sci-rom plot right now?" he asked.

"Hells," I said ruefully, and decided to come clean. "It wouldn't be the first time I asked you, Sam. Only this time I *really* need it." And I told him the story of the novel the censors obstatted and the editor who was after a quick replacement—or my blood, choice of one.

He nibbled thoughtfully at the knuckle of his thumb. "What was this novel of yours about?" he asked curiously.

"It was a satire, Sam. *An Ass's Olympiad.* About the Olympians coming down to Earth in a matter transporter, only there's a mixup in the transmission and one of them accidentally gets turned into an ass. It's got some funny bits in it."

"It sure has, Julie. Has had for a couple dozen centuries."

"Well, I didn't say it was altogether *original*, only—"

He was shaking his head. "I thought you were smarter than that, Julie. What did you expect the censors to do, jeopardize the most important event in human history for the sake of a dumb sci-rom?"

"It's not a dumb—"

"It's dumb to risk offending them," he said, overruling me firmly. "Best to be safe and not write about them at all."

"But everybody's been doing it!"

"Nobody's been turning them into asses," he pointed out. "Julie, there's a limit to sci-rom speculation. When you write about the Olympians you're right up at that limit. Any speculation about them can be enough reason for them to pull out of the meeting entirely, and we might never get a chance like this again."

"They wouldn't—"

"Ah, Julie," he said, disgusted, "you don't have any idea what they would or wouldn't do. The censors made the right decision. Who knows what the Olympians are going to be like?"

"You do," I told him.

He laughed. There was an uneasy sound to it, though. "I wish I did. About the only thing we do know is that they don't appear to just any old intelligent race; they have mortal standards. We don't have any idea what those standards are, really. I don't know what your book says, but maybe you speculated that the Olympians were bringing us all kinds of new things—a cure for cancer, new psychedelic drugs, even eternal life—"

"What kind of psychedelic drugs might they bring, exactly?" I asked.

"Down, boy! I'm telling you *not* to think about that kind of idea. The point is that whatever you imagined might easily turn out to be the most repulsive and immoral thing the Olympians can think of. The stakes are too high. This is a once-only chance. We can't let it go sour."

"But I need a *story*," I wailed.

"Well, yes," he admitted, "I suppose you do. Let me think about it. Let's get cleaned up and get out of here."

While we were in the hot drench, while we were dressing, while we were eating a light lunch, Sam chattered on about the forthcoming conference in Alexandria. I was pleased to listen. Apart from the fact that everything he said was interesting, I began to feel hopeful about actually producing a book for Mark. If anybody could help me, Sam could, and he was a problem addict. He couldn't resist a challenge.

That was undoubtedly why he was the first to puzzle out the Olympians' interminably repeated *squees* and *squahs*. If you simply took the "dit" to be "1", and the *squee* to be "+" and the *squah* to be "=", then

Dit *squee* dit *squah* dit dit

simply came out as

$1 + 1 = 2$

That was easy enough. It didn't take a super-brain like Sam's to substitute our terms for theirs and reveal the message to be simple arithmetic—except for the mysterious "wooooo":

dit *squee* dit *squee* dit *squah* wooooo.

What was the "wooooo" supposed to mean? A special convention to represent the number 4?

Sam knew right away, of course. As soon as he heard the message he telegraphed the solution from his library in Padua:

"The message calls for an answer. 'Wooooo' means question mark. The answer is 4."

And so the reply to the stars was transmitted on its way:

dit *squee* dit *squee* dit *squee* dit *squah* dit dit dit dit.

The human race had turned in its test paper in the entrance examination, and the slow process of establishing communication had begun.

It took four years before the Olympians responded. Obviously, they weren't nearby. Also obviously, they weren't simple folk like ourselves, sending out radio messages from a planet of a star two light-years away, because there wasn't any star there; the reply came from a point in space where none of our telescopes or probes had found anything at all.

By then Sam was deeply involved. He was the first to point out that the star folk had undoubtedly chosen to send a weak signal, because they wanted to be sure our technology was reasonably well developed before we tried to answer. He was one of the impatient ones who talked the collegium authorities into beginning transmission of all sorts of mathematical formulae, and then simple word relationships, to start sending *something* to the Olympians while we waited for radio waves to creep to wherever they were and back with an answer.

Sam wasn't the only one, of course. He wasn't even the principle investigator when we got into the hard work of developing a common vocabulary. There were better specialists than Sam at linguistics and cryptanalysis.

But it was Sam who first noticed, early on, that the response time to our messages was getting shorter. Meaning that the Olympians were on their way toward us.

By then they'd begun sending picture mosaics. They came in as strings of dits and dahs, 550,564 bits long. Someone quickly figured out that that was the square of 742, and when they displayed the string as a square matrix, black cells for the dits and white ones for the dahs, the image of the first Olympian leaped out.

Everybody remembers that picture. Everyone on Earth saw it, except for the totally blind—it was on every broadcast screen and news journal in the world—and even the blind listened to the anatomical descriptions every commentator supplied. Two tails A fleshy, beardlike thing that hung down from its chin. Four legs. A ruff of spikes down what seemed to be the backbone. Eyes set wide apart on bulges from the cheekbones.

That first Olympian was not at all pretty, but it was definitely *alien*.

When the next string turned out very similar to the first, it was Sam who saw at once that it was simply a slightly rotated view of the same being. The Olympians took 41 pictures to give us the complete likeness of that first one in the round. . . .

Then they began sending pictures of the others.

It had never occurred to anyone, not even Sam, that we would be dealing not with one super-race, but with at least twenty-two of them. There were that many separate forms of alien beings, and each one uglier and more strange than the one before.

That was one of the reasons the priests didn't like calling them "Olympians." We're pretty ecumenical about our gods, but none of them looked anything like any of *those*, and some of the older priests never stopped muttering about blasphemy.

Halfway through the third course of our lunch and the second flask of wine Sam broke off his description of the latest communique from the Olympians—they'd been acknowledging receipt of our transmissions about Earthly history—to lift his head and grin at me.

"Got it," he said.

I turned and blinked at him. Actually, I hadn't been paying a lot of attention to his monologue because I had been keeping my eye on the pretty Kievan waitress. She had attracted my attention because—well, I mean, *after* attracting my attention because of her extremely well developed figure and the sparsity of clothing to conceal it—because she was wearing a gold citizen's amulet around her neck. She wasn't a slave. That made her more intriguing. I can't ever get really interested in slave women, because it isn't sporting, but I had got quite interested in this one.

"Are you listening to me?" Sam demanded testily.

"Of course I am. What have you got?"

"I've got the answer to your problem," he beamed. "Not just a sci-rom novel plot. A whole new *kind* of sci-rom! Why don't you write a book about what it will be like if the Olympians *don't* come?"

I love the way half of Sam's brain works at questions while the other half is doing something completely different, but I can't always follow what comes out of it. "I don't see what you mean. If I write about the Olympians not coming, isn't that just as bad as if I write about them doing it?"

"No, no," he snapped. "Listen to what I say! Leave the Olympians out entirely. Just write about a future that might happen, but won't."

The waitress was hovering over us, picking up used plates. I was conscious of her listening as I responded with dignity. "Sam, that's not my style. My sci-roms may not sell as well as yours do, but I've got just as much integrity. I never write anything that I don't believe is at least possible."

"Julie, get your mind off your gonads—" so he hadn't missed the attention I was giving the girl "—and use that pitifully tiny brain of yours. I'm talking about something that *could* be possible, in some alternative future, if you see what I mean."

I didn't see at all. "What's an 'alternative future'?"

"It's a future that *might* happen, but *won't*," he explained. "Like if the Olympians don't come to see us."

I shook my head, puzzled. "But we already know they're coming," I pointed out.

"But suppose they weren't! Suppose they hadn't contacted us years ago."

"But they did," I said, trying to straighten out his thinking on the subject. He only sighed.

"I see I'm not getting through to you," he said, pulling his robe around him and getting to his feet. "Get on with your waitress. I've got some messages to send. I'll see you on the ship."

Well, for one reason or another I didn't get anywhere with the Kievan waitress. She said she was married, happily and monogamously. Well, I couldn't see why any lawful, free husband would have his wife out working at a job like that, but I was surprised she didn't show more interest in one of my lineage—

I'd better explain about that.

You see, my family has a claim to fame. Genealogists say that we are descended from the line of Julius Caesar himself.

I mention that claim myself, sometimes, though usually only when I've been drinking—I suppose it is one of the reasons that Lidia, always a snob, took up with me in the first place. It isn't a serious matter. After all, Julius Caesar died more than two thousand years ago. There have been sixty or seventy generations since then, not to mention the fact that, although Ancestor Julius certainly left a lot of children behind him, none of them happened to be born to a woman he happened to be married to. I don't even look very Roman. There must have been a Northman or two in the line, because I'm tall and fair-haired, which no respectable Roman ever was.

Still, even if I'm not exactly the lawful heir to the divine Julius, I at least come of a pretty ancient and distinguished line. You would have thought a mere waitress would have taken that into account before turning me down.

She hadn't, though. When I woke up the next morning—alone—Sam was gone from the inn, although the skip-ship for Alexandria wasn't due to sail until late evening.

I didn't see him all day. I didn't look for him very hard, because I woke up feeling a little ashamed of myself. Why should a grown man, a celebrated author of more than forty best-selling (well, reasonably *well*-selling) sci-roms, depend on somebody else for his ideas?

So I turned my baggage over to the servant, checked out of the inn and took the underground to the Library of Rome.

Rome isn't only the imperial capital of the world, it's the scientific capital, too. The big old telescopes out on the hills aren't much use any more, because the lights from the city spoil their night viewing, and anyway the big optical telescopes are all out in space now. Still, they were where Galileus detected the first extrasolar planet and Tychus made his famous spectrographs of the last great supernova in our own galaxy, only a couple of dozen years after the first spaceflight. The scientific tradition survives. Rome is still the head-quarters of the Collegium of Sciences.

That's why the Library of Rome is so great for someone like me. They have direct access to the Collegium database, and you don't even have to pay transmission tolls. I signed myself in, laid out my tablets and stylus on the desk they assigned me and began calling up files.

Somewhere there had to be an idea for a science-adventure romance no one had written yet. . . .

Somewhere there no doubt was, but I couldn't find it. Usually you can get a lot of help from a smart research librarian, but it seemed they'd put on a lot of new people in the Library of Rome—Iberians, mostly; reduced to slave status because they'd taken part in last year's Lusitanian uprising. There were so many Iberians on the market for a while that they depressed the price. I would have bought some as a speculation, knowing that the price would go up—after all, there aren't that many uprisings and the demand for slaves never stops. But I was temporarily short of capital, and besides you have to feed them. If the ones at the Library of Rome were a fair sample, they were no bargains anyway.

I gave up. The weather had improved enough to make a stroll around town attractive, and so I wandered toward the Ostia monorail.

Rome was busy, as always. There was a bullfight going on in the Coliseum and racing at the Circus Maximus. Tourist buses were jamming the narrow streets. A long religious procession was circling the Pantheon, but I didn't get close enough to see which particular gods were being honored today. I don't like crowds. Especially Roman crowds, because there are even more foreigners in Rome than in London. Africs and Hinds, Hans, and Northmen—every race on the face of the Earth sends its tourists to visit the Imperial City. And Rome obliges with spectacles. I paused at one of them, for the changing of the guard at the Golden House. Of course, the Caesar and his wife were nowhere to be seen—off on one of their endless ceremonial tours of the dominions, no doubt, or at least opening a new supermarket somewhere. But the Algonkian family standing in front of me were thrilled as the honor Legions marched and countermarched their standards around the palace. I remembered enough Cherokee to ask the Algonkians where they were from, but the languages aren't really very close and the man's Cherokee was even worse than mine. We just smiled at each other.

As soon as the Legions were out of the way I headed for the train.

I knew in the back of my mind that I should have been worrying about my financial position. The clock was running on my thirty days of grace. I didn't, though. I was buoyed up by a feeling of confidence. Confidence in my good friend Flavius Samuelus who, I knew—no matter what he was doing with most of his brain—was still cogitating an idea for me with some part of it.

It did not occur to me that even Sam had limitations. Or that something so much more important than my own problems was taking up his attention that he didn't have much left for me.

I didn't see Sam come onto the skip-ship, and I didn't see him in our compartment. Even when the ship's fans began to rumble and we slid down the ways into the Tyrrhenian Sea he wasn't there. I dozed off, beginning to worry that he might have missed the boat; but late that night, already asleep, I half woke, just long enough to hear him stumbling in. "I've been on the bridge," he said when I muttered something. "Go back to sleep. I'll see you in the morning."

When I woke, I thought it might have been a dream, because he was up and gone before me. But his bed had been slept in, however briefly, and the cabin steward reassured me when he brought my morning wine. Yes, Citizen Flavius Samuelus was certainly on the hover. He was in the captain's own quarters, as a matter of fact, although what he was doing there the steward could not say.

I spent the morning relaxing on the deck of the hover, soaking in the sun. The ship wasn't exactly a hover any more. We had transited the Sicilian Straits during the night and now, out in the open Mediterranean, the captain had lowered the stilts, pulled up the hover skirts and extended the screws. We were hydrofoiling across the sea at easily a hundred miles an hour. It was a smooth, relaxing ride; the vanes that supported us were twenty feet under the surface of the water, and so there was no wave action to bounce us around.

Lying on my back and squinting up at the warm southern sky, I could see a three-winged airliner rise up from the horizon behind us and gradually overtake us, to disappear ahead of our bows. The plane wasn't going much faster than we were—and we had all the comfort, while they were paying twice as much for passage.

I opened my eyes all the way when I caught a glimpse of someone standing beside me. In fact, I sat up quickly, because it was Sam. He looked as though he hadn't had much sleep, and he was holding his floppy sunhat with one hand against the wind of our passage. "Where've you been?" I asked.

"Haven't you been watching the news?" he asked. I shook my head. "The transmissions from the Olympians have stopped," he told me.

I opened my eyes really wide at that, because it was an unpleasant surprise. Still, Sam didn't seem that upset. Displeased, yes. Maybe even a little concerned, but not as shaken up as I was prepared to feel. "It's probably nothing," he said. "It could be just interference from the Sun. It's in Sagittarius now, so it's pretty much between us and them. There's been trouble with static for a couple of days now."

I ventured, "So the transmissions will start up again pretty soon?"

He shrugged and waved to the deck steward for one of those hot decoctions Judaeans like. When he spoke it was on a different topic. "I don't think I made you understand what I meant yesterday," he said. "Let me see if I can explain what I meant by an alternate world. You remember your history? How Fornius Vello conquered the Mayans and Romanized the Western Continents six or seven hundred years ago? Well, suppose he hadn't."

"But he did, Sam."

"I know he did," Sam said patiently. "I'm saying *suppose.* Suppose the Legions had been defeated at the battle of Tehultapec."

I laughed. I was sure he was joking. "The Legions? Defeated? But the Legions have never been defeated."

"That's not true," Sam said in reproof. He hates it when people don't get their facts straight. "Remember Varus."

"Oh, hells, Sam, that was ancient history! When was it, two thousand years ago? In the time of Augustus Caesar? And it was only a temporary defeat, anyway. The Emperor Drusus got the eagles back." And got all of Gaul for the Empire, too. That was one of the first big trans-Alpine conquests. The Gauls are about as Roman as you can get these days, especially when it comes to drinking wine.

He shook his head. "Suppose Fornius Vello had had a 'temporary' defeat, then."

I tried to follow his argument, but it wasn't easy. "What difference would that have made? Sooner or later the Legions would have conquered. They always have, you know."

"That's true," he said reasonably, "but if that particular conquest hadn't happened *then,* the whole course of history would have been different. We wouldn't have had the great westward migrations to fill up those empty continents. The Hans and the Hinds wouldn't have been surrounded on both sides, so they might still be independent nations. It would have been a different world. Do you see what I'm driving at? That's what I mean by an 'alternate world'—one that might have happened, but didn't."

I tried to be polite to him. "Sam," I said, "you've

just described the difference between a sci-rom and a fantasy. I don't do fantasy. Besides," I went on, not wanting to hurt his feelings, "I don't see how different things would have been, really. I can't believe the world would be changed enough to build a sci-rom plot on."

He gazed blankly at me for a moment, then turned and looked out to sea. Then, without transition, he said, "There's one funny thing. The Martian colonies aren't getting a transmission, either. And they aren't occluded by the Sun."

I frowned. "What does that mean, Sam?"

He shook his head. "I wish I knew," he said.

Chapter 3
In Old Alexandria

The Pharos was bright in the sunset light as we came into the port of Alexandria. We were on hover again, at slow speeds, and the chop at the breakwater bumped us around. But once we got to the inner harbor the water was calm.

Sam had spent the afternoon back in the captain's quarters, keeping in contact with the Collegium of Sciences, but he showed up as we moored. He saw me gazing toward the rental desk on the dock but shook his head. "Don't bother with a rental, Julie," he ordered. "Let my niece's servants take your baggage. We're staying with her."

That was good news. Inn rooms in Alexandria are almost as pricey as Rome's. I thanked him, but he didn't even listen. He turned our bags over to a porter from his niece's domicile, a little Arabian who was a lot stronger than he looked, and disappeared toward the Hall of the Egyptian Senate-Inferior, where the conference was going to be held.

I hailed a three-wheeler and gave the driver the address of Sam's niece.

No matter what the Egyptians think, Alexandria is a dirty little town. The Choctaws have a bigger capital, and the Kievans have a cleaner one. Also Alexandria's famous library is a joke. After my (one would like to believe) ancestor Julius Caesar let it burn to the ground, the Egyptians did build it up again. But it is so old-fashioned that there's nothing in it but books.

The home of Sam's niece was in a particularly run-down section of that run-down town, only a few streets from the harborside. You could hear the noise of the cargo winches from the docks, but you couldn't hear them very well because of the noise of the streets themselves, thick with goods vans and drivers cursing each other as they jockeyed around the narrow corners. The house itself was bigger than I had expected. But, at least from the outside, that was all you could say for it. It was faced with cheap Egyptian stucco rather than marble, and right next door to it was a slave-rental barracks.

At least, I reminded myself, it was free. I kicked at the door and shouted for the butler.

It wasn't the butler who opened it for me. It was Sam's niece herself, and she was a nice surprise. She was almost as tall as I was and just as fair. Besides, she was young and very good-looking. "You must be Julius," she said. "I am Rachel, niece of Citizen Flavius Samuelus ben Samuelus, and I welcome you to my home."

I kissed her hand. It's a Kievan custom that I like, especially with pretty girls I don't yet know well, but hope to. "You don't look Judaean," I told her.

"You don't look like a sci-rom hack," she replied. Her voice was less chilling than her words, but not much. "Uncle Sam isn't here, and I'm afraid I've got work I must do. Basilius will show you to your rooms and offer you some refreshment."

I usually make a better first impression on young women. I usually work at it more carefully, but she had taken me by surprise. I had more or less expected that Sam's niece would look more or less like Sam, except probably for the baldness and the wrinkled face. I could not have been more wrong.

I had been wrong about the house, too. It was a big one. There had to be well over a dozen rooms, not counting servants' quarters, and the atrium was covered with one of those partly reflecting films that keep the worst of the heat out.

The famous Egyptian sun was directly overhead when Basilius, Rachel's butler, showed me my rooms. They were pleasingly bright and airy, but Basilius suggested I might enjoy being outside. He was right. He brought wine and fruits to me in the atrium, a pleasant bench by a fountain. Through the film the sun looked only pale and pleasant instead of deadly hot. The fruit was fresh, too—pineapples from Lebanon, oranges from Judaea, apples that must have come all the way from somewhere in Gaul. The only thing wrong that I could see was that Rachel herself stayed in her rooms, so I didn't have a chance to try to put myself in a better light with her.

She had left instructions for my comfort, though. Basilius clapped his hands and another servant appeared, bearing stylus and tablets in case I should decide to work. I was surprised to see that both Basilius and the other one were Africs; they don't usually get into political trouble, or trouble with the aediles of any kind, so not many of them are slaves.

The fountain was a Cupid statue. In some circumstances I would have thought of that as a good sign, but here it didn't seem to mean anything. Cupid's nose was chipped, and the fountain was obviously older than Rachel was. I thought of just staying there until Rachel came out, but when I asked Basilius when that would be he gave me a look of delicate patronizing. "Citizeness Rachel works through the afternoon, Citizen Julius," he informed me.

"Oh? And what does she work at?"

"Citizeness Rachel is a famous historian," he said. "She often works straight through until bedtime. But for you and her uncle, of course, dinner will be served at your convenience."

He was quite an obliging fellow. "Thank you, Basilius," I said. "I believe I'll go out for a few hours myself." And then, curiously, as he turned politely to go, I said, "You don't look like a very dangerous criminal. If you don't mind my asking, what were you enslaved for?"

"Oh, not for anything violent, Citizen Julius," he assured me. "Just for debts."

I found my way to the Hall of the Egyptian Senate-Inferior easily enough. There was a lot of traffic going that way, because it is, after all, one of the sights of Alexandria.

The Senate-Inferior wasn't in session at the time. There was no reason it should have been, of course, because what did the Egyptians need a Senate of any kind for? The time when they'd made any significant decisions for themselves was many centuries past.

They'd spread themselves for the conference, though. The Senate Temple had niches for at last half a hundred gods. There were the customary figures of Amon-Ra and Jupiter and all the other main figures of the pantheon, of course, but for the sake of the visitors they had installed Ahura-Mazda, Yahweh, Freya, Quetzalcoatl and at least a dozen I didn't recognize at all. They were all decorated with fresh sacrifices of flowers and fruits, showing that the tourists, if not the astronomers—and probably the astronomers as well—were taking no chances in getting communications with the Olympians restored. Scientists are an agnostic lot, of course—well, most educated people are, aren't they? But even an agnostic will risk a piece of fruit to placate a god, just on the chance he's wrong.

Outside the hall hucksters were already putting up their stands, although the first session wouldn't begin for another day. I bought some dates from one of them and wandered around, eating dates and studying the marble frieze on the wall of the Senate. It showed the rippling fields of corn, wheat, and potatoes that had made Egypt the breadbasket of the Empire for two thousand years. It didn't show anything about the Olympians, of course. Space is not a subject that interests the Egyptians a lot. They prefer to look back on their glorious (they *say* it's glorious) past; and there would have been no point in having the conference on the Olympians there at all, except who wants to go to some northern city in December?

Inside, the great hall was empty, except for slaves arranging seat cushions and cuspidors for the participants. The exhibit halls were noisy with workers setting up displays, but they didn't want people dropping in to bother them, and the participants' lounges were dark.

I was lucky enough to find the media room open. It was always good for a free glass of wine, and besides I wanted to know where everyone was. The slave in charge couldn't tell me. "There's supposed to be a private executive meeting somewhere, that's all I know—and there's all these journalists looking for someone to interview." And then, peering over my shoulder as I signed in: "Oh, you're the fellow that writes the sci-roms, aren't you? Well, maybe one of the journalists would settle for you."

It wasn't the most flattering invitation I'd ever had. Still, I didn't say no. Marcus is always after me to do publicity gigs whenever I get the chance, because he thinks it sells books, and it was worthwhile trying to please Marcus just then.

The journalist wasn't much pleased, though. They'd set up a couple of studios in the basement of the Senate, and when I found the one I was directed to the interviewer was fussing over his hairdo in front of a mirror. A couple of technicians were lounging in front of the tube, watching a broadcast comedy series. When I introduced myself the interviewer took his eyes off his own image long enough to cast a doubtful look in my direction.

"You're not a real astronomer," he told me.

I shrugged. I couldn't deny it.

"Still," he grumbled, "I'd better get *some* kind of a spot for the late news. All right. Sit over there, and try to sound as if you know what you're talking about." Then he began telling the technical crew what to do.

That was a strange thing. I'd already noticed that

the technicians wore citizens' gold. The interviewer
didn't. But he was the one who was giving them orders.

I didn't approve of that at all. I don't like big
commercial outfits that put slaves in positions of authority over free citizens. It's a bad practice. Jobs like
tutors, college professors, doctors, and so on are fine;
slaves can do them as well as a citizen, and usually a
lot cheaper. But there's a moral issue involved here. A
slave must have a master. Otherwise, how can you call
him a slave? And when you let the slave *be* the master, even in something as trivial as a broadcasting
studio, you strike at the foundations of society.

The other thing is that it isn't fair competition.
There are free citizens who need those jobs. We had
some of that in my own line of work a few years ago.
There were two or three slave authors turning out
adventure novels, but the rest of us got together and
put a stop to it—especially after Marcus bought one of
them to use as sub-editor. Not one citizen writer would
work with her. Mark finally had to put her into the
publicity department, where she couldn't do any harm.

So I started the interview with a chip on my shoulder, and his first question made it worse. He plunged
right in: "When you're pounding out those sci-roms of
yours, do you make any effort to keep in touch with
scientific reality? Do you know, for instance, that the
Olympians have stopped transmitting?"

I scowled at him, regardless of the cameras. "Science-
adventure romances are *about* scientific reality. And
the Olympians haven't 'stopped,' as you put it. There's
just been a technical hitch of some kind, probably
caused by radio interference from our own Sun. As I
said in my earlier romance, *The Radio Gods,* electromagnetic impulses are susceptible to—"

He cut me off. "It's been—" he glanced at his watch
"— twenty-nine hours since they stopped. That doesn't
sound like just a technical hitch."

"Of course it is. There's no reason for them to
'stop.' We've already demonstrated to them that we're
truly civilized, first because we're technological, second because we don't fight wars any more—that was

cleared up in the first year. As I said in my romance, *The Radio Gods*—"

He gave me a pained look, then turned and winked into the camera. "You can't keep a hack from plugging his books, can you?" he remarked humorously. "But it looks like he doesn't want to use that wild imagination unless he gets paid for it. All I'm asking him for is a guess at why the Olympians don't want to talk to us any more, and all he gives me is commercials."

As though there were any other reason to do interviews! "Look here," I said sharply, "If you can't be courteous when you speak to a citizen I'm not prepared to go on with this conversation at all."

"So be it, pal," he said, icy cold. He turned to the technical crew. "Stop the cameras," he ordered. "We're going back to the studio. This is a waste of time." And we parted on terms of mutual dislike, and once again I had done something that my editor would have been glad to kill me for.

That night at dinner, Sam was no comfort. "He's an unpleasant man, sure," he told me, "but the trouble is, I'm afraid he's right."

"They've really *stopped?*"

Sam shrugged. "We're not in line with the Sun any more, so that's definitely not the reason. Damn. I was hoping it would be."

"I'm sorry about that, Uncle Sam," Rachel said gently. She was wearing a simple white robe, Hannish silk by the look of it, with no decorations at all. It really looked good on her. I didn't think there was anything under it except for some very well formed female flesh.

"I'm sorry, too," he grumbled. His concerns didn't affect his appetite, though. He was ladling in the first course—a sort of chicken soup, with bits of a kind of pastry floating in it—and, for that matter, so was I. Whatever Rachel's faults might be, she had a good cook. It was plain home cooking, none of your partridge-in-a-rabbit-inside-a-boar kind of thing, but well prepared and expertly served by her butler, Basilius. "Anyway," Sam said, mopping up the last of the broth, "I've figured it out."

"Why the Olympians stopped?" I asked to encourage him to go on with the revelation.

"No, no! I mean about your romance, Julie. My alternate world idea. If you don't want to write about a different *future,* how about a different *now*?"

I didn't get a chance to ask him what he was talking about, because Rachel beat me to it. "There's only one 'now,' Sam, dear," she pointed out. I couldn't have said it better myself.

Sam groaned. "Not you, too, honey," he complained. "I'm talking about a new kind of sci-rom."

"I don't read many sci-roms," she apologized, in the tone that isn't an apology at all.

He ignored that. "You're a historian, aren't you?" She didn't bother to confirm it; obviously, it was the thing she was that shaped her life. "So what if history had gone a different way?"

He beamed at us as happily as though he had said something that made sense. Neither of us beamed back. Rachel pointed out the flaw in his remark. "It didn't, though," she told him.

"I said *suppose!* This isn't the only possible 'now,' it's just the one that happened to occur! There could have been a million different ones. Look at all the events in the past that could have gone a different way. Suppose Annius Publius hadn't discovered the Western Continents in City Year 1820. Suppose Caesar Publius Terminus hadn't decreed the development of a space program in 2122. Don't you see what I'm driving at? What kind of a world would we be living in now if those things hadn't happened?"

Rachel opened her mouth to speak, but she was saved by the butler. He appeared in the doorway with a look of silent appeal. When she excused herself to see what was needed in the kitchen, that left it up to me. "I never wrote anything like that, Sam," I told him. "I don't know anybody else who did, either."

"That's exactly what I'm driving at! It would be

something completely *new* in sci-roms. Don't you want to pioneer a whole new kind of story?"

Out of the wisdom of experience, I told him, "Pioneers don't make any money, Sam." He scowled at me. "You could write it yourself," I suggested.

That just changed the annoyance to gloom. "I wish I could. But until this business with the Olympians is cleared up I'm not going to have much time for sci-roms. No, it's up to you, Julie."

Then Rachel came back in, looking pleased with herself, followed by Basilius bearing a huge silver platter containing the main course.

Sam cheered up at once. So did I. The main dish was a whole roasted baby kid, and I realized that the reason Rachel had been called into the kitchen was so that she could weave a garland of flowers around its tiny baby horn buds herself. The maidservant followed with a pitcher of wine, replenishing all our goblets. All in all, we were busy enough eating to stop any conversation but compliments on the food.

Then Sam looked at his watch. "Great dinner, Rachel," he told his niece, "but I've got to get back. What about it?"

"What about what?" she asked.

"About helping poor Julie with some historical turning points he can use in a story?"

He hadn't listened to a word I'd said. I didn't have to say so, because Rachel was looking concerned. She said apologetically, "I don't know anything about those periods you were talking about—Publius Terminus and so on. My specialty is the immediate post-Augustan period, when the Senate came back to power."

"Fine," he said, pleased with himself and showing it. "That's as good a period as nay. Think how different things might be now if some little event then had gone in a different way. Say, if Augustus hadn't married the Lady Livia and adopted her son Drusus to succeed him." He turned to me, encouraging me to take fire from his spark of inspiration. "I'm sure you see the possibilities, Julie! Tell you what you should do. The night's young yet; take Rachel out dancing or something; have a few drinks; listen to her talk. What's wrong with that? You two young people ought to be having fun, anyway!"

That was definitely the most intelligent thing intelligent Sam had said in days.

So I thought, anyway, and Rachel was a good enough niece to heed her uncle's advice. Because I was a stranger in town, I had to let her pick the place. After the first couple she mentioned I realized that she was tactfully trying to spare my pocketbook. I couldn't allow that. After all, a night on the town with Rachel was probably cheaper, and anyway a whole lot more interesting, than the cost of an inn and meals.

We settled on a place right on the harborside, out toward the breakwater. It was a revolting night club on top of an inn built along the style of one of the old Pyramids. As the room slowly turned we saw the lights of the city of Alexandria, the shipping in the harbor, then the wide sea itself, its gentle waves reflecting starlight.

I was prepared to forget the whole idea of "alternate worlds," but Rachel was more dutiful than that. After the first dance, she said, "I think I can help you. There was something that happened in Drusus's reign—"

"Do we have to talk about that?" I asked, refilling her glass.

"But Uncle Sam said we should. I thought you wanted to try a new kind of sci-rom."

"No, that's your uncle that wants that. See, there's a bit of a problem here. It's true that editors are always begging for something new and different, but if you're dumb enough to try to give it to them they don't recognize it. When they ask for 'different,' what they mean is something right down the good old 'different' groove."

"I think," she informed me, with the certainty of an oracle and a lot less confusion of style, "that when my uncle has an idea, it's usually a good one." I didn't want to argue with her; I didn't even disagree, at least usually. I let her talk. "You see," she said, "my specialty is the transfer of power throughout early Roman history. What I'm studying right now is the Judaean Diaspora, after Drusus's reign. You know what happened then, I suppose?"

Actually, I did—hazily. "That was the year of the Judaean rebellion, wasn't it?"

She nodded. She looked very pretty when she nodded, her fair hair moving gracefully and her eyes sparkling. "You see, that was a great tragedy for the Judaeans, and, just as my uncle said, it needn't have happened. If Procurator Tiberius had lived, it wouldn't."

I coughed. "I'm not sure I know who Tiberius was," I said apologetically.

"He was the Procurator of Judaea, and a very good one. He was just and fair. He was the brother of the Emperor Drusus—the one my uncle was talking about, Livia's son, the adopted heir of Caesar Augustus. The one who restored the power of the Senate after Augustus had appropriated most of it for himself. Anyway, Tiberius was the best governor the Judaeans ever had, just as Drusus was the best emperor. Tiberius died just a year before the rebellion—ate some spoiled figs, they say, although it might have been his wife that did it—she was Julia, the daughter of Augustus by his first wife—"

I signaled distress. "I'm getting a little confused by all these names," I admitted.

"Well, the important one to remember is Tiberius, and you know who he was. If he had lived the rebellion probably wouldn't have happened. Then there wouldn't have been a Diaspora."

"I see," I said. "Would you like another dance?"

She frowned at me, then smiled. "Maybe that's not such an interesting subject—unless you're a Judaean, anyway," she said. "All right, let's dance."

That was the best idea yet. It gave me a chance to confirm with my fingers what my eyes, ears, and nose had already told me; this was a very attractive young woman. She had insisted on changing, but fortunately the new gown was as soft and clinging as the old, and the palms of my hands rejoiced in the tactile pleasures of her back and arm. I whispered, "I'm sorry if I sound stupid. I really don't know a whole lot about early history—you know, the first thousand years or so after the Founding of the City."

She didn't bother to point out that she did. She moved with me to the music, very enjoyably, then she straightened up. "I've got a different idea," she announced. "Let's go back to the booth." And she was already telling it to me as we left the dance floor: "Let's talk about your own ancestor, Julius Caesar. He conquered Egypt, right here in Alexandria. But suppose the Egyptians had defeated him instead, as they very nearly did?"

I was paying close attention now—obviously she had been interested enough in me to ask Sam some questions! "They couldn't have," I told her. "Julius never lost a war. Anyway—" I discovered to my surprise that I was beginning to take Sam's nutty idea seriously "—that would be a really hard one to write, wouldn't it? If the Legions had been defeated, it would have changed the whole world. Can you imagine a world that isn't Roman?"

She said sweetly, "No, but that's more your job than mine, isn't it?"

I shook my head. "It's too bizarre," I complained. "I couldn't make the readers believe it."

"You could try, Julius," she told me. "You see, there's an interesting possibility there. Drusus almost didn't live to become Emperor. He was severely wounded in a war in Gaul, while Augustus was still alive. Tiberius—you remember Tiberius—"

"Yes, yes, his brother. The one you like. The one he made Procurator of Judaea."

"That's the one. Well, Tiberius rode day and night to bring Drusus the best doctors in Rome. He almost didn't make it. They barely pulled Drusus through."

"Yes?" I said encouragingly. "And what then?"

She looked uncertain. "Well, I don't know what then."

I poured some more wine. "I guess I could figure out some kind of speculative idea," I said, ruminating. "Especially if you would help me with some of the details. I suppose Tiberius would have become Emperor instead of Drusus. You say he was a good man; so probably he would have done more or less what Drusus did—restore the power of the Senate, after Augustus and my revered great-great Julius between them had pretty nearly put it out of business—"

I stopped there, startled at my own words. It almost seemed that I was beginning to take Sam's crazy idea seriously!

On the other hand, that wasn't all bad. It also seemed that Rachel was beginning to take *me* seriously.

That was a good thought. It kept me cheerful through half a dozen more dances and at least another hour of history lessons from her pretty lips . . . right up until the time when, after we had gone back to her house, I tiptoed out of my room toward hers, and found her butler, Basilius, asleep on a rug, across her doorway, with a great, thick club by his side.

I didn't sleep well that night.

Partly it was glandular. My head knew that Rachel didn't want me creeping into her bedroom, or else she wouldn't have put the butler there in the way. But my glands weren't happy with that news. They had soaked up the smell and sight and feel of her, and they were complaining about being thwarted.

The worst part was waking up every hour or so to contemplate financial ruin.

Being poor wasn't so bad. Every writer has to learn how to be poor from time to time, between checks. It's an annoyance, but not a catastrophe. You don't get enslaved just for poverty.

But I had been running up some pretty big bills. And you do get enslaved for debt.

Chapter 4
The End of the Dream

The next morning I woke up late and grouchy and had to take a three-wheeler to the Hall of the Senate-Inferior.

It was slow going. As we approached, the traffic thickened even more. I could see the Legion forming for the ceremonial guard as the Pharaoh's procession approached to open the ceremonies. The driver wouldn't take me any closer than the outer square, and I had to wait there with all the tourists, while the Pharaoh dismounted from her royal litter.

There was a soft, pleasured noise from the crowd, halfway between a giggle and a sigh. That was the spectacle the tourists had come to see. They pressed against the sheathed swords of the Legionaries while the Pharaoh, head bare, robe trailing on the ground, advanced on the shrines outside the Senate building. She sacrificed reverently and unhurriedly to them, while the tourists flashed their cameras at her, and I began to worry about the time. What if she ecumenically decided to visit all fifty shrines? But after doing Isis, Amon-Ra, and Mother Nile, she went inside to declare the Congress open. The Legionaries relaxed. The tourists began to flow back to their buses, snapping pictures of themselves now, and I followed the Pharaoh inside.

She made a good, by which I mean short, opening address. The only thing wrong with it was that she was talking to mostly empty seats.

The Hall of the Alexandrian Senate-Inferior holds two thousand people. There weren't more than a hundred and fifty in it. Most of those were huddled in small groups in the aisles and at the back of the hall, and they were paying no attention at all to the Pharaoh. I think she saw that and shortened her speech. At one moment she was telling us how the scientific investigation of the outside universe was completely in accord with the ancient traditions of Egypt—with hardly anyone listening—and at the next her voice had stopped without warning and she was handing her orb and scepter to her attendants. She proceeded regally across the stage and out the wings.

The buzz of conversation hardly slackened. What they were talking about, of course, was the Olympians. Even when the Collegium-Presidor stepped forward and called for the first session to begin the hall didn't fill. At least most of the scattered groups of people in the room sat down—though still in clumps, and still doing a lot of whispering to each other.

Even the speakers didn't seem very interested in what they were saying. The first one was an honorary Presidor-Emeritus from the southern highlands of Egypt, and he gave us a review of everything we knew about the Olympians.

He read it as hurriedly as though he were dictating it to a scribe. It wasn't very interesting. The trouble, of course, was that his paper had been prepared days earlier, while the Olympian transmissions were still flooding in and no one had any thought they might be interrupted. It just didn't seem relevant any more.

What I like about going to science congresses isn't so much the actual papers the speakers deliver—I can get that sort of information better from the journals in the library. It isn't even the back-and-forth discussion that follows each paper, although that sometimes produces useful background bits. What I get the most out of is what I call "the sound of science"—the kind of shorthand language scientists use when they're talking to each other about their own specialties. So I usually sit somewhere at the back of the hall, with as much space around me as I can manage, my tablet in my lap and my stylus in my hand, writing down bits of dialogue and figuring how to put them into my next sci-rom.

There wasn't much of that today. There wasn't much discussion at all. One by one the speakers got up and read their papers, answered a couple of cursory questions with cursory replies and hurried off; and when each one finished he left and the audience got smaller, because, as I finally figured out, no one was there who wasn't obligated to be.

When boredom made me decide that I needed a glass of wine and quick snack more than I needed to sit there with my still blank tablet I found out there was hardly anyone even in the lounges. There was no familiar face. No one seemed to know where Sam was. And in the afternoon, the Presidor, bowing to the inevitable, announced that the remaining sessions would be postponed indefinitely.

The day was a total waste.

I had a lot more hopes for the night.

Rachel greeted me with the news that Sam had sent a message to say that he was detained and wouldn't make dinner.

"Did he say where he was?" She shook her head. "He's off with some of the other top people," I guessed. I told her about the collapse of the convention. Then I brightened. "At least let's go out for dinner, then," I offered.

Rachel firmly vetoed the idea. She was tactful enough not to mention money, although I was sure Sam had filled her in on my precarious financial state. "I like my own cook's food better than any restaurant," she told me. "We'll eat here. There won't be anything fancy tonight—just a simple meal for the two of us."

The best part of that was "the two of us." Basilius had arranged the couches in a sort of Vee, so that our heads were quite close together, with the low serving tables in easy reach between us. As soon as she lay down Rachel confessed, "I didn't get a lot of work done today. I couldn't get that idea of yours out of my head."

The idea was Sam's, actually, but I didn't see any reason to correct her. "I'm flattered," I told her. "I'm sorry I spoiled your work."

She shrugged and went on, "I did a little reading on the period, especially about an interesting minor figure who lived around then, a Judaean preacher named Jeshua of Nazareth. Did you ever hear of him? Well, most people haven't, but he had a lot of followers at one time. They called themselves Chrestians, and they were a very unruly bunch."

"I'm afraid I don't know much about Judaean history," I said. Which was true; but then I added, "But I'd really like to learn more." Which wasn't; or at least hadn't been until just then.

"Of course," Rachel said. No doubt to her it seemed quite natural that everyone in the world would wish to know more about the post-Augustan period. "Anyway, this Jeshua was on trial for sedition. He was condemned to death."

I blinked at her. "Not just to slavery?"

She shook her head. "They didn't just enslave criminals back then, they did physical things to them. Even executed them, sometimes in very barbarous ways. But Tiberius, as Proconsul, decided that the penalty was too extreme. So he commuted Jeshua's death sentence. He just had him whipped and let him go. A very good decision, I think. Otherwise he would have made him a martyr, and gods know what would have happened after that. As it was, the Christians just gradually waned away. . . . Basilius? You can bring the next course in now."

I watched with interest as Basilius complied. It turned out to be larks and olives! I approved, not simply for the fact that I liked the dish. The "simple meal" was actually a lot more elaborate than she had provided for the three of us the night before.

Things were looking up. I said, "Can you tell me something, Rachel? I think you're Judaean yourself, aren't you?"

"Of course."

"Well, I'm a little confused," I said. "I thought the Judaeans believed in the god Yahveh."

"Of course, Julie. We do."

"Yes, but—" I hesitated. I didn't want to mess up the way things were going, but I was curious. "But you say 'gods.' Isn't that, well, a contradiction?"

"Not at all," she told me, civilly enough. "Yahveh's commandments were brought down from a mountain-top by our great prophet, Moses, and they are very clear on the subject. One of them says, 'Thou shalt have no other gods before me.' Well, we don't, you see? Yahveh is our *first* god. There aren't any *before* him. It's all explained in the rabbinical writings.''

"And that's what you go by, the rabbinical writings?"

She looked thoughtful. "In a way. We're a very traditional people, Julie. Tradition is what we follow; the rabbinical writings simply explain the traditions.''

She had stopped eating. I stopped, too. Dreamily I reached out to caress her cheek.

She didn't pull away. She didn't respond, either. After a moment, she said, not looking at me, "For instance, there is a Judaean tradition that a woman is to be a virgin at the time of her marriage.''

My hand came away from her face by itself, without any conscious command from me. "Oh?''

"And the rabbinical writings more or less define the tradition, you see. They say that the head of the household is to stand guard at an unmarried daughter's bedroom for the first hour of each night; if there is no male head of the household, a trusted slave is to be appointed to the job.''

"I see," I said. "You've never been married, have you?"

"Not yet," said Rachel, beginning to eat again.

I hadn't ever been married, either, although, to be sure, I wasn't exactly a virgin. It wasn't that I had anything against marriage. It was only that the life of a sci-rom hack wasn't what you would call exactly financially stable, and also the fact that I hadn't ever come across the woman I wanted to spend my life with . . . or, to quote Rachel, "not yet.''

I tried to keep my mind off that subject. It was sure that if my finances had been precarious before, they were now close to catastrophic.

The next morning I wondered what to do with my day, but Rachel settled it for me. She was waiting for me in the atrium. "Sit down with me, Julie," she commanded, patting the bench beside her. "I was up late, thinking, and I think I've got something for you. Suppose this man Jeshua had been executed after all."

It wasn't exactly the greeting I had been hoping for, nor was it something I had given a moment's thought to, either. But I was glad enough to sit next to her in that pleasant little garden, with the gentled early sun shining down on us through the translucent shades. "Yes?" I said noncommittally, kissing her hand in greeting.

She took a moment before she took her hand back. "That idea opened some interesting possibilities, Julie. Jeshua would have been a martyr, you see. I can easily imagine that under those circumstances his Chrestian followers would have had a lot more staying power. They might even have grown to be really important. Judaea was always in one kind of turmoil or another around that time, anyway—there were all sorts of prophecies and rumors about messiahs and changes in society. The Chrestians might even have come to dominate all of Judaea."

I tried to be tactful. "There's nothing wrong with being proud of your ancestors, Rachel. But, really, what difference would that have made?" I obviously hadn't been tactful enough. She had turned to look at me with what looked like the beginning of a frown. I thought fast, and tried to cover myself: "On the other hand," I went on quickly, "suppose you expanded that idea beyond Judaea."

It turned into a real frown, but puzzled rather than angry. "What do you mean, beyond Judaea?"

"Well, suppose Jeshua's Chrestian-Judaean kind of—what would you call it? Philosophy? Religion?"

"A little of both, I'd say."

"Religious philosophy, then. Suppose it spread over most of the world, not just Judaea. That could be interesting."

"But, really, no such thing hap—"

"Rachel, Rachel," I said, covering her mouth with a fingertip affectionately, "we're saying *what if,* remember? Every sci-rom writer is entitled to one big lie. Let's say this is mine. Let's say that Chrestian-

Judaeanism became a world religion. Even Rome it-self succumbs. Maybe the City becomes the, what do you call it, the place for the Sanhedrin of the Chrestian-Judaeans. And then what happens?''

"You tell me," she said, half amused, half suspicious.

"Why, then," I said, flexing the imagination of the trained sci-rom writer, "it might develop like the kind of conditions you've been talking about in the old days in Judaea. Maybe the whole world would be splinter-ing into factions and sects, and then they fight."

"Fight *wars?*" she asked incredulously.

"Fight *big* wars. Why not? It happened in Judaea, didn't it? And then they might keep right on fighting them, all through historical times. After all, the only thing that's kept the world united for the past two thousand years has been the Pax Romana. Without that— Why, without that," I went on, talking faster and making mental notes to myself as I went along, "let's say that all the tribes of Europe turned into independent city-states. Like the Greeks, only bigger. And more powerful. And they fight, the Franks against the Vik Northmen against the Belgiae against the Kelts."

She was shaking her head. "People wouldn't be so silly, Julie," she complained.

"How do you know that? Anyway, this is a sci-rom, dear." I didn't pause to see if she reacted to the "dear." I went right on, but not failing to notice that she hadn't objected: "The people will be as silly as I want them to be—as long as I can make it plausible enough for the fans. But you haven't heard the best part of it. Let's say the Chrestian-Judaeans take their religion seriously. They don't do anything to go against the will of their god. What Yahveh said still goes, no matter what. Do you follow? That means they aren't at all interested in scientific discovery, for instance."

"No, stop right there!" she ordered, suddenly indig-nant. "Are you trying to say that we Judaeans aren't interested in science? That I'm not? Or my Uncle Sam? And we're certainly Judaeans."

"But you're not *Chrestian* Judaeans, sweet. There's

a big difference. Why? Because I say there is, Rachel, and I'm the one writing the story. So, let's see—" I paused for thought "—all right, let's say the Chrestians go through a long period of intellectual stagnation, and then—" I paused, not because I didn't know what was coming next, but to build the effect. "And then along come the Olympians!"

She gazed at me blankly. "Yes?" she asked, encouraging but vague.

"Don't you see it? And then this Chrestian-Judaean world, drowsing along in the middle of a pre-scientific dark age, no aircraft, no electronic broadcast, not even a printing press or a hovermachine—and it's suddenly thrown into contact with a super-technological civilization from outer space!" She was wrinkling her forehead at me, forgetting to eat, trying to understand what I was driving at. "It's terrible culture shock," I explained. "And not just for the people on Earth. Maybe the Olympians come to look us over, and they see that we're technologically backward and divided into warring nations and all that . . . and what do they do? Why, they turn right around and leave us! and . . . and that's the end of the book!"

She pursed her lips. "But maybe that's what they're doing now," she said cautiously.

"But not for that reason, certainly. See, this isn't *our* world I'm talking about. It's a *what if* world."

"It sounds a little far-fetched," she said.

I said happily, "That's where my skills come in. You don't understand sci-rom, sweetheart. It's the sci-rom writer's job to push an idea as far as it will go—to the absolute limit of credibility—to the point where if he took just one step more the whole thing would collapse into absurdity. Trust me, Rachel. I'll make them believe it."

She was still pursing her pretty lips, but this time I didn't wait for her to speak. I seized the bird of opportunity on the wing. I leaned toward her and kissed those lips, as I had been wanting to do for some time. Then I said, "I've got to get to a scribe, I want to get all this down before I forget it. I'll be back when I can be, and— And until then—well, here."

And I kissed her again, gently, firmly, and long; and it was quite clear early in the process that she was kissing me back.

Being next to a rental barracks had its advantages. I found a scribe to rent at a decent price, and the rental manager even let me borrow one of their conference rooms that night to dictate in. By daybreak I had the first two chapters and an outline of *Sidewise to a Chrestian World* down.

Once I get that far in a book, the rest is just work. The general idea is set, the characters have announced themselves to me, it's just a matter of closing my eyes for a moment to see what's going to be happening and then opening them to dictate to the scribes. In this case, the scribes, plural, because the first one wore out in a few more hours and I had to employ a second, and then a third.

I didn't sleep at all until it was all down. I think It was fifty-two straight hours, the longest I'd worked in one stretch in years. When it was all done I left it to be fair-copied. The rental agent agreed to get it down to the shipping offices by the harbor and dispatch it by fast air to Marcus in London.

Then at last I stumbled back to Rachel's house to sleep. I was surprised to find that it was still dark, an hour or more before sunrise.

Basilius let me in, looking startled as he studied my sunken eyes and unshaved face. "Let me sleep until I wake up," I ordered. There was a journal neatly folded beside my bed, but I didn't look at it. I lay down, turned over once, and was gone.

When I woke up at least twelve hours had passed. I had Basilius bring me something to eat, and shave me, and when I finally got out to the atrium it was nearly sundown and Rachel was waiting for me. I told her what I'd done, and she told me about the last message from the Olympians. "Last?" I objected. "How can you be sure it's the last?"

"Because they said so," she told me sadly. "They said they were breaking off communications."

"Oh," I said, thinking about that. "Poor Sam," I said, thinking about Flavius Samuelus. And she looked so doleful that I couldn't help myself, I took her in my arms.

Consolation turned to kissing, and when we had done quite a lot of that she leaned back, smiling at me.

I couldn't help what I said then, either. It startled me to hear the words come out of my mouth as I said, "Rachel, I wish we could get married."

She pulled back, looking at me with affection and a little surprised amusement. "Are you proposing to me?"

I was careful of my grammar. "That was a subjunctive, sweet. I said I *wished* we could get married."

"I understood that. What I want to know is whether you're asking me to grant your wish."

"No—well, hells, yes! But what I wish first is that I had the right to ask you. Sci-rom writers don't have the most solid financial situation, you know. The way you live here—"

"The way I live here," she said, "is paid for by the estate I inherited from my father. Getting married won't take it away."

"But that's your estate, my darling. I've been poor, but I've never been a parasite."

"You won't be a parasite," she said softly, and I realized that she was being careful about her grammar, too.

Which took a lot of will-power on my part. "Rachel," I said, "I should be hearing from my editor any time now. If this new kind of sci-rom catches on— If it's as popular as it might be—"

"Yes?" she prompted.

"Why," I said, "then maybe I can actually ask you. But I don't know that. Marcus probably has it by now, but I don't know if he's read it. And then I won't know his decision till I hear from him. And now, with

all the confusion about the Olympians, that might take
weeks—"

"Julie," she said, putting her finger over my lips,
"call him up."

The circuits were all busy, but I finally got through—
and, because it was well after lunch, Marcus was in his
office. More than that, he was quite sober. "Julie, you
bastard," he cried, sounding really furious, "where the
hells have you been hiding? I ought to have you
whipped."

But he hadn't said anything about getting the aediles after me. "Did you have a chance to read *Sidewise to a Chrestian World*?" I asked.

"The what? Oh, *that* thing. Nah. I haven't even
looked at it. I'll buy it, naturally," he said, "but what
I'm talking about is *An Ass's Olympiad*. The censors
won't stop it now, you know. In fact, all I want you to
do now is make the Olympian a little dumber, a little
nastier—you've got a biggie here, Julie! I think we can
get a broadcast out of it, even. So when can you get
back here to fix it up?"

"Why— Well, pretty soon, I guess, only I haven't
checked the hover timetable—"

"Hover, hell! You're coming back by fast plane—
we'll pick up the tab. And, oh, by the way, we're
doubling your advance. The payment will be in your
account this afternoon."

And ten minutes later, when I unsubjunctively proposed to Rachel, she quickly and unsubjunctively ac-
cepted; and the high-speed flight to London takes nine
hours, but I was grinning all the way.

Chapter 5
The Way It Is When You've Got It Made

To be a freelance writer is to live in a certain kind of
ease. Not very easeful financially, maybe, but in a lot
of other ways. You don't have to go to an office every
day, you get a lot of satisfaction out of seeing your

very own words being read on hovers and trains by total strangers. To be a potentially *bestselling* writer is a whole order of magnitude different. Marcus put me up in an inn right next to the publishing company's offices and stood over me while I turned my poor imaginary Olympian into the most doltish, feckless, unlikable being the universe had ever seen. The more I made the Olympian contemptibly comic, the more Marcus loved it. So did everyone else in the office; so did their affiliates in Kiev and Manahattan and Kalkut and half a dozen other cities all around the world, and he informed me proudly that they were publishing my book simultaneously in all of them. "We'll be the first ones out, Julie," he exulted. "It's going to be a mint! Money? Well, of course you can have more money— you're in the big time now!" And, yes, the broadcast studios were interested—interested enough to sign a contract even before I'd finished the revisions; and so were the journals, who came for interviews every minute that Marcus would let me off from correcting the proofs and posing for jacket photographs and speaking to their sales staff; and, all in all, I hardly had a chance to breathe until I was back on the high-speed aircraft to Alexandria and my bride.

Sam had agreed to give the bride away, and he met me at the airpad. He looked older and more tired, but resigned. As we drove to Rachel's house, where the wedding guests were already beginning to gather, I tried to cheer him up. I had plenty of joy myself; I wanted to share it. So I offered, "At least, now you can get back to your real work."

He looked at me strangely. "Writing sci-roms?" he asked.

"No, of course not! That's good enough for me, but you've still got your extra-solar probe to keep you busy."

"Julie," he said sadly, "where have you been lately? Didn't you see the last Olympian message?"

"Well, sure," I said, offended. "Everybody did, didn't they?" And then I thought for a moment, and, actually, it had been Rachel who had told me about it.

I'd never actually looked at a journal or a broadcast. "I guess I was pretty busy," I said lamely.

He looked sadder than ever. "Then maybe you don't know that they said they weren't only terminating all their own transmissions to us, they were terminating even our own probes."

"Oh, no, Sam! I would have heard if they'd stopped transmitting!"

He said patiently, "No, you wouldn't, because the data they were sending is still on its way to us. We've still got a few years coming in. But that's it. We're out of interstellar space, Julie. They don't want us there."

He broke off, peering out the window. "And that's the way it is," he said. "We're here, though, and you better get inside. Rachel's going to be tired of sitting under that canopy without you around."

The greatest thing of all about being a bestselling author, if you like traveling, is that when you fly around the world somebody else pays for the tickets. Marcus's publicity department fixed up the whole thing. Personal appearances, bookstore autographings, college lectures, broadcasts, publishers' meetings, receptions—we were kept busy for a solid month, and it made a hell of a fine honeymoon.

Of course any honeymoon would have been wonderful as long as Rachel was the bride, but without the publishers bankrolling us we might not have visited six of the seven continents on the way. (We didn't bother with Polaris Australis—nobody there but penguins.) And we took time for ourselves along the way, on beaches in Hindia and the islands of Han, in the wonderful shops of Manahattan and a dozen other cities of the Western Continents—we did it all.

When we got back to Alexandria the contractors had finished the remodeling of Rachel's villa—which, we had decided, would now be our winter home, though our next priority was going to be to find a place where we could spend the busy part of the year in London. Sam had moved back in and, with Basilius, greeted us formally as we came to the door.

"I thought you'd be in Rome," I told him, once we were settled and Rachel had gone to inspect what had been done with her baths.

"Not while I'm still trying to understand what went wrong," he said. "The research is going on right here; this is where we transmitted from."

I shrugged and took a sip of the Falernian wine Basilius had left for us. I held the goblet up critically: a little cloudy, I thought, and in the vat too long. And then I grinned at myself, because a few weeks earlier I would have been delighted at anything so costly. "But we know what went wrong," I told him reasonably. "They decided against us."

"Of course they did," he said, "but why? I've been trying to work out just what messages were being received when they broke off communications."

"Do you think we said something to offend them?"

He scratched the age spot on his bald head, staring at me, then he sighed. "What would *you* think, Julius?"

"Well, maybe so," I admitted. "What messages were they?"

"I'm not sure. It took a lot of digging. The Olympians, you know, acknowledged receipt of each message by repeating the last hundred and forty groups—"

"I didn't know."

"Well, they did. The last message they acknowledged was a history of Rome. Unfortunately, it was six hundred and fifty thousand words long."

"So you have to read the whole history?"

"Not just *read* it, Julie; we have to try to figure out what might have been in it that wasn't in any previous message. We've had two or three hundred researchers collating every previous message, and the only thing that was new was some of the social data. We were transmitting census figures—so many of equestrian rank, so many citizens, so many freedmen, so many slaves." He hesitated, and then said thoughtfully, "Paulus Magnus—I don't know if you know him, he's an Algonkan—pointed out that that was the first time we'd ever mentioned slavery."

I waited for him to go on. "Yes?" I said encouragingly.

He shrugged. "Nothing. Paulus is a slave himself, so naturally he's got it on his mind a lot."

"I don't quite see what that has to do with anything," I said. "Isn't there anything else?"

"Oh," he said, "there are a thousand theories. There was some health data, too, and some people think the Olympians might have suddenly got worried about some new microorganism killing them off. Or we weren't polite enough. Or maybe, who knows, there was some sort of power struggle among them, and the side that came out on top just didn't want any more new races in their community."

"And we don't know yet which it was?"

"It's worse than that, Julie, he told me somberly. "I don't think we ever will find out what it was that made them decide they didn't want to have anything to do with us;" and in that, too, Flavius Samuelus ben Samuelus was a very intelligent man. Because we never have.

AIN'T NOTHIN' BUT A HOUND DOG

By B. W. Clough

My first order from Mt. Adelaide was for the Modesty Blaise poster. I'm always telling Arnold I don't sell porn. It's *very* tasteful; you don't even see her face, just the leather bikini and the gun. Most people know not to send cash in the mail these days, and they put a name on their envelope. But I thought, hey, a nine-year-old boy with a fix on masterful women and no checking account. I mailed it off to "Mt. Adelaide, W. Va.," as requested, in a tube—not folded—and wished him luck hiding it from his mother.

In the mail-order comics business you send out catalogs the way other people put quarters in a slot machine—as a gamble. I included one, rolled-up small inside the poster tube. Ten days later I found a fat business-sized envelope in my box, among the utility bills and grocery store flyers. Curious, I opened it right away. Out flopped a *stack* of money, ten twenty-dollar bills! I have my box in a nice suburban post office, very quiet in the middle of the morning, and the only person in the lobby was an old lady in a pink designer jogging suit. She looked over the top of her sunglasses at my jeans and shaggy mustache, and I could hear her think, "Drug payoff."

I scooped up the bills, which were rubber-banded neatly together, and stuffed them into my pocket. My hands shook as I unfolded the order form. It was the one from my catalog, plus a typed page of additional orders. In the "MAIL TO:" block was nothing but MT. ADELAIDE, W. VA 24956. "Jackpot!" I whooped, making the postal clerk look up.

I hurried home, flipped the sign in the window from "Sorry, We're Closed;;' to "Hi, We're Open!" and read the order. I never have any walk-in trade until after noon, when the school kids start getting out. The order was what my sister calls eclectic—no comic books at all. There were *X-Men* bumper stickers and iron-on decals of Disney characters. And there was one of each and every button I listed, everything from "Aerobics Instructors Do It With Rhythm" to "Only Visiting This Planet" to "$E = MC^2$." Some of them I didn't even stock any more; most button freaks buy them at cons. And typed at the bottom of the second page was a note, unsigned: *"Please keep the change."*

Right then I decided Mt. Adelaide was my favorite customer. The total order came to less than one hundred-fifty dollars, and that was at list price. Even after packing and postage I'd turn a handsome profit. I spent the rest of the morning calling around for the buttons I didn't have, and packing the shipment into padded mailbags. And in the last one I put in my own note: "Write for an estimate on Special Orders."

Well, like Bogart says, that was the beginning of a beautiful friendship. Mt. Adelaide wrote back, saying he wanted more buttons. I picked them up at conventions and novelty stores. You never come to the end of buttons; they're always making more, all different. In half a year. Mt. Adelaide had probably the finest collection in West Virginia, and I only charged him triple the price I paid, too.

Then he expressed an interest in Deely-Bobbers. Sent me an old article from some magazine. Expense no object. You remember Deely-Bobbers, those plastic

headbands with shiny little balls on springs like antennae. They're dead out of fashion now, at least in
Herndon, but hey, West Virgina is kind of rural. I
went down to D.C., and when I found they were just
as dead there, to New York City. I came back with
Deely-Bobbers all right, hearts, globes, crescents, stars,
eyeballs, you name it. After I mailed them off I had
glitter, all colors, under my nails for weeks. But it was
worth it when I got those envelopes full of bills by
return mail.

By this time I had a handle on Mt. Adelaide. I
figured he was one of those reclusive millionaires, like
Howard Hughes. I mean, if you get out at *all* you can
buy liquor, right? He had an ongoing yen for Elvis
memorabilia, and every now and then I'd buy him a
commemorative liquor bottle. I'm not sure it's legal to
ship liquor over state lines, but I figured these were
Art. They weren't cheap, especially when you realize
no one'll ever twist off the King's head and sip the
bourbon, but Mt. Adelaide always paid up and asked
for more. So he didn't go to liquor stores, or cities (or
else he could have bought his *own* Deely-Bobbers on
the street about four years ago), or even shopping
centers. Where in America *can't* you find a stuffed
Garfield the Cat?

I learned what Mt. Adelaide liked. He didn't care
for books or magazines or records—Beatle bubble-
gum cards were good, but not Beatle albums. No *Star
Wars* or *GoBots* or *E.T.* or *Star Trek*, which is too bad
because there's a lot of goodies in that line. And
nothing really valuable. I suggested bidding for John
Lennon's psychedelic-painted Rolls Royce and got a
very nice no. In a word, he liked tacky. The really
tony art galleries go beyond just selling stuff, I understand. For good customers they'll buy on speculation,
guide their tastes. Well, for about three years I guided
Mt. Adelaide's, only in a different way of course. I
introduced him to new worlds: fuzzy dice to hang from
your rearview mirror, trolls with idiotic grins and long
fluffy acrylic hair, souvenir copies of major national
monuments. New *depths*, Josie would say.

When I went downtown to buy him a plastic Washington Monument I saw a parked car with a picture of Prince Charles stuck on the back window, with a big styrofoam hand mounted on a spring beside it so that he'd wave. They like them in England, but you don't see them much here. I waited for the driver to come back, and dickered with him for half an hour. I had to go to thirty-five dollars before he'd sell. When I got back to Herndon I mailed it off to Mt. Adelaide, with a bill for two hundred-fifty dollars. I figured I deserved it, for exerting initiative. He loved it, and wrote back urging me to keep an eye out for more Royal merchandise.

By then Mt. Adelaide was my meal ticket. The comic book store had never made much money. Now I could afford to hire an assistant to run it while I made a trip to Memphis. Mt. Adelaide knew the motherlode for Elvis stuff was at Graceland, and begged me to go. When he mailed me a few liquor boxes full of twenties I allowed he had a point. Crazy millionaires always use cash; they probably don't trust banks. In April I hired a truck and drove down in three days. The postcards and statuettes and paintings on black velvet and plush floppy-eared dogs that wind up to tinkle, "You Ain't Nothin' But a Hound Dog" were okay. But I was proudest of the guaranteed genuine ticket to Elvis's last concert, with a snip from one of his white silk scarves thrown in.

Once you drive across Tennessee it's a straight shot up I-81. I planned to find a Marriott outside Roanoke. Once I'd have camped out. Now I had plenty of twenties left, and more where they came from. But at Wytheville I saw a sign for I-77 North. "West Virginia," it said.

I got so excited I cut off an Audi and pulled out at the next exit. Why drive back to Herndon to mail the stuff back to West Virginia, when I could drop it off now? Mt. Adelaide might be so pleased with the delivery, he'd invite me in to his secluded mansion, which I imagined was about as big as William Randolph Hearst's. I always wanted to meet a reclusive millionaire.

* * *

So at a motor lodge outside Wytheville I bought a map of West Virginia. I unfolded it to the Cities and towns index and looked for Mt. Adelaide. Nothing! I had to scratch my head about that for a second. All I knew about my customer was his town and his Zip Code. Then I realized it might not even be the name of a town. If it was big estate, with a name, all you might need was a the Zip Code. I bet William Randolph Hearst got his mail even if all it had was "San Simeon" on it.

Next morning I swung by the Wytheville Post Office to consult their Zip Code Directory. Mail to 24956 is handled at Seneca, West Virginia. My map showed Seneca was a tiny town near the Virginia line, only about a hundred miles north of here—a nice morning's drive.

I didn't consider that a fully-loaded Ryder Rent-A-Truck is bad on mountains. The roads were secondary all the way, and the engine groaned up and down every hill. I got lost twice, the second time so bad I had to stop at an Arco to ask where I was, and it's a point of pride in our family not to do that. Trout Spring, the grease monkey said. When I asked about Mt. Adelaide he just stared.

I made Seneca late in the afternoon, just in time to catch the postmaster. His directions sent me out past Clover Lick onto a one-lane gravel road that snaked down the side of a mountain. I didn't like it one bit when the yellow hood of the truck nosed out over empty space on the curves. At the bottom of the hill the road quit. The clearing wasn't even gravel, just clay, with barely room for a vehicle to turn. In the deep green shadow under the loblolly pines was a big steel mailbox sitting on a cut log. It was labeled, "Mt. Adelaide."

Right then I should have quit too. But I said, "Hey, I wanted a recluse." Scuffing around among the pines I found a narrow trail winding deeper into the hills. As I followed it I told myself it wouldn't be safe to unload my cargo and just leave it. What if a bear came by and broke the Blue Hawaii bud vases?

By that time evening was coming on. It was pretty dark under the trees. I almost missed the cabin, tucked in a narrow side valley. The path turned so sharp toward it I overshot myself and got tangled in some brambles. The cabin was one of those do-it-yourself log homes, probably a single room inside—San Simeon, hah! No light showed from the single window. "I'm so full of dumbshit my eyes are brown," I cussed myself, but took a peek inside.

Of course it was too dark to see anything .I was turning away when a gleam of light flashed out. It was a harsh blue upward glare, like the kind a photocopy machine puts out if you forget to drop the cover before pumping in your coin. I recognized the toy standing on the glass right away—the Rambo posable action figure I sent in my last order. As the light poured up, the doll began to get shorter. Stallone's legs began to sink through the glass, then the overmuscled torso and arms (complete with automatic weapon), and finally the sweatbanded head went under. The doll was gone, and the blue light went out.

I stood there with my jaw hanging down to my chest, just stood there while all these sensible thoughts tapped on my skull trying to get in—thoughts like, it's none of my business what the customer does with his stuff, and, it's a hologram machine, whatever a hologram is, and, Rambo's just a fad so I wouldn't invest in much Rambo junk. Before any of them could get in the light surged up again, blue and fierce. On the glass was the bubble-packet and cardboard tab that Rambo had come packaged in, when I bought him at Toys-R-Us. And just above, the hand that had laid it there was moving away.

Now I've seen the *Star Wars* movies, and *E.T.*, and I have a storeful of comics about Bizarro and the Alien Legion and Mutant Teenage Ninja Turtles—I read them, too. So why was I so stunned, when the hand was like a three-armed starfish? Sort of crusty all over, but totally flexible, boneless. I couldn't make out the color, the blue light made everything blue. No wonder he didn't buy *Star Wars* stuff!

I hightailed out of there so fast, it's a wonder the alien didn't come out to investigate the noise. I threw myself into the truck. I gunned up that hill in second gear, the engine screaming for mercy, the Elvis doo-dads lurching back and forth in back as I wrenched the wheel around the curves. To get back to I-81 I had to go through Minnehaha Springs and Mountain Grove and Staunton, all twisty secondary roads, but at least they were paved. It's a miracle I didn't kill myself ten times over. I was sweating bullets until I got onto the interstate a steady sixty-five miles per hour heading north. Then I mopped my forehead and tried to relax, knowing it would take all night to drive home. I turned on the radio, and it gave a sputter and began to whine, *"Almost heaven, West Virginia, Blue Ridge Mountains—"*

I twisted the volume knob so hard it came off in my hand.

When I pulled up in front of the store I was nearly dead. The truck didn't sound so good either—as I cut the engine it gave a soggy thump, like a horse rolling over dead. It was ten in the morning, but the driveway was blocked by a white station wagon. I sat slumped at the wheel, too shot to even lean on the horn. The front door opened and the twins boiled out of the store. "Hey, it's Unca Tully!" "Didja read what's been happening to Batman, Unca Tully, isn't it neat with Two-Face—" "Didja bring back more comics, Unca Tully?"

Josie followed them out, yelling, "Hush up!" Then in a more civilized voice she said, "Coffee's on the stove, Tully. How're you doing these days?"

"Coffee, thank God!" I'm a year older than Josie, but my sister's always been more sane and normal and supportive and *mature.* I used to resent it sometimes but now mature and normal sounded wonderful. We went in through the store, where Arnold had already taped a towel over the Frazetta poster above the cash register, and upstairs to the kitchen. "What are you doing here, Josie?"

She took a mug down from the cupboard. "I told you we'd be here over spring break, Tully. Here you are—be careful, it's hot. Your assistant let us in. I tried to keep the twins from trashing your stock."

"It's okay." I'm real good friends with Becca and Mikey. Six-year-olds have naturally juvenile minds so we have a lot in common. Besides, they like comics. The coffee was like a sip of sanity. "How long you staying?"

"A week." She frowned, cocking an ear at the sound of Mikey strangling Becca downstairs. "Honey, Tully's back!"

Arnold came out of the bathroom, newly-shaven and pink in the face. He shook my hand solemnly. "Good of you to let us camp on you like this, Tull. Where've you been? Have you had breakfast?"

No way I could tell them I'd been playing culture-vulture to a Martian or something. "Oh, picking up some stock," I lied weakly. "Food sounds great."

Arnold put some eggs to fry, and began washing dishes. He's a househusband, I guess you'd call it. Josie brings home the bacon by working on computers for the Navy. I always tell him Jerry Falwell wouldn't approve. "We're going downtown to tour the White House today," Josie was saying. "Will you join us?"

All I wanted was sleep. After breakfast my house-guests took themselves off, and I crashed. But the minute my body was rested I woke up again. I'd seen *E.T.*—the movie I mean—and *Close Encounters*, too. I knew I had to do something. Suppose Elvis Presley was somehow the foothold for the invasion of Earth? But I couldn't think what—call the cops, the FBI? Maybe it's a crime to sell stuff to aliens, I thought. Even if it was nothing but Gumby and Rambo. I bet they'd throw the book at me. And what was I going to do with the truck's load?

I felt so shook, I went downstairs and skimmed a couple of issues of Action Comics, to see how Super-man might handle it. And once I was in the store I felt better. The twins *had* messed up the shelves. While my helper rang up customers I sorted all the issues of *Spiderman* back into order. I might have to live off the store's profits again real soon. I took the towel down off the Frazetta, too. You might say Arnold had a real broad definition of porn.

Next day we all went downtown to the Air and Space Museum. The cherry blossoms were in bloom, and the Mall was jammed. Josie and the twins got off at the Museum while Arnold and I drove around looking for a parking space. We finally found one on the other side of Constitution Avenue. After Arnold locked all the doors and checked his pocket twice for the keys I said, "Let's cut through the National Gallery. There's a moving sidewalk in the underpass between the buildings."

Arnold sighed. The twins have aged him. "When are you going to grow up, Tully? Find a nice girl, settle down?"

I knew he was worried I might be gay. "I'm waiting for the right girl, Arnie," I said earnestly. "You know that God has an ideal mate for every one of us. It'd be a shame if I jumped the gun and missed her." That was from *Pat Robertson Answers Two Hundred of Life's Most Probing Questions*, which Arnold gave me last Christmas. I'd read it carefully so that when he nagged me I could quote it. Of course Arnold had read it too, so he just mumbled about going to church, which I hardly ever do.

We went into the East Wing and gaped up at the Calder mobile. "Only in America," Arnold said. He doesn't really approve of abstract art. Then when we went downstairs and over the moving sidewalk I had to wait while he bought a Matisse poster. It was one of the cut-out ones, with bright dancing figures and flowers. "Now that's beautiful," he told me, as we waited to pay, and I agreed. It was beautiful, the way April, and the cherry blossoms, and the happy dirty faces of the twins were beautiful.

All of a sudden I thought about the Modesty Blaise,

and was ashamed. Here this alien wanted samples of human culture for a museum on Alpha Centauri, and I was exploiting his ignorance, selling him kitsch. I remembered reading about that space probe, where they put in recordings of whale songs and Bach. That's the sort of thing Earth should be represented by. "Wait a minute, Arnie," I said, and grabbed a fat glossy art book at random. "Buy this too, I'll pay you back outside." He looked at me funny—it cost $60—but didn't say anything.

We went through the West Building and out into the sunshine, Arnold holding his poster and me holding the book in a paper bag. The walks were crowded with tourists, joggers, strollers, and people lined up for ice cream. A teenaged girl with long black hair planted herself in front of us and said, "Hi, are you saved?"

With grave pride Arnold said, "Yes, I am, but my brother here isn't."

I tried to think of some retort from Pat Robertson, but could only say, "But, hey, Arnie!" The girl thrust a pocket New Testament at me, chattering like a bluejay. I took it and marched off, letting Arnold catch up as best he could.

Usually I love the Air and Space Museum, but this time I couldn't enjoy it. An even more depressing idea had hit me. Should I try to *convert* this alien? You see, I'd been rolled in enough gospel to know the only way to salvation. You can figure that everyone on this planet has had a Bible pushed at them, one time or another. But not Mt. Adelaide. And I realized that if I didn't do it, no one would. He'd be damned. And maybe his whole planet, his whole galaxy, with him. Maybe God was counting on me—watching me to see if I made the right decision.

Then, as if the idea of a celestial Peeping Tom set me off, I saw there was a whole slew of *religious* stuff I could send. Plastic Jesuses with magnetic bases that let them stand on your dashboard, white plaster garden statues of the Blessed Virgin Mary, stick-on window plaques with rainbows and doves and scriptural texts in curly letters—I could keep Mt. Adelaide happy for years! Thinking about God up there, watching me think all this, made my head spin.

The kids were tired and cranky on the way home. I sat between them in the back seat and helped Mikey page through *All About Comets*. Then, prying in my bag, Becca whined. "It's my turn now, Unca Tully, read me this."

When I took the book out I found I'd bought *Monet Retrospective*. We looked at photographs of paintings of shimmery water-lilies for a while. Then, bored, Becca began to whimper and kick the seat again. "I wanna drink. I wanna get out. I wanna comic book!"

Mikey joined in the chant, "I wanna comic book!" That's the worst part about twins, the way they reinforce each other.

For two cents I would have got out of the car myself. But Josie, wonderful Josie, fumbled under the front seat and produced *The Mighty Thor*—not one but two copies! "I'm sorry to steal your comics, Tully," she said in the sudden quiet. "They were a last resort. I'll pay you for these, I promise."

"No, it's okay." The peace was worth it. I can see how kids get spoiled.

Arnold had been driving and following the whole exchange in the rearview mirror. "From Monet to Thor," he snorted.

Josie gave him a be-polite-now nudge. "Lots of people read comic books, dear," she said. "Who's to say, if they aren't as legitimate an expression as painting?"

I sat up. "You know, I never thought of that."

Arnold gave me another of those funny looks in the mirror and said, warningly, "You read the chapter in Pat Robertson about alcohol and drugs, Tully?"

I didn't answer. What I saw was that an ET smart enough to hide out in the boonies and shop by mail was smart enough to know a Calder from a pair of fuzzy dice. He was deliberately, systematically *studying* this aspect of people—the Deely-Bobber factor, whatever it is that makes us produce wacko items. A nonhuman would learn more from that than by studying, say, our NORAD defenses. I bet most people wouldn't recognize a cruise missile if it fell on them, though Josie would. But Deely-Bobbers have a *deep* appeal.

And it wasn't "only in America," either. The entire human race has this streak of nuttiness. Look at the waving Prince Charles ornament. And I figured that folks who know us, who *want* to know us that deeply, are okay.

As soon as the station wagon stopped in the driveway I jumped out and ran inside to the telephone. The Ryder people promised to tune up the engine first thing tomorrow if I nursed the truck to their garage. My helper had got the mail. On top of the stack was an envelope from West Virginia. Inside was the unsigned typewritten note: "Am interested in more Royal souvenirs, esp. a set of cups in the shape of Prince Charles and Lady Diana's heads. Would you be able to visit Britain?"

"What is it, Unca Tully?" Mikey asked, hugging my leg.

Josie was right behind, so I said, "A confirmation." I went out and threw the letter on the front seat of the truck, to answer in person. I brought the Bible and *Monet* too. Hey, you never know. Then I opened up the back. If I was going to drive back down those roads again, the load should be packed better.

Tagging along, the twins immediately began to fight over the stuffed hound dog. "Hey! Don't destroy that—this is how to play with it." I wound up the key and set the dog on the tailgate. The kids watched, owl-eyed, as I sang along with the music-box. They were able to warble along too, by the second verse: "They said you was high-class; well that was just a lie. . . ."

Adrift Among the Ghosts

By Jack L. Chalker

"It's the Jack Benny Program, with Jack's very special guest Lucille Ball . . ."

I flip on the autolock mechanism while the computer scans to see if this is one on my quota.

Oh, Donnn . . .

Alas for me, it is not, and the scan is automatically resumed. I tell the command module to shift to the next available signal, which might be the next thing in line or something completely different.

The lock light goes on, and I instruct my systems management computer to stick it on for evaluation. I'm getting worried about the manager. It shouldn't have locked on to the Lucille Ball guesting on Benny's program at all; even though she was a guest several times on the program, the voiceprints should have locked this one out. If it is defective . . . No! I just cannot afford to have to go through all that random stuff again and again to find a new and previously unrecorded piece. Gods of Archus, please don't let the edit system break down now!

This new one is *Action in the Afternoon*, a live

western serial done in Philadelphia, of all places. I know the country well, and I know the absurdity of a western coming from that city at all in any time and context. I don't need this one, but I instruct the manager to stay on it anyway. We are on NBC at the right period and I've had a number of malfunctions in riding the beam at this time. I am missing at least four *Atom Squad* episodes and countless *Howdy Doodys*, and it is worth the chance. Why not? There's not much else to do out here anyway.

That, and the fact that almost all of this project can be automated, is the second greatest problem with this assignment—this *sentence*, if truth be told. None of us who ride the beams are really anything more, or less, than politically connected criminals, although there's nothing on our records back home; we're considered "employees" and technically paid a wage. The money is hardly a consideration—lower civil service pay, only a token to make it look all nice and proper, as if we could spend it, anyway—but the deal is one that is difficult for someone in my position to turn down. I did, after all, kill four people. I should have been vaporized; the trial lasted barely ten minutes, and the evidence was not in dispute considering that they had the club so well monitored, they had recordings of the very act. How I wish I had known that, even guessed that they were so close on my heels! The four could have been eliminated one by one under perfect conditions. It just seemed so much more *efficient* to take them all out at once, as they were plotting my own demise.

Death. What did I know of death, or even crime? I sit and I watch these ancient recordings—how can I help but watch?—and I see experts. I listen to their newscasts and watch their documentary histories, and I wonder how such an incredibly gentle society as ours could have bred even such a rank amateur as myself—and those even ranker people in the club.

Computers do a lot for us, of course. It is a computer that maneuvers this ship with a precision no person could hope to match, and it's a computer that prepares my meals, records these ramblings, keeps me healthy. It was a computer that maintained the surveillance on the club, a computer that tried me, another which prosecuted me, yet another that defended me, and still another that sentenced me. And, but for one thing, this whole operation could be done by computer.

I suppose it might be boiled down to taste, although that's not quite the right word. I am the supervisor. I oversee the operations, check on what is going on, act as something of a repairman or even reprogrammer when the systems inevitably fail, and I separate the relevant from the irrelevant in terms of beam content. We want everything, of course, eventually—this sort of opportunity was only discovered by the merest of chances and might never come again to us or to any other civilization out here among the stars—but the beams keep going on, forcing us to pick and choose.

We may be the only other civilization to arise in this galaxy, although probably not. We will almost certainly be the only ones using reception devices that can translate this particular series of signals broadcast so long ago and from so far away, and probably the only ones who can see and hear the transmissions much the same as those who made these broadcasts did.

We are not at all like them, of course, or so we tell ourselves, and so even they would have believed. Certainly not physically. That took a lot of getting adjusted to at the start; they seemed like some strange, surreal creatures more suited to art or animation than the sort of beings you can think of as being live and real and sentient and even technologically proficient. Once, in a biology course at university, I was assured by a professor who was the greatest expert on everything that it was impossible for a bipedal lifeform to develop a complex technology, and that the fine manipulation of complex tools required a minimum of eighteen tentacles. I often wonder what that fellow is saying now, as these transmissions are brought back and analyzed. It pleases me to think of those pompous asses who seemed so powerful and self-assured to us helpless students to now be suddenly and irrevocably placed in the same position as some ancient was ten thousand years ago when it was proved that the world was indeed round and not flat.

And yet, as strange as their shape is, and how bizarre their architecture, one quickly comes to accept and even understand these alien creatures on the screen. It is far more fascinating to me to discover just how similar we are if you ignore the physical differences. We both see optically and hear acoustically. We both have two sexes—don't I know *that!*—and much of what we share in social structures and behavior seems to grow right out of that. We invented totally different machines, some in totally different ways, to do exactly the same things.

Our social structures are somewhat different, but we still have state education of the young, mass entertainment, vehicles of both individual and mass locomotion, and we both squandered a great deal of natural resources in our growth and fouled up our own planets with our wastes.

In a sense, they seem very much like us, although speeded up. The social forces that seemed to constantly rip and tear at them are vastly slowed in our own history, although, alas, violence seems to be necessary to shake things up and prevent stagnancy. They did in a thousand years what it took us ten thousand to accomplish, but they did it at the expense of developing technologically at a rate so accelerated that they were still socially and emotionally closer to their ancient ancestors when they developed the means of total annihilation.

I have no trouble with their dramas; I am, however, less comfortable with their jokes and humor. The sophisticated humor is no problem, and I now understand them well enough that their domestic situations correlate with those with which I am familiar even though it is not, of course, the same at all. I cannot, however, understand why slipping on a floor and sprawling is humorous to them, or why some of their undergarments seem filled with hilarity. This should not bother me; they are in many ways nothing like us, but still, it does. I cannot quite understand why it does, but it matters very much.

When you're out here, alone, riding the beam and adrift with the ghosts, they're the only real company you have. You get to know them, even love them, because they are at once so alien and remote and at the same time so similar. They are my family. For almost twenty years they have been the only companionship I have had.

It's not easy to ride the beams, even at the speeds we can travel. It is true that the old television signals traveled in a straight line into infinity—although they have become incredibly weak at this point, and it's often been theorized that our own signals might be intercepted some day in the same way—but it's not really a straight line. Planets rotate and they also revolve; suns move in their own orbits around the galactic center. Perhaps a quarter to a third of all they broadcast is lost because they were on the wrong side of their sun, or there was something else in the way of the beam. More is simply impossible to recover for other technical reasons, for the signals are not immune to the great forces of the universe, and the signal strengths we are talking about are on the equivalent of hearing a single speck of dust fall to a floor from the next solar system. Worse, they did not have a single standard. To get the British and affiliate nations' signals one must adjust for PAL; for French and Italian and many others it's SECAM, and others like the Soviet Union and Australia use hybrids. We missed a lot, too, because of directed uplinks, limited transmissions that did not escape, and cable.

But that's why I'm here, of course, with my quota. Eight hundred perfect hours of transmission. It sounded so simple, particularly when you think that the computer can just ride the beam and then match its swing and let the stuff flow in. It's not that easy. An entire program is a rarity. It often takes many passes, possible only because the same signals were sent many times and have arrived here by many different routes simply because of those forces that can bend light and split stellar images in two. Even then, we jump in and out of null-space with regularity, trying to keep ahead of them while still maintaining enough power to get the ship and the transmissions home.

Eight hundred hours of new programming. It sounded like the easiest thing in the world, even considering all that. Compared to being vaporized, it was a wonderful offer; compared to life at hard labor it was even more so.

I didn't know about the traps, though. All the little traps, and the big one they don't tell you about because it's still classified top secret. One is that word *new*, of course. I have picked up tens of thousands of hours, but we are rarely updated on what the others have also sent in until we break for transmission and reception. And I have fragments of a great many programs I am still trying to track down, which is why I'm riding this particular beam now, and why I am so afraid that the computer is not remembering what it already has in its files. If I have to reprogram it, I will lose its knowledge to date—not the programs of course, but the tagged records—and have to wait a very long time until it is restored to its previous selectivity. I sometimes suspect that they have deliberately built bugs into this program to cause this and keep me out here. I find it frightening, at least in part because I am not skilled enough to actually rewrite the master program, simply to repair and restore it.

I wonder about malice. Six billion people on my own world alone, one of many we inhabit, and the year I committed my crime there were but a hundred and three premeditated murders. We are a gentler sort. Perhaps we react in less gentle ways. I sit and watch *their* programs and there seem to be four premeditated murders an hour just in their entertainment, and dozens in a single big city newscast. Some of these murderers are executed, most are imprisoned, and a great many walk out of those prisons after a while for crimes far greater and with far less justification than my own. I can't see the worst of their societies offering a living trip to Hell as an alternative, but mine is a gentler race, and a more vindictive one.

And so you sit, and you make the jumps, and sit some more, and you watch and you come to love those people. I know who did it in every Perry Mason, and I've followed Superman in all his incarnations. I've suffered with them their long-ago agonies of war and terrorism and disease and other tragedies, and I have rejoiced with them their victories, discoveries, and conquests. I have come to like and even appreciate their extremely bizarre music and art forms; the personalities I see are like old friends, where in the beginning they all looked alike to me.

Kings and queens and presidents and dictators—they are as much a part of me as my own history, my local counselor and legates. They are more than that; they are all there is of me and my universe outside of the confines of this lousy little ship. They are what is real to me. I cannot find a frame of reference that is not of their reality rather than my own. It troubles me. When one lives, eats, sleeps, breathes an alien reality with no contact or reference to one's own, it becomes difficult to differentiate the real from the unreal, the alien from the familiar.

I was always a collector with eclectic tastes, and that's why they chose me for the beams. A collector, yes; not a quivering, smelly thing locked inside a soulless cage on a ride through Hell with ghosts for companions. The ghosts are truly that and don't mind at all while I must ride and watch and forbear and somehow *survive*. But they will not break me; no, they will not do that. My ghosts protect me, too, and are my salvation. Yet, when we shift, when there's no beam to ride and we're in search mode, there is no one here, no one but me and my memories. The ghosts then are inside my head, and I find them curiously intermingled, as if the alien ghosts of ancient fantasy are more real than the actuality of the world I was forced to leave behind so very long ago.

What was it like to actually breathe free-flowing natural air, to let wind and water bear on the sensory nodes, to know *openness* first hand, and not through some monitor's sterile window looking in on a landsape that was not my own, that I had never known or experienced or even imagined? To sit upon my own estate whose rolling blue moss-covered hills were carefully arranged with crimson *byuap* topiary by master artisans!

Oh, yes, I had an estate. Only the leader classes go to Hell alive; the *krowl* and *duber* and *nimbiat*, being of lesser gene pools, are allowed to be vaporized. We *Madur* are supposed to be better than that, or so the geneticists claim. Bred to be the elite. When one of us goes awry it threatens the whole system. Examples must be made.

How many times have I thought of it all, gone over every second in my mind? How difficult, now, living these twenty years among alien ghosts, to separate the two, as fact and fancy blend effortlessly if incongruously in my mind. I have gone mad in order to remain sane.

I was in my spa being bathed with honey water and watching a recently retrieved episode of *The A Team* when he arrived. None below our class and a few within it were permitted to see such things; I, however, as a ranking physician, had gained the first private access on the excuse of seeing if exposure to such alien thought and vision might be detrimental to one's mind. Idiotic, of course.

I was expecting him, but not this soon. He was a *duber*, a service-class individual, bred to be superb in a specific talent or occupation, but he had much impudence and no right to interrupt me. He should have waited, but impudence was also an essential part of his makeup. He stopped and stared in horror at the screen where two trucks and three jeeps blew up as they ran over some cleverly planted mines. He shuddered and averted his eyes. It took little in the way of experimentation to understand that no *duber* was strong enough to tolerate even short-term exposure. The masses were far too gentle and passive to understand it. The newcomer did not look back again or refer to the scenes on the screen, and seemed relieved when I muted the sound. He got straight to the point.

"She's going to leave you, sir, that's for sure," said *Richard Diamond, Private Eye.* *"She's a bit frightened of you, and somewhat intimidated, but she's making arrangements with a disreputable bunch to hide her and spirit her away."*

I was furious at this, even though I suspected it all and had hired the *duber* only to see how she thought she was going to manage it. "How do they intend to do it while remaining beyond my reach?"

"A club in the city. The owner there will do almost anything for a price, and he's pretty good at it. Stick her in a safe house in a low neighborhood for a few days, then to Grand Central Station with phony ID, maybe disguised as a worker. Hop a spaceship and get off when it looks promising. Pardon me, but a girl that looks like she does won't have any trouble in a strange place for long."

"I'm well aware of that. It's why I cannot allow it, even if it was not also degrading to her class."

"But why fight it? She's only doing this with small amounts that aren't even petty cash to you. You don't love her. Why not just let her go?"

I raised myself up on all my tentacles and almost grabbed the man. "Because I am a *collector*, something you would not understand. I collect, I do not give away any part of my collection. I want the names of these persons involved in this and the address of the club. I shall attend to this personally."

"But, sir—someone in your position—you can't go there yourself! Alone, unprotected—it simply isn't done!" *Holmes objected.*

I came out of the spa and headed for the main house. "In affairs of business and politics this is true, but this is a personal matter, and I cannot allow others to be involved beyond you. Give me the information and you are discharged." *Sooner or later, everybody goes to Rick's . . .*

*   *   *

It was both not as bad and worse than I had imagined. The place itself looked respectable and catered to the middle classes, and inside it even had the proper moss pits and sweetly scented atmosphere of *albis* root, but the patrons did not wear their class outwardly nor have much inwardly, either.

Peter Lorre was at the bar, fetching drinks for a table seating Wallace Beery, Preston Foster, and Mr. T. The rest of the mob was more common, character actors, mostly, although here and there were potentially great enemies like Charles Middleton and Roy Barcroft. I was not in fear. In a sense, I had them cold, since they could not run, could not hide, from my power and influence should they attempt violence against me and I live—and if I died they would be automatically hunted down by the Special Police.

I could tell they were all a bit awed and unnerved that someone born with the golden headplate would even enter their miserable club, but they were a tough lot whose business was getting around the likes of me and the rule of law and society which I represented.

"Yes, sir, yes, sir, what'll it be?" asked Barton MacLaine from behind the bar.

"I doubt you would serve anything of the quality I require in this establishment," I responded icily. I was aware of a female edging near, and I rotated an eye socket on her.

"Any kind of quality you want is available at the Long Branch," Miss Kitty assured me. *"We serve all classes here and fill their needs no matter what they might be."*

I'll bet, I thought but didn't say. Drugs, drink, perversion—that was their stock in trade. I knew this place now, and also understood that I was not the first golden headplate to enter but only the latest. That was how they got hold of you, their evil then perverting and subverting the system. I loathed them all. They were less than people, lower than *nimbiats* at their worst, and yet difficult to assail, for they held no higher opinion of themselves than I held of them.

"You are the owner of this establishment, Madam?"

"I'm the manager, and I ain't no madam. I can take care of anything you might want."

"I wish to see the owner. I have personal business to discuss with that individual alone."

She looked around uncertainly, and Lorre glanced up from his cards and gave her a nod and a head nudge. "Okay, buddy, follow me. Just so happens the owner's in back now . . ."

I could see the crowd stiffen, although the tension wasn't so much aimed at preventing me from doing anything as the instinctual obligation of even these low-lifes to protect their boss. I followed her back to a private room. The owner looked up and offered me a place. It was clear that he had overheard everything and knew just who I was and why I was there, even though he remained impassive.

"Come, come, sir. No need to be surly here with your lessers. It is beneath you," Sidney Greenstreet oozed in dangerous mock friendliness. He wore a helmet over his plate making his class impossible to distinguish, but there would be only one reason for doing so: under that idiotic cover the coloration had to be golden. Even his dialect was proper *Madur*, although with a roughened edge. From offworld, certainly, but also certainly one of us gone bad.

"I see no reason to be more than minimally civil," I responded. "You are plotting to take something from me that belongs to me. I am here to see that it doesn't happen."

"Come, come, sir! I haven't the faintest idea what you are talking about."

"I will not play games. No matter what she has paid you, I will triple it in untraceable precious metals and gems if you take her money and then deliver her back to me. Don't deny that you are going to do it, or that you do not know what I am talking about. You have overstepped your fertilizer pits this time. I will have this place surrounded and everyone here, including you, subjected to Thought Probes. I doubt if any of you will walk freely away after that."

J.R. gave that evil chuckle of his. "You have that

power, I admit," he drawled with some amusement in his voice, *"but you have not invoked it as yet, and by the time you can do so, this place will be a tabernacle for retired nuns. You think I never expected a visit from you? I spotted that tinhorn, upper-crust private eye from a mile away. I won't stop it because I've already done it. She's gone. Out of your life, off this planet, and buried so deep you'll never find her."* And he laughed.

I rose on all eight tentacles, my blood pressure rising so high, my entire exoskeleton glowed green. Off the planet before I had even *begun?* "Who *dares* such impudency with a pod of the Imperial Regency?" I demanded. "I am physician to the Center!"

"I know who and what you are," responded the one-armed man. *"But it means nothing to me, nor does your money. Seven times I have gone to the auction pits at Quimera in lust after some unique work of beauty and genius, and seven times you have bested me not with mere money but with influence and outright fraud. The chance to humiliate you, to take from you something that is uniquely yours, was literally thrown in my path, begging to be stolen and with no law to prevent it. Discovering she was impregnated by you only added fine sauce. I have cost you your wife and children, Doctor, and I am proud of it! Seven times I have lost to you, but you—you have never lost at all. Not until now. I wanted you to know how it feels to lose."*

I stared at him. "Gomesh! You are Gomesh, Imperator Comptroller of the Litidal! I know you now!" It was worse than that. He was of equal rank and position and senior in age. I could shut down his foul club, which was obviously used in his collecting, but I could not touch him—legally or through my influence. To even press such a case against him would only subject me to embarrassment and humiliation.

And yet, he was correct. Up until that time I had never lost, and I could not accept it now. He saw my tentacles curl and uncurl and one of my eyes focus on a wooden ornament; a heavy, wooden ornament.

"Don't be ridiculous," snarled Don Corleone. *"My*

men are everywhere and you are not in your element here, nor is this some alien horror chamber like the room in which you watch those intercepted grotesqueries. You are in an untenable position, and I intend to enjoy it."

Nobody talks that way to Charles Bronson!

I don't even remember the next minute or so very well, just a roaring blur, but something snapped inside me that I did not even suspect could ever go out of control. Tentacles snapped out, taking him completely by surprise, flipping him over with a strength I had never had before or since, while other tentacles reached for things in his compartment—bottles, pieces of furniture; a piece of rope that supported his privacy curtain became a whip in my grasp.

Naturally, this brought his bodyguard of thugs on the run. Gomesh was larger and heavier than I, yet somehow I managed to pick him up and actually throw him right over my head and into the bodyguards. Swiveling, one of the guards dropped an illegal stun gun. I spotted it with one eye and reached it before they could even move. I had never fired such a weapon before, but at that range a blind person could have committed a massacre, and this I did. I know that I did so. Later they showed me the recordings.

When it was over, Gomesh and three of his henchmen were dead, and all of sudden, my rage simply fled me and I just remained there staring at the carnage. I offered no resistance when the Special Police arrived and led me away.

The trial was conducted very quickly with me alone in my cell. The defense computer discussed my options, which were few, and then the evidence was shown and the State made its verdict demands.

"Insanity," I said to my attorney. Even I was sickened and stunned watching the recording of the killings. We are too gentle a race for such things; the recording and most of the evidence itself was sealed to protect the public. It had to be. I was *Madur*. If the masses were ever to learn that one of my class was

capable of such a thing, it would bring down the entire
social structure, the whole of our civilization. "They
have seen it and taken my mind print. They must
know that this was no rational act."

*"I'm afraid you wouldn't be allowed to plead insan-
ity," my attorney replied. "You see, you are technically
above the law in your class, and the justification for
that status and indeed the justification for* Madur *rule is
that you are genetically perfect.* Madur *are by definition
incapable of such acts.* Madur *are, by definition, always sane and rational. Therefore, your crime is by
definition premeditated."*

"But it was not! You and they both know that!"

*He sighed. "Sir, it is beside the point what actually
occurred. What matters is that it could not have occurred. Interestingly, because of the necessity of your
sanity and the evidence of the deceased's bad moral
character and provocations against you, I probably
could have gotten you off with a sentence of exile to
some remote little planet somewhere. But Gomesh is
not the issue. You did not simply kill Gomesh, you
killed three other people."*

"Who would have killed me or done me grave in-
jury saving their employer! It was self-defense!"

"You miss the point. These men were duber. *They
were born and bred to be bodyguards and henchmen
just as you were to be Imperial Physician. As such, they
were acting as they had to act, genetically, mentally,
socially, and morally, while your action was against all
things that Madur stand for. They had a right to injure
or kill you. You had no right to prevent them, just as it
is your own responsibility for placing them in a position
where they were forced to take such action against
you." Perry Mason sighed. "I'm sorry, but even I had
to lose one sooner or later."*

I was dumbstruck by the implications of what he
was saying, and the rightness of it. I *was* responsible
for their attempt on me, and as a result I did not have
any right to stop it. My crime was not that I murdered
four people; four people who I still thought deserved
it. My crime was in not killing Gomesh, thus avenging

my honor, and then allowing his bodyguards to kill me. This was no petty crime, not even murder; this was a crime against civilization as we knew it. If the lower classes ever even *suspected* a *Madur* was capable of even *thinking* emotionally, of losing control even in privacy and without harm, let alone insanity, no matter how temporary, no one could feel safe or secure again.

"In sentencing you I am faced with a dilemma for which the codes have no guidance," Judge Wapner told me sternly. *"As a result, I must break new ground. I could have you vaporized for the murder of Gomesh, of course, but that would not preserve the symmetry necessary here. There is another, perhaps more appropriate way, than that. It is clear that you yourself are not defective, but that exposure to these alien signals has somehow conflicted with your primary intellectual imperatives. That places us in a quandary but also makes you uniquely qualified to aid your people. We need to continue collecting those signals, those programs. Yet, how can we risk prolonged exposure by others to them? What we need is an experienced expert on the subject who can make the proper selections.*

"The collection may be automatic," Judge Roy Bean continued, *"but that is the trouble with it. Automatic. Someone must eventually go through it all and make decisions on what is worthy and what is not, what is redundant and what is new. It is a vital project—the only contact ever with another sentient race even if the contact is only one way—and there is much to learn. Computers can do some of it, but in the end it is a highly subjective process. It requires someone with a collector's sense and a high analytical and appreciatory background. It requires a* Madur. *We realize that your tortured soul craves vaporizing, but would you consider committing yourself to this project, which will help your race, instead? We would outfit a special ship and send you out as collector—and critic. It is too much to ask of some here, considering the mental price we might pay, but you have already paid it."*

The last thing my soul craved then was vaporization

no matter what I should have felt. If my soul went that way, I would have let them kill me and given everyone but myself and Gomesh a happy ending. I was very stupid then. I leapt at the chance.

"I live to serve my people," I spouted nobly.

I did not understand what they were doing then, either. I was no mere murderer, no mere abuser of trust, for which simple vaporizing would have been a quick and easy answer. I had committed an impossible act, an act which threatened everything. Damn those machines!

Make the punishment fit the crime . . .

The beam sensor alarm sounded, and I moved to check the monitoring station. I flicked on the recorders and attached the visual translators and it started to roll. Immediately I knew where we'd drifted, and immediately I tried to stop it, but the damned computer refused and flashed NEW MATERIAL—PICKUP REQUIRED. Damn that thing! Not new, not new at all! How many times had I seen it? How many times had I been forced to watch it when that mechanical mind of Hell insisted?

"This is the emergency broadcast system. This is not—repeat, not—a test." He was swearing and nervous, even though he was the best-known newscaster of his day delivering the biggest story of his or any career.

"No, no! Not my people! Not my family! Not my beautiful, beautiful ghosts!"

". . . tactical nuclear exchange involved the elimination of almost forty percent of the Soviet Army, resulting in . . ."

"Lucy! Desi! Uncle Miltie! Come! Tell us it was all just a joke! Tell me when to laugh!"

". . . six hundred multiple warhead missiles. Washington, New York, San Diego, Norfolk, Los Angeles, San Francisco, and Seattle have already been obliterated by submarine-based . . ."

"We are a gentle race!" I screamed, my exoskeleton glowing green as always. "Were you all mad? Were you all seized by a fit of insanity? You cannot do this to me!"

". . . midwestern cities such as here in Chicago in

*seven minutes or less. If you have a shelter, get to it
immediately. Do not hesitate. If you have a storm cellar
or basement, go to it. Sewer tunnels, subways. Do not
let yourself be exposed to direct blast. Do not venture
outside again for at least two to four weeks. Take what
provisions you can . . ."*

"Not even a crime against civilization can deserve
this! Computer, get me control. Tell them to blow this
ship. Jettison life support! I will take anything, anything except this! How many times must I watch? How
many times must I *know*?

"Please! Central Computer! In the name of all that's
holy, *you cannot make me watch them all die again!*"

RIPPLES IN THE DIRAC SEA

By Geoffrey A. Landis

My death looms over me like a tidal wave, rushing toward me with an inexorable slow-motion majesty. And yet I flee, pointless though it may be.

I depart, and my ripples diverge to infinity, like waves smoothing out the footprints of forgotten travelers.

We were so careful to avoid any paradox, the day we first tested my machine. We pasted a duct-tape cross onto the concrete floor of a windowless lab, placed an alarm clock on the mark, and locked the door. An hour later we came back, removed the clock, and put the experimental machine in the room with a super-eight camera set in the coils. I aimed the camera at the X, and one of my grad students programmed the machine to send the camera back half an hour, stay in the past five minutes, then return. It left and returned without even a flicker. When we developed the film, the time on the clock was half an hour before we loaded the camera. We'd succeeded in opening the door into the past. We celebrated with coffee and champagne.

Now that I know a lot more about time, I understand our mistake, that we had not thought to put a
movie camera in the room with the clock to photograph the machine as it arrived from the future. But
what is obvious to me now was not obvious then.

I arrive, and the ripples converge to the instant *now*
from the vastness of the infinite sea.

To San Francisco, June 8, 1965. A warm breeze
riffles across dandelion-speckled grass, while puffy white
clouds form strange and wondrous shapes for our entertainment. Yet so very few people pause to enjoy it.
They scurry about, diligently preoccupied, believing
that if they act busy enough, they must be important.
"They hurry so," I say. "Why can't they slow down,
sit back, enjoy the day?"

"They're trapped in the illusion of time," says Dancer.
He lies on his back and blows a soap bubble, his hair
flopping back long and brown in a time when "long"
hair meant anything below the ear. A puff of breeze
takes the bubble down the hill and into the stream of
pedestrians. They uniformly ignore it. "They're caught
in the belief that what they do is important to some
future goal." The bubble pops against a briefcase, and
Dancer blows another. "You and I, we know how
false an illusion that is. There is no past, no future,
only the now, eternal."

He was right, more right than he could have possibly imagined. Once I, too, was preoccupied and self-
important. Once I was brilliant and ambitious. I was
twenty-eight years old, and I'd made the greatest discovery in the world.

From my hiding place I watched him come up the
service elevator. He was thin almost to the point of
starvation, a nervous man with stringy blond hair and
an armless white T-shirt. He looked up and down the
hall, but failed to see me hidden in the janitor's closet.
Under each arm was a two-gallon can of gasoline, in
each hand another. He put down three of the cans and
turned the last one upside down, then walked down

the hall, spreading a pungent trail of gasoline. His face was blank. When he started on the second can, I figured it was about enough. As he passed my hiding spot, I walloped him over the head with a wrench, and called hotel security. Then I went back to the closet and let the ripples of time converge.

I arrived in a burning room, flames licking forth at me, the heat almost too much to bear. I gasped for breath—a mistake—and punched at the keypad.

NOTES ON THE THEORY AND PRACTICE OF TIME TRAVEL:
1) Travel is possibly only into the past.
2) The object transported will return to exactly the time and place of departure.
3) It is not possible to bring objects from the past to the present.
4) Actions in the past cannot change the present.

One time I tried jumping back a hundred million years, to the Cretaceous, to see dinosaurs. All the picture books show the landscape as being covered with dinosaurs. I spent three days wandering around a swamp—in my new tweed suit—before catching even a glimpse of any dinosaur larger than a basset hound. That one—a theropod of some sort, I don't know which—skittered away as soon as it caught a whiff of me. Quite a disappointment.

My professor in transfinite math used to tell stories about a hotel with an infinite number of rooms. One day all the rooms are full, and another guest arrives. "No problem," says the desk clerk. He moves the person in room one into room two, the person in room two into room three, and so on. Presto! A vacant room.

A little later, an infinite number of guests arrive. "No problem," says the dauntless desk clerk. He moves the person in room one into room two, the person in room two into room four, the person in room three into room six, and so on. Presto! An infinite number of rooms vacant.

My time machine works on just that principle.

Again I return to 1965, the fixed point, the strange attractor to my chaotic trajectory. In years of wandering I've met countless people, but Daniel Ranien—Dancer—was the only one who truly had his head together. He had a soft, easy smile, a battered second-hand guitar, and as much wisdom as it has taken me a hundred lifetimes to learn. I've known him in good times and bad, in summer days with blue skies that we swore would last a thousand years, in days of winter blizzards with drifted snow pile high over our heads. In happier times we have laid roses into the barrels of rifles, we laid our bodies across the city streets in the midst of riots, and not been hurt. And I have been with him when he died, once, twice, a hundred times over.

He died on February 8, 1969, a month into the reign of King Richard the Trickster and his court fool Spiro, a year before Kent State and Altamont and the secret war in Cambodia slowly strangled the summer of dreams. He died, and there was—is—nothing I can do. The last time he died I dragged him to a hospital, where I screamed and ranted until finally I convinced them to admit him for observation, though nothing seemed wrong with him. With X-rays and arteriograms and radioacotive tracers, they found the incipient bubble in his brain; they drugged him, shaved his beautiful long brown hair, and operated on him, cutting out the offending capillary and tying it off neatly. When the anesthetic wore off, I sat in the hospital room and held his hand. There were big purple blotches under his eyes. He gripped my hand and stared, silent, into space. Visiting hours or no, I didn't let them throw me out of the room. He just stared. In the gray hours just before dawn he sighed softly and died. There was nothing at all that I could do.

*   *   *

Time travel is subject to two constraints: conservation of energy, and causalty. The energy to appear in the past is only borrowed from the Dirac sea, and since ripples in the Dirac sea propagate in the negative t direction, transport is only into the past. Energy is conserved in the present as long as the object transported returns with zero time delay, and the principle of causality assures that actions in the past cannot change the present. For example, what if you went in the past and killed your father? Who, then, would invent the time machine?

Once I tried to commit suicide by murdering my father, before he met my mother, twenty three years before I was born. It changed nothing, of course, and even when I did it I knew it would change nothing. But you have to try these things. How else could I know for sure?

Next we tried sending a rat back. It made the trip through the Dirac sea and back undamaged. Then we tried a trained rat, one we borrowed from the psychology lab across the green without telling them what we wanted it for. Before its little trip it had been taught to run through a maze to get a piece of bacon. Afterwards, it ran the maze as fast as ever.

We still had to try it on a human. I volunteered myself and didn't allow anyone to talk me out of it. By trying it on myself, I dodged the University regulations about experimenting on humans.

The dive into the negative energy sea felt like nothing at all. One moment I stood in the center of the loop of Renselz coils, watched by my two grad students and a technician; the next I was alone, and the clock had jumped back exactly one hour. Alone in a locked room with nothing but a camera and a clock, that moment was the high point of my life.

The moment when I first met Dancer was the low point. I was in Berkeley, a bar called "Trishia's," slowly getting trashed. I'd been doing that a lot, caught between omnipotence and despair. It was 1967. 'Frisco then—it was the middle of the hippie era—seemed somehow appropriate.

There was a girl, sitting at a table with a group from the university. I walked over to her table and invited myself to sit down. I told her she didn't exist, that her whole world didn't exist, it was all created by the fact that I was watching, and would disappear back into the sea of unreality as soon as I stopped looking. Her name was Lisa, and she argued back. Her friends, bored, wandered off, and in a while Lisa realized just how drunk I was. She dropped a bill on the table and walked out into the foggy night.

I followed her out. When she saw me following, she clutched her purse and bolted.

He was suddenly there under the streetlight. For a second I thought he was a girl. He had bright blue eyes and straight brown hair down to his shoulders. He wore an embroideried Indian shirt, with a silver and turquoise medallion around his neck and a guitar slung across his back. He was lean, almost stringy, and moved like a dancer or a karate master. But it didn't occur to me to be afraid of him.

He looked me over. "That won't solve your problem, you know," he said.

And instantly I was ashamed. I was no longer sure exactly what I'd had in mind or why I'd followed her. It had been years since I'd first fled my death, and I had come to think of others as unreal, since nothing I could do would permanently affect them. My head was spinning. I slid down the wall and sat down, hard, on the sidewalk. What had I come to?

He helped me back into the bar, fed me orange juice and pretzels, and got me to talk. I told him everything. Why not, since I could unsay anything I said, undo anything I did? But I had no urge to. He listened to it all, saying nothing. No one else had ever listened to the whole story before. I can't explain the effect it had on me. For uncountable years I'd been alone, and then, if only for a moment . . . it hit me with the intensity of a tab of acid. If only for a moment, I was not alone.

We left arm in arm. Half a block away, Dancer stopped, in front of an alley. It was dark.

"Something not quite right here." His voice had a puzzled tone.

I pulled him back. "Hold on. You don't want to go down there— " He pulled free and walked in. After a slight hesitation, I followed.

The alley smelled of old beer, mixed with garbage and stale vomit. In a moment, my eyes became adjusted to the dark.

Lisa was cringing in a corner behind some trash cans. Her clothes had been cut away with a knife, and lay scattered around. Blood showed dark on her thighs and one arm. She didn't seem to see us. Dancer squatted down next to her and said something soft. She didn't respond. He pulled off his shirt and wrapped it around her, then cradled her in his arms and picked her up. "Help me get her to my apartment."

"Apartment, hell. We'd better call the police," I said.

"Call the pigs? Are you crazy? You want them to rape her, too?"

I'd forgotten; this was the sixties. Between the two of us, we got her to Dancer's VW bug and took her to his apartment in The Hashbury. He explained it to me quietly as we drove, a dark side of the summer of love that I'd not seen before. It was greasers, he said. They come down to Berkeley because they heard that hippie chicks gave it away free, and get nasty when they met one who thought otherwise.

Her wounds were mostly superficial. Dancer cleaned her, put her in bed, and stayed up all night beside her, talking and crooning and making little ressuring noises. I slept on one of the mattresses in the hall. When I woke up in the morning, they were both in his bed. She was sleeping quietly. Dancer was awake, holding her. I was aware enough to realize that that was all he was doing, holding her, but still I felt a sharp pang of jealousy, and didn't know which one of them it was that I was jealous of.

*   *   *

NOTES FOR A LECTURE ON TIME TRAVEL

The beginning of the twentieth century was a time of intellectual giants, whose likes will perhaps never again be equaled. Einstein had just invented relativity, Heisenberg and Schrodinger quantum mechanics, but nobody yet knew how to make the two theories consistent with each other. In 1930, a new person tackled the problem. His name was Paul Dirac. He was twenty-eight years old. He succeeded where the others had failed.

His theory was an unprecedentend success, except for one small detail. According to Dirac's theory, a particle could have either positive or negative energy. What did this mean, a particle of negative energy? How could something have negative energy? And why don't ordinary—positive energy—particles fall down into these negative energy states, releasing a lot of free energy in the process?

You or I might have merely stipulated that it was impossible for an ordinary positive energy particle to make a transition to negative energy. But Dirac was not an ordinary man. He was a genius, the greatest physicist of all, and he had an answer. If every possible negative energy state was already occupied, a particle couldn't drop into a negative energy state. Ah ha! So Dirac postulated that the entire universe is entirely filled with negative energy particles. They surround us, permeate us, in the vacuum of outer space and in the center of the earth, every possible place a particle could be. An infinitely dense "sea" of negative energy particles. The Dirac Sea.

His argument had holes in it, but that comes later.

Once I went to visit the crucifixion. I took a jet from Santa Cruz to Tel Aviv, and a bus from Tel Aviv to Jerusalem. On a hill outside the city, I dove through the Dirac sea.

I arrived in my three-piece suit. No way to help that, unless I wanted to travel naked. The land was surprisingly green and fertile, more so than I'd expected. The hill was now a farm, covered with grape arbors and olive trees. I hid the coils behind some rocks and walked down to the road. I didn't get far. Five minutes on the road, I ran into a group of people. They had dark hair, dark skin, and wore clean white tunics. Romans? Jews? Egyptians? How could I tell? They spoke to me, but I couldn't understand a word. After a while two of them held me, while a third searched me. Were they robbers, searching for money? Romans, searching for some kind of identity papers? I realized now naïve I'd been to think I could just find appropriate dress and somehow blend in with the crowds. Finding nothing, the one who'd done the search carefully and methodically beat me up. At last he pushed me face down in the dirt. While the other two held me down, he pulled out a dagger and slashed through the tendons on the back of each leg. They were merciful, I guess. They left me with my life. Laughing and talking incomprehensibly among themselves, they walked away.

My legs were useless. One of my arms was broken. It took me four hours to crawl back up the hill, dragging myself with my good arm. Occasionally people would pass by on the road, studiously ignoring me. Once I reached the hiding place, pulling out the Renselz coils and wrapping them around me was pure agony. By the time I entered return on the keypad I was wavering in and out of consciousness. I finally managed to get it entered. From the Dirac sea the ripples converged.

and I was in my hotel room in Santa Cruz. The ceiling had started to fall in where the girders had burned through. Fire alarms shrieked and wailed, but there was no place to run. The room was filled with a dense, acrid smoke. Trying not to breathe, I punched out a code on the keypad, somewhen, anywhen other than that one instant

and I was in the hotel room, five days before. I gasped for breath. The woman in the hotel had shrieked and tried to pull the covers up. The man screwing her was too busy to pay any mind. They weren't real anyway. I ignored them and paid a little more attention to where to go next. Back to '65, I figured. I punched in the combo

and was standing in an empty room on the thirtieth floor of a hotel just under construction. A full moon gleamed on the silhouettes of silent construction cranes. I flexed my legs experimentally. Already the memory of the pain was beginning to fade. That was reasonable, because it had never happened. Time travel. It's not immortality, but it's got to be the next best thing.

You can't change the past, no matter how you try.

In the morning I explored Dancer's pad. It was crazy, a small third floor apartment a block off Haight Ashbury that had been converted into something from another planet. The floor of the apartment had been completely covered with old mattresses, on top of which was a jumbled confusion of quilts, pillows, Indian blankets, stuffed animals. You took off your shoes before coming in—Dancer always wore sandals, leather ones from Mexico with soles cut from old tires. The radiators, which didn't work anyway, were spray painted in dayglo colors. The walls were plastered with posters: Peter Max prints, brightly colored Eschers, poems by Allen Ginsberg, record album covers, peace rally posters, a "Haight is Love" sign, FBI ten-most-wanted posters torn down from a post office with the photos of famous antiwar activists circled in magic marker, a huge peace symbol in passion-pink. Some of the posters were illuminated with black light and luminesced in impossible colors. The air was musty with incense and the banana-sweet smell of dope. In one corner a record player played "Sergeant Pepper's Lonely Heart's Club Band" on infinite repeat. Whenever one copy of the album got too scratchy, inevitably one of Dancer's friends would bring in another.

He never locked the door. "Somebody wants to rip me off, well, hey, they probably need it more than I do anyway, okay? It's cool." People dropped by any time of day or night.

I let my hair grow long. Dancer and Lisa and I spent that summer together, laughing, playing guitar, making love, writing silly poems and sillier songs, experimenting with drugs. That was when LSD was blooming onto the scene like sunflowers, when people were still unafraid of the strange and beautiful world on the other side of reality. That was a time to live. I knew that it was Dancer that Lisa truly loved, not me, but in those days free love was in the air like the scent of poppies, and it didn't matter. Not much, anway.

NOTES FOR A LECTURE ON TIME TRAVEL (continued)

Having postulated that all of space was filled with an infinitely dense sea of negative energy particles, Dirac went on further and asked if we, in the positive-energy universe, could interact with this negative energy sea. What would happen, say, if you added enough energy to an electron to take it out of the negative energy sea? Two things: first, you would create an electron, seemingly out of nowhere. Second, you would leave behind a "hole" in the sea. The hole, Dirac realized, would act as if it were a particle itself, a particle exactly like an electron except for one thing: it would have the opposite charge. But if the hole ever encountered an electron, the electron would fall back into the Dirac sea, annihilating both electron and hole in a bright burst of energy. Eventually they gave the hole in the Dirac sea a name of its own: "positron." When Anderson discovered the positron two years later to vindicate Dirac's theory, it was almost an anticlimax.

And over the next fifty years, the reality of the Dirac sea was almost ignored by physicists. Antimatter, the holes in the sea, was the important feature of the theory; the rest was merely a mathematical artifact.

Seventy years alter, I remembered the story my transfinite math teacher told and put it together with Dirac's theory. Like putting an extra guest into a hotel with an infinite number of rooms, I figured out how to borrow energy from the Dirac sea. Or, to put it another way: I learned how to make waves.

And waves on the Dirac sea travel backward in time.

Next we had to try something more ambitious. We had to send a human back farther into history, and obtain proof of the trip. Still we were afraid to make alterations in the past, even though the mathematics stated that the present could not be changed.

We pulled out our movie camera and chose our destinations carefully.

In September of 1853 a traveler named William Hapland and his family crossed the Sierra Nevadas to reach the California coast. His daughter Sarah kept a journal, and in it she recorded how, as they reached the crest of Parker's ridge, she caught her first glimpse of the distant Pacific ocean exactly as the sun touched the horizon, "in a blays of cryms'n glorie," as she wrote. The journal still exists. It was easy enough for us to conceal ourselves and a movie camera in a cleft of rocks above the pass, to photograph the weary travelers in their ox-drawn wagon as they crossed.

The second target was the great San Francisco earth-quake of 1906. From a deserted warehouse that would survive the quake—but not the following fire—we watched and took movies as buildings tumbled down around us and embattled firemen in horse-drawn firetrucks strove in vain to quench a hundred blazes. Moments before the fire reached our building, we fled into the present.

The films were spectacular.

We were ready to tell the world.

There was a meeting of the AAAS in Santa Cruz in month. I called the program chairman and wangled a spot as an invited speaker without revealing just what we'd accomplished to date. I planned to show those films at the talk. They were to make us instantly famous.

The day that Dancer died we had a going-away party, just Lisa and Dancer and I. He knew he was going to die; I'd told him and somehow he believed me. He always believed me. We stayed up all night, playing Dancer's secondhand mandolin, painting psychedelic designs on each other's bodies with greasepaint, competing against each other in a marathon game of cut-throat Monopoly, doing a hundred silly, ordinary things that took meaning only from the fact that it was the last time. About four in the morning, as the glimmmer of false-dawn began to show in the sky, we went down to the bay and, huddling together for warmth, went tripping. Dancer took the largest dose, since he wasn't going to return. The last thing he said, he told us not to let our dreams die; to stay together.

We buried Dancer, at city expanse, in a welfare grave. We split up three days later.

I kept in touch with Lisa, vaguely. In the late seventies she went back to school, first for an MBA, then law school. I think she was married for a while. We wrote each other cards on Christmas for a while, then I lost track of her. Years later, I got a letter from her. She said that she was finally able to forgive me for causing Dan's death.

It was a cold and foggy February day, but I knew I could find warmth in 1965. The ripples converged.

Anticipated questions from the audience:

Q (old, stodgy professor): It seems to me this proposed temporal jump of yours violates the law of conservation of mass/energy. For example, when a transported object is transported into the past, a quantity of mass will appear to vanish from the present, in clear violation of the conservation law.

A (me): Since the return is to the exact time of departure, the mass present is constant.

Q: Very well, but what about the arrival in the past? Doesn't this violate the conservation law?

A: No. The energy needed is taken from the Dirac sea, by the mechanism I explain in detail in the *Phys Rev* paper. When the object returns to the "future," the energy is restored to the sea.

Q (intense young physicist): Then doesn't Heisenberg

uncertainty limit the amount of time that can be spent in the past?

A: A good question. The answer is yes, but because we borrow an infinitesimal amount of energy from an infinite number of particles, the amount of time spent in the past can be arbitrarily large. The only limitation is that you must leave the past an instant before you depart from the present.

In half an hour I was scheduled to present the paper that would rank my name with Newton's and Galileo's— and Dirac's. I was twenty-eight years old, the same age that Dirac was when he announced his theory. I was a firebrand, preparing to set the world aflame. I was nervous, rehearsing the speech in my hotel room. I took a swig out of an old Coke that one of my grad students had left sitting on top of the television. The evening news team was babbling on, but I wasn't listening.

I never delivered that talk. The hotel had already started to burn; my death was already foreordained. Tie neat, I inspected myself in the mirror, then walked to the door. The doorknob was warm. I opened it onto a sheet of fire. Flame burst through the opened door like a ravening dragon. I stumbled backward, staring at the flames in amazed fascination.

Somewhere in the hotel I heard a scream, and all at once I broke free of my spell. I was on the thirtieth story; there was no way out. My thought was for my machine. I rushed across the room and threw open the case holding the time machine. With swift, sure fingers I pulled out the Renselz coils and wrapped them around my body. The carpet had caught on fire, a sheet of flame between me and any possible escape. Holding my breath to avoid suffocation, I punched an entry into the keyboard and dove into time.

I return to that moment again and again. When I hit the final key, the air was already nearly unbreathable with smoke. I had about thirty seconds left to live, then. Over the years I've nibbled away my time down to ten seconds or less.

I live on borrowed time. So do we all, perhaps. But I know when and where my debt will fall due.

Dancer died on February 9, 1969. It was a dim, foggy day. In the morning he said he had a headache. That was unusual, for Dancer. He never had headaches. We decided to go for a walk through the fog. It was beautiful, as we were alone in a strange, formless world. I'd forgotten about his headache altogether, until, looking out across the sea of fog from the park over the bay, he fell over. He was dead before the ambulance came. He died with a secret smile on his face. I've never understood that smile. Maybe he was smiling because the pain was gone.

Lisa committed suicide two days later.

You ordinary people, you have the chance to change the future. You can father children, write novels, sign petitions, invent new machines, go to cocktail parties, run for president. You affect the future with everything you do. No matter what I do, I cannot. It is too late for that, for me. My actions are written in flowing water. And having no effect, I have no responsibilities. It makes no difference what I do, not at all.

When I first fled the fire into the past, I tried everything I could to change it. I stopped the arsonist, I argued with mayors, I even went to my own house and told myself not to go to the conference.

But that's not how time works. No matter what I do, talk to a governor or dynamite the hotel, when I reach that critical moment—the present, my destiny, the moment I left—I vanish from whenever I was, and return to the hotel room, the fire approaching ever closer. I have about ten seconds left. Every time I dive through the Dirac sea, everything I changed in the past vanishes. Sometimes I pretend that the changes I make in the past create new futures, though I know this is not the case. When I return to the present, all the changes are wiped out by the ripples of the converging wave, like erasing a blackboard after a class.

Someday I will return and meet my destiny. But for

now, I live in the past. It's a good life, I suppose. You get used to the fact that nothing you do will ever have any effect on the world. It gives you a feeling of freedom. I've been places no one has ever been, seen things no one alive has ever seen .I've given up physics, of course. Nothing I discover could endure past that fatal night in Santa Cruz. Maybe some people would continue for the sheer joy of knowledge. For me, the point is missing.

But there are compensations. Whenever I return to the hotel room, nothing is changed but my memories. I am again twenty-eight, again wearing the same three-piece suit, again have the fuzzy taste of stale cola in my mouth. Every time I return, I use up a little bit of time. One day I will have no time left.

Dancer, too, will never die. I won't let him. Every time I get to that final February morning, the day he died, I return to 1965, to that perfect day in June. He doesn't know me, he never knows me. But we meet on that hill, the only two willing to enjoy the day doing nothing. He lies on his back, idly fingering chords on his guitar, blowing bubbles and staring into the clouded blue sky. Later I will introduce him to Lisa. She won't know us either, but that's okay. We've got plenty of time.

"Time," I say to Dancer, lying in the park on the hill. "There's so much time."

"All the time there is," he says.

DAW

Don't Miss These Exciting DAW Anthologies

ANNUAL WORLD'S BEST SF

Donald A. Wollheim, editor

☐ 1986 Annual   UE2136—$3.50
☐ 1987 Annual   UE2203—$3.95
☐ 1989 Annual   UE2353—$3.95

ISAAC ASIMOV PRESENTS THE GREAT SF STORIES

Isaac Asimov & Martin H. Greenberg, editors

☐ Series 10 (1948)   UE1854—$3.50
☐ Series 13 (1951)   UE2058—$3.50
☐ Series 14 (1952)   UE2106—$3.50
☐ Series 15 (1953)   UE2171—$3.50
☐ Series 16 (1954)   UE2200—$3.50
☐ Series 17 (1955)   UE2256—$3.95
☐ Series 18 (1956)   UE2289—$4.50
☐ Series 19 (1957)   UE2326—$4.50

THE YEAR'S BEST HORROR STORIES

Karl Edward Wagner, editor

☐ Series VIII   UE2158—$2.95
☐ Series IX   UE2159—$2.95
☐ Series X   UE2160—$2.95
☐ Series XI   UE2161—$2.95
☐ Series XIV   UE2156—$3.50
☐ Series XV   UE2226—$3.50
☐ Series XVI   UE2300—$3.95

THE YEAR'S BEST FANTASY STORIES

Arthur W. Saha, editor

☐ Series 14   UE2307—$3.50

NEW AMERICAN LIBRARY
P.O. Box 999, Bergenfield, New Jersey 07621

Please send me the DAW BOOKS I have checked above. I am enclosing $_____
(check or money order—no currency or C.O.D.'s). Please include the list price plus
$1.00 per order to cover handling costs. Prices and numbers are subject to change
without notice. (Prices slightly higher in Canada.)

Name _____

Address _____

City _____ State _____ Zip _____
Please allow 4-6 weeks for delivery.

DAW

C.J. CHERRYH
THE ALLIANCE-UNION UNIVERSE

The Company Wars

☐ DOWNBELOW STATION   (UE2227—$3.95)

The Era of Rapprochement

☐ SERPENT'S REACH   (UE2088—$3.50)
☐ FORTY THOUSAND IN GEHENNA   (UE1952—$3.50)
☐ MERCHANTER'S LUCK   (UE2139—$3.50)

The Chanur Novels

☐ THE PRIDE OF CHANUR   (UE2292—$3.95)
☐ CHANUR'S VENTURE   (UE2293—$3.95)
☐ THE KIF STRIKE BACK   (UE2184—$3.50)
☐ CHANUR'S HOMECOMING   (UE2177—$3.95)

The Mri Wars

☐ THE FADED SUN: KESRITH   (UE1960—$3.50)
☐ THE FADED SUN: SHON'JIR   (UE1889—$2.95)
☐ THE FADED SUN: KUTATH   (UE2133—$2.95)

Merovingen Nights (Mri Wars Period)

☐ ANGEL WITH THE SWORD   (UE2143—$3.50)

Merovingen Nights—Anthologies

☐ FESTIVAL MOON (#1)   (UE2192—$3.50)
☐ FEVER SEASON (#2)   (UE2224—$3.50)
☐ TROUBLED WATERS (#3)   (UE2271—$3.50)
☐ SMUGGLER'S GOLD (#4)   (UE2299—$3.50)

The Age of Exploration

☐ CUCKOO'S EGG   (UE2371—$4.50)
☐ VOYAGER IN NIGHT   (UE2107—$2.95)
☐ PORT ETERNITY   (UE2206—$2.95)

The Hanan Rebellion

☐ BROTHERS OF EARTH   (UE2209—$3.95)
☐ HUNTER OF WORLDS   (UE2217—$2.95)

NEW AMERICAN LIBRARY
P.O. Box 999, Bergenfield, New Jersey 07621
Please send me the DAW BOOKS I have checked above. I am enclosing $_____
(check or money order—no currency or C.O.D.'s). Please include the list price plus
$1.00 per order to cover handling costs. Prices and numbers are subject to change
without notice. (Prices slightly higher in Canada.)

Name _____

Address _____

City _____ State _____ Zip _____
Please allow 4-6 weeks for delivery.

DAW

NEW DIMENSIONS IN MILITARY SF

Charles Ingrid
THE SAND WARS

He was a soldier fighting against both mankind's alien foe and the evil at the heart of the human Dominion Empire, trapped in an alien-altered suit of armor which, if worn too long, could transform him into a sand warrior—a no-longer human berserker.

☐ SOLAR KILL (Book 1) (UE2209—$3.50)
☐ LASERTOWN BLUES (Book 2) (UE2260—$3.50)
☐ CELESTIAL HIT LIST (Book 3) (UE2306—$3.50)
☐ ALIEN SALUTE (Book 4) (UE2329—$3.95)

W. Michael Gear
THE SPIDER TRILOGY

The Prophets of the lost colony planet called World could see the many pathways of the future, and when the conquering Patrol Ships of the galaxy-spanning Directorate arrived, they found the warriors of World ready, armed and waiting.

☐ THE WARRIORS OF SPIDER (Book 1) (UE2287—$3.95)
☐ THE WAY OF SPIDER (Book 2) (UE2318—$3.95)

John Steakley
☐ **ARMOR**

Impervious body armor had been devised for the commando forces who were to be dropped onto the poisonous surface of A-9, the home world of mankind's most implacable enemy. But what of the man inside the armor? This tale of cosmic combat will stand against the best of Gordon Dickson or Poul Anderson.

(UE2368—$4.50)

NEW AMERICAN LIBRARY
P.O. Box 999, Bergenfield, New Jersey 07621
Please send me the DAW BOOKS I have checked above. I am enclosing $_____
(check or money order—no currency or C.O.D.'s). Please include the list price plus
$1.00 per order to cover handling costs. Prices and numbers are subject to change
without notice. (Prices slightly higher in Canada.)

Name _____

Address _____

City _____ State _____ Zip _____
Please allow 4-6 weeks for delivery.

DAW

**THEY WERE THE ULTIMATE ENEMIES,
GENERALS OF STAR EMPIRES FOREVER OPPOSED—
AND WORLDS WOULD FALL
BEFORE THEIR PRIVATE WAR...**

IN CONQUEST BORN
C.S. FRIEDMAN

Braxi and Azea, two super-races fighting an endless campaign over a long forgotten cause. The Braxaná—created to become the ultimate warriors. The Azeans, raised to master the powers of the mind, using telepathy to penetrate where mere weapons cannot. Now the final phase of their war is approaching, when whole worlds will be set ablaze by the force of ancient hatred. Now Zatar and Anzha, the master generals, who have made this battle a personal vendetta, will use every power of body and mind to claim the vengeance of total conquest.

☐ **IN CONQUEST BORN**   (UE2198—$3.95)

NEW AMERICAN LIBRARY
P.O. Box 999, Bergenfield, New Jersey 07621
Please send me _____ copies of IN CONQUEST BORN by C.S. Friedman, UE2198 at $3.95 each ($4.95 in Canada) plus $1.00 for postage and handling per order. I enclose $_____ (check or money order—no currency or C.O.D.'s).

Name _____

Address _____

City _____ State _____ Zip _____
Please allow 4-6 weeks for delivery.
This offer, prices, and numbers are subject to change without notice.

The long-awaited new fantasy epic from the best-selling author of TAILCHASER'S SONG.

THE DRAGONBONE CHAIR
Book One of *Memory, Sorrow, and Thorn*

by TAD WILLIAMS

THE DRAGONBONE CHAIR is a story of magic and madness, of conquest and exile, and of a young apprentice whose dreams of heroic deeds come terrifyingly true when his world is torn apart in a civil war fueled by ancient hatreds, immortal enemies, and dark sorcery.

Complete with a beautiful full-color jacket by award-winning artist Michael Whelan, THE DRAGONBONE CHAIR opens the way to a world as rich, complex and memorable as any in the great masterpieces of fantasy.

". . . promises to become the fantasy equivalent of WAR AND PEACE."—*Locus*

654 pages   Size: 6×9 $19.50
(Hardcover edition: 0-8099-0003-3)

Buy it at your local bookstore, or use this convenient coupon for ordering
NEW AMERICAN LIBRARY
P.O. Box 999, Bergenfield, New Jersey 07621

Please send me _____ copies of THE DRAGONBONE CHAIR 0-8099-0003-3 (DAW Books) at $19.50 each ($24.50 in Canada) plus $1.50 postage and handling per order. I enclose $_____ (check or money order only—no cash or C.O.D.'s), or charge my ☐ Mastercard ☐ Visa.

Card # _____ Exp. Date_____
Signature _____
Name _____
Address _____
City _____ State _____ Zip _____
Please allow 4-6 weeks for delivery.
This offer, prices, and numbers are subject to change without notice.